FATAL FOREVER

THE FATAL FAE SERIES: BOOK FOUR

TEACUP
DRAGON
PUBLISHING

To those who waited with more patience than a dragon for this book, thank you.
I hope Rori, Therron, Cian, and Nikala made the wait worth it.
All my love, Forever.

BOOKS BY TAMERI ETHERTON

*Song of the Swords**

The Prince of Dragons

The Stones of Resurrection

The Temple of Sacrifice

The Ruins of Betrayal

The Veils of Deception

The Keeper of Stars

*The Fatal Fae**

Fatal Illusion

Fatal Assassin

Fatal Legacy

Fatal Forever

Fatal Destiny

*Court of Stars**

Sunset in Shadow

*Chronicles of Eidyn**

Dragon Mage

*Daring Ever Afters**

Enchant

Short Stories

UnBroken

*Books that are part of the Aetherverse: The fantastical realms of Tameri Etherton. Characters and storylines intersect within the books with magical consequences.

FATAL FOREVER

THE FATAL FAE SERIES: BOOK FOUR

USA TODAY BESTSELLING AUTHOR

TAMERI ETHERTON

❦   1   ❦

Dead dads are dicks.

Fucking monster. Scalding water seared Cian's skin, but he didn't care. He scrubbed hard, as if trying to remove the stain of shame that covered every inch of his body like a rash without a cure. The floral-scented soap mocked his anger. His *father*—the man who had raised him, had taught him right from wrong, had showed him how to wield his magic, and a million other tiny things that led to big decisions and sometimes irrevocable regrets—was the monster responsible for kidnapping fae. For fifteen years, Cian had believed Hagan MacNair died on the cobblestones of Edinburgh Castle. He thought a shadow man had murdered his father while he watched, helpless, hopeless, and heartbroken.

Lies. All lies. An elaborate deception meant to free Hagan from the confines of Faerie so that he could live anonymously under a new name—Hunter Pearson.

His own fucking father. He should've known. Should've sensed something, anything, but there was nothing left of the man he'd worshipped all his life. It defied logic how the same man who raised him with a strict yet loving hand could become this deranged psychopath. And what he did to Nikala? Cian choked back a retch at the memory of Hunter's lab.

The cold shower with hooks in the ceiling from which Hunter had hung Nikala for hours on end, the multitude of torture devices, the tubes and contraptions Hunter used for his experiments horrified Cian. Hunter had broken Nikala so many times it was a miracle she was alive.

A miracle. Yes, that's what she was. A bloody fucking miracle.

One cobbled together from a macabre mix of magical creatures molded into the perfect killing machine. Well, near perfect. She still had a soul and a conscience. Without those, Hunter would possess the most lethal weapon ever created: a woman who could pass for human, murder without guilt, and disappear into the ether without being seen.

And she'd been programmed to kill Cian.

Yet she hadn't. Even at the house in Chelsea after they'd killed Hunter's assassins and the madman was mentally taunting them, she'd defied him and not murdered Cian as commanded. Only time would tell whether he would get a second reprieve from her. Or whether the next kill order would be fatal.

At least now they knew what had happened to the kidnapped fae. What Hunter had done to them—it made Cian shudder with disgust. All those lives lost. They must've suffered, and for that, Hunter would pay with his own life.

Cian refused to take responsibility for his father's deception. He rinsed the last remnants of rage from his hands and turned off the water. He'd have to tell Eirlys about everything that had happened, including Rowan's duplicitous treachery. She wouldn't be glad of the news. Rowan had served the two queens of Faerie for several centuries. Both Eirlys and Midna would be livid to learn he had deceived them. But that was a tomorrow problem. Tonight, their priority was finding his sister Rori.

He stared at the face in the mirror, barely recognizing himself. He was exhausted. They all were. Jumping through doorways from one place to another, constantly chasing an enigma who seemed to always be five steps ahead of them— it was infuriating as well as physically taxing.

And there, just behind the fear, was the question he dared not ask aloud. If this whole time Rowan had been working with Hunter, who else in Faerie wasn't to be trusted? How far did the deception go? Dammit all. He was a shitsucking spy if he couldn't even see the guilty when they were right in front of him. Well, no more. He'd not let loyalties and familial ties blind him ever again. Everyone was suspect. Almost everyone.

"None of this is your fault, you know." Nikala leaned against the doorframe of the large bathroom, looking small and frail.

"I should've known. Should've protected Rori." He glared at his reflection. "It's my fault she's in danger now."

"No." Nikala shook her head fiercely and moved to his side. She stared at his reflection in the mirror, her eyes filled with an intensity that sent a chill down his spine. "Hunter has been planning this since before you were born. Rowan wasn't lying back at the manor about Rori being Hunter's first experiment. It was called the Dawn Project. She has something inside her that Hunter desperately wants, but he can't find."

"Any idea what that might be?" Cian dried his hands on a soft towel and dragged his fingers through his hair, sighing loudly. His imagination ran wild with what their father might do to Rori.

She shook her head, frowning. "I wish I did, but if it's important to Hunter, he'll stop at nothing to get it. I'm sorry, Cian."

The unspoken threat that Hunter would destroy Rori, kill her ruthlessly, hung between them. It was a reality Cian wasn't prepared to accept yet knew in his heart was true. Their father was gone.

"I was just thinking how some dads are complete dicks. Dead ones even more so." He saw the pinch of her eyes and corrected himself. "Not that I'm saying your dad is or was."

"Oh, he definitely was." Sadness pulled her features low and guilt bit against his heart. None of this would've happened without Hunter.

"How can you even stand to look at me? What my father—Hunter—did to you...all those years of torture and abuse...I wouldn't blame you if you hated me right now."

Nikala turned him to face her and held his face between her warm hands. The intensity in her eyes flared with passion. "You're not him. You're nothing like Hunter. I don't see him when I look at you. I see Cian MacNair. I see you." She stood on tiptoes and brushed his lips with her own.

If only he could forgive himself so easily. It was his job to be there for his baby sister.

Instead, he'd been too busy chasing shadows. Too

concerned with finding Nikala. He should've never left Rori at Rowan's cottage. But then, if he'd stayed, they never would've learned of the wizard's deception. They'd played right into his hands. He and Rori trusted Rowan with their lives, and now, his baby sister was about to—what? Die? No, Hunter needed her, but Cian didn't know why.

"Where do you think he'd take her?"

Nikala shook her head and stepped back to lean against the wall. "There are a dozen places I can think of, but I don't know for certain."

"We need to find him and Rori before Hunter gets whatever he's after." Cian slipped her hand into his as he passed and walked them both to the office where he'd first met Malcolm only a short time ago.

Therron glanced their way from where he stood at the huge window that overlooked the Thames and London's Southbank.

"I know what your father wants."

He said it casually, but Cian saw the torment etched into his features, the sorrow in his crystal-blue eyes.

"That demented shitgibbon is not my father. Hagan MacNair died in Edinburgh fifteen years ago." Cian glared at the elf, as if daring him to say otherwise.

"I'm sorry." Therron put his hand over his heart and inclined his head. "I'm angry and frightened and looked to put some of that blame on you. Forgive me."

Surprised at the admission and apology, Cian faltered in his step. He had to remind himself that Hunter had very nearly killed Therron only a few hours earlier. They were all angry and wanted revenge. They all cared about Rori. Even the elf. It was a truth he'd denied but had to accept.

Cian mimicked the elf's action and placed his hand over his heart with a dip of his head. "We are not enemies, Your Highness. I didn't always see it that way, but I do now. We have a common desire to see Hunter destroyed, and I am grateful for your help."

Therron nodded, a cheeky smirk on his lips, his gaze once again focused on something outside SIRE's building. "It would please me if you only called me Therron. At least, outside of Elvenwood." The grin faltered. "This man, Hunter…it was his face I saw behind my father in the throne room at my palace. His reach is vast and should not be underestimated. His power, immense. The queens should be made aware of these new revelations, but I am loath to leave without Rori." Therron cast a glance to Cian. "Did you see the image of Hunter behind my father? Do you know why he would corrupt the elven court?"

Cian blew out a breath and shook his head. "I was too focused on the light show that woman put on. Now that's power. If we could get her on our side, we just might win."

A low hum came from the elf. "Her name is Taryn. Lady Delarainne believes she and her partner Rhoane are the gods who created Cilachaem. I am inclined to believe her. They…know things about our world, our people. But I feel they are not meant to fight this battle for us."

"Taryn and Rhoane?" Nikala gasped. "The couple with the huge white dog? They're gods?" She whistled low and slow. "I suppose I shouldn't be surprised. They were scary powerful." She flexed her fingers, a wild look in her eyes. "Explains a lot, though. Elven princes, gods walking among mortals…bloody hell, what next? No, don't answer that." She waggled a finger as if in warning. "I need to process the fact that I might've met actual, real gods. Who, in my defense, looked pretty damn normal when they weren't using their power."

"If I am understanding it correctly," Therron spoke softly, as if to keep the information from whatever he watched from the window, "they are not yet gods, but mere mortals. It is complicated."

Nikala slouched onto a sofa and rubbed her eyes. "What about any of this isn't complicated?"

She wasn't wrong. Cian went to the sideboard to fill a tumbler with whisky but decided against alcohol. He needed to keep his wits sharp. Gods, enhanced assassins—the super soldiers Hunter experimented on—indeed, what next? A tiny voice in the back of his mind whispered his darkest fear, and he hid a tremble of anxiety. War. Wasn't that Hunter's ultimate objective? But did he crave war just in the human realm, or Cilachaem? Or, war between those two worlds? Somehow Rori played a role in his plans, but how?

They had to find her before Hunter turned her into a weapon like he'd done to Nikala. He grabbed a soda from the small refrigerator beneath the sideboard and offered one to the others. Therron declined, but Nikala took a can and tapped the top before opening the tab. Such a small thing, but her caution over a fizzy drink's ability to surprise her with an unwanted spray to the face made Cian's belly tighten in all the best ways. He loved this woman. It didn't matter what Hunter had done to her; he loved the ferocious fighter and the quietly suspicious soda sipper.

"What does Rori have that Hunter wants?" Nikala

asked Therron before taking a long drink straight from the can.

Cian watched, mildly intrigued as her throat constricted and loosened with her swallowing. When the can was empty, she crushed it in her hand and joined the elf at the window, tossing the mangled aluminum into the trash on her way. Impressed despite himself, Cian studied the pair. Similar facial features, both with lithe bodies and pale-blonde hair; she could easily have passed for elven if her ears were pointed.

For the hundredth time, he wondered about her lineage. Malcolm was her father, but who was her mother? Possibly elven. A fae father and elven mother? It would explain why she was raised far from Faerie's two queens, and Elven-wood's bigotry. Nikala turned toward Therron, and in the moonlight, she looked one hundred percent fae.

A vision taunted him, of a sweet face and strawberry-blonde hair, but he couldn't place the woman. A soft giggle brushed his thoughts and he touched his temple, half expecting the vision to explode to life.

A ping sounded from the lift in the outer reception area and startled him. Tension filled the room as they waited. Nikala turned from the window and reached for a drawer in the huge desk he knew held a gun. Cian snatched his from the waistband of his trousers. Therron merely watched the door, his hands loose at his sides.

"Expecting someone?" Cian asked, and Nikala shrugged.

"It'll either be Hunter or Maxx."

Therron's jaw tightened so hard Cian feared he might break his back molars.

The seconds ticked by as they waited. Cian's insides coiled, and he prepared himself for the worst. If Hunter Pearson walked through that door, he'd be met with a bullet through his chest. Father or not, the man had to be stopped. Even as the thought went through his mind, a sharp pain cut into his skull, and he flinched from the severity. He looked to Nikala with deepest dread and knew, whatever fuckery Hunter had done to her to prevent her from killing him, he'd manipulated Cian as well. And most likely Rori, too. His own children. There was no end to his treachery, but somehow, Cian would find a way to end it. Everything depended on Hunter being stopped.

The door creaked open, and he held his breath.

Please, he prayed to whatever gods might be listening, let Rori be alive. And let me kill my father before he destroys everything I love.

❦   2   ❦

Therron. Rori fought through the darkness to find him. How many jumps had they made? Four? Six? Too many doorways to count, and always with the man's arm crooked around her neck, nearly suffocating her. It was to keep her pliable, she knew, and to keep her from seeing too much. Eventually, they'd stopped leaping from doorway to doorway, but by then, she'd blacked out.

Her head ached from repairing and replacing wards the man had destroyed in that first brutal attack in the manor home that was strangely familiar. He'd been searching for something and had nearly found it. His violent yet efficient search had come close—too close—to discovering her secret, but powerful wards had kept him from tearing into her completely and uncovering her every vulnerability. Wards she'd not known were there, nor did she know who placed them, or when. Desperation had clung to him like cat fur on a black jumper, and she'd understood in the very depths of her soul that he was intent on finding the thing to destroy it. And then, to end her.

She flinched from the realization, and magic seared against her wrists, burning her flesh with persistent fury. Rage-fueled magic. Snickertits. She didn't have to ask whose magic it was, or why he was angry. A smile crept to her lips. His anger meant he still hadn't gotten what he wanted. Which meant her wards were working. Though she could feel his magic in the bonds holding her captive, her body was too lethargic to move, her lids too heavy to open. Unnaturally so.

Once more, she searched for Therron, only to be dissuaded by a persistent suggestion to forget him entirely. The message came from inside her mind, the same as it did every time she imagined ways to kill her captor. With each new idea, a subtle nudge pushed the thought away. Once, after their second leap through a doorway, she'd reached for the dagger on her hip, but that time, a sharp pain slashed against the inside of her skull. The message was clear: she couldn't kill the man.

Now, her mind suggested she sleep—to give in to the sweet lullaby of the eternal nothingness. This wasn't a darkness she recognized. It wasn't the void of the doorways, nor was it the silence of the dead forest she'd woken up in a few weeks earlier. This was something altogether worse.

A faint scent of lycenum tickled her nose, and she stifled a sneeze. Not a poison, but just as deadly if used improperly; she'd ingested enough over time to make herself mostly invulnerable to its effects. The only explanation she had for blacking out was that someone had overdosed her. But was it out of caution? Or was she dealing with a novice?

Whoever it was, they couldn't know that she would metabolize the substance quicker than most. Or perhaps they did know, hence the overdose. If they knew that, they could know far more about her than she'd thought. The question of how they would have such personal information about her pinged against her brain.

She'd never told a soul about her immunity to poisons or potions. Not even Meg. But of course, the healer had worked on her enough she might have sussed it out. Even so, Meg wouldn't tell anyone her secret. She was as close to family as one could get.

Rori visualized her blood purifying the potion, a trick she'd learned long ago that served her well. Relief spread over her like a comfortable blanket when the fog began to clear. She kept her body limp, as if still under the drug's influence.

Recollections came to her slowly, as if her mind woke from a centuries-long sleep. She cast back to the attack, searching for clues in what she could remember. A deluge of images flashed in her mind, and her heart stammered.

The manor house. The scarred man with violence in his eyes. The pain, dear goddess, the pain of his brutal assault. Then, beyond that, she saw a shining light, as if a star sent from the heavens had walked through the door.

Therron.

Where was he? Did he live?

Her blood chilled, and she withheld a gasp as new images flooded her skull. Before the manor, there had been the clinical room with an acrid scent, the wooziness that made her feel drunk and out of control. The nausea. And finally, Therron collapsed on the floor in a lifeless heap. A pit burned in her belly, and her nostrils flared with suppressed rage. The man had done that to him. Neither she nor Therron had seen him in the stark room, which meant he'd been hiding, or he had access to a doorway somewhere close by.

It stood to reason there was a doorway in the lab; how else had he gotten her to the manor so quickly? Which meant he wielded powerful magic. Was he fae or elf? Or something else?

Whatever he was, he'd left Therron to die. The elf was trying to protect her and got caught in a deadly trap. If only he knew she'd gladly give her life for his.

Without thinking, she lifted her arm to rub her temple and was stopped by the magic bonds that held her strapped to a chair. A fresh wave of burning seared her skin, and she took several long, slow breaths to calm the rampant beating of her heart. Where the bloody hell had the man taken her? She lived, but for how long? She already knew the answer to that question: until he discovered her secret.

A new memory stirred, of a family friend who had betrayed them.

Although her mind knew the truth, her heart refused to believe Rowan would do such a horrendous thing. He was a kindly wizard who served Cilachaem's queens. Yet he'd been in the house. A shiver raked her spine at the memory of how creepy he'd acted. Completely unlike the wizard she'd grown up with. Maybe she was mistaken, and it hadn't been Rowan. After all, she was in the throes of being mentally violated and could've thought she saw him. Yet she knew Rowan had been there, and that Therron had been right to suspect him of nefarious intentions. Rowan salaciously said something about her being a new plaything, which Rori didn't understand, nor did she know why he'd been so interested in the man's cellar. But she could imagine what someone like him would have hidden beneath his house.

Futnuckers and bumblesticks. Rowan was considered family, same as Meg. And both of them knew too many of their secrets and vulnerabilities.

A shudder slithered across her skin, and she kept herself as still as possible. The magic bonds burned anew, and she struggled to calm her nerves. What role did Rowan play in all this? He'd seemed on intimate terms with the man. What had he called him? Hunter. The name stirred a memory, but it escaped before fully forming. In its place was a sense of foreboding and doom. This was bad.

She kept her eyes closed and listened. Sounds came to her from someone nearby. His steady breathing and slight shuffling of his feet gave no hint to what he was doing. Beyond his noises, there was a muted silence that unnerved her. She knew what that odd quiet meant.

They were in a soundproof room. A room perfect for torture. The cellar Rowan had mentioned? Somewhere else?

Rori opened her eyes slowly and blinked against the stunningly bright lights. After a few moments, her vision adjusted, and she saw the looming figure of the man who'd kidnapped her. The madman had his back to her as he hunched over a table set out with tools meant for torture. She recognized many of them; others were a curious mystery to her. Images of what each implement could do flashed through her mind, and just as quickly, she shunted them away.

Her gaze shifted to the walls, which were covered by

thick padding, just as she'd suspected they would be. A small table sat off to the side, and a hospital bed with thick straps snugged against the wall on her left. An antique display cupboard, the kind with drawers below and glass-fronted shelves above, looked oddly out of place in the otherwise sterile modern setting. Bottles and vials crowded the shelves, some bearing the same symbols she saw on the glass prisons she'd taken from Acelyne. How many lives had they stolen over the years? Hundreds? Thousands?

Nausea churned in her gut, and her gaze slid back to the man. He turned slightly, his face in profile, and she was reminded of another man, one whom she'd loved with her entire being, and feared half as much. A man who'd criticized and complimented, who'd challenged and cheered, a man who'd given her life.

The sense of familiarity pitted in her already unsettled belly, and from somewhere deep within the core of her soul, a wail of despair threatened to erupt from her clamped lips.

No. No dear gods, please, no.

The pleas were useless. There was no denying the inescapable nightmare that her realization brought. She could hide from it all she wished, but it wouldn't make the truth of her situation disappear.

Tears stung her eyes as she studied the slope of his shoulders, and the way his fingers flexed as he considered each tool. Those two seemingly unimportant details were clues that this man, this monster, was her father. Hagan MacNair, now the infamous Hunter Pearson. Fuckity fuck fuck. She was fucked.

A sliver of annoyance spread through her veins. She should've recognized him. Should've known him the moment he violently attacked her at that house she felt vaguely familiar in, but there was nothing fatherly in the way he had violated her mind, searching the expanse of her memories without care to her consent or comfort.

Rage burned the last of the lycenum from her system, and her mind fully cleared as if clouds had blocked the sun. The memory of how close he'd come to finding her secret ripped through her with agonizing anxiety. He'd nearly found it—and destroyed her in the process. Thank the gods for that traitor Rowan. In a way, he'd saved Rori's life. If she ever saw him again, she'd thank him before kicking his scrawny ass.

She flexed her bound hand and tried again to slip it from the magical bonds, to no avail. Hunter Pearson was nothing like her father. Damn, it annoyed her she didn't recognize him, but there was precious little to connect him to her memories. His damaged face looked nothing like the man she'd grown up idolizing. His voice, distorted and raspy from whatever had caused his deformity, wasn't the same she heard in her mind. Even his scent was off. She breathed in and scrunched her nose at the acridness that filled her senses. An open bottle sat on the edge of the table, its contents the cause of the odor.

Mistlethwain. A poison she knew well. And, lucky her, one of the one hundred thirty-seven she was immune to. Would he know that? She had to assume he knew everything about her life now. A jag of self-pity cut at her thoughts, but she shut it down. Now was not the time to feel sorry for herself. Her dad was dead. This man wished her dead. End of discussion. Focus, MacNair.

His damaged hand passed over a set of tools, as if he

were a tarot reader choosing a card. She couldn't see his face, but imagined his eyes were closed, allowing the instruments to speak to him. It was something he'd taught her how to do when she was six. His physical features might have changed, but it was those unconscious habits that gave him away. The young girl in her longed for the father who had challenged her to extreme limits, but always had a cuddle for her at the end of the day. That man was long gone. The sooner she accepted it, the better for everyone.

Idly, she wondered what could have marred his features and affected his speech. What would do that to a person? Several poisons that she could think of, or a whole host of chemicals. Perhaps it was from an illness. His olive-toned skin was once smooth, but now pockmarked and his damaged cheek pale with purplish veins crisscrossing his features. The beard he wore hid the deformity well enough, as did a black turtleneck. What he couldn't hide, and what worried her most, were his eyes.

Once filled with softness and love, they were hardened pits of brown that belonged to a stranger. It made her wonder what happened in the years he'd been gone. What had so thoroughly destroyed her dad and left in his place this abomination?

Was it something external? Or had he done this to himself?

A tremor of anxiety rippled down her back. She could only guess at his endgame. More questions crashed against her skull, frightening in their intensity and emotion. All of them ended with why, why, why? Then, a simple question nudged to the forefront of her mind. One she wasn't sure she wanted the answer to but had to ask.

"Does Mum know you're still alive?" The bonds that held her captive tightened, and her father's hands shook ever so slightly. She might've missed it had she not been staring at them.

"You always were clever. I'd hoped you'd lost that irritating quirk during your time at the Academy. I certainly paid Dorchmeir enough to bully it out of you." He turned fully toward her, a sneer on his broken lips.

His reply stunned her into silence. He hadn't tried to deny it, to ask forgiveness, to deflect or stall. Instead, he admitted to being responsible for the abuse she'd suffered at the hands of a stupid boy.

Her magic flared, and she saw the mean little glint light up his eyes. This was what he wanted—for her to get angry and lose control. Well, he was in for a huge disappointment. Instead of railing and lashing out like she wanted to, she nodded solemnly and withdrew her magic.

"That explains a lot. I always wondered why he had such a hard-on for me. I suppose it's nice to know it wasn't personal."

"Oh, trust me, it was. It was his hatred that made him vulnerable and easily manipulated."

Ouch. And fuck that asshole. Both of them.

"And your cash." She kept her derision contained, but only just.

Hunter chuckled. "That too."

Disgusting festering pustule of a man. Paid someone to bully his own daughter. At least she knew the level of depravity she was working with.

"Why go through all that trouble?" She glanced at the

magic bonds holding her captive and pretended innocence. "What's so special about me?"

A scalpel glinted in the harsh lights. His magic, clearly visible, swirled around the blade. "You tell me."

She allowed tears to fill her eyes and swallowed a very real lump of fear. Magic-infused torture. Just flipping great. How the hell was she to hide her unicorn now?

❦ 3 ❦

The Thames looked like an obsidian snake as it twisted its way through London. Nikala could just make out a couple walking on the other side of the river, their bodies close, heads bent. She shouldn't be able to see that far, but then, she wasn't human, was she?

A chill scraped across her skin, and she crossed her arms close over her chest. What she was, exactly, was still open to debate. Her gaze flicked to the pub a short distance from SIRE's offices. Magical portals, fairytale worlds, and a goddamned elf prince standing not more than six paces from her. If she hadn't seen the immense magic he and Cian had used to destroy Hunter's manor, she might still be in denial. But she did see it—and felt it. More intense than the little tickles that Cian's magic had given her when they made love, the intensity of Therron and Cian's magic as it whirled through stone and earth was terrifying. And intoxicating.

She pressed her hand against the glass, the cool against her skin calming her erratic nerves. She had magic, too.

One day, she might even command it as easily as the men had. Idly, she wondered whether she had as much power as them…deep down, suppressed beneath all of Hunter's experiments and modifications. Another shiver, this one full of caution. She hadn't gone into a killing rage when the men used their magic. In fact, she hadn't felt anything but relief as they destroyed her childhood home and place of torture.

The lift pinged in the outer reception area, and she turned from the window, her heart beating quickly. She pulled open a drawer to retrieve the gun she kept for these exact situations. Best to be overcautious and prepared than surprised. Cian reached for his gun tucked into his waistband. Therron merely faced the door, hands loose, eyes intent.

"Expecting someone?" Cian rolled his shoulders.

"It'll either be Hunter or Maxx." Please be the latter, she silently added.

Therron shot her a look that held daggers. Whatever he was about to say went unspoken as the door opened and an apprehensive-looking Molly peered into the room, her eyes wide.

"Blimey! Don't shoot." She held her hands up in surrender; fear crowded her soft-brown eyes.

"What are you doing here, Jones?" Cian swore as he returned the gun to his waistband.

"I brought those notebooks you gave me to scan. I figured you'd want them back and, well, was told it's safest here." She tugged a suitcase into the center of the room with a grunt.

Genuine joy at seeing the sweet woman's face washed

over Nikala like a cool shower in the hot sun. She set the weapon atop the desk in case she needed it in a hurry. Cian reached to help Molly with the suitcase, and a flash of bright red caught in the corner of Nikala's eye. A moment later, a second figure entered the office and closed the door behind her. A brightly colored scarf covered her head, and large glasses obscured her face, but she'd know her anywhere.

"Maxx!" Relief weighed heavy in Nikala's tone.

Cian's brows dipped low, but now was not the time to rehash how upset he'd been that she had hired the traitorous assassin. She had her reasons—and explained them to him several times—but from the snarl on his lips, he still hadn't made peace with the idea.

To her right, she heard Therron hiss and a moment later, a sword flew through the air and plunged into the door not an inch from Maxx's expensive head covering.

"What the hell, Therron?" Nikala turned on him, but the elf ignored her and stormed toward Maxx with death in his eyes.

Molly squeaked and rushed to stand behind Cian, using him as a shield. She couldn't blame her. Molly was an analyst, unused to the messy business Nikala often found herself embroiled in.

"Everywhere you go, destruction follows. I told you in the pub you were a traitor and deserved to die, and that is still my belief," Therron accused Maxx.

To her credit, Maxx neither flinched nor lashed out. Instead, she inclined her head to Therron. "You speak true, Your Highness." With absolute calm, she placed two fingers on the wobbling steel blade and puckered her lips. "Either your aim is terrible, or you do not wish me dead just yet."

Therron snatched his sword from the door and held it to the spy's throat. "Where is Rori? What has that fiend done with her?"

Maxx looked to Nikala, fear in her eyes. "Hunter has her? How long?"

"A few hours." Nikala tapped her nails on the desk, frowning. Her phone sat impotent a few inches from her fingers, and she itched to try her tracking app one more time. "I can't locate him. Is it possible he went back to the other place?" Fuck. Why couldn't she say the name of Cian's homeworld? More mind fuckery, perhaps, or a general discomfort with knowing there were worlds beyond Earth. She guessed the former, with a smidge of the latter. It was all still too new, too fresh, too wild to comprehend.

"Faerie? Impossible. The queens would know," Cian insisted.

"Not impossible." Maxx ignored Therron's sword and explained, "There are three doorways I know of in Faerie that are hidden from the queens. One in the Seelie Palace, another in the Unseelie Palace, and the third at Rowan's. If Hunter were stupid enough, he could hide there, especially if he was absolutely certain Rowan wouldn't disturb him." The accusation lingered in her tone, and Cian nodded as if to confirm Rowan was dead. "Well, that's a relief. He was getting far too uppity lately." Her glance flicked to Nikala and back to Cian. "We must hurry. If Hunter has Rori, there isn't much time."

"Why does he need her?" Nikala slid the phone off the

desk and tucked it into her back pocket. She'd try the app again in a minute. Hunter couldn't have just disappeared.

Maxx closed her eyes a moment before replying. "I don't know. I've spent the past two decades trying to find out, but I'll tell you this—if he gets what he's after, we have more than war to worry about." She removed the overlarge glasses and met Therron's intense gaze. "Either slit my throat or let me go. The choice is yours, but this is rather tedious."

Therron hesitated a moment before he sheathed his sword. A heartbeat later, it vanished. Nikala's small gasp echoed in the suddenly silent room. Everyone watched as the elf prince placed his hand over the gash his sword had made in the wood. The words he spoke made the hairs on her arms raise, and she fought the urge to wipe the man's magic from her skin. Not that it hurt, but the tenderness she sensed, the pure devotion she felt in the healing, made her yearn for something that had been lost the day her father had given her to Hunter. She glanced at Cian and saw that he, too, was affected by what Therron was doing.

Maybe he also yearned for something lost the day his father faked his own murder. Something neither of them would ever get back, but perhaps together, could give each other. They could love and mourn and heal together. Forever, if he'd have her. The admission surprised her, and she looked away quickly before Cian caught her in the sappy moment.

Therron finished his healing, or whatever it was he did, and bent his head as if praying. What god would elves pray to? Her mind spun to Taryn and Rhoane, and a fresh shudder ran its course down her back and she wondered if she'd ever get used to this. Elves. Gods. Faeries. She sucked in a breath and rubbed her hands down her jeans. She had no choice. Adapt or die, she always said. But this time, it was personal.

"Be a dear and unpack the bag." Maxx indicated the suitcase, and Cian hefted it onto the sofa.

Methodically, he began to remove the notebooks she had stolen from Hunter's manor. Molly slipped from behind him, her gaze locked on Therron.

"Is he, is that, oh my golly gosh. You're Therron Mistwalker. An elven prince, here." It was barely a whisper, yet Molly's words filled the room. "Are all elves this pretty? He is stunningly gorgeous. Why's his hair short? I thought elves only wore their hair long. Wait." Molly turned to Cian. "Why is an elf in the human realm?" Now her tone turned serious and frightened. Her naturally strawberries-and-cream skin paled to an ugly ashen shade.

"Who is this?" Therron indicated Molly, and Nikala moved to protect the girl, but Cian stood to his full height and stared the elf down.

"Molly Jones. She works for an agency that maintains peace between our world and here, and I consider her a friend." The implied threat in his last words weren't lost on anyone.

Molly smiled up at him with a sweet blush, and Cian grinned. "Aw, MacNair, I always knew you cared."

"Don't let it go to your head, Jones," Cian teased. "Hate to break it to you, but this one has some sort of complicated relationship with my sister." He motioned to Therron.

"Of course he does. All the gorgeous ones are taken." Molly mock sobbed, winking at Nikala.

"You'll find your own Prince Charming someday, Jones.

I've no doubt." Cian put an arm around her and gave a gentle squeeze. To Therron, he added, "You said you know what Hunter needs from my sister."

Therron's glance flicked to Maxx and back. "I do not have confidence that what I share will stay between us, and I cannot risk Rori's life until I know for certain these two are to be trusted. Especially her." He jabbed a finger toward Maxx.

They all looked at Maxx, who held up her hands and smirked. "I mean, he's not wrong. I am a traitor, after all. But Molly's loyalty shouldn't be questioned." The joking tone didn't go over well, and she sighed. "Fine. What do we have to do to prove our loyalty?"

A thin golden thread of magic appeared between Therron's outstretched fingers. "Invoke the Oath of Ainech."

Molly gasped and covered her mouth, eyes huge with dread and shaking her head.

"The fuck?" Nikala whispered as she looked to Cian for an answer.

He half shrugged, as if he had no idea what the oath meant, but from Molly's reaction and the way the color drained from Maxx's face and her lips flatlined, Nikala guessed it was some serious shit.

"Therron," Nikala cooed as she cautiously stepped toward him. "We're all friends here. Yes, Maxx is a spy and assassin. So is Cian. So am I. We're not bad people. Well, maybe a little bad, but for a good reason." She was rambling, but something in her knew that this oath was forbidden.

She reached out to touch Therron's hand, to try to convince him the oath wasn't necessary. The golden thread of magic leapt to her outstretched fingers and wrapped around them with such force she squeaked like a damn mouse. Her! Famed killer, emotionless bitch, Nikala St. James was afraid of a single thread of magic.

Therron's eyes bulged, and he clasped her hand in his own. The air whooshed around them; a moment later, they stood in an old-fashioned room with luxurious fabrics covering a huge bed with four posters and curtains.

Who the hell slept like that anymore? Nikala's head buzzed and her legs felt weak, as if they were about to collapse at any moment.

"What did you do to me?" She snatched her hand from Therron's grip, not liking the way his eyes were filled with confusion and worry.

"I didn't do this. You did." He stared hard at her, his lips pale. "Who are you? Truly?"

The urge to tell him everything about her life, what she knew, what she guessed, what she feared overwhelmed her with its ferocity. She opened her mouth to speak but shut it with a snap.

The truth was, she had no idea who she was.

4

Nikala pulled her gaze from Therron's stern glare and froze with a new kind of fear she'd never had. Too many firsts were happening with her lately. She didn't like this. Not one fucking bit. She took in their surroundings, more confused than ever how the bloody hell they'd gotten there.

The room was lovely, with feminine fabrics in luxe silks and rich velvets in shades of green and pink covering every surface of the walls and furnishings. Lush, thick rugs lay over wood flooring stained a dark shade of mahogany. It reminded Nikala of the manor in Aberdeen, and she suppressed a shudder of revulsion. Except this room felt heavy with history and lived lives. Yet there was a lightness to it, as if joy were a daily occurrence here. There was an ethereal playfulness in the decorations. Especially in the paintings which, if she looked too closely, were almost pornographic.

In one, set against a backdrop of rolling green hills, several groups of what could only be described as fairytale creatures picnicked in a lovely meadow. All very idyllic, except for the fact that every single person was naked and a few of the groups were actively involved in orgies. When she squinted to better see the creatures, she could swear they moved. She looked away from the painting and kept her eyes focused on the dressing table, which was innocuous enough. Only a silver hairbrush and comb were laid out on the glossy surface. Her fingers itched to touch the brush, to feel the bristles against her skin.

A prickling ran along her arms, making goose bumps rise and the tiny hairs on her arms quiver. Whose room was this? There was a familiarity in the place that unnerved her. It wasn't anywhere Hunter had taken her; she was sure of it. She knew most of his labs, and this wasn't one of them. Her gaze went to Therron and balked at the glare he gave her. His spoken question hung between them, and she shook her head in answer.

She didn't know where they were, or how they'd gotten there. A nagging little tremble in the back of her skull mocked her, as if she should know this place.

"Where are we?" She avoided answering the elf's other question.

"The Unseelie Palace in Faerie. I've not been in this particular room, but it's similar enough to the rest of Midna's palace that it's safe to assume. The question is, why here?" Therron gazed at the bedchamber, his eyes narrowed as if in deep thought.

"More importantly, how did this happen? I know I didn't do this." Her hand clasped over her mouth, and she whimpered as a shot of pain struck her skull. "That's a lie. I did bring us here. But I don't know how." She hadn't meant to lie, or to confess she hadn't told the truth, but she was compelled to all the same. As if a force beyond her own free will dragged it from her. "I don't like it here. No, that's not right. I'm confused and scared." What the hell? Was she going to confess every fucking sin she'd ever made? Why couldn't she shut up?

Therron took her hand and smoothed it like a parent would a child, a very intimate thing to do, but it seemed appropriate in the moment. And honestly, she welcomed his touch. It reminded her she was real. He was real. This wasn't some fucked-up nightmare. It wasn't the room she feared, but something else. Elusive, yet nearly within reach.

"You brought us somewhere locked in your memories. Either you've been here before, or someone very special to you has and you're channeling their memory." Therron kept his tone level, deliberate.

If he was trying to calm her, then he must've been totally freaked out.

"I swear to you, I didn't intend this. I didn't even mean to touch your magic. That's what it was that did this, right?" She looked at her slightly trembling fingers in wonder.

"I'm equally at a loss as to how this happened. I had not yet spoken the oath, but I was thinking the words when you reached out." His eyes narrowed and head cocked. "Somehow, we are bound to the oath. And to each other."

She pulled away, hands held up in defense. "No. I didn't consent to this. Take it back." She moved farther into the room, rubbing her arms as if slaking his magic from her.

"I can't, Nikala. Whatever you did, it activated the oath."

Now he'd pissed her off. She was trying to be reasonable, but to blame her for something she didn't do, or even know how to do, was too much.

"I didn't do anything, you stupid elf. I was trying to stop you from forcing your oath on Maxx and Molly." Her voice rose to just below shrill. She glanced from one side of the room to the other, looking for an escape and finding none. Wherever they were, Therron had to get them out of there. The knot of panic swelled in her gut. It was only a matter of time before the manic urge to destroy magic users would take over her senses.

"I don't understand how this happened. The oath was meant only for those two women, not for you or me. This I promise you."

"She doesn't know what she is, Therron." A feminine voice sounded beside him, and he turned to stare in the direction the voice had come from. But there was no one there. "She has no control over these events and is frightened, which is a new feeling for her. Be gentle with her. Everything depends upon it."

"What do you mean?" Therron glanced at her, and she glared at him as if he had completely lost his marbles. Perhaps he had. Perhaps she had.

Nikala crossed her arms, her brows dipped dangerously low with her sneer. "Are you asking me? Or that disembodied voice I'm hearing? Please, God, tell me you hear it, too."

"You can't see her?" Therron looked from her to the window and back.

"See who? The rude voice that says I don't know what I am? Um, human, you obsequious blob of nothing. Also, fuck you."

Therron winced at her harsh words. But who the hell was she-it-they to talk about her like that?

"It's difficult to explain, but the voice you hear is Ishnara. Well, her ghost anyway. Why can't she see you?"

The last part, Nikala assumed was said to the ghost.

Nikala processed what Therron had told her and stood stock-still, afraid to move or speak or do anything that might cause her heart to stop beating or her murderous urge to burst forth. She'd finally reached the point of not trusting herself or reality. A slow coolness started at her brow and moved down across her skin, leaving her damp with an apprehension she'd never experienced before. Ghosts. Talking ghosts. Her father's ghost hadn't frightened her, but this one did. At least she couldn't see the damned thing.

"I don't wish her to."

Ishnara's voice sounded close to Nikala. Too close. She refused to scream, but the effort not to was unbearable.

"There is a darkness in her I cannot name. It worries me."

The fuck? The ghost was messing with her. Had to be. What sort of nonsense was that? But she knew, deep down, what Ishnara meant, and it worried her as well.

"She was tampered with by the same man who is controlling my father, and who is responsible for kidnapping fae," Therron explained, as if it were a simple thing.

The man had a name. Hunter Pearson. Maybe Ishnara wouldn't recognize the name—or, even more troubling, she might.

The air around them vibrated. "Where is this monster? I shall see to it he never harms our kind again, for it is not just fae he has taken." An intense, angry tone filled Ishnara's words.

"He's in the human realm." Therron held his hands up in supplication. "Beyond your reach, I'm afraid." He hesitated a moment before adding, "He kidnapped Rori."

"No." It was barely a whisper and spoken like a mother who loved her child very much. The amount of emotion in that one tiny word was enough to ignite Nikala's jealousy that she'd been denied a mother by two selfish men only interested in their own agendas.

The trembling air suddenly stilled, like the calm at the center of a tornado, and Nikala braced—for what, she wasn't certain. But a pissed-off ghost couldn't be good.

Ishnara shimmered into a semi-transparent form, and Nikala gasped. The ghost was gorgeous. Dark, nearly black hair, brown eyes that held a lifetime's worth of sadness, pale skin, and soft-pink lips that drooped into a frown. She wore a lavender gown that revealed more than it covered but was tastefully designed to leave just enough to the imagination. The filmy fabric floated as if by its own accord. Peeking from behind the woman were gossamer wings that caught the sunlight drifting in through the window.

Nikala wasn't sure whether she should bow, curtsey, or shit herself. The latter was definitely winning, and that alone was horrifying.

"Settle, little one. I am Queen Ishnara of the Unseelie Court, dead these many centuries, but unable to leave this realm." Her glance flicked to Therron and then back to Nikala. "I mean you no harm."

Nikala took a step backward, half tempted to bolt through the closed door. Wherever it led had to be better than this nightmare she couldn't escape. Ghosts. Dead queens. She dared not ask what next. Thus far, that had only provoked more chaos.

Ishnara studied her a moment before drifting close enough their noses touched. Every cell in Nikala's body screamed at her to jump away from the creature, but she forced herself to stand still. Her eyes widened, and she was sure they filled with awe. Or horror. She really couldn't say.

"You truly don't know who you are, do you?" Ishnara pulled away, tears sparkling in her long-dead eyes. "Oh, sweet child. I'm sorry you've been kept in the dark for so long."

Nikala crossed her arms with a snort. The nerve of the woman! "I know perfectly well who I am. Who the hell is she to say I don't?" She glared at Therron. This was becoming tedious. "I'd like to go home now."

The sound of a key turning alerted them to potential danger, and Therron ushered Nikala toward the dressing room behind them. Her heart ratcheted up again, beating so hard she could barely breathe. What now? No, she didn't want to know. And yet, she desperately needed to know how this nightmare played out. For that's what it had to be —a dream, nothing more. Ghosts. Blargh!

"They can't see you," Ishnara said. "You aren't fully here, though I am unsure how you've managed to be here and yet not."

If her words were meant to calm, they did the opposite. Nikala was about to question her when a woman rushed into the room, hair mussed, eyes wild.

"Mairead! My darling sister, you've come home." She looked around the bedchamber, confusion dawning in her features. "Mairead? This is no time to play your hiding game. Come out now, I command you." But there was more fear in her voice than force. "Sweetheart, please. I've missed you. The entire court has missed you. Please, don't do this to me."

Mairead. She'd heard wrong. Had to have. Nikala slowly shook her head against the voices in her mind telling her what her heart couldn't comprehend. Maybe Mairead was a popular name in Faerie. Perhaps it was just a bizarre coincidence in a string of strange occurrences.

"That is Midna, present queen of the Unseelie Court," Therron whispered. "Mairead is her sister, missing now for several months."

The queen's sister? No, it wasn't possible. Nikala chewed the inside of her cheek and winced at the pain she caused. Ishnara caught her eye and gave a slow nod as if to confirm what Nikala tried to deny. Nikala answered with a quick shake of her head and glance at Therron. He couldn't know. None of them could know. Ever.

She swallowed hard, trying to deny the truth that battered against her very existence. The reason the room was familiar made perfect sense now. And yet she still sought to hide from what was right in front of her. Tears filled her eyes, and she blinked furiously against them. A sense of belonging, of finally finding her home, wrapped around her with protective warmth, and she sighed with a lifetime's worth of longing.

Midna's wings vibrated with her angst, and Nikala gave an unconscious twitch to her shoulder blades. What had Cian told her about faerie's wings? She racked her brain to recall his words. Something about all fae had them, but only royalty showed them. Nikala nearly gasped, but covered it with a cough. Therron glanced at her, and she scowled in reply. None of this made sense.

And yet just there, in the way the queen held herself, in the angle of her jaw, the slope of her nose, Nikala saw the resemblance to the woman who had come to her when she held the pendant.

The woman had called herself Mairead.

In those resemblances, she saw herself.

Cian had said she was fae. Cian had called her princess. Did Cian know? Or was it another coincidence? She'd have to ask when they returned to SIRE's offices. Her gaze went to Midna, and then to Ishnara. Did Midna know Mairead had a child? Ishnara reached out to grip Nikala's hand, as if she could read her thoughts. No, Midna didn't know. And now the queen mourned the loss of her missing sister.

Mairead. The queen's sister. Nikala embraced the truth with her whole heart and accepted—finally—that the woman in the pendant was the same Mairead Therron said was missing from the Unseelie Palace. Her mother.

At last, she knew who and what she was. Cautious elation turned to harrowing worry—her mother was one of the kidnapped fae. She had to save her before it was too late. Before Hunter found her and learned the truth of who Nikala was. Before Hunter destroyed everything. Before he destroyed her chance at happiness. Destroyed her family.

5

Despite their sometimes adversarial relationship, it broke Therron's heart to see Midna dart from the bedchamber to the bathing chamber, back to the outer sitting room, and finally to the dressing room in search of her sister. The fear clear in her features, the agitation of her vibrating wings, and the sorrow in her voice was too much. This queen, so fierce and brave and strong, who never showed vulnerability or weakness, was caught in a spiral of despair that she had to hide in the privacy of her sister's rooms.

She passed them several times without even a glance in their direction. With a sob, she returned to the bedroom, and they followed. Tears shone in her lovely eyes. Her hair, vibrant pink upon entering, turned a dull yellow, and her wings lost their luster.

Several soldiers stood uncomfortably in the doorway, shifting from foot to foot, unsure what to do.

Midna waved them off. "Search the grounds. If there was an intruder to my sister's apartments, I want them caught and brought to me. Whoever is playing this cruel joke will pay."

The soldiers left and quietly closed the door behind them. When they'd gone, Midna crawled upon the great bed and curled into a tight ball. The sound of weeping came from her, and Therron hesitated a moment before reaching out to comfort the Unseelie queen.

Ishnara stopped him before his hand made contact and indicated he stay away from her kinswoman.

Silently, he obeyed, though it tore at him to do so. She needed someone by her side in these moments. Someone she could trust. Someone to confide in. Someone to love. Only the first two he could offer, and love only as a friend.

"Dear sister, where are you? What has become of you?" Midna mumbled into the blankets. After a long pause, she sat up and wiped the tears from her eyes before pushing her hair off her face.

Therron studied Midna's actions, a revelation forming in his mind that was unsettling, and yet made perfect sense. It wasn't so much the way Midna huffed as she stood, nor the imperial way she strode into a room, but it was the small things: A flick of her wrist. The slope of her nose in profile. The curve of her lips. He glanced at Nikala and saw that she, too, saw the similarities between the Unseelie queen and herself. Her scowl deepened, and Therron hid a grin. She knew. And now she knew he knew.

"Come back to me, please." Midna kissed the pillow on Mairead's bed and smoothed her gown before leaving the room.

None of them spoke for several moments until finally Therron broke the silence. "Have you seen Midna before?"

The question was meant for Nikala, and Ishnara watched them both intently.

"No."

"It looked like you recognized her."

"I told you, I don't know her. Therron, I don't want to be here. Please take me home."

He took Nikala's hands in his own and held them tightly. It was time he told her a truth of his own. One he wasn't too happy to reveal.

"The oath that binds us—it prevents us from lying to each other, but that is for us alone. I swear on my honor as an elven prince, I will not tell anyone anything you share with me." His gaze bore into her, and he hoped she understood the deeper meaning of his words.

"You mean, I can't lie to you? Ever? About anything?"

Her hands trembled in his grip, and he reminded himself she was a spy and an assassin. Her entire life had been a lie. Telling the truth was most likely a hazard she avoided as often as possible.

"You cannot. Nor I, to you. If you try to break the oath and lie, you will suffer great pain, possibly even death. Most likely death."

Her eyes narrowed and nostrils flared. A manic look settled in her eyes, and he tensed, unsure what it meant, or what she would do next. She closed her lids and breathed deeply. When she opened them again, the mania was gone. Finally, she gave a slight nod.

He wanted to know about Mairead, but had to be gentle.

Nikala grinned and cocked her head. "No lying to me, huh? How'd you get that scar on your face?"

Therron winced at her directness. No one had ever dared ask him about his scar before, though he suspected many wished they could. There was no point trying to evade the question, or even to lessen the importance of it. The oath forced him to tell the truth, but he could decide how much of his sad tale to share with her.

"I'll tell you when we're back in London."

"Tell me now."

It wasn't so much a demand as a test. He stamped down his irritation. Fine. He'd answer her question and then corner her about her knowledge and relationship with Mairead. Two could play the petty game.

"I am cursed, and I bear this mark as a symbol of my fate." Therron pointed to Ishnara, who had been hovering between them and the door Midna left through. "By her. It's a long, sordid tale, but I'll sum it up. Many centuries ago, when Ishnara was still a princess, she was betrayed by two elven princes, my ancestors. She was understandably hurt and angry, and consequently set a curse upon my family. Once every generation, a prince would be born who was the bearer of her curse. When this prince met his fated mate, she must publicly declare her love within three moonturns. If she does not, the prince will die a horrible death."

"You added that last part. I never said horribly. Just that the prince would die," Ishnara corrected.

"Apologies. The prince would die. Still not great for the prince, but I digress. The cycle would continue until the woman—who I should mention could not and would not be born of high status, but a commoner without any noble blood—until the woman chosen as the fated mate breaks the curse. To date, no woman has declared their love within the time frame."

"And Rori is your fated mate, I assume?" Nikala watched him, horror in her eyes.

He could only imagine what she was thinking, but honestly, it probably wasn't so different than how he'd felt for all these many years.

"Correct. Even if she weren't, she stole my heart the moment I saw her playing darts in the pub." His features softened at the memory, then immediately hardened at the image of Acelyne attacking her. The witch had already suffered the consequences of her actions; Hunter would as well. Just as soon as they found him. "Now you know. We should return to London."

"Not yet." Nikala breathed out a long, steady stream of air, her cheeks puffing with the effort. "So, Ishnara's ghost is stuck here until you break the curse, is that right? And now that you've met Rori, if she doesn't declare her love for you within three months, you'll die. That's one fucked-up curse, Therron. And all because an elven prince broke your heart?" This was directed to the dead queen.

"There's more to it than that, but in simple terms, yes." Ishnara's ghostly form drifted from one side of the room to the other, her agitation clear in the disrupted air around them. "I did try to revoke the curse, but once said, it's impossible to take back. I am not so much stuck here as I choose to be here to help where I can. Lady Rainne finding my book, for instance. Therron collecting the ring that controls the demon in the void."

Therron patted his pocket where the ring was hidden. Fury, bright as a spark, sped through him, cumulating in a swirling rage in his belly. "Rowan set that thing to attack Rori?"

"He stole the ring from your brother's rooms, and yes, commanded the demon to kill Rori. But she is much stronger than she seems. I'm sure this vexed Rowan very much." Ishnara chuckled in an eerie, hollow sort of way. "I will not miss him. Horrible man. I only wish I saw his deception earlier, but my focus has been on your family and Midna's. I don't have the energy to spare to watch over all Cilachaem."

"Did you know Rori would be my fated mate?" An unsettling question formed in his mind, and he pushed it aside.

"I have never known who the mate would be until the connection is made. Once you saw Rori in the Shoogly Dragon, only then did I become aware of her. Although, I should've guessed before then."

Nikala stood beside a dressing table and picked up a silver hairbrush. Her face went all soft as she stroked the bristles.

"What do you mean? Why should you have known?" Therron dragged his attention away from Nikala, back to Ishnara.

"She and her brother have always been special."

At this, Nikala glanced up, her focus fully on the Unseelie queen's ghost. "Special how?"

Ishnara's wings fluttered, and she looked to Therron, as if seeking permission. "I have no oath with this woman. What I share might change the course of not just your path, but hers."

"Tell us." Therron's throat went dry, and prickles of

apprehension stung his skin.

"Though Cian and Rori are not noble born, they are descended from a fierce warrior called Neve. She was my personal guard, and the best friend a queen could ever wish for. She had a rare talent I'd never seen before—she could command Pegasus. She didn't have a Pegasus soul, nor could she shift into one, but they obeyed her implicitly. It was truly remarkable. She loved my brother, the crown prince, and was to marry him, but before the wedding, he was killed in battle." Ishnara cast Therron a dour glance. "It was an elven arrow that stopped his heart. I was sent to the elven palace as a peace offering of sorts. My father did not want war and wished to form an alliance with the elves. I suppose you could say I was a gift for the princes."

Nikala sucked in her breath, but Ishnara stopped her protests.

"I went willingly. And, truth be told, I once loved the princes. But that is a story for another day. Neve eventually found love again and sired two children, a boy and a girl. The boy had no remarkable abilities, but the girl had the soul of a Pegasus." Another gasp from Nikala drew a smile from Ishnara. "Through the matrilineal line of succession starting with Neve, there were always two children born, a boy and a girl. And always the boy held no special soul, but the girl did. It changed from child to child, but there was always something unique about the girls. It was the same with Cian and Rori, with one notable exception."

Therron and Nikala sat upon the bed, fully engrossed in Ishnara's story. He knew what was hidden in Rori, but not her brother. If Cian possessed a mythical soul, it could be anything. His fingertips brushed the scar on his cheek and the question tickled his mind yet again. Cian might be the dragon Rhoane had seen in Therron's future.

"It wasn't until you healed the lycan that I fully understood. If not for Taryn, we may never have discovered Rori's true soul." Ishnara's gaze was far away as she continued. "Never in the history of Neve's legacy was there a unicorn, until now. Yet you only discovered one part of her secret, Therron. There is something else, something elusive I've not yet been able to name. As for Cian, I am still uncertain what lurks in his soul. It is dark, that I do know. But not all darkness is dangerous. It could be that he has the ability to command creatures, or perhaps even shift into one. We will not know until it manifests, if it ever does." She held up her hands, shrugging. "I suspect their mother and grandmother knew they were special because both children were heavily warded since birth."

"Warded? As in, blocked from that power? Why?" Nikala's eyes were huge and filled with wonder. Quick as a carlix, they clouded. "Never mind. I know why. To protect them from Hunter."

"Not just protect them," Ishnara whispered. "To protect all Cilachaem. All signs point to this being the time of change for our world. Rori and Cian are at the epicenter of that change. One drop of their blood could alter the course of history."

Her ghostly eyes bore into Therron, and he felt the warning lurking in their depths like a physical blow to his sternum. Through Hunter's children, he could command immeasurable power. He could destroy an entire world or even two worlds.

❧ 6 ❧

A stream of crimson made a lazy path across Rori's skin, mesmerizing in its languid procession. She stared, transfixed, as Hunter gathered her blood into another vial. That made twelve so far, with another eleven empty vials waiting patiently on the table to her right. They were nothing like the glass pendants she and the other fae had been imprisoned in. Those were simple trinkets compared to the elaborate bone and silver pieces Hunter lovingly stroked, with each topper placed to hold her blood securely within its confines. He'd bragged about how clever he was to have discovered that if he lined the inside of the vial with pure silver, it would keep her blood from turning to glitter. Snickertits. She'd rather hoped it would evaporate or something before he could use it for whatever evil purposes he intended.

"What kind of bone is that?" Her voice came out raspy, and she had to expend too much effort just to say the few words.

"Dragon. Now hush. You don't want me to force more magic down your throat, do you?"

She shook her head, more out of incredulousness than acquiescence. Dragon bone? He'd said dragon bone; she was sure of it. A memory of Taryn insisting Cilachaem had dragons forced its way past his magic. He'd drugged her with more lycenum, this time adding a wicked spell that made her nauseous and sleepy. He was testing her limits, she knew, and yet her curiosity wouldn't let her remain docile.

"Where did you find a dragon?"

The sound he made could've been a chuckle or an irritated grunt; she wasn't sure. "Still so clever and curious, even when it behooves you not to be."

Despite the consequences, she searched his words for any sort of affection, and felt the bitter sting of disappointment when she found none. It was merely a statement of fact said without emotion.

He put a stopper in the vial and breathed in as if it were an expensive perfume made just for him. Another vial was placed against the underside of her forearm, where he'd made several incisions to collect her blood.

Her head ached from the drugs, and she was woozy from the loss of blood, even though it wasn't more than a cupful. Seeing his reaction with each vial filled made her want to retch—and kick his ass. He studiously ignored her question and focused on gathering every drop of the crimson liquid. When the stream ran dry, he cursed and flashed his scalpel to make yet another cut along her arm.

"Why must you heal so quickly? It's rather irritating."

"Maybe it has to do with my wild magic."

A twitch of his lips, a slight pause of the scalpel. "What makes you think you have wild magic?"

Even now, locked in a room somewhere far from the Faerie queens, it made her heart quicken to say the words aloud. They were a death sentence if someone from Faerie heard, and now she'd admitted to her captor something she could barely admit to herself for most of her life.

"The day you died—disappeared—I was practicing spells you'd taught me. Without warning, I lost control of my magic. It spun in a tempest so terrifying, I clamped my magic shut and never told a soul what happened. After that, I didn't use magic unless absolutely necessary. I couldn't risk Eirlys discovering my secret." She watched his reaction to the deliberate use of the word and was pleased when his gaze flicked to her, eyes intent.

"That's what you're hiding? Wild magic?" Disappointment dripped from each syllable. He rubbed his chin with his damaged hand and grunted. "It makes sense, and yet, Acelyne thought there was more to you."

At the mention of the enchantress, Rori stiffened. Of course they were business partners, but the way he said her name was more of a caress for a loved one than indifference for a casual acquaintance. He filled another vial and added the stopper. This time, he didn't inhale the scent but merely set it with the others and grabbed a new vial. Her admission had distracted him, which was exactly what she wanted.

"She told me I was perfect," Rori said quietly. "Just before I killed her."

Anger flashed in Hunter's eyes, and his lips tightened with a snarl. "She underestimated you. We all did."

His voice lowered to a soft tone. Was that pride she

heard? Or was that wishful thinking? After all this time, she was still trying to gain his approval. What a fucking nutjob she was.

"We? You mean you, Acelyne, and Rowan? Was Dorchmeir part of your plan? Or did Acelyne drag him along for funsies?"

"Funsies? Are you a child?"

A shake of his head showed his disgust, and Rori hid a smile. The more she could anger him, the better.

"My association with Dorchmeir ended when you left the Academy. Acelyne thought it fitting we use him as bait. She always hated the boy. In that, you had something in common."

Again, the softer tone.

Her belly twisted with the realization that he had feelings for Acelyne. Wicked imaginings pierced her skull, hurting as deeply as when she learned her father had died. Only this was worse because now she knew he had deceived everyone, especially her mum. She had to know how far the lies went, yet at the same time didn't wish to know.

"Were you lovers?" she blurted before she could think better of it.

Again, that sound that could've been a chuckle or a grunt came from him. She felt his magic wrap around her skin, seducing her to sleep.

"We weren't lovers, no." His scratchy voice held a hint of melancholy. "But I did love her as a brother would his sister. I'm sure you can understand that kind of love."

Something in his tone, in the way he held her arm more gently as he spoke, intrigued her. Taking advantage of his distracted vulnerability, she locked her mind against him and slipped a thread of her own magic into his touch, and then to his thoughts. Just a whisper of magic, not enough to notice or cause alarm. Warmth infused her, and her head filled with images of him and Acelyne. Years and years of memories played out in vignettes, each more confusing than the first.

This wasn't her magic's doing.

"Why are you showing me this?" She wished he'd stop, but at the same time needed more to understand fully what he was trying to tell her.

"So that perhaps you don't hate me so much."

"I don't hate you." Not fully. He was, after all, still her father. Even if he was hardly recognizable as the man who raised her, his genetics, his history were a part of her.

A snort answered. "You should. I've done reprehensible things. Things I can never atone for, nor do I wish to."

"Why do them? What do you hope to accomplish?"

He swiped her arm with the pad of his forefinger and sucked the blood he'd gathered. A repulsive groan rumbled from his chest, and his eyes rolled up in ecstasy.

She held back the disgust that roared from her belly and threatened to spew over his stupid face. So fucking gross.

"Do you know how close you were to freeing the captives in Acelyne's pendants? Just one drop of your blood accompanied with the words you used would've freed them all. But now, you'll never have the chance." A vicious little grin marred his already ugly features.

She shuttled aside the fact that he knew about something that had happened in the privacy of Eirlys's rooms. Something no one should've known about except the three people present: her, Therron, and the Seelie queen. Unless there had been a servant present. She couldn't recall, but there were almost always servants in Eirlys's bedchamber or close by.

She circled her thoughts back to what he said about her never having the chance to free the captured fae. The meaning dug into her love of the man who had raised her like a worm burrowing through an apple, leaving a hole in its wake.

"I suppose now that you have my blood, you'll kill me?" This cat-and-mouse game he was playing was exhausting. For every question she asked, he introduced several more without giving coherent answers.

"Something like that."

"Something worse than death? What, you'll keep me in an animated state, but unconscious so that you can feed from me whenever necessary like some deranged vampire?"

She imagined herself imprisoned in a glass coffin, alive yet not. If Hunter expected her to allow herself to be his snack anytime he wished, he was in for a huge disappointment. Even then, she could feel her unicorn stirring with a desire to annihilate the bone vials and the man who sat before her. It shocked her how vicious the need to destroy was. Weren't unicorns all sparkles and rainbows? Apparently not hers. And she was delighted with the revelation.

"If only you hadn't broken out of your pendant, none of this would've happened." He glanced at the small room with disdain. "One of my modern labs would've made the process so much easier." A frustrated sigh flared his nostrils. "What's done is done."

The images stopped abruptly, and Rori reeled with how quickly he was able to control his magic. One final memory lingered…whether by Hunter's choice or not, she couldn't say. He and Acelyne were in Meg's cottage, making potions using the very cauldron Rori had used dozens of times when she'd visited Meg. It hurt her heart to think that her friend was involved, but from the memory, she sensed Meg had no idea what Hunter and Acelyne were up to. Gods, she hoped not.

It would kill her mum to learn that they'd been betrayed by the healer as well. It occurred to her that she'd not recognized Maxx's name when Eirlys questioned Dorchmeir, and that her mum had most probably warded her from remembering her dearest friend. If her mum had the forethought to ward Rori from future pain, then she most certainly had suspicions about not only her best friend, but her allegedly dead spouse.

A visit with her mum was long overdue, and now Rori had a list of questions she needed answers to. That would have to wait. A heavy drowsiness crept in, and she only had a short time before Hunter made good on his promise of "something else."

"If you must know, Acelyne and Meg are my half-sisters," Hunter said casually, before he blew out a breath and made a weird sort of maniacal laugh that sounded like helium released from a balloon. "Do you know how long I've wanted to tell someone? You're the first to know. Well, besides Acelyne and myself. Even Meg doesn't know." He leaned back and looked to the ceiling. "Thank you, Aurora. Thank you for letting me confess this one thing."

She scrunched her face in drowsy confusion. What the absolute fuck?

"You're welcome?" Her brain struggled to make the

connections of how they could possibly be half-siblings, coming to the only logical conclusion. "Papa MacNair cheated on Nana. What a dick. Wait, does that mean Meg is part of your sordid plan?" He'd said she didn't know, but what did that mean, exactly?

He placed a stopper in the final vial and set it with the others without the creepy inhale.

"Acelyne and Meg's father Tomas couldn't sire children for whatever reason. Their mother and my father had an affair, yes. Though I don't like the word. They loved each other fiercely. My mother never knew, nor did Tomas. He was a good man and raised both girls as his own. Even though Meg didn't know she was blood related, she loved you and your brother as if you were kin. There was an instinctive special bond that she showed the pair of you. That closeness made her not to be trusted. And there's her friendship with your mother. So no, she isn't involved, although at one time I did consider blackmailing her to help. Acelyne talked me out of it. She thought Meg could be better manipulated if she knew nothing of our schemes."

To know Meg hadn't betrayed them gave Rori some comfort, but not much. "How long have you been planning all this?" If she could keep him talking, it would give her time to metabolize the drugs without falling into a coma-like sleep.

"Oh, since before I met your mother." He leaned back in his chair, arms crossed over his chest, eyes narrowed in memory. "I was fifteen when Acelyne first approached me. Of course, I didn't believe her. You see, I adored my father. He was strong and brave, and everyone admired him. But when I confronted him, he admitted it was true. He knew about the first baby and even though he couldn't publicly claim her, he surreptitiously found ways to be part of her life. The same with Meg when she arrived several years later."

Rori let that churn in her mind a moment, her brain making connections she didn't like. "Your father is the source of our dark magic, isn't he?"

"Baltus MacNair, dark wizard, and not a soul knew his secret. Not even my mother. She died never knowing about his hidden talents, or about his bastard daughters. Pity he passed on before you were born. I'm sure he would've enjoyed instructing you in the ways of the dark. He would've found a way to harness your wild magic, I'm sure of it."

Hunter's eyes gleamed with an inner light that she found disturbing. It was almost fanatical in its luminescence.

"So Papa MacNair, you, and the enchantress cooked up this scheme to destroy Faerie and the human realm? I assume that's your plan. Kill everyone, and you alone come out the victor."

"I could give a rat's ass about Faerie. I just need those two meddling cows to stay out of my business here. I have no intention of ruling Faerie or this godforsaken world." He leaned forward with a grin that made her insides recoil. "If you think you're clever in getting me to confess, I suggest you consider the source. Am I to be trusted? Am I feeding you lies to take back to the queens?"

Despite his mocking tone, she saw the fear lurking in the depths of his eyes. He'd spoken the truth—too much of it—and regretted it.

She half shrugged and blinked as if sleepy. "What does it matter? I'll be dead or something soon. Who could I tell? I am curious, though, did you conduct any experiments on Cian? Or just me?" It was a question she'd been asking herself since she learned of the Dawn Project.

"Just you. Acelyne traced your lineage back to the Unseelie Court several millennia in the past, and it appears there's a unique power that's passed matrilineally through the women to female offspring. Cian is useless to me." His lip quirked to the side. "I hope I'm there when Nikala kills him. Her final test. Once that's complete, then I'll know she's ready."

The words hit Rori like a blow. She sucked in a breath and steadied her rampant heartbeats.

"That's your son you're talking about. Have you no compassion for your children at all?"

The intensity of his glare could've polished a rough diamond. "My children are disappointments I'd rather forget. You had your chance to earn my respect, and you failed." He held a vial beneath his nose and breathed in her essence. "Acelyne believed there was something special about you, but I don't see it. Perhaps your blood will give me answers you cannot. Pray there is a use for you after all." That mangled, maniacal laugh filled the small space.

Rori pretended to flinch against it, affecting a look of hurt and failure, but inside she seethed. Her rage burned through the lycenum and his sleeping spell. In the far reaches of her soul, something dark and powerful stirred, and she welcomed it wholly.

7

Therron shuddered at the importance of what Ishnara was telling him and Nikala. Cian and Rori, innocent of their role in Cilachaem's future, were the key to everything happening not just in his world, but in the human realm, too. Somehow, he was supposed to tell them the news without terrifying them. Not to mention Ishnara's warning that if Hunter—or anyone with evil intent—were to somehow claim or command their powers, only the stars knew what could happen. Their blood could be used for good or ill; it all depended on who controlled them first.

Therron's father's erratic behavior in the throne room came to mind. For one terrible moment, he worried that his father knew about the MacNair siblings' secret. But then he recalled how he'd summarily dismissed Cian and refused to acknowledge Rori. If his father knew how powerful the pair were, he would've kept them at the palace, where he could use them. And if his father didn't know, then for now,

Hunter also didn't know. Which meant they had time. Not much, but hopefully enough.

Heat wafted off Nikala, and he understood her rage. His own blood boiled with this new information. The fact that Rori's mother and grandmother had felt the need to protect the children at birth meant on some level, Labhruinn knew there was a danger. It was possible she and her mother warded the children out of another precaution. It could be they feared the queens discovering the children's secrets, or they were worried both had wild magic. Therron never understood why wild magic was feared and despised in the Faerie lands. Like everything, even wild magic had its uses; it just needed nurturing and someone strong enough to control their power.

The maze of possibilities, of what-ifs and whys was complicated and difficult to traverse. The only way he could know for certain why Labhruinn had warded her children was to ask her personally. He'd only met her once, and briefly at that, but he knew instantly she was not a woman to defy. Her power wasn't just through magic, but an intimidating physical presence that she exuded. No wonder Queen Eirlys had been reluctant to let her retire.

A disturbing thought crashed into his mind, and he shuddered. "Labhruinn may have had her reasons for keeping Cian and Rori's secrets, but Taryn forced Rori to expose herself. Is she in danger now?" He didn't care whether Taryn and Rhoane were gods; if they put Rori at risk, he'd have their heads.

Ishnara's lips quirked in thought. "I can't say. She was warded still when she left Elvenwood with you, and I sensed a barrier of protection from Taryn and Rhoane. Perhaps they understood her situation better than I and did what they could to mitigate the peril."

"Who is this Lauren person? I keep hearing that name." Nikala cocked her head. "Is it Lauren, like Loren? I feel like when you said it, it sounded different, more like Lahwrenn."

"It's an ancient name with many interpretations." Ishnara spelled out Labhruinn's name in the air using her magic.

That a ghost could use magic intrigued him, and worried him. He liked to believe that death stopped bad people from doing bad things, but if they were still allowed to wield magic beyond the grave—well, he understood now why Midna had been so brutal to Acelyne when destroying her body.

Nikala sighed. "That's beautiful. So, who is she?"

"She is Cian and Rori's mother," Therron answered.

Her lips tightened, and she nodded slowly. "It all makes sense now."

When she didn't continue, he gently prodded, "What does?"

"Hunter. He's terrified of Labhruinn. And I do mean terrified. Anytime her name was mentioned, he'd shit bricks."

"Why is he frightened of her?" Ishnara drifted to the window and back, her eyes misty.

Therron hesitated, but Nikala nodded and gestured to the queen. He inhaled sharply against a need to protect Rori. "What I tell you now, will you promise to hold sacred? You cannot tell anyone. I must have your promise before I say another word."

Ishnara placed her hand over her breast. "You have my word as the Unseelie queen that what you say will stay with me."

"Hunter Pearson is Hagan MacNair. He staged his own death to look like murder and has been living all these years in the human realm."

The dead queen gasped and a puff of smoke came from her lips. "The villain! Your brothers must be made aware! This man must be captured and face punishment."

"You promised, Ishnara. You cannot tell my brothers or anyone else. Not yet. Once we've captured Hunter, then the truth will come out, but not before." Therron stood to his full height and withdrew his sword. "Place your palm upon my blade and swear an oath of secrecy." He knew damn well it wouldn't hold considering she was dead, but it made him feel better all the same.

Ishnara did as asked, her eyes flinty. "Because you have sworn me to silence, I would ask the same of you. There is more to your curse than you know."

Therron looked at her, alarmed. "What else could there be?"

Ishnara glided to the door and then through it. He hesitated, unsure whether he was meant to follow. Just when he took a step, she returned.

"I hold no oath over you, but what I am about to tell you cannot go further than your ears, do you understand?" The ghost looked first to Therron, and then to Nikala.

They both nodded, though he wasn't sure what was so important it had been kept secret all this time. His curse wasn't well-known, but no one tried to hide it.

"When I cursed your family, I was angry, and hurt. I

loved the princes, truly, I did, but they deceived me in a very public, humiliating way. When I placed the curse, something happened—I am unsure what, but the curse became tangled. I have watched over the Unseelie rulers throughout the millennia. All of them, king or queen, were able to produce an heir. All of them except Midna. I have read the dark books in Elvenwood's library, and it is my fear that Midna's barrenness is somehow tied to your curse, and she cannot conceive until the curse is broken. Further, what I have surmised is, if Midna does not conceive within three moonturns of the curse being broken, she will die—painfully and hideously." Her dark eyes met his, and he saw the anguish that lurked in them.

Her curse, meant to punish elven princes, was also a death sentence to her future kin. His gaze went to the closed door, and his heart broke anew for Midna. All this time, she'd been desperate to conceive and had no idea that her fate was bound to his and Rori's.

Therron's mind whirled with all the information he had gathered. Plans whipped into formation, only to vanish when a new idea came to him. Through them all, he knew he must alert the palace. With his brother Thaddeus missing, and his father under the influence of Hunter, it was up to Theo to protect Elvenwood in his absence. It was his duty to go, but he was loath to leave Rori until he knew she was safe.

"Ishnara, are you able to get a message to my brother?"

"I can." She eyed him suspiciously. "Why can't you tell him yourself?"

"There are things I must take care of in the human realm before I return. First and foremost, I must find Rori.

Do not let Theo know she's in danger. I need him to stay strong for my mother and the kingdom. Tell him to take on the mantle of rulership without appearing to do so. He and Lady Delarainne must gain the trust of the court, and their support. I don't trust my father, not with this monster controlling him. If Taryn and Rhoane are still at Elvenwood, I could use their counsel." He thought for a moment, debating what else to share with his baby brother. "Let him know of Rowan's deception, but that it must be kept confidential to only himself and the Faerie queens for now. I believe my father wants war with Faerie not for his own desire, but for the shadow man. Tell Theo he needs to meet with Faerie's queens and conspire to thwart my father's idiocy."

"That's treason, Your Highness." The grin on Ishnara's lips belied the foul words.

"I know. But I have a death sentence anyway—why not push the sword deeper?"

"Rori loves you, Therron. Anyone could see that." Nikala's words were meant to soothe, but instead hurt.

"Perhaps, but we don't know who or what she'll be when next we see her." His gaze bore into hers, his meaning clear.

Nikala herself had showed them what Hunter was capable of. By the time they rescued Rori, she might be nothing more than a beautiful weapon, devoid of compassion. That is, if she survived Hunter's treatments.

"At least now we know what he wants from her." Nikala shook her head and snorted a laugh. "I must really be losing it because when Ishnara told us Rori had a unicorn soul, I didn't even blink. An hour ago, I would've laughed my ass off in disbelief. Faerie queens—one dead, no offense—lycans, gods, magic, and now a motherfucking unicorn!" Her eyes narrowed and tone sobered. "What could Hunter do with her unicorn soul?"

Ishnara shimmered, and her wings fluttered. "He could heal—regenerate as many times as necessary. He would be immortal."

"Are you saying Rori is immortal?" Fae didn't live as long as elves, and Therron had always assumed he'd die from the curse. But if there was a chance of him and Rori living long lives together, that gave him hope he'd never dared have.

The dead queen shrugged. "You saw Rori when she returned from the void with that demon's fang in her. What do you believe?"

Bloody hell, she was right. Rori had survived when she should've perished. If she wasn't immortal, then her blood was powerful enough to heal the most grievous of wounds. Blood Hunter would gleefully corrupt to his vile needs.

At least now they knew what Hunter wanted from her, and why.

"Ishnara, do you know how we return to the human realm? Would a doorway work?"

She smiled at him as if he were a dimwitted child. "Nikala brought you here. It is she who must take you back."

"But I told you, I don't know how." Frustration tinged Nikala's words.

"Wish it so." Ishnara reached a ghostly hand to smooth Nikala's cheek. "You have great power within you. Never forget this. You are the daughter of queens." She leaned forward and kissed Nikala's lips. "You are descended from me, my sweet. What that man did to you, turn it against him and use it to your advantage."

In those few statements, Ishnara confirmed Therron's suspicions. Mairead was Nikala's mother.

Nikala's eyes grew large and shimmered with unshed tears. She reached a finger to her lips as if in a dream. "I see it now. Yes. Thank you."

Whatever information Ishnara shared with her, Therron wasn't privy to, but from the way Nikala's mouth curved in a smile, he knew it would help the assassin understand who she really was.

"Are you ready, Your Highness?" He smirked as he stretched a thread of magic the same as he had in SIRE's office and held his hand for her to clasp.

"Get bent, elf man. Don't you ever call me a—" With a whoosh, the air stilled. Nikala squeezed his hand tighter. "Fucking princess."

Bright lights momentarily blinded him, and Therron blinked at the three bewildered faces of Molly, Maxx, and Cian. They stood in the exact positions from when he and Nikala were whisked to Faerie. If he had to guess, no time had passed for the others, so Nikala's outburst came as a surprise.

"What's going on?" Cian took a step toward him, and Nikala gasped at the realization she'd brought them back to the human realm. "Who's fucking a princess?"

"What?" Without missing a beat, Nikala pulled her hand away, shrugging. "I just think we don't need stupid elven oaths that have who knows what consequences. Therron can just pull his fancy sword from thin air, and we all place our hand on it with a promise that what is said between us stays between us. Yeah?" She glared at Therron and strode to the suitcases. "We've got work to do."

Cian looked from him to Nikala and back, confusion clear in his face. Maxx watched with narrowed eyes, and Molly stared in awe. Nikala was right. A simple promise would have to suffice. With a sigh, he withdrew his sword.

8

The scar on his cheek burned with an intensity he'd never felt before. Therron placed a hand over the mark, willing it to settle. He stood at the broad window overlooking the city that made his heart shrink in awe at the vastness of this world. Cilachaem was a village compared to this monstrosity of buildings and people and noise. So much noise. Constant, unrelenting chaos. No wonder Hunter had chosen this as his playground.

It was easy to get overlooked or forgotten here. It was the perfect place to hide.

To his left, the jolly human called Molly had taped a map of this world, Earth, to the window. He'd thought London was the largest city of this sprawling world and was surprised to realize they were on an island, with other cities as large as, or larger than London. This world, with its massive continents and huge expanses of water, gave him anxious shudders. How the hell were they going to find Rori with so much land and sea to cover?

Molly had circled cities in blue ink to indicate known locations of Hunter's labs, with yellow sticky flags marking possible outposts. Nearly two dozen places to search. And time was running out.

Behind him, the sound of papers rustling and quiet conversation were a balm, and an irritant. He could speak their language, could even read it, but not the swirling loops and coded symbols of Hunter's handwriting. They were a mystery to him, which meant he could not help in the search for Rori by those means. He had other means—his elven magic, but it would take vast amounts and Cian had cautioned him to refrain from using too much of his power. To do so would be like sending a beacon to Hunter and his enhanced soldiers, giving them their location. Therron didn't give a damn if they knew where they were, but he wouldn't do anything that would risk Rori's life.

And using large amounts of magic would not only do that, but according to Molly, it would cause friction between this world and others. Including Cilachaem.

The best he could do was gather food from the pub and make sure they were fed. Remnants of their meal were spread across the tables, giving Therron a twitch. Did they expect him to clean up after them as well?

He swallowed a harsh rebuke and reminded himself yet again that everyone in the room was worried for Rori. Everyone, including Molly, had a relationship with Rori. As much as he wished he were unique in that regard, it gave him comfort to know they all, in their own way, loved and valued her. Though she was only blood related to Cian, Therron had the sense that each of them looked on her as a sister.

Nikala tapped at a keyboard on her computer, a completely foreign object to him, but of great importance to her. Every so often, one of the small group would swear or exclaim, followed by a brief explanation of what was found. Notes were made, more scribbles were etched into paper, more keys were clacked, and yet they did nothing.

Hunter's network of spy bases and laboratories was too widespread to jump willy-nilly from one to the next. They needed a plan. Although Therron understood why, it chafed that they were several hours into their search and hadn't a clue where to start. At the moment, all he could do was stand at the huge window and cast his thoughts across the skies in the hope that Rori heard him and replied. He couldn't let his emotions override sense. Patience was needed. Yet he and patience had never been great allies.

With the coming morn, his mood darkened. Where was she? Why hadn't she tried to contact him? He refused to believe she was dead, but her continued silence played tricks with his mind. He couldn't allow himself to entertain the idea that Hunter had found her unicorn soul and destroyed her. Or worse, he was keeping her alive just enough to continue to extract whatever he needed from her.

Would she know him the next time they met?

Would she love him?

The scar seared against his flesh, and he swore a curse his mother would be mortified to hear come from his lips. Damn the pain.

"What is it?" Nikala stood next to him, her eyes full of concern.

"My scar is burning and I don't know why." From the corner of his eye, he could see Cian watching them. Ever since they'd returned from the odd trip to Faerie, the spy had been suspicious, and for good reason. He'd not had the opportunity to discuss the situation with Nikala and thus, neither mentioned it.

"We'll find her, Therron. You must have hope." She placed her hand on his shoulder and gave a slight squeeze.

"I feel impotent and useless." It was the harsh truth he'd been denying even to himself.

"You are neither of those. Can you use your magic to translate Hunter's text?"

He shook his head. Because it only took a small amount of magic and therefore was allowed by Cian, it was the first thing he'd tried. Hunter's writing was too erratic for his magic to decipher. Molly and Maxx had no problem reading and understanding what they found in the notebooks, which only made him feel less necessary. Cian had designated himself the collator of information gathered and made several lists. Nikala then took those lists and searched her computer for mentions of locations, buildings, or people who could help in the search.

It was exhausting for them, and frustrating for him. Yet none of them complained.

He straightened his shoulders and gave Nikala a wan smile. "I can keep trying."

Pivot, iterate, and try again. It's what Rori would do.

Nikala nodded, but instead of returning to her laptop, she bit her lower lip and looked out the window. His gaze met Cian's, and he nodded to the spy. There was no reason for Cian to be jealous of him, but sometimes emotions made little sense.

"I need to ask you something." Nikala indicated he

follow her to the conference room, where an enormous desk dominated the space. She closed the door and turned to him. "Can you make it private in here?"

He cocked his head, curious why she'd want to leave the others out of their conversation after she'd made everyone swear on his sword. His magic cocooned them in a small bubble, providing the privacy she requested.

"It is safe to speak. What's so important you don't want the others to hear?"

She rubbed her arms and glanced at the closed door. "Did that really happen? You know, back there with Ishnara and stuff? Was it a dream?"

"It was real."

"But no time passed here and we were gone at least half an hour." She walked around the huge desk, his magic stretching to encompass her path. "How is that even possible?"

"How is it possible that an elven prince is standing in your office? How is it possible you survived Hunter's experiments? Perhaps, right now, for you it's best not to ask what's possible, but rather to accept that everything in your life is about to change. You're going to see and experience things your human upbringing won't understand. You have to trust that the impossible is possible."

"Right. Okay. So, that means what Ishnara said about Rori is true. She's a unicorn and something elusive. What does that even mean?" Her gaze flicked to the door. "We have to tell Cian, but how do we do that without sounding like we've lost our freaking minds?"

"Cian grew up in Faerie. The fae live alongside trolls,

brownies, and ogres. Yes, a unicorn is rare—actually, unheard of—but he is accustomed to the extraordinary."

She nodded, her fingertips tapping her biceps. "And the other stuff…with Mairead and Midna. That's all true, too?"

Therron stood where he was, even though his heart longed to comfort her. He couldn't imagine what she was going through, or the confusion it would cause, but he knew what it felt like to want to hide from a difficult truth, and it pained him that she had been raised unknowing of her heritage. Being thrust into royalty was enough of a shock, but then to realize she had a family, one who would love her if she could accept who she was…he didn't envy her situation.

"What does your heart tell you?"

She glared at him, but there was no bite to her hard stare. "I learned long ago to shut my heart down." She flinched, her face scrunching. "Bloody oath. Fine. My heart tells me Mairead is my mother, and Midna is my aunt. There. Happy?"

"Incredibly so. Give yourself time to process everything. But don't take too long to tell Cian. He's worried about you."

"All of this is so new. I don't know what to do with all these emotions." A little laugh burst through her lips. "I really, *really* hate this truth serum you forced upon me."

A knock at the door startled them both, and Therron withdrew his magic circle of protection.

Cian stuck his head into the room and gave them both a long scrutiny before fully entering. "Everything okay?" Concern laced Cian's words.

"Yeah. Fine. Therron was asking about some of Hunter's less savory experiments, but didn't want to upset Molly if she overheard."

Cian's lips thinned, as if he didn't believe her. His head swiveled toward Therron. "You said you knew what Hunter wants with Rori. What is it?"

"Her blood." Therron could sense Nikala's unease with the situation, and her blatant lie to Cian was warning enough that what happened in Faerie was to stay between them for the time being. So he kept his explanation truthful, but not complete. "She heals rapidly, and I believe it's this facet of her that Hunter wishes to examine more closely. To discern if there is any quality of her healing properties he can exploit."

Cian nodded and rubbed a finger along his upper lip. "Makes sense. If our healing abilities didn't come from him, of course he'd want to explore them further. Do you think this means he'll leave her unharmed?"

At this, Nikala snorted. "Hunter doesn't know how to conduct experiments without some form of torture. Whether it's physical, mental, or emotional, he gets off seeing his subject suffer." As if realizing what she'd said, she clapped a hand over her mouth. "I'm sorry. That was incredibly insensitive of me."

Therron's gut twisted with imagined horrors Hunter was putting Rori through at that very moment. "If that's the case, then we're wasting time."

He left the pair in the conference room and strode to his place by the huge window. His thoughts tumbled and whirled, his heart pinching against the truth of Nikala's words. Insensitive, yes, but honest. He'd had only a glimpse of the hell she had survived. He couldn't allow himself to imagine the horrors Hunter had in store for Rori.

His scar burned anew, and he flinched against the searing. In his reflection, he watched in revulsion as his skin peeled away to reveal dark scales. When his fingertips touched the scar, his flesh was intact, but the image in the window remained. He closed his eyes to avoid seeing the awful thing and focused on Rori. It was her face he sought, her scent he longed for, her touch he craved.

His breathing slowed and the terrible image dissipated from his mind. *Rori.* He looked out over the sleeping city and sent his thoughts across the skies in the hopes they would reach her, wherever she was. *We are searching for you. Don't lose hope. We'll find you.* He desperately wanted to add that he loved her and would move worlds to find her, but he held back.

Tell her, a voice said, and his eyes snapped open.

A large, scaled snout just outside the window startled him into stunned disbelief.

His gaze traveled up the scales to a pair of glowing amber eyes, and further still past a horned head down a sleek neck to the creature's back. Wings beat gently, keeping his huge body aloft.

Therron stood still for a moment, letting the realization seep into every cell of his body. His chest swelled against the rampant beating of his heart, his head went woozy, and his knees turned to a wobbly mess.

Impossible.

His words to Nikala only moments earlier mocked him now.

What he saw outside the window couldn't be possible. Especially in the human realm.

Yet, he knew in the depths of his heart his eyes did not deceive him. Not more than two sword lengths from him was a dragon.

9

The aircon gently blew cooled air through the room, but it had little effect on the blood boiling in Cian's veins. The door snicked shut with Therron's departure, and he took a long breath to calm himself. He wasn't overreacting. Something had happened between the elf and Nikala. Something in the blip of a moment, but he felt it. And now, private meetings. He hated that he was jealous.

"What happened between you and Therron?"

Nikala's head swiveled toward him, her eyes narrowed. "Nothing. I told you, he was asking difficult questions."

"Not in here." Cian jerked his head toward the other room. "Out there. Therron was pulling magic into a thread and then," he snapped his fingers, "there was a moment of…" He searched for the word, but came up short. "Nothing. As in, I couldn't feel your presence anymore. Then," he snapped his fingers again, "you were back and talking about fucking princesses."

She shrugged and stepped toward him, a Cheshire Cat

grin on her lovely face. "Have you?" She reached for his belt and unfastened it.

"Have I what?"

"Fucked a princess?"

A gleam lit in her eyes, and he swallowed hard. Damn, she was sexy. He knew she was distracting him; hell, he'd perfected the art of fucking for distraction, or information, or whatever was needed in the moment.

"Not to my knowledge." His words came out low, husky. Two could play this game.

He reached to unbutton her shirt, but she gave a shake of her head with a glance to the closed door.

"It's locked." He threaded magic through the keyhole just to be sure. "We won't be disturbed for as long as you want."

"No time. Quick and dirty. You know how I like it."

His cock jumped when she pulled his pants to his knees. She'd be the death of him. He was sure of it. And if he died with his cock balls-deep in her pussy, so be it.

He made quick work of shimmying her pants to her boots and stepped between her legs. With a swift lift, he had her ass on the table and his cock nudging her already wet outer lips. It was hot how ready she was for him. How he would've loved to go down on her and spend a good hour bringing her to climax after climax. Instead, he pushed into her, swallowing a gasp of delirium. Fucking her always made him light-headed and his thoughts turn to candy floss. She was his dream. She was his doom. She was every-thing he ever wanted.

His hands smoothed up her torso; the soft cotton of her shirt rubbed against his palm and he cupped her breasts in his hands. Despite her quip about no time, he kept the pace leisurely, delighting in the way Nikala groaned and squirmed. His thumbs flicked across her nipples several times, each making her flinch and quiver against his cock.

"You tease." It came out almost a growl, but the smirk on her lips told another story.

"You love it."

Fucking her was different than the other women he'd been with. Deeper, more meaningful. This wasn't a shag for information, or a quick release with an unmemorable face. With Nikala, he was attuned to her body, as if there were a tether from her heart to his. Delighting her was important, not his wants or needs. Even when he tried to deny it, the truth was there—in the back of his mind, and in his heart —that this was special. Nikala was special. If only she'd trust him enough to tell the truth about what happened with Therron.

The thought of Therron pulled his mind away from the soft pleasures of Nikala's body, and he moved instinctively into the rhythm he often used to coax confessions from unwilling subjects. A thread of his magic swirled through him, and he realized with a shock what he was doing. With an irritated grunt, he released the thread. It would be easy to wrap Nikala in his magic and find out what she was hiding from him. Too easy.

And a terrible way to break any trust she'd already given.

He kept his power embracing her, but didn't employ his sex magic to elicit her secrets. When she was ready, she'd tell him. And if she never did, so be it. He trusted her.

She moaned and arched so that her pussy ground into

him, but that wasn't what caused his heart to flutter. Her neck lay exposed, begging to be nipped. Circling his arm around her back, he pulled her in close, his pace increasing with his excitement. The scent of their quick and dirty sex bored into his nostrils, and he inhaled deeply as if to memorize this moment. His lips brushed against the bare skin of her neck, and a little whimper wrapped itself around his heart.

Damn, he had it bad. His tongue lashed her jaw before he sunk his teeth into the soft flesh of her throat and nipped playfully. She cried out, but not in pain. By the way her pussy clenched, there was only pleasure in her cries.

Emboldened by her response, he sucked hard, but not too hard to leave a mark. She squirmed and bucked, her breath catching in tiny pants that made his belly tighten. This woman—this fragile, fierce, beautiful woman—had captured his heart so thoroughly, he couldn't imagine a day without her in it. Didn't want to think about a future without her.

His entire body buzzed with the realization, and he pulled her even closer, as if to bury himself in her until they became one.

"Marry me." He whispered the wish against her skin.

Nikala cried out and ground against him, his whisper lost to the sounds of her orgasm. A corkscrew of relief and sorrow went through him. He'd meant the words, but didn't want to freak her out. Didn't want to scare her. Didn't want her to run from his love.

He tightened his hold and pumped into her orgasm, his own cresting with delicious tingles scratching at his skin.

Yes. This. This was what he wanted. Nikala in his arms,

forever. That's why making love to her was different—with her, *he* was different. He wanted to be a better man, a better partner, a better everything.

He came hard, his heart beating with wild abandon as his thoughts took hold. He would marry her right then if he could. Never in his life had he been so sure of anything as he was at that moment.

His fingers brushed along her forehead and down her cheek to her parted lips. "You are fucking amazing."

"You're not half bad yourself." She lifted until her lips were against his and took them between her teeth.

He grunted against the slice of pain and grinned. "Keep doing that and we'll never leave this room."

"Tease."

"You love it." He turned her words back on her with a cocky grin.

"I do." She chuckled and flicked a glance to where their bodies melded into one, her face scrunching in the most adorable way. "I should probably clean up before rejoining the others."

"Good point." He twirled his hand and a warm towel appeared on his palm. "Allow me."

He made short work of gently wiping her sensitive areas before taking the moist towel to himself. When he'd finished, he swished his hand again, and the towel vanished.

Nikala watched him the entire time, her eyes wide, a curious expression in them.

"Neat trick. But, you know, there's a bathroom just there." She jutted her chin to a closed door in the corner. "And a bedroom, now that I think of it." Her throaty laughter filled the room. "It's probably a good thing I didn't remember that until just now. I'm not sure I would let you leave."

Her legs gripped him until he was pressed against her nakedness.

"Careful, lass."

"Or what?"

Oh, gods, but he wanted to fuck her again and again and again. The way she bit her lip as she looked up at him, the tilt of her head, the slight peek of her cleavage from her shirt…it drove him wild with desire.

"You'll get your wish, that's what." He lifted her, and she snuggled into him, her lips nuzzling his neck.

Instead of taking her to the bedroom like his heart told him to, his head prevailed and he pivoted to break her legs' hold on him and set her down before stepping out from between her legs. Her pouty whimper was cute and all, but they had more pressing matters.

She wriggled off the table and pulled her jeans up in one swift motion. "Someday, I'd like to have more than a few stolen moments with you. Promise me, when this is all over, we'll go away somewhere no one can find us."

He secured the button on his trousers and held her face between his hands. "That is a promise I gladly make. You and me. No phones, no laptops, nothing but the sun on our faces and our toes in the sand."

"Sounds perfect."

He kissed her nose. "You're perfect."

Her snort was delightful. "Yeah, we'll see about that when Hunter enacts his kill code. I hate that he has this power over me." She stepped back and eyed Cian with a purposeful glint in her eyes. "That thing you did with the facecloth. Can you teach me to do that?"

"Of course. Unless Hunter's blocked you from your magic, I should be able to teach you anything you want to learn." He fastened his belt, his mind sifting through lessons learned decades earlier. He'd been a child when his mother first showed him how to wield his magic. It shouldn't be too difficult to instruct an adult—unless, of course, they'd been mentally manipulated to fight magic and destroy those who used it against them. No problem.

Nikala smoothed her blouse and ran her fingers through her tousled hair. "Presentable?"

"Always." He took her hand and kissed her palm. "Let's see if they have anything new to share."

When he and Nikala entered the large office area, neither Molly nor Maxx looked up. They hunched together on the sofa, their heads close as they studied one of Hunter's notebooks. Cian scanned the room for the elf, but didn't see him. His gaze went to the open door of the bathroom on the other side of the room, and then to the closed office door.

"Where's Therron?" Nikala asked before Cian had the chance.

Molly and Maxx turned toward them, eyes clouded. Whatever they'd been studying had pulled their entire attention.

"He was just there." Maxx pointed to the large window that overlooked the Thames. "Only moments ago."

Nikala strolled to the bathroom and flicked on the light before returning with a frown on her pretty face. She checked the reception area and then entered the smaller office where she kept her belongings. Cian stood near the door where he could hear her muttering to herself. A minute later, she reappeared and passed him without a word.

At the window, she stood with her arms crossed, her fingers tapping along her biceps.

"Are you sure he didn't leave? Did you hear the lift ping? Did he say he was going to get something to eat? Some fresh air? He couldn't have just disappeared."

Worry dripped from every syllable, and Cian vacillated between wanting to go to her, to hold her and reassure her that Therron was fine, and being slightly jealous that she cared so much for the elf.

"We were focused on something we found in this notebook, but I'm sure we would've heard him if he left," Molly offered, but it didn't sound convincing.

Maxx stood and walked to the door. She placed her hand upon the wood, her lips moving. Cian tried to trace her magic, but it was undetectable.

Finally, she said, "He didn't leave. At least not through this door."

There was only one way into or out of the office. If he didn't use the door, then he'd found another way.

"A portal?" Nikala asked.

"We would've felt it." Cian rubbed his arms, certain he'd not sensed any magic other than his own. But then, he'd not felt Maxx's only moments earlier.

"Well, I, for one, think it's rude to just disappear." Molly crossed her arms and glared at them.

Indeed. Therron was a lot of things, but rude wasn't one of them.

Molly squinted and pursed her lips. Without saying anything, she walked to the window and bent to pick something off the floor.

Cian cocked his head to better see.

"What's that?" Maxx drew close, but held back.

Cian gave the assassin a swift glance, a question in his eyes. Maxx shook her head and jutted her chin toward Molly, who inspected a metal-looking disc held tightly between her fingers.

"I'm not certain, but if I had to guess, I'd say it was a dragon scale." Molly looked cheerfully at the others. "Of course, I'll need to have it tested and verified."

Nikala started to laugh, low and slow at first, but then her chortle bellowed into a full-fledged belly laugh that had her bending over and gasping for breath.

"I see nothing humorous about the situation," Maxx warned, but Nikala ignored her.

"Dragons. In London." She wheezed. "Nothing is impossible."

More laughter followed, but Cian didn't join in her raucous acceptance of mythical creatures—even in Faerie, dragons were considered lore, nothing more. His gaze went beyond the window to the clouds.

"Molly, grab your coat. I'll escort you to MI6. Do not lose that disc," Maxx ordered.

"Scale," Molly corrected, and Maxx made a sour face.

"Whatever. Cian and Nikala, find Rori. If Hunter has somehow taken Therron right under our noses, then whatever time we didn't have before, we have less of now."

Nikala pulled herself together and picked up her phone. A final hiccup laugh escaped her lips, and she snarled to cover the gaff. "You don't seriously believe Hunter took Therron, do you?"

"I don't know what to believe anymore." Maxx looked first to Nikala, and then to Cian. "There's an old saying in Elvenwood that when dragons return, it will signal the beginning of the end. I need to get word to the queens." She looked at Molly. "I can't believe I'm saying this, but you might be the only option we have."

Molly's eyes grew large, and a smile overtook the bottom half of her face. "You'd let me go to Faerie? Oooh, yes, please."

"I said maybe. That's not a yes."

Maxx ushered Molly out the door without saying farewell, leaving Cian and Nikala staring after them.

"You don't think she'll really send Molly to the queens, do you? Is that safe?"

"She'd be a fool if she did. Humans aren't exactly welcomed in Faerie." Cian stared at the door debating if he should chase after the women.

Nikala cricked her neck and stretched her back. "What do you think Maxx meant about dragons? Could that happen?"

He blew out a breath and ran his hands through his hair. "Like you said, nothing is impossible." He glanced out the window, his heart tumbling in his chest. "The only thing is, when nothing is impossible, that leaves a whole lot that is possible."

The beginning of the end. If only he knew whether that meant a new beginning, or the end of everything.

❧ 10 ❧

Wind rushed past Therron's face with a crispness that ignited something deep inside. Instead of being terrified, he relished the speed and dizzying heights the dragon reached. His fingers curled around a mottled grey scale, his knees gripping the dragon's sides as if he were riding a horse. It was invigorating and thrilling, this sense of freedom. His back itched, as if he longed for his own wings to unfurl and fly unfettered.

Far below, they flew over a wide channel he recognized from the map taped to the window of SIRE's office. He'd never had need to study the human realm's geography and only learned the one language of English because his mother had insisted. Now, Therron wished he'd taken a keener interest in Earth and studied the maps hidden in the forbidden section of Elvenwood's library. They were tucked beside the old tomes that held the myths and legends of Cilachaem, including the dire warnings that one day, darathi vorsi—dragons, in the common tongue—would return.

When they did, the tales told of a time of struggle for Elvenwood, but that a glorious rebirth would dawn for the elven kingdom. Those stories, Therron had read again and again until he knew them by heart.

In none of the books did they mention dragons living in the human realm.

Yet here he was, flying high above the land on a dragon that spoke to him in his mind. A talking darathi vorsi. Not even his trusting brother Theo would believe such a tale.

The dragon hadn't said why he needed to go with him, nor had Therron asked; he'd simply understood that this was important. He hoped it had something to do with finding Rori.

They made a quick descent, spiraling lower and lower until the dragon set down atop a building that could've been taken straight out of the lovely city of Cere. Thinking about Cere made him ache to see Rori again. It was in that city where he first saw her with her friends at the pub, and then later when she broke out of the amulet Acelyne had trapped her in. He held the memories tight and gently nudged them to a safe corner of his mind.

He needed to focus. The dragon had come to him in London for a purpose.

"Where are we?" Therron slid from the beast's back to stand on hard stone.

"Paris. Atop Notre Dame, specifically." The dragon scanned the area, his snout lifted. His nostrils flared and settled before he returned his attention to Therron. "I am Aimon. This is where I live sometimes. It is also where I first met Aurora."

Therron rubbed his chin as he recalled Rori mentioning

a confrontation with Dorchmeir atop a church in the human realm. She hadn't mentioned a dragon.

"It was an Academy outing, I believe. She was young."

"Not so young to not know how to save an ailing dragon." Aimon flicked his left wing so that Therron could see a fine line in the membrane. "A crossbow quarrel. Nasty business. I was up here a good two centuries before she found me."

"May I?" Therron stepped to the wing, but did not reach out to touch it.

"For what purpose? If you seek to check Aurora's work, then you will be sorely disappointed. She is an exceptional healer."

"She's an assassin." The words were out before he had a chance to bite them back.

"Yes, funny that. An assassin by choice or by trade, it matters not, for what she truly is has not yet been discovered by her."

Aimon flicked his wing toward Therron, and he gently felt along the outer bones before running his fingertips over Rori's healing. Even after so many years, he felt her magic in the thin line. The dragon hadn't lied when he said the healing was exceptional.

"What do you mean, she hasn't discovered what she truly is?" Therron kept his tone level, but his heart quivered in his chest that the dragon knew Rori's secret. If he knew, then others might as well, and right then, keeping Rori alive and safe meant keeping knowledge of her unicorn hidden.

"That's enough, Aimon. You always were too chatty," a stern voice commanded from behind Therron, and he turned to see a tall gentleman wearing human clothing stride toward them.

Therron barely had time to register the man before a sword appeared in his right hand and he lunged forward. Therron pulled his sword from the scabbard he kept hidden from human eyes and blocked the attack. Another swing, another block, followed by a wild attack that only appeared chaotic, but Therron recognized as one that was meant to unbalance him.

This man, whoever he was, didn't know Therron's swordmaster delighted in the very same type of lessons with him and his brothers. The more chaotic his attacks, the calmer Therron became. He only defended himself, never going on the offensive, which seemed to annoy the stranger.

Far superior in his sword skills, Therron could have ended the fight at any time. Instead, he studied the man, his form, his movements, all the while asking himself why the man would attack him, yet not voicing the question. He could learn more from the man's actions than his words. At least, for the moment. When the fighting finished, Therron would get the information he desired.

Sweat beaded on the man's brow, and a dark stain spread beneath his armpits and across his chest, but Therron was barely winded. If the man meant to intimidate or frighten him, he would be sorely disappointed.

Aimon stood still, never moving if the fighting got too close, nor did he do anything to help either combatant. When Therron flicked a glance at the dragon, he appeared like stone; if he didn't know better, he would've thought Aimon a statue similar to those dotted around the roofline of the building.

The man lunged for a slice, his movements sluggish. If they continued, someone would get injured, and it wouldn't be Therron.

"Enough!" Therron held up his hand and flicked his wrist, sending the other man's sword clanging to the ground. "Who are you and why have you attacked me?"

Annoyance flashed in the man's eyes. Even though he was clearly winded, he kept his calm as he answered. "I am called Kaen. One of the Dragon Lords of London. You are in our territory without permission or cause, an infraction worthy of detainment. Aimon brought you here against our wishes."

"Yes, but he did so at the behest of the lords of Paris." Another gentleman stepped from the shadows. Where Kaen was fair-haired, this man had raven locks and deep-set dark eyes that seemed lit from within.

"What could be so important you broke the treaty and took an otherworld creature from our kingdom?" Kaen retrieved his sword and sheathed it. A moment later, it disappeared.

Therron kept his own sword firmly in his grasp.

"Not just an otherworld creature, Kaen. This is His Royal Highness Therron Mistwalker, heir to the Elvenwood throne."

Kaen looked as if he would breathe fire. "What the hell is Donyatella playing at? If she knew a prince was in London, she should've alerted us."

"Donyatella and her boys hold to their own allegiances. Perhaps she felt you didn't need to know or be involved. You have been busy of late." The man seemed to remember Therron and turned to him. "Apologies, Your Highness. I am

Lucien de Montague, a Dragon Lord of Paris. You've met Kaen, and our esteemed young friend, Aimon." Lucien pointed first to himself, then Kaen, and finally the dragon who vacillated between scale and stone. "I'm sure you have many questions."

"Only one," Therron growled. "Where's Rori?"

Kaen's head snapped toward Lucien. "Tell me you had nothing to do with this."

Lucien shook his head and glanced at the morning sky. "I swear to you, I did not, nor any of my brethren. Perhaps now you will understand why it was imperative we brought Therron here. Rori was taken by her father, the one who calls himself Hunter Pearson."

Kaen's face paled. "So it is true?"

Lucien nodded slowly.

"Someone tell me what is happening this moment, or I shan't control my temper any longer." Therron lifted his sword level with their faces. "You know who I am—you know about Rori and her father. What else do you know that you aren't telling me?"

Kaen shared a glance with Lucien, who nodded.

"The dragon lords keep watch over the realms. We do not interfere unless absolutely necessary," Kaen stated, his gaze intense. "Certain events over the past several years have caused us to reconsider our involvement with the human realm. Namely, the chaos Hunter Pearson is causing."

"Do you know what his objective is?" Therron sheathed his sword, but kept his hand close just in case it was needed in a hurry.

Lucien shook his head. "Not entirely. Thus far, he's unleashed his enhanced soldiers and scyvers on the world, but there doesn't seem to be any rhyme or reason to it. He's not made any demands or made a power grab. We're flummoxed."

"He sows chaos. That's what the London dragon lords believe is his end goal. Create panic and chaos from within and let the world destroy itself." Kaen crossed his arms with a grunt.

"Why?" Therron glanced over the city. The sun peeked from behind the short buildings, its rays lengthening into the clear sky. It looked peaceful from where he stood. Serene.

"We don't know." Lucien gripped Therron's shoulder. "We were hoping you could shed some light on his intentions."

"I don't know anything about Hunter Pearson beyond the fact he has Rori, and when I meet him face-to-face, I will destroy him." The ignominy of being poisoned by the man still stung. Never again would he let the craven dog best him. "He is powerful, more so than any fae should be, but his power is not natural."

The dragon lords shared a look.

"He has been experimenting on humans and other-world creatures. One of them is your travel companion, Nikala St. James. Can she be trusted?"

Therron flexed his hand, the oath still fresh in his memory. "She wants to see Hunter destroyed as much as I do." He eyed the men, hoping they were allies. "Will you revoke your neutrality and help us?"

"Are you asking as the darathi vorsi prince?" Lucien watched him closely, as if waiting for a specific response.

"I don't understand what you mean. What is the prince of dragons?"

Disappointment pulled at Lucien's features. "We were told the darathi vorsi prince was in London. You are the only Eleri in London; therefore, we assumed the prince was you."

A conversation with Rhoane drifted through his mind. He'd called Therron Eleri, but said the elves had lost the meaning of the word over time. He hadn't mentioned anything about a dragon prince, however.

"I'm sorry to disappoint you." The sun rose higher in the sky, and Therron stepped to the edge of the building. Far below, people dotted the walkways…some walking briskly, others meandering. "I've wasted too much time. Do you know where I can find Rori?"

Lucien stood on his left, and Kaen on his right. Both men looked out across the city. In profile, he could've sworn he saw dragon scales beneath their human flesh. His gaze flicked to Aimon, now looking fully alive without a hint of stone.

"You call yourselves dragon lords. Are you darathi?"

"We are human yet have darathi souls." Kaen looked as if he would say more but held back. "We can shift into dragons."

Therron gaped at him, remembering his manners a second too late. He pressed his lips closed to keep the cascade of questions from spilling out. Rori was the priority, and yet, he felt this revelation was something he needed to understand.

"After you settle this business with Hunter Pearson, find us. We have much to discuss." Lucien pointed in the opposite direction they faced. "We have it on good authority Hunter took Rori to Venice. The precise location, we don't know." Lucien gripped the stone balustrade. "Rori is known to us, as is her brother. We know who they are, and what they do here in the human realm. Although we do not condone such actions, we've also witnessed much kindness from them both. Neither of them are entirely what they appear. Especially Rori." His gaze flicked to Aimon. "We owe her a great deal." He placed a hand over his heart and took a step back from the stone barrier keeping them from falling to their deaths. "May the winds grace your wings, my new friend."

Therron inclined his head, more confused than ever. Venice wasn't circled on the map taped to the window at SIRE.

"How will I find you?" His glance swept over Aimon, who once again looked made of stone.

"You'll know," Lucien said cryptically before heading to a door tucked between two pillars. "It's too light for us to fly, but you may use one of your portals from here as long as you don't pull too much magic."

With that, he and Kaen disappeared into the darkness of what Therron assumed was a stairwell. Therron stepped lightly to a shadowed area and lifted his hand to make a doorway back to London.

"Your Highness, please find Rori," Aimon said from his left, and he looked to see the misty-hued dragon watching him intently. "She saved my life. And no matter what Lucien or Kaen say, I will fight for her. And you, my prince." He knelt low as if in a bow.

"There is no need for formality, my friend." Therron

reached to pat his snout, marveling at the warmth of his scales. A flash of recognition whipped through his mind, followed by images of Lucien, Kaen, and thousands of other darathi, some shifters like the two lords. He snatched his hand away to stop the images, but they continued to pelt his brain.

Aimon's eyes grew large, and his lips lifted in a grin. He'd seen the images, too.

One last vision danced in Therron's mind—of a midnight-blue dragon wearing a golden crown embedded with dragon eggs that glittered like jewels. The Crown of Awakening.

His scar burned anew and his back itched as if his skin meant to tear open to unleash something impossible.

Twenty-three dragon bone vials sat nestled in a glass box on top of the workspace. Not an equal two dozen, which annoyed Rori. There had to be a special meaning to the number, or it could be Hunter didn't care whether he had an odd amount of her blood. No, it had to be relevant. She tucked the information away for later, when she could research the possibilities.

Though, she wasn't sure later would ever come. Hunter had left her ages ago, and she was beginning to think he meant to leave her there to die. Alone.

What an absolute bellend.

She skimmed the walls in front of her, glancing quickly over the curio with the decorated vials similar to the one she'd been held in when Acelyne kidnapped her. A shudder ran its way down her spine, and she flinched against the burn of Hunter's magical restraints on her wrist. Her stomach growled its unhappy state. She had no idea how long she'd been there, wherever there was. Hours, days… there was no way to tell in the padded room.

Rori cocked her head and listened for a sound, anything beyond her own breathing and the grumblings of her belly. Behind her, she heard a soft inhale. Barely perceptible, but it was there. The air was still as she trained her ear toward what she couldn't see.

Another inhale, followed by the slow release of breath.

She turned as much as she could, ignoring the pinch of magic against her skin.

Hunter watched her, his dark eyes intent on her face as if waiting to see her reaction. She decided to play along and affected a surprised, and slightly frightened expression.

"Jesus fudgebuckets! How long have you been there, watching me like some deranged creeper?"

"I'm trying to decide what to do with you." He casually slid off the medical bed and strolled to the curio that housed the vials from Faerie. "I would like to study you, test you, but this lab is insufficient for my needs." He removed a silver and glass vial, his eyes narrowed and lips pursed. "You intrigue me, Aurora. The amount of poison I've given you should've killed you four times over by now, yet here you are." He dangled the vial between two pinched fingers. "Alive, unlike these subjects."

Her stomach twisted with the realization that the vials weren't empty but contained the bodies of those poor souls Acelyne kidnapped. They must not have survived the journey, or even worse, the spell to release them might've killed them. She desperately hoped the spell she'd given Eirlys didn't harm any of those imprisoned.

"Then let's go to one of your other labs where you can experiment on me all you'd like." She kept her tone cheerful, as if she couldn't think of anything better than being poked and prodded by the madman.

Pretending to be interested in his other labs was part ruse, part genuine curiosity. She actually did wish to know how he got the imprisoned fae out of the amulets and what he did to study them. But she had zero interest in being his test subject. What she really hoped for was that he'd release her from the binds keeping her prisoner, and she could escape.

"Yes, I'd like that. But you see, I'm afraid as soon as we leave this room, that bloody elf could find us. You're connected to him in ways I can't break. You might not have announced your affections publicly and broken the curse yet, but you've done something to strengthen your bond with him. I felt it in London. Strange, though, I don't sense it coming from you." He set the vial inside the curio and rubbed his chin. "I could use this to my advantage."

Rori's mind whirled with this new information. She thought Hunter had killed Therron, but from his words, it sounded as if he wasn't successful. A warm flush rose from her sternum, and she pushed the elation down before Hunter noticed. There would be time to celebrate later. When she wasn't a specimen trapped in Hunter's web.

"You mean use me as bait. Why do you need Therron dead?"

"Not dead…something else." A wry smile cricked his lips, making him look uglier in the artificial light. "His brother proved to be a huge disappointment." His hand swept over the dragon bone vials, and he inhaled deeply. "Why were you chosen to break his curse? All those years and no one else came close. But you…" He picked up a vial and turned toward her. "Could it be the dark magic flowing through you? Your wild magic, as you say?"

"I'm assuming those are rhetorical questions because I have no idea. I didn't even like Therron at first. I'd been convincing myself I should study with Midna when I met him."

"Midna? Why?"

Rori shrugged as much as she could, being confined to a chair and bound by his magic. "Why not? You and everyone else always told me I was too emotional, that a spy was worthless if they let emotions get in the way of the mission. I figured Midna could," she paused to find the right word, "*condition* that out of me."

To her astonishment, Hunter laughed. "I suppose if anyone could, it would be that bitch."

Rori watched his features, surprised at the hatred that filled his eyes.

"She rejected you as a student." It wasn't a question. She could feel his tortured anguish at being turned away.

"Midna is a desperate, aging queen without an heir. Her opinion of me is of little consequence." He glared at Rori so hard she feared he might take his acrimony of the queen out on her. "You didn't need her to strip you of compassion. You only needed to remember what I taught you as a child."

Ah. He was bitter that she'd forgotten his teachings and sought another instructor. Or, he was angry that she'd intentionally ignored his lessons. Either way, he definitely would take out his frustrations on her if she wasn't careful.

"I was so young when you left. All I ever wanted was more time with you. Teach me all you know now. I'm here. I'm willing to learn."

His eyes softened, and she hoped he believed her lies.

"I could teach you wonders that would blow your mind. Everything you thought impossible is not only possible, but could be yours for the taking." He unfastened the stopper of the vial and tipped it to pour into his palm.

Instead of a stream of her blood, glitter-like dust made a pile on his skin.

The air vibrated with his fury, and Rori internally braced—for what, exactly, she didn't know. She instinctively understood this was bad. Real bad.

"What have you done?" Hunter shrieked the words, his fists shaking.

"I didn't do anything. I swear!"

He opened three more vials, only to find more glitter. Somehow, her blood had turned to dust even though he'd made special vials to prevent exactly that from happening. She was as flummoxed as he.

"I will fucking end you and then I will kill your brother myself." This wasn't a shriek; his voice went quiet, which was even more terrifying than hearing him bellow.

"I don't know what happened." Her lips went dry, and panic cut her breathing short. "You gotta believe me. I didn't, I wouldn't." Real tears spilled over her cheeks, and she blinked through the haze. "Dad, I promise—"

"Your father is dead. I am Hunter Pearson, you insolent twit."

Time slowed and stretched with an eerie countenance. She watched his features twist in rage, making the spider-webbed pockmarks turn bright red. His lips lifted with a snarl, and his fist rose as if to strike. The magic bonds burned against her wrists, but she didn't flinch against them, nor did she hide from the blow that was about to come.

This was it. The end of it all. She'd never get to see Therron's handsome face again, or hold his hand, or kiss him with a hunger only he could satiate. A deep mourning settled in her heart for a future she'd never live. A future stolen from her by a madman hell-bent on a narcissistic crusade to destroy everything she held dear.

From the gleam in Hunter's eye, Rori knew in the deepest, darkest depths of her being, her father meant to kill her. And he would enjoy it.

❦ 12 ❦

Hunter's fist slammed into Rori's cheek too hard and too fast for a normal fae, with a force powerful enough to end her life. She heard the crack of her cheekbone shattering a split second before pain ricocheted across her face, followed by the stinging of torn flesh. The impact of the punch knocked her sideways to the tiled floor, her shoulder taking the brunt of her weight. A fresh wave of agony swept from her shoulder down her arm, and across her back. Pain was good. Pain meant she wasn't dead yet.

Rori lay still, stunned at the violence her father had inflicted upon her. Hunter had warned her, but she didn't want to believe that the man who she'd loved was truly gone. Now she knew the truth. Except, Hunter was wrong; her father wasn't dead—he lived inside this monster, like some kind of macabre reincarnation. With the same sorrow she'd felt when she first learned of her father's death, she understood and accepted that this had always been who

Hagan MacNair was, at his core. A new name only made him more violent, more of an asshole.

This time, she wouldn't mourn him.

"Pathetic." Hunter scoffed. "To think you were created from my DNA. I'm ashamed to admit I ever saw something in you. Get up, Aurora." The threat of more violence hung on his command.

Her breathing came in ragged pulls as she dragged herself to all fours. It was eerily reminiscent of when she'd first woken up in the silent forest all those days—or were they weeks—ago. The pain, the feeling of being examined under a microscope, the sound of her father's voice telling her to get up. *If she didn't win, she was dead.*

The splintered chair lay in ruins, and she slipped her hands free of the magical restraints. Either Hunter wasn't aware they'd loosened, or he didn't care. Either way, she was free of the nasty things. Her hair hung like a curtain across her face, blocking her vision higher than his ankles. She could imagine the look of disgust on his stupid face and used that as fuel to propel her upward.

Every muscle protested her movement. She'd been trapped in the chair for hours, maybe even days. Standing took effort she could not afford, but she couldn't appear weak. Not now. Her right hand brushed her hip, and she felt a pulse of energy from the daggers she always wore. Hunter must not have considered her a threat if he allowed her to keep them. Idiot.

Or maybe he couldn't touch them. Eirlys always said they were for her use alone.

Or it had been a test. No idea whether she passed or failed, nor did she care.

Rising to her full height, she glared at the man she once considered the single most important person in her life. There was a time she would've done anything he asked. The need for his approval slid off her like an oily substance, and she twitched her shoulder blades against the invisible ickiness. He'd used that eagerness to please to his advantage ever since she was a baby.

Red ringed her vision—not from rage, but from the internal injuries his punch caused. Although, her fury probably added depth to the shade of crimson. She pulled her dagger free, ignoring his taunting chuckles.

"You can't kill me." His lips twisted into a rictus grin, and his gaze went to the table that held the dragon bone vials.

A pair of syringes—one slim, the other fat—sat innocently together. Beside the fat syringe were several small glass capsules with filaments inside. The slim syringe was empty, its purpose a mystery.

"I wasn't afforded the time that I had with Cian and Nikala to mentally manipulate you, which is a shame. I had to go the easy route and implant a microchip into your skull. Should you try to kill me, your brain will explode. Messy, but effective." He held his hands up, as if it couldn't be helped.

"And the glass capsules?"

"Crude trackers. Again, if I'd had my equipment at another lab, it would've been so much more eloquent. Alas, must needs and all that." He waved his hand as if it were a trifle annoyance.

She glanced down and saw a red stain on her shirt. A quick feel of her abdomen sent a chill through her. He'd implanted the tracker beneath the skin, where she could see and feel it. A constant reminder that she couldn't escape him. And if she tried, the microchip would certainly implode her brains.

Fresh blood dripped from her damaged cheek to the tiled floor. Her head ached and legs wobbled, but she fought through the sickness that churned in her gut. She would never escape him. Even if he let her go, he could hunt her down at any time. Fear, deep and primal, squeezed her already upset belly, inching its way up her sternum to her throat. Her vision blurred, and ears rang with a high-pitched whine that might've been her own keening.

The darkness she sensed earlier returned, and with it, a clear path to freeing herself from Hunter's control. It involved invoking a spell he himself had taught her. Oh, the delicious irony. The fact the spell might kill her pushed against her skull, but she casually ignored the warning. Death would come for her eventually, like it would for everyone. But hopefully, not today.

She inched closer, pretending acquiescence, limping like a feeble child. Slowly, she brought her right hand to Hunter's throat, where her dagger hovered close to, but did not touch, his skin. Even at that small distance, she could feel the invisible push against her will. The fingers of her left hand gripped her other dagger, ready if needed. Hunter's expression remained passive, but she saw the pinch of concern in his eyes. He wasn't totally confident in the microchip's proficiency. She might not need the dark spell to remove it and break Hunter's control, but he didn't need to know any of that.

"You asked me at the manor if I remembered the words

I was taught when I was little." She smiled wryly, ignoring the flash of pain the action caused her injured cheek. "I do."

The memory of when she was barely two years old, played in her mind. In it, she saw how Hunter had poisoned her with a mixture of blood from other races. When she was near death with fever, he'd held her close and whispered the words, *"Ignacium docromanun iglattio favenoria."* Die by the light to be reborn to the dark. Then he told her, "Fight, Aurora. Fight for your true life."

Even at that young age, she understood the choice.

She chose the light.

Rori stared into Hunter's eyes. "Shall I tell you what they are?"

A wild delirium whipped across his features. "Yes."

"Eat a bag of dicks, you malignant piece of shit."

She brought her knee up hard, connecting with his balls. The pain-fueled groan he made delighted her a little too much. Taking advantage of his distress, she stepped back enough to allow her leg to swing wide in a roundhouse kick that caught the side of his head. Hunter slammed to the floor, spewing curses. Due to her fear of risking the microchip exploding in her head, she didn't plunge her dagger into his aorta like she wanted. Instead, she wrapped her magic around his limbs in much the same way he'd restrained her. He struggled and fought against the bonds, earning a bash to his head with the butt of her dagger. Blessed silence followed.

She couldn't kill him, but apparently, she could injure him. It would have to do for now.

Without knowing how long he'd be out, or even if he was unconscious, she wasted no time grabbing her leather jacket from where it had been tossed into a corner. Her gaze took in the rest of the room, noting details she'd recall later. Right then, her priority was to get out and as far from him as possible. But not without the dragon vials. She swept everything off the worktable into the pouch she made with her jacket before collecting all the amulets from the curio. If there was a chance she could save any of the trapped fae, she had to try.

Hunter didn't move as she stepped around him to the hallway. A few steps later, she passed an open doorway. It took her addled brain a moment to realize what she was staring at—a half dozen stainless-steel tables, all gleaming beneath bright lights. Each with a small sink at the end. Autopsy tables. This wasn't a lab; it was a morgue. Her father had brought her here to dissect her.

Rage-fueled adrenaline spiked her blood, and she shook with the need to destroy everything in her path. Her gaze flicked across the tables, noting the mortuary cabinets in the wall, before landing on a closed laptop.

She rushed to the computer and gently set down her bundle. When she opened the laptop, a display popped up, asking for Hunter's password. Bollocks and snickertits. It would take ages to decipher his possible passwords. She was about to slam the lid closed when she noticed the little tab for a fingerprint.

Aware time was slipping away, she rushed to where Hunter lay inert on the tile floor and grabbed his hand, her own shaking as she pressed his right forefinger onto the pad. A moment later, the screen blipped and Hunter's entire world opened to her in one glorious window after another. She returned to the morgue and quickly changed the password to one only she would know, taking an extra moment to clear the fingerprint command from the computer. A messenger bag hung from the back of a chair, and she tossed the laptop inside, but kept the vials and amulets wrapped in her jacket.

She rooted through the contents of the bag, relieved when she saw his phone was tucked into a pocket. He might have another on him, but she dared not search him and risk him waking up. She wiped her sweaty forehead, wincing at the pain that shot through her face from her wound.

Precious seconds ticked by as she debated her next move. If Hunter could track her, she didn't want to risk the others by giving away their location. She needed to take the vials to Faerie, but again, if he followed her there, then the entire kingdom was in danger. What she needed was to disappear. Be completely untraceable for a few days. Super easy with a microchip in her skull.

Fuckity fuck fuck snickertits.

With one last glance at the man she'd mourned for most of her life, she turned and raced down the hallway. At the bottom of a short set of steps, a thick curtain the same hue as the walls caught her boot. She tripped into a half-hidden door, ripping the curtain from its rings in her rush to escape. The door swung open with her push, and she stepped into yet another hallway. Sound rushed to her from all angles, and she was overpowered with smells and scents that were at once foreign and familiar. A thought whipped through her brain that Hunter had taken pains to sound-proof the entire upper floor, but not here.

When her head cleared and her cheek wasn't throbbing

in pain, maybe then she could unravel why. For the moment, she didn't have the spoons left to care. She needed an escape, and quickly.

A buzzing came from the other end of the hallway, and she ran toward it, hoping it was a doorway she could use to portal out of this hellhole. Her anxious breaths lengthened in relief when she saw the faint outline of Hunter's magic on a nondescript door tucked into a small alcove. Knowing full well he could follow her, she said the words that would open a portal and stepped into the doorway with a plan to leap from one doorway to another, hopefully confusing Hunter in the process. Her mind, however, overrode those plans and chose to focus on the one thing she absolutely needed to keep from her thoughts: Therron.

The portal closed behind Therron with a soft snap, and he shook out his shoulders to center himself. The small office off SIRE's reception area afforded him the privacy and quiet he needed. His mind whirled with what had just occurred. Dragons in the human realm. Dragon lords in London and Paris. Men who had a dragon soul and could become the great beasts. He'd never heard of such things, nor had he ever expected to see a dragon up close.

A part of him wanted very much to race to Elvenwood, where he hoped Rhoane was, and demand an explanation. This all started when that sly Eleri arrived at Elvenwood. And yet Therron knew that wasn't true. He'd been cursed upon his birth from a millennia-dead princess. Elves and fae were being kidnapped long before Taryn and Rhoane made an appearance in his father's throne room.

Whatever was happening in Cilachaem affected what happened in the human realm, and vice versa. These things had been churning unnoticed for who knew how long and now were converging. It wasn't a coincidence, he was certain of it.

He dared not tell the others until he could make sense of it. Not until he had something more substantial to share than he met a dragon and two men who claimed to have dragon souls. And certainly not until he understood what it all meant, and what part he played in events.

His scar thrummed and he rubbed it absently, mentally preparing to see the others. They had to have noticed his absence by now. If only he had food, he could pretend he'd gone to the pub for breakfast. It wasn't too late to do so, but that would take precious time away from finding Rori. Now that he had a location, he wouldn't waste another moment.

He brushed past the receptionist's desk just as the lift doors opened and Maxx walked out.

"If it isn't the intrepid flyboy. I see you've returned from your mysterious mission." Her chin jutted toward Nikala's closed office door. "They were worried about you."

"But you weren't?" It was a childish question to ask, but he didn't yet trust Maxx. She seemed to know things she shouldn't, and her comment about him flying set his nerves on edge.

"I tend to not worry about those who can take care of themselves."

"I'll take that as a compliment rather than a confirmation of your indifference."

She eyed him suspiciously. "We found an unusual silver disc near the window where I last recall you being. Molly has her machines analyzing it. Any idea what she might find?"

"Whatever it is, I'm just as interested in the results as

you." Two could play the twisting words and meanings game. He truly was interested in what Molly found, but not for the same reasons as the spy.

Before Maxx could ask a question he'd rather not answer, he strode to the closed door and held it open for her. She stalked into the room, her lips tight. Therron suppressed a chuckle as he entered the expansive office. The spy must've hated not being able to interrogate him. She'd get answers when he was ready to give them, and not a moment sooner.

Nikala saw him first, her eyes narrowed in that way he now knew meant she had questions for him. Damned spies and their incessant need to know more.

"Any updates?" Cian asked.

He and Nikala hunched over the desk, their focus on her computer.

"I sent Molly home to get some rest, much to her disappointment. I should never have suggested it and get her hopes up. As much as I believe the queens need to know what's happening here, I'm not yet convinced Molly is the one to tell them. She's too soft. Besides, she's got her computers analyzing that disc we found. We'll have answers soon enough." Maxx slid a challenge-fueled glance to Therron. "Anything you'd like to add?"

"I know where Rori is. A place called Venice. To the south of here, I believe."

Nikala's face paled, and she shared a worried look with Maxx.

"What is it?" Therron took a step forward, ready in an instant to draw his sword and fight.

"Venice isn't a lab so much as a morgue. It's where

Hunter takes the test subjects who don't survive his experiments." Maxx's face softened. "I'm sorry, Therron."

"This doesn't mean Rori is dead." He flexed and straightened his hand, wishing Hunter's face was near enough to take the impact of his fury.

"He's right. Hunter might've chosen Venice for exactly that reason—he didn't think we'd consider that location. It's actually the perfect place for him to hide out for a few days, to plan his next step. Until we know for sure, we must assume Rori is alive." Nikala stepped around the desk and took Therron's hands in her own. "What does your heart tell you?"

Cian's look of surprise matched Therron's. Nikala wasn't a touchy-feely kind of person. But she was right—his heart told him the dragon lords were correct. Rori was in Venice, and she was alive.

"It tells me we're wasting time. Let's go to Venice."

Nikala's lips quirked with a cheeky grin. "And we will." She released his hands and stepped to the desk. "But it will take a bit of planning. If Hunter is there, we need stealth and caution." More to herself, she added, "That would explain why I'm not getting a hit on him." She looked up at the others. "There are rooms at the villa built for certain activities that are best kept quiet. He's reinforced the walls and added padding. It's a relative dead zone, no pun intended. No signals in or out. No Wi-Fi, nothing. Which means," she tapped several keys on her computer, "he won't know that I just told his security system to loop recordings every fifteen seconds."

"Therron, can you take us through a doorway to Hunter's villa?" Cian drew a finger across one of the maps from where they were in London to where Therron assumed Venice was located. "Where in Venice is his villa located, specifically?"

"A private portal is too dangerous," Maxx cautioned. "We've already used too much magic in the human realm. We can't afford to draw the queens' attention now. We'll use the doorway in the pub to one I know of in a church not far from Hunter's."

They spent a tense few minutes sketching out a plan for how they would access the villa before Nikala shoved her laptop into a bag and slung the strap over her head.

"Right. Are we all ready to die?" She gave a nervous chuckle Therron didn't appreciate in the least.

"I will not die today. Nor will I die on human soil. We'll find Rori." He said the words to soothe himself as much as her.

"What aren't you telling us about this villa?" Cian pierced Nikala with a look that could wither the bravest warrior. "Have you spent time there?"

"Not as a captive." Nikala left the rest unsaid, but Therron understood her meaning that she, too, had participated in some of Hunter's unsavory experiments. Whether voluntary or not was the question he didn't wish to know the answer to.

"We'll all know soon enough what's waiting for us at the villa. Let's go." Maxx jerked her head toward the door, and they filed out in silence. In the reception area, she turned to Therron and Cian. "You two, put wards on these rooms. We can't assume Hunter won't return."

Therron gripped Cian's shoulder. "If we combine our

power, it will strengthen the warding." He saw the indecision in the spy's eyes, followed quickly by acquiescence.

With a solemn nod, Cian opened his magic, and Therron was taken aback by not just the power the man wielded, but by the tinge of darkness he felt in the threads. He pulled at those threads especially, weaving them into his own magic to create a fortified web of security cloaking the rooms. Then, he expanded their wards to the entire building. Not an easy task, nor one he relished, but keeping Hunter from the lab on the floor below was imperative. Destroyed or not, it had already proved to be a place where the madman felt confident in his vile abilities. Therron's heart thudded in his chest and sweat dotted his upper lip by the time they finished. To his relief, it appeared the effort had been difficult for Cian as well.

Nikala bent over the receptionist's desk to scribble a note before stalking to the lift. She jabbed a finger on the button that called the terrifying metal box that propelled them up and down with dizzying momentum. It opened immediately, and they all stepped inside.

After a moment, Nikala said, "I left a note for Darla."

"It's Sunday. Does she normally come in on the weekend?" Cian asked.

"I don't actually know." Nikala's brows scrunched upon her forehead.

"She doesn't," Maxx answered.

"Hmm." Nikala stared at the closing doors. "I suck at being a CEO."

"It wasn't what you were trained in, darling," Cian offered and took her hand. Nikala gave him a grateful look that held deep meaning meant only for the two of them.

Seeing the affection between the pair was sweet, and made Therron miss Rori all the more. They would find her. Alive. Once they rescued her, he'd return them both to Elvenwood, where they would be safe from Hunter, if only for a short while.

The group walked in silence to the pub, barely acknowledging Donyatella or her boys as they made their way to the cellar. Maxx opened the doorway and, one by one, they stepped inside. Within moments, another doorway opened, and Therron found himself in darkness near as total as the in-between.

Again, Maxx took the lead and lit a torch that hung from a wall sconce, giving Therron the impression she used the doorway frequently. Up several flights of stairs, and through a maze of hallways, they stepped into a dimly lit area with a domed roof. Beneath the decorative ceiling, white marble walls were interspersed with painted frescoes, and a huge statue took up nearly an entire wall at the back of the room. A woman holding a baby was at the center of the statue, with admirers seeming to crawl toward her. It made no sense to him, but then, few human things did.

People clad in modern clothing wandered aimlessly through the space.

"Is this a palace?" Although, it looked a tad small to be a full palace.

"It's a church. Keep walking." Maxx led them across the pale-red and cream checked floor to a set of double doors. Outside, she took a deep breath and cricked her neck. "The villa is just there." She pointed to their right, where a canal wound between the buildings. "And the entrance is down this way."

Instead of turning to the right, she crossed a bridge and went to the left. The group followed, passing shops with human-like statues posed in unnatural positions. Other shops held shoes and bags, again with the odd figurines with arms bent at strange angles. People stopped to admire what the statues were displaying. He'd seen similar windows in London and drew his gaze over the busy street, where shoppers held bags with the shops' names emblazoned across them.

Tucked into a doorway beside the fancy shop windows were a pair of men, hair unkempt, blankets crumpled around their sleeping bodies. Therron glanced at the people walking toward him, but none of them seemed to notice the pair. Sorrow laced through his thoughts and heart.

It was the same everywhere—from Elvenwood to Faerie to the human realm. Wealth lived beside poverty in an uncomfortable existence.

"You coming?" Maxx broke him out of his reverie, and he hastened his steps.

Nikala waited impatiently in front of a locked wrought-iron gate. Beyond the gate was a tidy courtyard and a slightly less tidy building with green shutters covering all the windows. The exterior looked to be in some need of repairs, with missing plaster revealing bare brick. It was the same with several other villas along the street. What he couldn't decipher was whether this shabbiness was intentional or simply the wearing of time.

To have such an exterior in Elvenwood would be an outrage, but he wasn't in the elven kingdom. He was far from home in a city he didn't know, desperate to find Rori.

Nikala pressed several keys on a discreetly hidden black

box and then placed her hand on the gate's handle before drawing a long breath. "I don't know what we'll find in there. Brace yourself for the worst."

Before anyone could question her, she opened the gate and strode across the courtyard to the villa's front door.

Therron sent a plea to the old gods of Cilachaem. Whatever they found, please let Rori be alive. It wasn't his curse he was thinking about in that moment; it was Rori and only Rori—the woman he loved. The only woman he'd ever love. The woman he'd die fighting to protect.

❧ 14 ☙

Flashes of light whipped past Rori in the in-between, and she kept her focus straight ahead, too terrified to look to the side for fear she might encounter the snake-dragon-demon again. The newly healed wound the beast had given her throbbed with her accelerated heartbeats, and she drew a long breath to settle her nerves.

The flashes stretched and yawned, as if doorways opened and then closed at indiscriminate intervals. Something had happened to the in-between. Something she hoped was good and not the alternative. Time drifted. What should've been a short jump through the portal felt as though it, too, stretched into infinity. Anxiety twisted her muscles. She should've been through by now. This was taking far too long. She'd never, not once in all the times she'd used the doorways, gotten lost, but she was beginning to think there was a first time for everything.

Focus, MacNair.

Therron.

She kept her thoughts on his face, his smile, the light that danced in his eyes when she said something ridiculous. That scar.

Focus. Breathe.

She recalled the way Therron touched her when they lay naked in that huge bed at Midna's palace. The way his fingers trailed along her skin, igniting a fire beneath the flesh, making her yearn for more than his touch. She wished to be consumed by his flames. To drown in his heat.

A shimmering appeared, and she raced toward it with all the strength she could muster.

Therron.

Wildly, she leapt through the opening before it was fully formed, tumbling to a hard stone surface. Her abused body protested, and fresh waves of agony swept along her muscles. She lay on her back, panting through the pain, blinking against the morning sun that momentarily blinded her. She lifted a hand to shield the brightness, just as a hulking shadow blocked the light. Rori squinted to better see, and stared up at something remarkable. Something she recognized from a school trip taken almost a decade earlier. Something she'd never expected to see again. A charcoal-grey scaled snout sniffed the air above her battered body.

Definitely not her Therron. She clung to the messenger bag with one hand and her jacket in the other with a protective hold as she rolled to a kneeling position. From that angle, she could just make out disc-like scales, soft amber eyes, and the hint of wings she remembered being as soft as gossamer.

"It's you." She blinked away tears that refused to hide.

"Yes, and it's you." His deep voice vibrated through her nerves.

Somehow, in her mad escape, when all she'd thought of was Therron and safety and falling into his strong embrace, she'd instead managed to maroon herself on the rooftop of Notre Dame Cathedral in Paris. Snickertits times a million.

The gravity of her situation crashed into her, and she shuddered against the fear that sought to strangle her thoughts.

"We need to hide. He'll track me here, and you absolutely don't want him to see you." Rori rose on unsteady legs, ignoring the pins that shot throughout her body, robbing her of breath.

"Who are we hiding from?"

"Hunter. My fa—" She started to say *father*, but the word stuck in her throat. "A madman who is a danger to this world and Cilachaem. To all worlds, actually."

"I see." His eyes shuttered, and he made little harrumphing sounds. "Come." The dragon lumbered to a shadowed corner and settled himself before indicating she should slink between his legs.

"But he'll see you." Her gaze went from his taloned feet to the horns atop his head. "You've grown, Aimon."

A grin widened his snout. "You remembered my name. I'm well pleased you have. Now, get inside. I promise, he won't know we're here. You're safe with me, Aurora."

She crouched beneath his bulk and sunk to the ground, her back against his belly. He was surprisingly warm for a scaled creature. From where she sat, she could see the doorway she'd fallen through, and most of that section of the rooftop. It was a decent vantage point. She was grateful for the dragon's confidence, but if she could see the door, then Hunter could see her. Yet there was nowhere else to hide, and she didn't have the time or strength to make another leap through the doorway.

Not that it would matter. Hunter would track her wherever she went. She slid her precious bundle to her side and tucked the jacket and bag against the stone wall. Her fingers flicked open the sheath on her hip, and she withdrew her dagger. The slim blade had saved her life more times than she could recount, and she prayed to the First Goddess that it would do so once more.

Before she could put much thought into what needed to be done, she lifted her shirt and found the implanted tracker in her abdomen. One long breath was all she allowed to steady her nerves. A swift flick of the blade made a clean cut into her skin, the stinging pain more of a nuisance than anything. As calmly and carefully as possible, she used the tip of the blade to work the tracker free from the tissue layer that had already formed around it. This caused a fraction more pain, and she breathed through it the best she could. Small whimpers escaped her lips, and she struggled to stay calm and not do more damage to her broken body.

Tears pricked her eyes, and she blinked hard to stop their flow. Futnuckers, it hurt. Everything hurt. Her body, her heart, her mind were all overwhelmed with the kind of pain that came from betrayal and a loss of something cherished that could never be regained.

The glass capsule plopped onto her belly, and she placed it on the stone surface before smashing it with the butt of her dagger. Several curses filled the air as she wished hellfire upon Hunter a thousand-fold.

Next, she wiped her bloodied hands on her jeans and slid the laptop from the leather bag. Her fingers shook as she opened the lid and typed in her password. The same windows she saw in Hunter's morgue sprang to the screen. Her nerves tightened and fingers curled as she read the file name of the first window: The Dawn Project.

And there, blinking half a foot from her face, was her history. Later, when she had the time and brain space to parse the files, she'd learn everything the monster had done to her. But now, she needed to find a way to rid herself of the microchip Hunter had embedded in her skull.

She scanned several pages, her mind snagging on certain words that made her heart ache and belly recoil. He was so much more than a monster. A mad scientist hell-bent on destroying two worlds. With her as his weapon.

With Herculean effort, she pushed the dire thoughts aside and kept scrolling until finally, she found what she was looking for—an innocent-looking page with her name, the identification number of the microchip, date injected, and there, at the bottom of the page were two words: Activate and Deactivate.

The former was bright green, which she assumed meant Hunter had already activated the microchip. He hadn't lied. At any moment, he could manipulate her to do his bidding. Or blow up her skull.

Her breaths came in shallow pulls and nostrils flared with each inhale. It might be a trap. He might've planted the laptop in the hopes she would steal it. He might even have seeded the idea that she search for her name and click on the Deactivate button, thereby killing herself.

"Is everything all right, Aurora?" The dragon bent his neck so that he could peer at her between his long legs.

"I'm trying to decide if Hunter set me up to fail. If he did, then I die."

"Does he want you dead?"

A stress-filled chuckle rumbled up her chest. "Not completely, but close."

"What does your gut tell you?"

"That it wants to spill what little is left in there all over your lovely scales."

His dark lips pulled into a grin. "What happens if you don't die?"

Her fingertip hovered over the touchpad. "I free myself from his control."

She mashed her finger down, clicking the Deactivate button.

Nothing happened. There was no sense of freedom, or of relief. Nothing.

The screen blipped and a new line appeared on the page. It read, "Microchip number 19785362 is no longer active."

A wave of relief swept over her, and she took a deep breath to clear the fear that had lodged in her psyche. This wasn't over, not yet.

Rori cricked her neck and set the laptop aside. She closed her eyes and called forth her magic, only allowing a tiny thread to form. She didn't need the spell her father had taught her when she was little. That was her fail-safe if she couldn't find another way to rid herself of the microchip.

Yet she needed to use the dark magic infused in her blood to pull the chip from her brain. She didn't know how she knew, but she did. She trusted her gut.

Not even her unicorn soul could do what had to be done. To say she was terrified was an understatement. Ever since that day her dad disappeared and she'd lost control of her magic, she'd feared this day. Feared her wild magic—or what she believed was wild magic.

"I'm here, Aurora." The dragon nudged her boot with his snout.

"Can you feel my dark magic?"

"Aye. I won't let anything happen to you."

She directed her magic to the base of her head, where she felt a small incision in her skin. Gently, she opened the incision and coaxed the microchip out, using her fingertips and magic in tandem. Sweat rolled down her forehead to pool on her closed eyelids. Each worrying thought that entered her mind was immediately silenced. She couldn't afford to doubt herself now.

With a final shove of her magic, and a strong squeeze of her fingertips, the chip broke through her skin, and she pinched it so tightly it cut into her flesh. She wiped the sweat from her eyes on her shirt and looked at the tiny metal square. No bigger than her pinkie fingernail, it amazed her that something so small could cause such destruction.

Her magic subsided with a slow tugging at her nerves, as if it were reluctant to return to the shadows. If she hadn't been so focused on ridding her skull of the microchip, she would've noticed the seductive nature of her dark powers. Even then, as she leaned against the dragon's belly, she felt the lure of pleasure her magic promised. Sensual pleasure. Dangerous pleasure. The kind of pleasure that sucks you in and destroys you.

No thank you very much.

Tucking the darkness away, Rori drew on her lighter powers, immediately feeling the sense of renewal and healing her unicorn soul brought. She swirled a thread of magic to form around the chip, creating an amethyst cabochon encased in a bed of silver. Curlicues crept up the smooth sides, and a long silver chain dangled from her fingertips. She slid the pendant over her head, pulling her hair free so that the amethyst nestled in the crevice of her breasts.

She gripped the crystal in her fist. "A little reminder of how demented Hunter Pearson is, and to never, ever underestimate him."

The adrenaline that had given her the extra energy needed to not only escape the villa, but then to remove the tracker and microchip, left her body with a chilling rapidity. Completely spent, she leaned against the dragon. Blood oozed down her side, and her face throbbed against her splintered cheekbone.

She knew she should reach out to Therron, but her thoughts were chaotic and full of emotions she knew would only worry him. When her heart rate slowed, and fear didn't stalk her words, then she would send a message.

A drop of water splashed on the top of her head and ran down the back of her skull to where she'd forced the chip from her brain. A larger drop, heavy and thick as if from a summer thunderstorm, plunked upon her forehead, and she blinked against the rivulets that ran into her eyes. Another splash, followed by several more, covered her face. She looked up to see Aimon angling his head so that his tears fell onto her. Too dumbfounded to speak, she lifted her face to him, her own tears mingling with his.

The left side of her face tingled with oddly painful pins unlike she'd ever experienced. He shifted his head so that his tears moved from her face to her exposed belly. She watched in fascination as the wound she'd made cutting out the tracker healed; the blood turned not to glitter, but to smoke as if it were paper being burned. Yet there was no pain now. Not in her face, nor her abdomen, nor her skull.

"You healed me." She half sobbed. "Thank you."

He moved his snout until it touched her forehead. "I owe you my life, Aurora MacNair. 'Tis an honor to do you this small kindness." One last tear trickled down his cheek to her chest, where it washed over her amethyst. "I will protect you as you once protected me. Sleep now."

His words sunk into her the same as his tears, and she gave in to his suggestion. Her body sagged and became heavy. She fought against it with the last of her energy reserves.

"I need to let Therron know where I am. I don't want him to worry."

His smile showed two huge fangs, and she nearly reached out to touch one.

"The dragon prince is looking for you. We'll make sure he knows you're safe."

A chilling thrill went through her at his words. *The dragon prince.* It seemed fitting, and yet strange at the same time. Therron was an elven prince. Cilachaem didn't have dragons.

Therron, she sighed before realizing what she'd done. Immediately, she shut her mind, sweeping aside all thoughts of the elf.

She couldn't risk reaching out to him. Hunter needed Therron for something, which meant she'd protect him no matter the cost. Fuck Hunter and his sadistic desires.

Cian. Her breath caught, and she choked back tears. She would have to tell him what their father had done to her. The man they had all mourned—she would be the one to expose him for the monster he was. A pit formed in her throat. Before she told Cian, she'd have to tell their mother.

After she healed. If she survived the night.

$\maltese$ 15 $\maltese$

The villa was exactly as Cian remembered it. Green shutters meant to keep the villa cool in the summer and warm in the winter. A crumbling exterior meant to give the villa a look of time-worn poverty that belied what was inside. Cian's hands trembled as he looked up to the small window he remembered as if from a dream.

He'd been there. Once, perhaps thrice, a long time ago.

His gaze slid to Nikala, his mind making calculations he'd rather not realize.

"What is it?" Nikala placed a hand on his shoulder, and he struggled to hide the chill that wormed its way down his back.

"I'm not sure."

She gave a reassuring squeeze before confidently reaching behind a planter and moving a brick to retrieve a key hidden there.

"Whatever we find inside, I'm here for you." Nikala took his hand in hers, the warmth strange yet needed. Her eyes narrowed a moment, as if she experienced his unease as her own. With a shake of her head, she unlocked the villa's door.

If only he could convey what troubled him. If only he could remember why this place gave him the creeps.

They stepped into a small entryway, and a memory seized Cian.

His father held him by the shoulders, his face serious. "You're becoming a man, son, and as such there are responsibilities you must accept."

Cian hadn't understood the seriousness or meaning of his father's words. Surely, he had a few years to be young and carefree before anything important was expected of him. He was, after all, only eleven years old. He wouldn't enter the Academy until he was fourteen. Even so, he'd lifted his chin and straightened his shoulders to show his father he was ready.

His father kept his grip on Cian and continued, "This villa, and all it represents, could be yours one day. But only if you prove you're worthy."

At this, Cian stood taller. His very existence had always been about showing his father he was worthy. Earning his father's approval was the single most important thing in his life. He'd do whatever was asked of him.

Hagan had guided him through the little entryway to a kitchen, where Cian had spied two coffee mugs near the sink. One for him, he'd thought; how nice of his father to consider his needs. But his father hadn't offered him a cup of the bitter drink that, in truth, Cian didn't like unless it had several cubes of sugar and enough milk to make it the color of his flesh. Candy coffee, his mum called it.

The memory of his mum teasing him about how sweet he liked his drink made him smile despite the memory or dreariness of the villa. The group passed the kitchen, and Cian snuck a look inside. There, next to the sink, was only one coffee mug. He wondered who the second one had been for, but then shut the thought down, knowing he might not like the answer. One day, perhaps he'd be ready to answer that riddle, but that day was not today.

"Upstairs," Nikala said.

Cian's stomach dropped.

He'd all but forgotten this villa and what had happened there, but now, the memories zoomed through his brain as if hopped up on high-grade meth.

Three closed doors led off the landing, only one of which was of any interest to Cian. Before he could stop himself, he opened the one to his right and peered inside. It was exactly as it had been that summer when his father first brought him to Venice. Pale-green walls, a single bed with an ancient floral quilt covering a tatty mattress.

His gaze drifted to the metal bed frame, to the railings that had once been used to confine him to the bed. Without thinking, he rubbed his wrists, surprised when he didn't see the red welts the ropes had left on his skin.

"Cian?" Nikala said softly beside him. "You okay?"

He wasn't. Not by a long shot.

"You're less than useless." His father's words pounded against his skull. "At only two years old, your sister is more powerful than you'll ever be. Such a waste of MacNair blood." The final words were hissed into Cian's face. "I should leave you here alone to rot."

But Hagan hadn't left him alone. Not for another two

full weeks, until he'd completed whatever bullshit experiments he'd needed to do to Cian.

"Yeah," he said at last to Nikala. "Let's continue."

He pulled his sleeve lower to hide the scars, lightened by time and Meg's healing, but still as painful today as they were when he first received them two decades earlier.

A terrible thought lodged in his throat, and he glared at Nikala. "When did Hunter first start his experiments with you?"

Her eyes narrowed, lips pursed. "When I was eight. Right after Malcolm gave me to him."

"Time of year. Winter? Spring?" He made a silent plea that she say any season but summer.

"In the summer, close to the solstice. Why?"

Fuck.

Timelines were falling into place like a mad game of Tetris.

Hagan was already calling himself Hunter by then. Cian would never think of his father as Hagan again. Hagan was the man he loved. Hunter was a monster Cian didn't know. What he understood now was that Hunter had used them all.

Rori's illness. Her miraculous recovery. His sudden interest in Cian, followed closely by his equally quick disinterest in him.

When Cian couldn't replace Rori, Hunter found a new victim.

"Did he bring you here that summer?" How close had he been to meeting the eight-year-old Nikala in this house of horrors? Solstice was only a few days after he'd left Venice and returned to Faerie. He remembered because he'd begged his father to let him stay for the celebrations.

"I don't think so. All I remember of that time is Scotland." Nikala touched his arm, and the warmth of her love traveled across his skin. "Cian, what's going on? Are you remembering something?"

His nod was slow and uncertain. "I was brought here when I was eleven." He wrung his hands, his voice unsteady. "I didn't please him. I failed."

Sadness filled Nikala's gorgeous eyes. "I'm sorry, Cian. I had hoped you'd been spared his torture."

"No, it wasn't like that. Not torture. Not like what he put you through. It was..." Cian paused, searching for the right words. "Tests."

Nikala cocked her head. "What kinds of tests?"

Cian rubbed his arm, felt a sudden phantom pain spasm across his back, recalled a scalpel dripping with blood.

"I don't know. I mean, I know what he did to me, but not why, or what he hoped to learn from the procedures. I only know he told me I was worthless. Less than worthless, actually."

"You know you're not worthless, right?" Nikala pushed his hair off his forehead. "Hunter's the worthless piece of shit for what he did to you."

"Did to us. All of us, starting with Rori."

Therron appeared behind Nikala and gave them a curious glance. "There's something you should see upstairs." Without waiting for a reply, he turned and disappeared down the hallway.

Cian took Nikala's hand in his own and kissed her fingers. "We're stronger together." He had no idea where the sentiment came from, but it was the absolute truth. Together, they would defeat Hunter.

"Damn right we are." She cupped his cheek a moment before pivoting to follow Therron.

Cian watched her back for a moment, before forcing himself to take a step. Her questions had rattled him, and he didn't know why. The tests had to have meant something, but his younger self was too wrapped up in gaining his father's approval to ask.

Parts of his past either he'd blocked from memory or were blocked from him were up the stairs Nikala and Therron were heading toward. As much as he didn't want to face what they might find, he had to confront what happened to Rori, and the truth of his past.

❧ 16 ❧

Cian took the stairs two at a time to catch up to the others. They skipped the second floor, where Cian recalled Hunter's study was located, along with his father's bedroom. Another room was used as storage. If there were more, he couldn't remember, nor did it matter at the moment. He trudged up the stairs to the top floor. At a small landing, he stopped to get his bearings. The air was heavier here, and the scent different—clear, crisp…as if this floor was cleaned often with harsh astringents. Sounds of the city dimmed to an eerie silence, and he glanced at the padded walls Hunter must've installed to make the place soundproof.

As they passed a doorway on Cian's left, he felt the pull of magic and paused, senses on alert. A curtain hung from several broken rings, but it was what he saw behind the curtain that drew his attention. A nondescript door—odd in this villa where every entranceway, every door had elabo- rate details etched into the woodwork. He pushed it open, half expecting Hunter to jump out at him. But there was no surprise attack, only another hallway, dimly lit. He squinted into the semi-darkness. At the other end, glowing softly like a siren's call, he saw what had pulled at him.

A door. But not just any door. A doorway.

He cast back in his memory, but there was nothing there involving this door. He and his father always arrived the same way the little group had this morning through the church.

Maxx appeared like a cat on silent feet and touched his arm. "He made this after your time here. There are a lot of renovations you wouldn't recognize."

Something in her eyes told him he wouldn't like the changes Hunter had made. Steeling himself for the worst, he followed her down a narrow hallway. She ignored the room to his left, but Cian stopped to look inside. His innards went cold at the sterile tables and wall of small cubicles. It was as Maxx had said back in London—a morgue.

His memory of the room was that it had been an attic, but even now, he recalled the beginnings of Hunter's personal mortuary in his home. There had been two tables back then, not with sinks, but buckets that Cian never let himself question their purpose. He'd been strapped to one of the tables, he was sure of it.

A jagged pain raced down his forearm, and he rubbed the spot where his memory told him Hunter had broken the bones. He didn't remember why or what he'd done to deserve the punishment, just that his father had snapped his forearm as if it were nothing.

Sick fuck.

His gaze traveled to every corner of the room, as if searching for something, or someone. Maxx stepped into view, and he was seized by yet another memory. He pushed the cuff of his sleeve high enough he could see his unmarked skin, where there should've been a scar from the broken arm. Warmth oozed from the spot—magic, but not his.

"You healed me." Cian met Maxx's even stare with his own. "Not just my arm, but many other injuries he gave me in this house. Why?"

Maxx blinked and looked toward the boxes inset into the wall. "I hated what Hunter was doing to you." She held up a hand. "I had no idea about Rori until much later, and have lived with the guilt of what I could've done to stop him ever since. But you...the tests he set up for you were nothing more than an excuse to hurt an innocent boy."

"Cian," Therron said from the doorway, but he ignored the elf.

"You're an assassin, not a healer," he challenged Maxx. At the Academy, they made the students choose one or the other, with the unspoken rule that they could never be both.

Therron shifted, his measured glance pinging from Cian to Maxx and back.

"I never saw the point of making us choose. Why can't I be equally as good at one as I am at the other?" Maxx lifted her chin as if in silent rebellion. "Neither Hunter nor the queens know, and I'd like to keep it that way. Although, I'm hardly the first nor the last."

At this, Therron drew in a sharp breath, and Cian

looked to him for an explanation. None came, but from the way his eyes narrowed in Maxx's direction, it was clear he had opinions on the matter.

"Something to add, Therron?"

A beat of silence, then Therron said, "There's something you should see."

Therron motioned for Cian to follow him to the room at the end of the hall. Nikala stood outside, her head stretched to peer inside as if she dared not enter. A slow burn of alarm started in Cian's gut and spiraled outward. His glance took in Therron's features, noting the anger that simmered in the tightness of his jaw, and the worry at the corner of his eyes.

"What did you find?" Cian asked the elf, not wanting any surprises when he looked into the room.

"Rori was here."

"And?"

Rage flashed across Therron's features. "See for yourself."

Therron stepped into the room, with Nikala following, then Cian, and finally Maxx. A quick scan showed a ransacked cabinet to his left, a worktable beside it. Tools he recognized and had on occasion used for torture were strewn across the wooden top. His gaze slowed on a lone scalpel, but he quickly moved on to the rest of the room. A broken chair lay splintered on the floor, and behind him to his right was a hospital bed that looked recently slept in.

Maxx bent and retrieved something from the floor. "A tracker. Crude, and low tech, but it's all he had available to him." She rose and held a tiny glass tube between her thumb and forefinger. "My guess is he also embedded a microchip in her skull."

"What use is this microchip?" Therron's gaze flicked from an empty apothecary cabinet to the broken chair on the floor.

"When he doesn't have enough time for mental conditioning, Hunter goes old school and implants a device to control his subject," Maxx explained.

"Are you saying he can control Rori's mind?" Therron's eyes narrowed and jaw hardened. His fists clenched and unclenched.

Cian understood only too well what the elf was feeling. Death was too good for the madman. Cian half hoped the faerie queens would go old school on Hunter and have him drawn and quartered before dissolving him into dust. He deserved far worse for what he'd done. He pulled his thoughts from the dark places they sought to wander and scanned the rest of the small room.

No bodies. No blood. Whatever the hell had happened here, he couldn't make out from the scant information his initial investigation provided. There was a fight, for sure, but the victor wasn't clear. Whatever secret Rori was hiding, it appeared Hunter spared no compassion in his attempt to uncover it.

"What was Hunter searching for in my sister? What could be so important he'd need to hide her away and torture her?" Cian asked the questions aloud, to no one in particular. He wasn't sure he wanted to know, but at the same time, needed to know who or what his baby sister was.

Instead of answering, Therron knelt near the broken chair and ran his hand over the tiled floor. A glittery substance Cian knew instinctively was faerie blood, now turned to dust in the human realm, was scattered across the pristine white marble.

"Is that Rori's?" Of course it was, but Cian also hoped it wasn't. He swallowed against the rise of emotion and reminded himself he was a decorated spy for his queen. Spies could not afford to be emotional, even for their loved ones. It was the first lesson they taught at the Academy. And the only one that almost got Rori kicked out her first year.

Cian rubbed his wrists, as if trying to hide the scars of his past. He knew the brutality his father was capable of. If Hunter had tortured Rori to discover her secret, he might've gone too far and killed her. Or, hopefully, Rori escaped.

"It's Rori's," Therron confirmed. Then, he did something remarkable that Cian had never witnessed before.

Therron placed his hand atop the shimmering motes of Rori's dried blood and closed his eyes. A moment later, what Cian could only describe as a movie played in the air in front of the elf.

Maxx gasped, and Nikala took Cian's hand. He felt a small tremor in her touch and gave a slight squeeze. It was easy to forget how new magic was for her. And probably terrifying.

There, suspended in midair, Cian watched as Hunter struck his only daughter with enough force to kill her. Rori took the blow to the side of her face and toppled to the floor from the impact. The room vibrated with the sound of Rori's cheek breaking, followed by the splintering of the chair she was bound to.

"Fuck me. What was Hunter thinking?" Maxx snapped.

Tears glinted in Therron's eyes as he cautioned, "There's more."

Cian heard the words as if through a viscous substance. The room swirled and rotated, the lights flickering as he fell to his knees. Instead of seeing what Therron showed them, Cian saw himself as a child, his bare arms held in front of him, his naked body bound to a wooden chair.

Hunter approached, a scalpel gleaming in the lights.

"Let's see what your sister's blood has done for you." A devilish chuckle left his father's mouth and a light shone in his eyes that burned Cian's soul with fear.

His father enjoyed this. Enjoyed hurting his son. Enjoyed testing him to beyond his limits.

Yet Cian didn't understand why. He couldn't fathom what he'd done to deserve such treatment.

A sharp pain splintered his thoughts, and his younger self looked down to see a crimson line of blood run from his elbow to the top of his hand. Tears stung his eyes, but he dared not let them fall. An agonized scream rent the air, deafening him to what his father was saying.

"Cian, you're safe. There's nothing to fear here. Come back to the present, Cian," a woman's gentle voice said from beyond the torment; for one joyous moment, he thought it was his mum.

"What's wrong with him?" another woman, one he loved with his whole heart, said to his left.

"He's remembering what happened here."

Someone rubbed his arms, and he looked down at the tear in his skin, amazed and horrified to see the skin knitting back together.

"Well, son, you've at least passed this test." Hunter patted him on the head as if to reward him for what a good boy he'd been.

Then his father left the room. Cian sat in the dark, bound to the chair, naked, confused, and alone. He swallowed the tears that threatened, and the shriek that begged to be loosened.

He would not, could not, show weakness.

Not if he hoped to survive.

17

Therron paced from the doorway back to the room where Cian lay still on the strange bed. Used in hospitals, Nikala had said, but Therron didn't understand the reference. Only when Maxx added that hospitals were where they treated people who were ill or injured did he realize it was similar to the healing wards at Elvenwood. Though, the bed looked more like a torture device than for healing.

Everything in this place had a sense of anguish to it. His gaze went to the worktable, where a scalpel lay innocently—but he knew it had been used on Rori. How recently, he could only guess. From the dried blood on the floor, he would say half a day, perhaps a bit more. Which meant she'd been alive that morning when Aimon came to see him.

They were wasting time.

"If Cian needs longer to rehabilitate, then perhaps Maxx can stay with him while Nikala and I investigate the doorways. I picked up two trails, each leading in separate directions."

"We're not leaving without Cian." Nikala glared at him, as if he'd told her the spy was dead.

"Then stay. I'll find Rori on my own." Therron's rage simmered through his blood. He stormed to the door and turned to face the others. "Can't you see that Rori is all that matters? Hunter doesn't need you or me. He needs Rori. She is the one who can break not just my curse, but Hunter's hold on both worlds, yours and mine. Without her, we are lost." He was nearly shouting but didn't care.

"Therron, I know you're upset." Nikala approached and smoothed a hand across his back in a comforting motion like his mother would do whenever he'd woken from a nightmare. "But now is not the time for histrionics." Her gaze went to a small contraption in the corner and to another one on the other side of the room. "Hunter has cameras everywhere. Whatever you say or do here, he can see."

"Cameras? Recording devices, yes?" Therron barely waited for Nikala's nod before he approached one of the metal boxes and pressed his face close to the round glass. "If you are watching, know this—I will hunt you through all the worlds. I will not bring you to court for your queen to administer justice—I will enact my own." He took a slow breath, head bowed, and then looked directly into the blinking red light. *Alseacht enora desedrias vectum de morte aneal alseacht enora.*"

Maxx gasped and covered her mouth.

"What did he say?" Nikala's blue eyes were huge as she looked from Maxx to Therron.

"It's an oath of the old language. Dark. Dangerous. Forbidden." Maxx's face was pale, and her lips trembled.

Cian swung his legs off the bed and stood to face Therron. "I'm fit for travel. Let's go find my sister before this lunatic gets us all killed."

Therron cast one last glance at the room; his gaze landed on the scalpel. With one swift movement, he grabbed the wretched thing and gently placed it into his coat pocket, wrapping a band of magic around the sharp blade to keep it from slicing the fabric or his skin.

At the doorway, he explained again that he couldn't decipher one signature from the other. They were equally filled with anger and pain.

"Knowing Rori, she made several stops before landing at her true location. She would know Hunter would follow her." Therron hoped his theory was correct. It was what he would've done if being followed. He smoothed his chest where his heart pinched with insidious frequency. "My heart tells me we should return to London, but I don't think she would go there, not yet."

"I agree. If she believes Hunter is chasing her, she'd go where he wouldn't think to look for her." Cian rubbed a finger along his upper lip. "The only problem is, I don't know where that would be."

"There might be a way to find her." Nikala met Maxx's gaze. "It's dangerous but could give us the answers we seek."

Maxx blew out a breath. "You'd risk taking a crown prince of Elvenwood there?"

Nikala shrugged. "We have no choice. We've spent hours poring over Hunter's journals. Everything we need is at the lab in Geneva."

"Then let us go." Therron pointed to the doorway. "Whatever dangers await, we can face when we get there."

No one spoke for a long moment, and Therron shifted with his annoyance. They were stalling, but he didn't understand why.

Finally, Maxx broke the silence. "Fine. We'll use Hunter's doorway straight to his office." She looked him directly in the eye. "Whatever happens, do not use your magic." He was about to ask why, and she held up a hand to stop his questions. "Just don't. There are things at the lab you don't need to know about. Things that can destroy you and your family. Trust me on this, Your Highness."

He had no love for her, nor any trust, but he saw in her steady gaze how important it was that he obey her command and gave a brief nod that he would do as she asked. He'd risk hellfire to find Rori.

She stepped around Therron and said the words that would take them to whatever or wherever Geneva was. He waited for the others to enter before following. Despite her cryptic warning, his heart rate ramped up and a tiny thread of hope they might find Rori made him eager to hurry them along. But he knew better than to be impatient in the inbetween. Time worked differently in there. Even though it was pitch black, his gaze flicked left to right, alert to any sign of the snake-dragon-demon that had attacked Rori.

A light blinked in the distance, and they collectively quickened their pace to reach it. The tiny cupboard they entered barely fit all four of them. Cian squeezed himself in a half circle to open a door that led to a blessedly large office. Machines whirred and blipped all around them. To the right, a large bank of monitors showed moving pictures of various rooms, and directly in front of them sat a huge desk.

Therron's nerves tightened as he glanced at the unfamiliar surroundings. Pain lived here. Pain and suffering on a scale he never could've imagined. His heartbeats quickened, and sweat slicked down his back. He twitched his shoulders in irritation, not understanding what prompted his unease.

Nikala strode to the panel of monitors. His gaze followed her and while she studied the screens, he found the source of his anxiety. In one of the moving pictures, about a dozen people milled about in a room devoid of machinery. Beds stacked one upon the other were pressed against the walls, but otherwise the room was empty. It wasn't the lack of furnishings that caught his attention.

The people looked human, but he sensed differences in all of them. One, a male, passed a camera and looked up, as if seeing Therron through the glass lens. In that moment, Therron saw into the man's spirit, saw the elf trapped somewhere dark. Saw the pain.

"What are these people?" He pointed to the screen.

Nikala pulled her attention away from the monitor she'd been studying, where three people moved about their business. "Scyvers. I don't see Hunter. Maybe we got lucky." She stepped closer and examined one picture in particular. "There's a computer in here." She tapped the glass. "I can hack into it and send information to my laptop." She tapped a separate panel with a lone man dressed in black. "Let me know if anyone surprises us." This was said to Maxx, who nodded her understanding.

The word buzzed in Therron's mind. Scyvers. Nikala had said it nonchalantly, as if they were a common nuisance, nothing more. Therron stared at the monitor. These were once his people. A female came into view, and like the man, she looked at the camera. Therron didn't sense elven in her, but something else he didn't recognize. He realized with a shock that not all of those in that room were from Cilachaem.

"What should we do while you're gone?" Cian asked Nikala.

"You're coming with me. Therron, stay here with Maxx. You're safest here." Her gaze swept the room. "It's the only office that doesn't have cameras."

She strode past a large glass partition with multicolored markings and out the door with Cian close behind.

"I thought they'd never leave." Maxx peered at the bank of monitors and tapped a different one than Nikala had. "Come on, we've work to do."

"But Nikala said to stay here."

"And you always do as you're told?"

Therron chuckled. "Hardly."

He followed her out the door and to the right, down a long white corridor. Doors were equidistantly placed on either side—some open, most closed. At the end of the hall, Maxx turned right, but not before checking to see whether the corridor was empty. She walked with purpose, but he sensed her constant vigilance in the way her shoulders stiffened with her hurried gait and the sweeping of her head from left to right with each open door.

Finally, she ducked into an office and closed the door behind Therron. He heard the lock click and cocked an eyebrow in question.

"Precautionary." When she turned, she sucked in a breath.

A wall of clear glass separated the office from another room. He stepped closer to better see and counted a dozen people milling about. They all wore grey tops and trousers, their feet bare, heads shaved. Six bunk beds flanked the sides of the room, with a large empty space in the center. It was the room he'd been watching on the monitor.

"Who are they?" Therron cocked his head toward the glass.

"No one you need bother with. Step back before they see you." Maxx sat at a desk with a large black monitor hiding her from those in the other room. She pressed a button on the side of the desk and the wall turned misty, the people becoming nothing more than shadowy shapes. "Don't touch anything," Maxx warned before she began to type furiously.

This close, he felt the scyvers' pain as if it were his own. An overwhelming need to rescue them, to take them back to Elvenwood to heal them, came over Therron. Even those who weren't elven, he felt compelled to rescue, as if it was his duty as the heir to the Elvenwood throne to protect them. Or die trying.

18

Therron glared at Maxx's back as she continued typing, oblivious to the scyvers only a few steps from where she sat. It enraged him that she and Nikala could so callously ignore the tormented people. He seethed as pictures flashed across her computer screen. The pictures and accompanying files meant nothing to him, but they were more important to Maxx than the suffering in the next room. This office was larger than the previous one, with several desks pushed against the side wall. More computers, more chairs, more places for people to sit and tippity-tap away on an ethereal machine that Therron would never fully understand.

On the other side of the opaque window, a low keening could be heard.

"We need to save them."

"No, we don't."

"They are in pain."

Maxx turned with a snarl, but her features softened when she looked at him. "Therron, *denatis desedrias ne de morte anadriel septivian golachna.*" Death is the only cure for these poor souls.

Therron stared at her as if she'd turned into a cockatrice. "They can be healed."

"They can't. Trust me, Your Highness. If there was a way, I have tried to find it, but Hunter's experiments are irreversible. I'm sorry."

In her eyes, nay, in her very being, he saw the bone-weary heaviness she carried and believed her words. He also, in that moment, saw not a spy or assassin, but a complicated woman who held her emotions in check even when it behooved her not to. His gaze flicked to the monitor where two pictures remained on the screen, and from what Therron could tell, they were father and son. Maxx gave him a wan smile.

"My family. My loves. I would do anything in this world and beyond to keep them safe, just as you would for Rori. Stay focused." She returned to the keyboard and started to type.

As much as he hated to hear it, she spoke the truth. That she'd chosen to speak in Eleri was not lost on him. She wasn't at all what she seemed. Admitting that she had a family was a risk, and he appreciated the trust she gave him in sharing the knowledge. He saw a bit of himself in her, which was a revelation he never thought he'd make. Stradling two worlds, with her heart tied to one while doing her best to protect the other. It was a precarious balancing act he admired. He wasn't too proud to admit he might've been wrong about her but would keep that tidbit to himself.

Seeing her devotion made him think about Elvenwood.

He knew he needed to return, as much to learn what was happening there as to share what was going on in the human realm, but not until Rori was safe. He was putting her above the throne, not a very kingly thing to do, but the throne was nothing without her. The pull of responsibility was new, and scary. The realization he was thinking of himself as king of Elvenwood was shocking enough, but to imagine himself on the throne with Rori as his queen felt right. And yet it didn't. He was the heir, yes, but he'd always known the throne wasn't for him.

The strange pinching of his heart agitated him. He wasn't meant to rule Elvenwood, nor did he believe Thad was, either. Which left Theo. But if Theo were to rule, where was Thad, and why wasn't he to be king? He was heir; the curse would soon be broken. Yet he knew with absolute certainty ruling wasn't his destiny. And yet he equally had no idea what that destiny involved. Lucien's belief, and Rhoane's cryptic words, about a darathi vorsi prince nudged at his skull. If only he knew what the pair meant. Or what a prince of dragons was.

His mind circled the thoughts until he felt dizzy from not grasping an answer. Find Rori. Then he could return to Elvenwood and all would be made clear. He'd demand Rhoane explain himself. He'd find his destiny.

He was about to insist Maxx finish whatever it was she was doing but was distracted by the rattling of the door handle.

Therron turned and faced the door, ready in case whoever was on the other side came through. Maxx glanced his way, saw his position, and returned to her work. Her typing became even more frantic. Clicks of the strange, hump-shaped thing they called a mouse interspersed with her swear words and keyboard clacks.

Whatever she was doing, she didn't wish to share with him.

The door handle jostled again, and this time he heard the scratch of a key being inserted.

"One more minute, just one more," Maxx whispered.

The door opened and a man dressed all in black entered. He stepped to the center of the room and looked first at Therron, then to Maxx, the surprise on his face changing rapidly to anger.

"You're not supposed to be here." He pointed a finger at Maxx. "The boss'll have your head for this."

"Hunter will never know," Maxx replied without looking to see who entered. "Take care of him, will you?"

Therron assumed she meant him and kicked the door closed. Before he could reach into his pocket to grip the scalpel, the first punch hit him in the solar plexus and nearly knocked the wind from him. He'd not thought humans were this strong, but how wrong he was. The second punch Therron ducked successfully and landed one of his own to the man's gut. He oomphed, but didn't stumble backward.

"Keep him busy, Therron. I need a bit longer."

The idiot man looked to see what Maxx was doing, giving Therron time to land a double punch, first to his chest and then to his jaw. The man spun with the impact, losing his balance. When he rose, he held a gun in his right hand.

"No more games." He cricked his neck and aimed the pistol at Therron's face. "Say goodnight, pretty boy."

Therron pulled a shield of magic over him and ducked just as a small flame burst from the tip of the gun. The bullet grazed his magic without injuring him. Maxx shrieked something, but all he heard was the screeching sound of the bullet ripping into the door. Pounding came from the opaque window, but Therron didn't take his gaze from the man determined to kill him.

"God dammit, Therron!" Maxx bellowed.

The man's face reddened with rage as he lifted the gun for a second shot. Therron ducked too quickly for the man to follow and slid behind him in one smooth movement. He pulled the scalpel from his pocket and rammed it into the man's neck. Bright-red blood spurted from the wound, making an arc from his body to halfway across the room. The gun slipped from his grip and clanged to the floor. He grabbed the scalpel with meaty fingers and jerked it free, unloosing even more blood. His eyes were full of shock and ill-placed anger as he went to his knees.

"How?" The man rocked forward, arms splayed against the white tile. A lake of red surrounded his lifeless body.

"Bloody hell. No pun intended." Maxx sat at the desk, her steady gaze taking in the entirety of the room.

"The scalpel was meant for Hunter. I suppose one of his henchmen will have to do."

"You think?" She turned back to the computer and made several more clicks. "There. Got it." A long sigh and a click later, the two pictures blinked from the screen.

On the other side of the window, faces pressed against the glass hard enough Therron could make out their features. The fervor intensified with unrelenting howls and screeches that sounded like someone being tortured.

"Fuck." Maxx clicked a few more keys and entered something into the computer.

A moment later, one by one, the scyvers' heads exploded. Therron jumped back, revulsion rippling through his gut. Blood and brains splattered the glass, and he gagged. As each person went down, they slid the gore beneath splayed palms. Although he'd seen a hint of Hunter's brutality, as each scyver died, he felt their relief at having their living nightmare ended. Glimpses of what Hunter had done to them tore through Therron's mind, and he reeled from the enormity of what they'd suffered.

This was what Eirlys and Midna were trying to prevent. He had to warn them, to tell them everything Hunter had done, was doing. If only he knew what Hunter's endgame was, then he could prepare the queens and his own kingdom. If his father would even listen.

"Why, Maxx?" He knew the answer. Still, he had to hear it from her.

"It was the most compassionate thing I could do. They would've suffered more had I not." She didn't look at the window but kept her focus on him. A softness lingered in her eyes, in the concern creasing her features.

"They might've been rehabilitated." He stubbornly refused to accept her decision.

The door opened, and Nikala stopped so suddenly Cian ran into her back. Her gaze went from the floor to the window, her expression full of emotion, anger especially. "So much for being discreet."

Cian peered over her shoulder. "Holy fuck. What happened?"

"There's no time." Maxx checked her watch. "We have

less than a minute to get out of here. I've wiped all the security cameras. We need to leave. Now."

Therron made his way around the dead man as best he could without touching the pool of blood. Maxx swooped down and grabbed the scalpel before shoving him out the door. His last glance was at the window with the remains of the poor souls in that room.

The weight of responsibility for their deaths hung from his shoulders. He'd used magic, and now, they were dead.

19

Dammit fucking all. Nikala pressed her knuckles into the desktop, ignoring the pain that flared up through her hands. Things were spiraling out of control. She glared at the polished wood, her mind dashing between thoughts. Her head pounded with all the decisions needing to be made. Not least among them, where everyone would be sleeping that night. And what the bloody hell they would have for dinner. Those were the easy questions. The more difficult ones, like what was Hunter really up to, and how best they should deal with his enhanced soldiers, circled the back of her brain…lurking, testing, irritating her need for control.

Therron stood at the huge window, staring into the distance at something she couldn't see. He'd said nothing since they returned from Geneva, but from his stony silence, she knew he was pissed. Her glance swept to Cian, who was hunched over a pile of notebooks. Maxx sat next to him, her foot tapping out her annoyance.

Tension hung in the air, oppressive, making it hard to think, hard to breathe.

She sat in the lush leather desk chair Malcolm had made specifically for her, but that she'd rarely used. Now it seemed her ass was permanently planted in the comfy seat. At least, it was when she wasn't chasing ghosts. She reached for her open laptop, hoping once again she might find answers in the files she'd stolen from Hunter's lab. They spread across the screen, making a mosaic of sorts. So much information, too much to wade through in one night. Her first priority was to find Rori, and thus far, there was nothing. Which meant, Hunter had the information stored somewhere else.

The lift pinged and everyone, including Nikala, looked at the open door to the office, wary of who might be coming through at six o'clock on a Sunday evening. A moment later, blonde hair bouncing with her jolly steps, Molly entered with a large basket clutched in her hands. Cian and Therron immediately went to help with the girl's burden.

"I thought you might be hungry," she said sheepishly. Her gaze flicked to the outer room. "Where's Darla?"

"It's Sunday. Apparently, she gets the day off," Nikala said, deadpan.

"Oh. Right." Disappointment clung to Molly's words. "Well, I hope you don't mind a shark cutie board. I myself would cut a bitch for a decent brie." Her giggles were warming and endearing, and exactly what they needed at the minute.

"I think you mean a charcuterie board," Maxx corrected.

"That's what I said. Shark cutie." Molly went to a wall of cupboards and opened the center section to reveal a huge television. "I'm assuming you haven't seen this yet." She withdrew a remote from a drawer and clicked the power button.

Immediately, the image of a burning building came into view, and everyone stopped what they were doing to stare at the screen.

There, plain for all the world to see, was Hunter's lab in ruins. The scroll across the bottom said a gas leak had caused a massive explosion, destroying the glass building and everything inside. Firefighters fought the blaze while a plume of black smoke clouded the sky.

As one, they turned to look at Maxx.

"What have you done?" Therron's rage showed in the veins protruding from his neck and forehead. "First those poor souls in that room, and now this? Have you no compassion?"

"It's because of my compassion that I did what I had to do. As for those 'poor souls'…please. They're scyvers, Therron. I know you see elves and fae, but Hunter stripped every spark of what made them elves and fae from them. He created magic junkies with no soul, no peace, and certainly no empathy. Had they reached you, they would've consumed all your magic and devoured your body as if you were a steak at a cookout. Stop seeing them as living beings. They might walk upright, but there is nothing left of the person they were."

Her words sounded harsh, even to Nikala. Therron stood tall and pushed his shoulders back as if personally affronted. "That's your opinion, but I disagree. I watched, nay, helped save the lycan as he lay dying. I felt Taryn and Rhoane restore his magic. It might be a shadow of what he once had, but he's been given the chance at rehabilitation. Don't you think these scyvers deserve the same?"

Nikala watched the pair, both convinced they were right, and understood both sides. She knew where Maxx was coming from, that she believed it was a mercy to spare the scyvers a life of addiction to something that would never truly fulfill them. Although she'd only just found her magic and didn't understand what it was they were denied, she knew the despair of needing something just out of reach.

Despite the warmth of the room, she rubbed her arms as if cold. Cian looked at her, eyes full of concern.

"Let's not argue over this. What's done is done." Nikala tried to bring brevity to the situation. "I, for one, will not mourn the loss of that lab." Or all the horrors done to her there, but they didn't need to know about those.

"But there are others," Therron countered.

"They're not alive, Therron. You must understand that. We need to destroy the remaining labs and everyone in them. Including the workers." Maxx glared at those in the room. "They are equally complicit in what Hunter's done. Every person who calls themselves a scientist and administered those tests, they knew what they were doing. Even the janitors knew. They're all complicit."

"As are we." Nikala spoke softly. "Do we deserve rehabilitation, Maxx? Or do we deserve to die?"

It was a question she'd asked herself all too often growing up. One that she could never fully answer.

"Everyone deserves a chance." Therron stood, his eyes

full of concern. "Yes, they are complicit, but what if they believe what they're doing is for the greater good?"

"Spoken like a true king." Maxx scoffed. "Isn't that counter to your family motto? Protect the elves, fuck everyone else. I've seen what your 'greater good' has done for marginalized societies."

Therron shook his head. "I can't undo what has been done, nor will I sit here and discuss murder on a grand scale. I was never meant to be king, but that doesn't mean I can't act honorably."

"Says the thief who killed a man with a scalpel not more than four hours ago," Maxx countered.

Cian stood and held out his hands to the pair. "Emotions are high right now. Decisions were made without consulting the group, fine, but now we need to rationally discuss our next move. Sit. Eat. Molly brought us dinner and it would be rude to ignore her generosity." He pointed to the closed basket. "Instead of arguing over semantics, help me unload this beast."

The three began setting up Molly's shark cutie board, Therron and Maxx with scowls crossing their features. Their enmity went beyond anything Nikala understood, seemingly to a history between the elves and fae.

Molly stood next to the television, the remote in her hand, eyes wide. "Shall I turn it off?"

"Please." Nikala squinted at the TV. "Wait."

The scroll along the bottom now read there were two people rescued from the Eris Building. It wasn't the survivors that caught her attention. A tickle in the back of her mind tugged at her with the memory of something important she'd forgotten. She sat in her chair and searched the laptop for any mention of the name Eris. It came up several times in the files she uploaded from the lab's mainframe computer, but also in Hunter's personal notes. She did a quick internet search, her belly tightening with each hit.

"Turn it off, please, Molly." Nikala gave the girl a wan smile. "We can plan after we eat."

Molly joined the men and within minutes, they had a spread worthy of the queen. Jams and chutneys, cheeses Nikala had never seen before, crackers, fruit, prosecco, wine…it was deliriously intoxicating. She couldn't remember the last time she'd eaten more than a quick bite from the pub.

The conversation was stilted as they ate, with Molly attempting to liven the mood with anecdotes of her time at MI6. Nikala half listened, her mind processing what she'd learned.

"Chaos. That's what Hunter wants. Specifically, cruelty through chaos." She shoved a cracker spread with Wensleydale and cranberry cheese into her mouth, taking a moment to savor the exquisite taste. "Cruelty was always the point."

The others stopped their chatter and watched her, expressions ranging from curious to confused.

"It wasn't until I saw the news that it registered. Hunter calls his umbrella project, the one that encompasses all the other projects including Rori, me, possibly even you, Cian, Eris. That building Maxx blew up was referred to as the Eris Building. I'd be willing to bet he named every lab Eris. Why? What's so special about that name?"

"Eris is the name of the Greek goddess of discord and strife," Molly offered, even though Nikala wasn't looking for an answer. "Eris spelled backward is SIRE. It's a semordni-lap." At their blank looks, she continued, "An anadrome."

"Right. Thank you, Molly. Excellently noted." Nikala chided herself that she could've just asked Molly for the information, but she didn't know the girl was wicked smart. She wouldn't underestimate her again. "So this Eris, she excels at causing chaos, often pitting men against one another to cause war." Nikala took another bite, her mind working through Hunter's motivations. "He wants war, but not *with* your world." At this, she looked at Cian and Ther-ron. "He's too much of a diva to get his hands dirty with politics. No, I think what he wants is for the leaders of this world, and also yours, to bring about a war that will end everything. Two worlds. Two wars. Utter destruction."

"You're talking about nuclear disaster." Maxx cocked her head. "I can see that for Earth, but there are no such things as nukes in Faerie or Elvenwood."

"No. But there is power. Magic. And what if there was someone or something that could ignite the spark that would take all that power and bind it together? What would happen?" Nikala's stomach tightened as she recalled Ishnara's warning. One drop of Rori's or Cian's blood could change the course of their world. And probably Earth.

Cian blew out a breath and looked at the ceiling. "Best guess? Make a magical nuke."

"But nothing that powerful exists," Maxx argued. "The queens would've recognized it for the destruction it could cause and eliminated it." She toggled her thumb to Cian and herself. "Why do you think we're here?"

Nikala shared a glance with Therron, and he gave the slightest shake of his head.

"That power does exist. It's been hidden for decades, but right under your noses." Nikala rose from behind the desk and sat beside Cian on the sofa. "It's what makes you and Rori so special. Your blood. Inherited from a warrior thousands of years ago, passed down matrilineally, growing stronger—more potent—with each child it manifested in until, finally, there were you and Rori."

Cian's face lost color. "What are you saying? I have the power to blow up a world? Rori does? How?"

Therron cleared his throat, his eyes misty. "Ishnara wasn't sure about what's inside you, Cian, but as for your sister, she holds within her one of the most mythical, powerful souls ever known—that of a unicorn." He spoke the words gently, as if to a child, his expression full of concern and worry.

Cian reeled back, and Maxx leaned forward. Molly sat with a glass of prosecco stalled at her lips.

"Did he say unicorn?" Molly took a sip and looked to the ceiling. "That would explain a lot. A LOT, lot."

"It explains everything. Especially why Hunter is so desperate to keep her under his control." Maxx blew out a long breath. "Fuck me. I never would've guessed that. Let's just hope Hunter hasn't, either."

"This stays between us." Nikala looked them in the eye, one at a time. "It's no longer just Rori's life that is threatened. The fate of Earth and Cilachaem hang in the balance."

They nodded in silent agreement, each processing the information in their own way. Nikala took Cian's hand in her own and gave a squeeze. They knew Rori's secret, but his was as yet unveiled. She picked up her phone with her free hand and pressed the app with Hunter's tracker. Still nothing. She told herself it didn't mean he was dead; after all, the tracker would still work even if he wasn't alive. With each passing minute, her anxiety rose. They had to find Rori before Hunter discovered what she was.

Nikala kissed Cian's knuckles, the realization hitting her in the solar plexus that her priority wasn't just about Rori's safety, but Cian's as well. Which meant, she had to protect him at all costs. If Rori had escaped Hunter's grasp, he might come for Cian next.

¾ 20 ¾

Birdsong filled her hearing, and Rori lay still, enjoying the sound. A momentary spasm of panic flitted through her veins, but this wasn't the silent forest she'd woken up in when Acelyne had kidnapped her. That forest was lifeless and devoid of sound. Birds meant living creatures. She just didn't know where she was.

Soft sheets hugged her clothed body, and beneath her head was a comfortable pillow. If she'd been kidnapped again, at least they were considerate assholes. She listened beyond the birdsong to what was in the room, hearing a soft snore to her left, and someone pacing several feet from the foot of the bed.

She wasn't alone.

She also wasn't dead. Whoever had taken her from the rooftop of Notre Dame wanted her alive. Always a good sign. She opened her eyes and stared at the cream-colored ceiling for a moment, trying to register the architecture. The slightly domed ceiling had a large medallion in the center, with a glittering chandelier hanging from a gold chain.

Once upon a time, it would've held candles, but now electric bulbs gave off soft light. Could be England, could be France. Could be anywhere. Her gaze traveled down to a set of long windows flanked by off-white shutters. Lovely. All of it was shabby-chic elegance with old-world charm.

A clear bag hung from a slim stand, blocking her view and startling her with the realization that the milky liquid inside was feeding a drip line that flowed down to her hand. She flexed instinctively and felt the sharp prick where a needle was embedded beneath her skin.

Fresh panic whipped through her, followed closely by anger.

"Easy, Aurora," a soothing voice said to her right, and she turned toward it. "You're safe here."

She knew that voice, but the face that accompanied it confused her.

"Did you drug me?" She reached to pull the needle from her skin, but he stopped her with a strong grip to her arm.

"You've been through quite a lot. We thought it best to keep you sedated at least for a little while so that we could build up your strength," a deeper, less gentle voice said from her left, and she looked to see a man unfolding himself from the confines of an overstuffed chair.

His dark hair looked black in the morning light, and his eyes, deep-set glints of shadow, seemed to glow as he moved.

"Where am I? Who are you?" She pushed herself to a sitting position, wincing at the jab of pain from the needle. "Can I take this out now?"

"I'll call for my healer." The man placed his hand over

his heart and bowed his head. "We mean you no harm, Aurora. Please call me Lucien." He motioned to the other side of the bed, where an attractive man with grey hair that belied his youthful looks watched her with concern in his amber eyes. "You've already met my accomplice."

"I don't think so." Rori shook her head slowly. "Though you do seem familiar."

The young man chuckled good-heartedly. "I would hope so. I am Aimon. This is my elven form."

Rori gasped despite herself. "Elven form? And on the roof of Notre Dame, that's your dragon form?"

"Aye. I am what my people call an aerlghot—half elven, half dragon."

"Your people?" She shifted on the bed, fascinated with where the conversation was heading. If he had a dragon soul, perhaps he could better help her understand what it meant to have a unicorn soul.

"I come from a world not yet known by your world or this one. I was sent to scout for darathi vorsi—dragons, in the common tongue—but was injured shortly after arriving. To stay alive, I became one of the stone statues you see atop the cathedral. When you healed me, I was finally able to shift back into my elven form."

He spoke plainly, without anger or contrition.

The room spun, and she leaned her head against the padded headboard. "You're a dragon shifter? Are those common on Earth?"

"Not so much as they once were," Lucien answered. "Though we are ever hopeful we can once again fly the skies without fear." He sighed, and Rori rolled her head to face him. Sadness hung in the dip of his eyes, the pull of his lips downward. "Now that the darathi vorsi prince has awakened, a new age is upon us."

"I feel like I woke up in a parallel universe. You're speaking English, but your words make no sense."

"They will in time, Aurora."

"Call me Rori, please." She gazed at the rest of the room, her vision landing on a table in the center of the large space. There, her jacket hung from a chair and the contents of her bag, along with the amulets she stole from Hunter's villa, were neatly laid out. "You don't work for Hunter, do you?"

A snort came from Aimon. "Hardly. He's an abomination. No offense."

"None taken." She scooched herself up further. "Why am I here?"

"We debated taking you to London, but since Therron wasn't there, we felt it best to secret you away somewhere Hunter couldn't find you. We've sent a message to your beloved that you are safe and well cared for."

Beloved. She nearly snorted at that, but at the same time, the word wrapped around her heart, comforting. She'd never had a beloved, or ever thought she might be a beloved. And now, it didn't seem so terrible.

"I…" She stopped herself, unsure of how she should phrase her words. "Hunter put something in my brain, and even though I removed it, I'm afraid of contacting Therron, or anyone through mind-speak in case Hunter can trace them." It sounded ridiculous when she said it out loud, but it was true.

"My tears healed you of your wounds, Au—Rori.

Hunter should not be able to find you now." Aimon reached a hand toward her. "May I?"

Despite herself, she flinched from his touch. "What are you going to do?"

Aimon looked to Lucien, who stepped closer to the bed. "We can search your mind for any lingering control Hunter might have over you and rid you of his presence. Only with your permission."

She flexed her fingers against the soft sheets. If they searched her mind, they might discover her unicorn soul. Or, any number of memories that could be used against her.

"If it will ease your worry," Lucien began, "I am what is known as a Dragon Lord. We are bound by similar oaths as Donyatella and her Stone Guardians. Dragon Lords all have a dragon soul and serve to protect the realm we are assigned. We mainly stay neutral, but in cases like yours, we are allowed to intervene. I promise you, there is nothing in your mind or memories that will be taken from you or used for nefarious purposes. This I, Lucien de Montague, do swear to you as a Dragon Lord of Paris." He kissed his thumb before touching it first to his forehead, then his heart, and finally his lips.

A warm tingling went through her, as if this action were symbolic of something important. A distant murmuring went through her mind, as if hundreds of people spoke at once. Again and again, she was told she could trust Lucien and Aimon. It reminded her of when she'd first met Taryn in the illusion inside the illusion and she'd told Rori to trust Therron.

"Fine. Just…I'm sorry for what you might find. I've done some terrible things."

"Haven't we all, darling." Lucien spoke softly and placed his hands on her head.

"Not very reassuring."

"It's better to speak the truth plainly than to conceal for ill purpose."

Aimon placed his hands on her head as well, and the whispering in her mind increased. A flood of emotions swept over her, none of them hers, but she didn't fight them. She'd trusted Taryn and Rhoane when healing the lycan, and that led to the discovery of her unicorn. She had to have faith that this would be beneficial as well.

Lucien made several grunts, his eyes closed as he pressed upon her skull. Aimon hummed a tune not familiar to her, his fingertips tapping along her forehead. It reminded her of Rhoane's song as they healed the lycan. Soothing, melodic, safe. She closed her eyes and quieted her mind as if to hear them better, but it was silent. In fact, she couldn't hear bird-song or the ticking of a nearby clock…nothing.

Then, a soft click, followed by a whooshing sound. Another, and once more, sound rushed in and she heard not just the birds, but a deer in the forest outside the windows somewhere. It bounded through the brush; its heartbeat rushed with adrenaline. There was more: Lucien's blood flowing through his veins, the strength of his dragon rippling through his muscles…the same with Aimon. A bug skittered across the wooden floor. She breathed in and out, letting the sounds linger where they would, or dissipate if they wished.

She floated through time and space, touching all creatures, hearing the cry of the snake-dragon-demon thing as if it were alone and frightened, which made zero sense to her. Her body didn't belong to her in those moments; she was one with the stars in the sky and the dirt of the earth. Her unicorn snorted and huffed, its strong hoof pawing the ground. She shimmered silvery-white in the bright sunlight, but there was something else, something elusive that she couldn't see. Shadows rose from the unicorn...dark, menacing.

Slowly, her hearing evened and the external sounds hushed until she felt grounded again, in her own body.

Lucien and Aimon released her head and both stood back.

"Well, that was something." Lucien leaned forward on the bed, his fingertips splayed on the duvet cover.

"Did you see it?" Rori asked quietly.

"See what?" Aimon looked to Lucien, who shook his head. "We cleared any remnants of Hunter's presence in your mind, of which there was very little. As for seeing anything—there was a vast swath of velvety blue, but otherwise, I saw nothing."

Lucien's eyes narrowed, and he cocked his head. "I did sense something. More a feeling than anything else. Serene is the only way I can describe it. A peace that I've not felt in many a century."

"Yes. I felt it too." Aimon crossed his arms and looked to the ceiling. "I would swear I had the same sensation when you healed me all those years ago, but I was consumed with so many other emotions, I didn't recognize it at the time."

"What does it mean?" She was relieved they hadn't seen

the unicorn, but this new revelation about peace and calm had her thoughts spinning.

"Only you can decide," Lucien said sagely. "Ah, here's Uthran with nourishment. Now, don't snaffle everything all at once. Your belly's shrunk and though the mixture we fed you helped, you are only still recovering from your trauma."

Rori looked to the doorway, where a creature entered, carrying a tray. Bluish-grey fur covered their wide head, long spiked ears, and their jaw, leaving the center portion of their face clear. Large brown eyes blinked at her, and she reminded herself staring was rude.

"Uthran is an oewling. He was left here as a baby, and I took him in." Lucien's gaze went to Aimon. "Another rescue, you might say. They do find their way to me."

Furry blue hands set the tray upon the bed, and Uthran hopped up to take her hand in his. "Be still." His touch was warm, his removal of the needle gentle. "Might bleed a little."

Lucien placed a finger over the hole in her skin the needle left, and she felt his magic as he healed the wound.

"Thank you, Uthran." Rori flexed her fingers, relieved when there wasn't pain. "Where are you from?" She'd never seen a two-foot-high furry blue creature during any of her travels on Earth.

Uthran looked to Lucien. When he nodded, the oewling slid the tray closer to her and hopped off the bed. "My homeworld is far from here. Behind two stars past the moon."

"We're still trying to figure out the name of his planet. Or how he came to be orphaned on Earth. What we do know is that he's been here around five hundred years,"

Lucien explained, his hand stroking between Uthran's ears. The oewling's eyes softened in a bliss-filled expression.

Rori picked up a sandwich and looked to Aimon. "Where are you from?"

"My kingdom is called Aerithilyn, on the world of Nasus."

Two worlds she'd never heard of. Her gaze went to the window and a chill snaked down her spine. Hunter might know of those worlds and many more. She pushed the duvet off her legs and swung them to the edge of the bed. She had to return to Faerie at once. The queens needed to know what was happening on Earth. The men protested, even Uthran made a tsking sound, but she would not be deterred. Her duty was to Cilachaem. She would get a message to Therron as soon as she reached the Seelie Palace.

As soon as she stood, she realized her mistake. Lack of food and bound to a chair, imprisoned for a few days, meant zero strength.

She went down hard, her legs buckling under her as she hit the hardwood. Pain shot up her back to settle in her head, and the room spun with terrifying intensity.

The queen would have to wait.

The slim brown disc sat heavy in Therron's hand. He absently passed it between his fingers as he stared at the river in the hopes it might provide answers to his burdened heart. People passed, their conversations a snippet on the wind before they drifted away to wherever they were going. Therron held the disc up to view it in the moonlight. It was unremarkable upon first viewing, but he saw the inscription meant only for him. A message encoded into a dragon scale.

Dragons existed. It was a wish he'd long had but never thought possible. And now he held proof that they lived in the human realm. He rubbed the scale between his thumb and forefinger, recalling Lucien's message as he watched the waves gently wash upon the river's shore.

Rori was safe. She'd found shelter with Aimon after escaping Hunter's villa, and Lucien had taken her to an undisclosed location so that she could heal properly. He would send word when he had an update.

There was more, some gibberish about accepting his

true fate, but Therron chose to focus on the news about Rori. She was alive. He exhaled a long, slow breath, feeling the weight of his worry lessen. He had no reason to believe Lucien would cause Rori harm, but he wasn't altogether ready to trust the man implicitly. For the moment, he was happy to know his beloved was being cared for.

He tucked the dragon scale into the same pocket he kept the ring hidden. His true destiny. Therron could only imagine what Lucien meant, but in his heart, he knew. Just as he knew when Rhoane and Taryn healed the lycan that they'd not only unlocked Rori's unicorn, they'd unleashed something inside Therron, too.

No longer could he feign ignorance. He felt it now, stirring in the depths of his spirit. A creature feared and honored, a myth equally as powerful as Rori's unicorn.

Yet he wouldn't name it.

Couldn't.

Not yet.

Not until he understood what this meant for his future. His whole life, he'd been told he would die before ascending the throne. Now that he'd found Rori, and would survive, he knew ruling Elvenwood wasn't his future. His destiny lay somewhere outside Elvenwood and even Cilachaem.

He stared at the waves, seeing beyond the way the moonlight turned their small peaks white. His vision turned to one of him soaring high above the land with Rori by his side. He couldn't see her, but he knew she was there. Her laughter filled the air and brought joy to all who heard.

Their destinies were entwined. She was more than an assassin and spy, and he was much more than a thief hiding from his curse.

He stretched his thoughts, trying to grasp more of the vision, but it sped faster, just out of reach.

Accept your true fate, Lucien had said through the dragon scale.

Several tears spilled from Therron's eyes to course down his cheeks, and he wiped them away with the backs of his hands.

The truth terrified him.

He'd known since a baby he would die of a broken heart. Had accepted it. Then, when he met Rori, he dared to believe in a different future. But this? This was beyond his comprehension.

A movement behind him brought his attention to the present, and he turned to see a woman approaching, her eyes wild, hair floating like a bird's nest above her head. A limp caused her to lean to one side and she looked close to falling over, yet she continued walking toward him. Her nose twitched with her constant sniffing the air. Then her head lowered, and her gaze settled on him. Mania twisted her features into a horrifying sight. A low keening came from her closed lips, much like the sound he heard in the Geneva lab.

A fissure of concern went through him that he was alone in a city he didn't know, with dozens of people in close proximity. Her focus was on him, but he had to protect those nearby. His instinct was to fight, yet the woman hadn't attacked him. The way she stared at him as she limped through the passersby made him believe she soon would.

Her mouth opened and a screech unlike anything he'd heard before issued forth, frightening those on the embankment. Several people swore at her, a few laughed, some darted away. Therron kept her gaze and didn't move.

"You smell of magic." She came closer and sniffed the air. A frantic sort of need entered her eyes, and she reached out to claw at him with pointed nails. "Give it to me."

A scyver. Blood and ashes, not now. He didn't need a public brawl.

Her nails came close to his face, and he grabbed both her wrists. The strength she possessed surprised him, and he clasped her hard.

"It's mine. Give it to me."

Rank breath assaulted him and rotted teeth shone in the moonlight.

"Need it."

She moved closer, mouth open as if to bite him, and he twisted her wrists above her head, spinning her as he did. She hissed and wailed, drawing the attention of a few men. They called out to him to leave the woman alone, one even coming near as if to help. The moment he saw her face, he backed away, hands up, apology spilling from his lips.

Therron fought against her wriggling body, losing his grip on her wrists. She ducked low and spun too quickly for him to move out of her way, her nails slashing across his face. Stinging warmth crisscrossed his cheek. She raised her fingers to her face and inhaled his scent, her eyes rolling to the back of her head. An instant later, her eyes snapped forward, and she reached for the pocket holding the dragon scale and Bastiaan's ring.

"Mine. Give to me."

Her guttural words held an urgency that frightened

him. He had no doubt she would kill him to get what she wanted. What she needed.

"What's going on here?"

Two males approached, wearing a uniform Therron recognized as the local constabulary. The woman reeled around and screamed at the men before lunging toward them. One fumbled at his side and a sharp bang was followed by a sizzling sound. The woman dropped to the ground, her body shaking with spasms caused by the wires sticking out from her torso.

Therron stared at the woman, and then the constables.

"She attacked him, sir. I saw it all." One of the men who'd yelled at him stepped from the gathering crowd.

"We'll need full statements from all of you." An officer pointed at Therron. "You should get that looked at."

Therron raised a hand to his face, and his fingers came away red. He waited until the constables had their backs to him and moved away from the scene, ignoring calls from the officers. He walked quickly to put as much distance between himself and the others as possible. He hadn't used magic, yet she could sense it on him. What rattled him most was the look she'd given him—it was filled with desperation, yes, but beneath that he sensed her desire for death.

At the pub, he sped past where Dony sat at the bar and went to the restroom to clean the wound on his face. He stared at his reflection in the mirror, aghast at what he saw. Ragged red marks, as if made from a wild beast, tore his skin from ear to nose. His scar raged red, even though she'd not touched it. Anger burst from his gut, and his hands shook as he gripped the cool sink.

She'd sensed the dragon scale and ring, both powerful with magic. He knew, without a single doubt, that she could've broken through his ribs and pulled his heart from his chest if given a chance. Whether the added strength was Hunter's doing or not, he could only guess.

The door opened, and Silar strode through. "Dony wanted me to check on you." He squinted, and he cocked his head. "Looks ghastly. Need a salve?"

"Please." Therron used a paper towel to clean the blood from the wounds, wincing with each pass. A scratch shouldn't hurt this much.

Silar returned, and Therron applied the salve before thanking the man. He nodded to Dony on his way out, grateful she didn't quiz him about what happened. He was sure she'd know within the hour. He kept vigilant on his way back to SIRE's offices, of scyvers and constables. It wouldn't be in his best interest to get hauled to the dungeons or wherever they took criminals in this realm.

The offices were dark when he exited the lift, and his senses went on high alert. Cian and Nikala had said they were going out for fresh air, but didn't say where, and Molly had gone home for the night. Maxx had offered to stay in case anything important came up. He walked toward the open office door, his hands loose, near the sword he always wore but kept hidden at his side with the tiniest amount of magic.

Maxx sat at Nikala's desk, her face lit from the computer screen. She was too engrossed in what she was doing to notice Therron had entered. Or she was ignoring him. He didn't care either way. Only when he stood directly in front of the desk did she look up.

"Pub brawl?"

"Pardon?"

She indicated his face. "Looks like a wolf attacked you. So, not a pub brawl."

"What are you doing with Nikala's laptop?"

Maxx sighed and ran a hand over her face, as if she wore the cares of the world and was weary of the burden.

"I know you don't agree with me, but there are three hundred fifty-seven scyvers in London. Half that many in Hunter's labs. Those are the ones I can track. Who knows how many more are spread across the world. Scyvers are vampires, Therron. They take magic from others, and by doing so, they then create another scyver. It's an epidemic that must be stopped." She held up her hand as if to halt his arguments, but he said nothing. "Scyvers are Hunter's failures. The ones who survived the tests, but didn't thrive. Hunter keeps them around as his first line of defense. Foot soldiers, if you will. They're the poor sods who rush in and get shot first, making way for Hunter's super soldiers. The real calvary."

"Nikala said Hunter didn't involve himself in war. He wants chaos."

"Yes, and what better way to cause chaos than a bunch of magic-hungry vampires?" She shrugged nonchalantly. "My guess? He's going to release them into the world like a virus. They feed on whatever magic they can find, create new scyvers, then move on to the next city. Think of the mayhem that would create. A pandemic without a cure."

"Do they not eat or drink or sleep?"

Maxx shook her head. "They feed only on magic." She peered closer at his face. "What caused that?"

He jerked his head as if to avoid her stare. "What's your plan?" He pointed to the laptop.

"I've modified their microchips. Instead of their heads blowing up, their hearts will stop. It'll be instantaneous and painless."

He touched the wound on his cheek and shivered as he recalled the woman's frantic scrabbling. "I still think they can be rehabilitated."

"And where would that happen? Huh? Are you prepared to find a place at Elvenwood for them?"

Earlier that day, he would've said yes. "Never. I wouldn't let them within a league of the palace. That would be setting a starved dog loose at a banquet."

Maxx smirked. "Now you're beginning to understand. These creatures aren't sick. They have been genetically mutilated. They have no compassion, no humanity if you will, nor do they possess the intellect to process what rehabilitation needs from them. They're barely living, Therron. Surely, you see that?"

The woman's screech sounded in his ears, and he shied away from the truth.

"You're a mother, Maxx. How can you condone the wholesale slaughter of these people?"

"It's precisely because I'm a mother that I have to." She reached a hand toward the laptop. "If this were my son, I'd want to mercifully end his suffering. Tell me you wouldn't do the same if it were Rori who scratched your face tonight."

He watched her hand hover over the keyboard, then moved his gaze up to see tears sparkling in her eyes. Damn the woman, she was right. Without waiting for his approval or not, she pressed a button and sat down, her tears unloosed upon her cheeks.

Therron staggered backward at the enormity of what she'd just done. From the look of angst upon her face, he knew she took no pleasure in her actions. He wasn't fully ready to accept it yet, but knew in his heart Maxx was right—they could not be healed. They'd been turned into a macabre mix of magic and science, with death their only escape.

"What's going on here?" Cian entered the office first, followed closely by Nikala.

"I need to see to my family." Maxx surreptitiously wiped her eyes and stood, closing the laptop. "I'll be gone a few days."

She left the room without another word, leaving the two of them to stare at him with questions dancing in their eyes. Questions he never wished to answer.

Therron turned away from the pair and retreated to the conference room. He needed a moment alone to gather his thoughts. Not just about Maxx, but Rori. If only he knew where she was, and could see for himself that she was being well cared for. He tapped his fingers on the mahogany table and admired the craftsmanship of the piece. It looked elven made. Malcolm was from Faerie; it very well could have been constructed by one of Therron's kin. A piece of home in a new world.

An idea came to him. It was wild and he wasn't sure it would work, but he lost nothing by trying. He opened a small portal, no bigger than the size of his hand, and spoke directly into the shimmering void.

"To the girl with the outlandish blue hair who has

completely captured my heart, I wish you well. I miss your laughter, and your touch. I miss everything about you. I know not where you are, but be assured my heart is with you, always. May you receive this message with all the love and warmth that I've sent with it. Yours forever, Therron." He blew a kiss and swirled his hand to close the portal.

"What are you doing?"

Therron jumped at the sound of Nikala's voice. He'd thought he was alone. Bloody spies, always creeping up on people. Even so, he grinned as he turned to her.

"I sent a message to Rori through the doorways."

"You can do that?"

"I have no idea, to be honest."

She rubbed her folded arms, nodding sadly. "We all miss her, Therron."

He held up the little brown disc. "I heard from the people taking care of her. We should tell Cian what I've learned."

She stepped aside and put a hand on his arm. "Would it be easier if you waited for her in Elvenwood?"

He shook his head. "My father was adamant that we leave the kingdom. A few days is not enough for him to calm down."

"I'm sorry, Therron. Truly. It must be difficult to be so far from home and family."

Cian entered the room and gave them an odd look. Not of jealousy per se, but there was something dark in his expression Therron didn't like.

Therron nodded to Cian and glanced at Nikala. "Rori is my family now. And by association, so are you." Emotion choked his words.

"Therron has news about Rori." Nikala took Cian's hand in her own. "Let's get comfy and hear what he has to say."

Therron followed the pair to the sofas in the office and settled himself to tell them about not only Lucien's message, but how he'd met the dragon lord. They listened without interruption and when he finished, Cian breathed a sigh of relief.

"I don't like not knowing where she is, but if you have faith in this Lucien, then we trust your opinion."

"I only met him once, but he seems honorable." Therron shifted on the sofa, uncomfortable with where the conversation might go. He wasn't up for examining how dragons came to be in the human realm, or what this meant for Cilachaem.

Nikala looked thoughtful for a moment, then turned to him with a question etched across her features. He braced himself for the inevitable.

"Where'd you get that scratch, and what was Maxx up to earlier?"

It wasn't the question he'd thought she'd ask, but one he dreaded all the same. Because it was Nikala who asked, he had no choice but to tell them the truth. No embellishment. No leaving out important information. He poured himself a glass of the fizzy drink he didn't much enjoy but gave his brain a nice fuzziness. Both Cian and Nikala watched him with the practiced assessment of experienced spies.

"I was attacked by a scyver, and Maxx sent a command on your laptop to execute all the scyvers who had tracking devices."

"Bloody hell." Nikala grabbed the fizzy drink and took a swig straight from the bottle.

"There's more."

Therron told them about Maxx's warning there were others without tracking devices and her mutterings that it was an epidemic. When he finished, both Cian and Nikala sat quietly.

Finally, Nikala said, "We need to destroy all the labs. All the machines, the research, everything needs to go. Then we'll find every single soldier Hunter enhanced and take them out. If Hunter wants chaos, we'll give it to him."

Therron touched the scar on his cheek and grinned. For the first time in a long time, he had hope that they just might get the jump on Hunter.

22

Tourists made assassin work easy most days. Thousands of people to blend into, most of them oblivious a stone-cold killer was in their midst. Then other days, like today, tourists annoyed the fuck out of Nikala. Their slow movements, and constant stopping to take photos, meant she had to keep alert to their whereabouts as well as the three men who tailed her little group.

They walked past a shop, and Nikala searched the window's reflection for Hunter's enhanced soldiers, spotting one across the street. Another was several meters in front of them, lounging by a streetlight with his phone close to his face, as if engrossed in whatever was on the screen. But she saw the furtive glances their way, noticed the earpiece he tried to hide in his thick, dark hair. She didn't know these men, hadn't trained them or worked with them, which was odd considering she thought she'd trained nearly all of Hunter's spies.

These were new. As she and the older vets used to say—their boots were shiny. Which meant, Hunter had recruited them within the past few years, when she'd been on her self-destructive sabbatical.

"Do you see them?" Cian whispered on her left.

"Yep. Three men. One in front, one behind on the left, the other across the street."

"What's your plan?"

"Ignore them."

As they passed the man leaning against the streetlamp, Nikala stared hard at him. He flinched and glanced away, a sure sign he was new and possibly ill-trained. She'd never allow her operatives to lose eye contact. Set a boundary, stay focused.

"Let's grab a cab." Nikala veered toward the street and hailed the first taxi that came into sight. From her periphery, she saw the three men scrambling. "Pfft, rookies." She nearly spat the word. Hunter would be livid to see these amateurs.

She, Therron, and Cian squeezed into the back seat of the cab. Hunter's Rome lab was several blocks away on the bank of the Tiber, but she asked the driver to take them to Vatican City near the Via di Porta Cavalleggeri. As they neared Piazza San Pietro, she asked him to stop and tossed him enough euros to cover the fare and a handsome tip. She darted across the square, with Therron and Cian keeping pace, all three dodging school groups and tourist groups alike. At the other side of Vatican City, Nikala steered the three of them toward a bus stop she knew would take them close to the lab.

They sat in the back row, where they could see the doors to the bus, and out the windows of both sides. If the three spies from the street followed them, she didn't see them now.

"They know where we're going." Cian adjusted his suit jacket over the crisp white shirt he wore.

"Do you ever wear jeans? Or T-shirts?" It amused her that he only ever seemed to wear suits.

"Never." He shrugged. "I'm comfortable."

"Hmmm." She couldn't believe his suit trousers were more comfortable than her jeans, and from the way Therron twitched in his clothing, she assumed he was wishing he had whatever elves wore in Elvenwood. "It makes you stand out."

"Maybe I want to stand out."

"How far until we reach the lab?" Therron gazed out the window, his back to her.

"Five, ten minutes max. Depends on traffic."

"I do not like this hotbox on wheels."

Nikala laughed at that. A good ole hearty guffaw that made her cheeks redden. "It's called a bus."

"Yes, well, I do not like a bus."

It wasn't her preferred method of transportation, but it often allowed protection within a group of strangers. She sat back and tried to imagine Earth from Therron's perspective. It would be loud and scary, with people everywhere. She recalled the rooms she'd visited at Midna's palace. If Therron's palace was anything like Midna's, he was definitely used to a life of luxury.

"Who's Ishnara?" Cian leaned against the seat, eyes closed.

The question surprised her. Anxiety curled around her gut, pulling her innards into knots. "Who?"

One eye opened to regard her, Cian's lips quirked in a half smile. "You mentioned her. She said Rori was a unicorn and I'm something, but she wasn't sure what. I did some searching, but the results were inconclusive. Is she a friend of Malcolm's?"

Therron snorted, and Nikala could've kicked him. Her heart rammed in her throat, and her head pounded to the beat. "She's, well, no, not a friend of Malcolm's. I mean, maybe she is now that he's dead. It's hard to explain."

Cian sat forward and looked her straight in the eye. "Are you saying a ghost said there's something inside me, but she doesn't know what?"

"Precisely." Nikala didn't breathe. She hoped Therron didn't take this opportunity to force her to tell Cian about their bizarre trip to Faerie.

"Huh." He leaned back and shrugged. "I don't feel like I have anything lurking in the depths of my soul. Hell, even my father told me I was useless. Maybe she's wrong."

Therron glanced over his shoulder, taking a break from studying the road outside the bus's window. "What if she's right? Do you believe Rori is a unicorn?"

Cian chuckled. "I one hundred percent believe that about my baby sister. She's amazing and beautiful and strong. I never thought she should be an assassin, but she seemed determined."

Nikala's shoulders relaxed, and she sent a grateful thanks to the stars that the moment had passed. She knew Cian deserved the truth, and would tell him, but when the moment was right.

"She has a healer's touch," Therron said simply before returning to the window. "I believe she went to the

Academy to earn her father's love, even though he was already presumed dead by then."

"You're not wrong." Cian leaned against the seat again. "We all make mistakes in a bid to earn our parent's love."

She knew he meant himself, and possibly Therron, but the words hit hard. None of what was happening would've been possible if not for her. She was so desperate for not just Malcolm's love, but also Hunter's, that she refused to see the evidence right in front of her of the turmoil they were generating.

"This is us." Nikala stood and pressed the button for the bus to stop. She gave a quick glance out the window but didn't see the soldiers.

She knew better than to hope they wouldn't show up. The best she could wish for was that there weren't several dozen inside. With Geneva in ruins, they would disperse to the last three labs—here in Rome, the one in Brussels, or the last in Sweden. Although, that one was too small for soldiers or scyvers. It was the first lab Hunter built to carry out his experiments that wasn't at his ancestral home in Scotland. As far as she knew, she'd been the only test subject he worked on at his home. All the others either started in Sweden, or one of the other labs.

She considered the newest lab in London, but Maxx had destroyed it before it was fully functioning. Just to be safe, they'd do a sweep of the floor once they returned.

"Keep alert." She strode from the bus stop toward a large building that had once belonged to the church.

A high brick wall with chain link fencing on top was added in the last decade, along with a sturdy metal gate for both pedestrian visitors and cars. She bypassed both of those and went to the secret entrance around the corner, where Hunter had shown her how to gain access undetected. Cian raised an eyebrow at the plain door. She winked and pressed her hand against a brick. A squealing sound, like metal upon metal, came from behind the brick, followed by a small keypad rising from a hollowed-out area.

She scanned the area, making certain they hadn't been followed, before she pressed her thumb against the pad and whispered, "Illitrium ventu verni." A bead of sweat ran down her forehead, and she wiped it with her sleeve.

Cian glanced at Therron, who shook his head. She'd always assumed it was Latin, but if Cian didn't recognize the language, it must be something else. A chill swept over her, and she buried her emotions deep. More games. More mind fuckery. Hunter was a clever sadist, she'd give him that much.

A locking mechanism ground on the other side of the door, and a moment later, it swung open. Relief swept over her, and she forged ahead, confident they weren't going to get shot.

Their plan was to investigate the three remaining labs and determine whether any scyvers remained. Once Therron had confessed to what Maxx had done, Nikala knew they had to close the labs for good. If there were scyvers still in residence, they'd agreed as a group to try to rescue them and sort out rehabilitation if possible.

Hunter's place in Scotland would've made an excellent home for the scyvers, but Cian and Therron had destroyed it. Even so, there was still the land. She'd have to check to see whether SIRE owned it. If she did, they could build a rehabilitation facility. But that would take time, and time was something they didn't have.

Nikala led the men through the building to Hunter's office on the second floor. They saw no one in the hallways or the open offices. A prickling fear started at the base of her neck, and made its way through her skin to her nerves.

Hunter's office door stood wide open, something that would never happen in normal circumstances. But these weren't ordinary times. She stepped into the room, wary. Papers were strewn about, drawers open, monitors tipped over as if someone had ransacked the place. Except, it looked too perfect.

"Someone's been busy," Cian drawled.

Nikala flicked the switch to turn on the multiple security screens Hunter had in his office in each of the labs. Empty. All the rooms, including the staff lounge, were empty. No scyvers, no employees, not even a janitor could be seen.

"Maybe they took the hint from Geneva and shut down before Maxx could do it for them permanently." Therron was eyeing the screens, lips thinned.

"No, something's off here." Nikala chewed a cuticle, her mind racing with possibilities.

Therron cocked his head and frowned. "People are coming. A dozen, I'd say. Their footsteps are muffled, but they wear heavy boots."

Nikala shared a glance with Cian before she looked back to the monitors. "No one is showing on the screens."

"Elven hearing is much better than fae." Therron shrugged. "It's a well-known truth."

"Kill the other two, but the pale-haired male we need alive."

Elven truth or not, Nikala heard the whispered words as if the person stood in front of her. "Therron, leave. Now."

"Why? I can fight."

"You didn't hear them? They need you for something."

Therron shook his head. "I only heard the footsteps. No words."

Cian went to the door and listened. "They're getting closer. What's the plan, Nikala?"

She pointed to a small door to their left. "Therron must leave. Us, they're going to kill, but him they need alive. That's what they said. Now, Your Highness, please. You have to leave. If their plan is to take you to Hunter, it's for a reason. To lure Rori out of hiding is my guess. But your life is in danger if you stay." She grabbed his hands, her own shaking. "Go to where you feel safest. Don't tell us. Just leave Earth. Now."

He wavered. She could see indecision dancing in his eyes. He didn't know what Hunter was capable of—she did. Therron wasn't safe.

"We'll find Rori." Her intense gaze was full of haste. Any second now, the men would burst into the room and then there would be no chance for escape.

"If I go, do you promise to tell Cian the truth about Ishnara?"

"This isn't really the time, Therron. Besides, I didn't lie."

"The whole truth."

Fuck. "You bastard. If it means you'll go, yes, I'll tell him everything."

His magic or the oath or something slithered up her

arm, straight to her heart. She winced against the sharp pain and pushed him toward the door. Therron opened it without a word, and a moment later, she sensed he was gone.

Cian watched her from where he stood, the look on his face unreadable. Tension snapped between them, and she knew she'd need to tell him everything or risk losing him.

But first, they had to survive the men who were mere steps away from the office door.

23

Just when he thought he could trust her, Cian realized that it was a sham. His love for her was real—too real—but apparently, she continued to keep secrets from him. That was no way to build a future. No way to live happily ever after as the fairy tales said. Fuck it. Fuck *her* if she couldn't be honest with him.

The soldiers were nearly to the door, but he didn't move. His gaze stayed rooted on Nikala's gorgeous face, his body remembering her smell, her taste, her touch. Dammit. Not now. He glared harder, trying to force his emotions into a tiny box, where they couldn't confuse the situation more than it already was.

She watched him, a look of resignation in her eyes.

"They said they'll kill us, Cian. We can discuss what Therron meant later. Right now, we need to fight."

"I didn't hear anything." He hadn't and that stung more than anything else. She and Therron had heard the men approaching, but he'd been in a vacuum of silence.

"Later. Please?" She stepped toward him, her hands out to grasp his.

The wounded part of him nearly jerked his hands away, but he fought through the hurt and clasped her to him. He desperately needed to trust her. Their lips met, and heat seared all the way from his mouth to his cock. Now was definitely not the time for that. She ground her hips against him, grinning with her kiss.

"Later for that, too." She ended the kiss and withdrew her gun from an ankle holster hidden beneath her jeans.

"The minute we're safe. You promise?"

"I promise."

He saw the conflicted sadness in her eyes and tried to guess what could cause her so much angst. That was a rabbit hole he couldn't afford to explore. She'd promised. He'd extend his trust a little further and see what happened once they were safe. He snorted a chuckle. As if they ever would be. He really should've chosen his words more carefully.

"I thought you hated guns."

Her shrug was adorable. "They're efficient, if messy."

"Kinda like us."

She grinned. "Exactly. You ready? They're here."

Muffled sounds came from the other side of the closed door, and Cian chose to wait and see what the soldiers brought to the party. There was a brief scuffle before the knob turned and the door slowly opened. Nikala leaned against the desk, arms crossed, gun held in her right hand, but concealed by her left arm. Cian stood to the side, body loose, ready.

"Ah, the prodigal daughter returns." A blond dressed all in black addressed Nikala.

"Good to see you, Soloman." Nikala raised her chin toward the others. "Quite the welcoming party. I don't know these gentlemen."

Four others crowded into the room, none of them the men who followed them earlier.

Soloman glanced toward Cian, eyes narrowed. "Where's the other one? Pale hair, pointy ears?"

"Just the two of us here, Sol."

"Nah, I saw three of you come in."

"You're getting on in years…perhaps your vision isn't what it used to be."

Sol snarled at Nikala and motioned for one of the men to check the two rooms that connected to the office. One of which was where Nikala had sent Therron.

No one moved while the men searched. Sol kept his gaze firmly on Nikala, his jaw tensing with each passing second. When the men returned and shook their heads, Sol swore under his breath.

"Where'd he go?" Sol demanded.

"I don't know who you're talking about. But, I am curious where everyone is. The scyvers, the staff…usually this place is a hive of activity. It's not a weekend, so why is it empty? I hope Hunter doesn't pop in for an impromptu visit. I'm certain he wouldn't be happy."

Sol's face was like a stone. He didn't flinch at the mention of Hunter. Despite himself, Cian was impressed with the man's self-control. Keep him talking, darling, he thought to himself. Nikala was masterful at getting information from even those trained to keep their lips sealed. Cian was damn proud of the woman, even if he was vexed with her at the moment.

But then, Sol thought he had the upper hand and could spill all his secrets because she and Cian would be dead soon. He watched the man closely, looking for tells. They were outnumbered, but not outclassed or outmagiced. It might be ill-advised to use in the human realm, but if needs must, Cian would damn sure use his magic to destroy these men.

"Closed out of precaution. I'm sure you heard about what happened in Geneva."

"Terrible accident." Nikala shook her head. "All those lives lost. Were they friends of yours?"

"Shut up, bitch. We know it was you who set off that explosion."

"You can't prove that."

Cian counted sixteen weapons between the five men, with more probably hidden beneath clothing. Hand grenades hung from utility belts beside hunting knives that he didn't relish seeing up close and personal. His gaze roved over the men, noticing when one of them moved their finger closer to the safety on his semi-automatic. A gun that size would do incredible damage in the small office. The soldiers wore bulletproof vests, whereas he and Nikala had thin layers of clothing for protection.

It would be a slaughter over within seconds. They'd walked into an ambush, too preoccupied to realize it until too late. Of course Hunter's men would be on high alert after Geneva. But Nikala had been certain the other labs would be operating on schedule. He should've argued harder to wait, but he'd wanted to see for himself whether all the scyvers had perished. Now, they not only didn't know whether any scyvers survived Maxx's purge, they had no idea where they were if they had.

The soldier's finger slid toward the trigger.

Sol and Nikala continued to parley, neither backing down.

"Do you remember our night at the Chelsea house?" Cian asked Nikala.

After a beat, she cocked her head. "Yeah?"

"Let's not do that."

"Quick and dirty?" she asked with a wicked smirk. "Love it."

On the count of three, shoot that motherfucker and run for the door Therron used. If this office is like the one in Geneva, Hunter will have a secret doorway hidden in there. It's our only way out of this situation. Cian sent the thought to Nikala.

The only problem was, the door was on the other side of the five men blocking Cian's path.

One.

"Where are the scyvers?" Nikala asked, halting his countdown.

Sol looked to the ceiling, his face red. "You know damn well where they are. Incinerated. Along with the scientists and staff, as per the boss's protocol. Same with the other labs." He glared at Nikala. "Tell me how you did it. How'd you make the scyvers' deaths look like a heart attack?"

Damn and hells fire, Cian hadn't expected that from Hunter. Incinerating the scyvers to cover his tracks, yes, but not killing his own scientists.

"I didn't have anything to do with that," Nikala said. "But I thank you for the information."

Two, three!

Nikala raised her gun and shot Sol in the face before turning the weapon on the man who had his finger already on the trigger of his semi. Cian dove toward one of the soldiers who'd been taken by surprise and knocked him to the ground. He rolled off, shooting him in the neck as he did. A single shot to the knee took a third soldier down, giving Cian the time necessary to grab Nikala's hand and drag her to the door.

A knife whizzed past Cian's head to puncture the wood. He snarled and turned back to the fallen soldiers, taking too much pleasure in emptying his gun in the nearest man's body. Nikala took out the final soldier before retrieving the knife and throwing it at the man Cian had shot in the leg. The blade struck him with a dull thud and his eyes rolled up until only the whites showed.

"And I thought they were enhanced super soldiers," Cian mocked.

"We caught them by surprise." She looked around the office, lips pinched. "This was staged." She pointed to one of the monitors. "I bet they have a picture plastered in front of the cameras on this floor. They knew we'd come. Probably the same waiting for us in Brussels and Sweden."

"Do you think there's any reason to search them?"

"Not unless we plan to take out all of Hunter's men, just the two of us." She kicked Sol's leg. "We can't just leave them here."

"Apparently, there's an incinerator."

She shivered visibly and made a face. "It gives me the creeps."

"You clean up and I'll take care of them. Just tell me how to get there."

An hour later, the place looked like they'd never been there. Sure enough, Sol had put static pictures in front of the cameras on not just this floor, but every major area they thought Nikala might search. She went to several of those rooms in the hopes she could find information on Hunter's whereabouts or how to find the rest of his soldiers, but came up empty.

While she was busy, Cian found the security room and deleted the footage from before they entered. He rerouted any future recordings to Nikala's laptop, preventing the need for him to sneak them out using a touch of his magic to keep from being noticed or caught on film. Out of an abundance of caution, he did so anyway.

Once outside, he wiped clean the keypad Nikala had used to gain them entrance to the building.

"What's our next move?" She stood beneath a tree, her back arched in a stretch, her gorgeous face lifted to the sky.

"You tell me what's going on between you and Therron."

Her entire body stiffened, and Cian prepared for the worst. She'd fallen for the elf. Who wouldn't? He was stunning in that damn elven way that made even Cian attracted to him. But Therron was destined for Rori, and if Nikala was in any way going to ruin that, it was a problem.

A huge fucking problem.

❧ 24 ❧

The doorway lengthened, and Therron stepped onto the cold stone slabs atop the cathedral in Paris. He should've gone straight to Elvenwood, but he couldn't leave Rori. His breath came in shallow huffs as he paced in a circle, his mind spinning with his harsh steps. How could Nikala hear the men and not him? Elves had excellent hearing.

He stopped, his gaze snapping to where his doorway blinked out. *Unless she had something inside her implanted by Hunter.* He spun toward the doorway to return and warn Nikala, but a shimmering to his left halted his progress.

It wasn't just the glimmer, but a pull toward a wall half in shadow. He cautiously approached, his gaze sweeping the empty roof. He lifted his foot and paused midair before gently placing it back on the stone tiles. There, barely noticeable, was more of the glittery substance he'd found at Hunter's lab in Venice. Rori's blood.

His heart thudded in his throat, making swallowing

difficult. He breathed through his nose, his nostrils flaring with his anxiety. She'd been here. This was where she'd found safe harbor with Aimon when she escaped Venice. They'd been so close. Therron bit down on his cheek to keep his jealousy in check. Aimon had helped her. He couldn't be mad at the dragon for protecting Rori.

No, he was angry at himself.

He'd spent too much time chasing possibilities. Therron breathed out and looked to the sky. Fluffy white clouds floated past, but they didn't bring him calm. He knelt and smoothed the dried blood with his fingertips. Sparkling motes stuck to his skin as he whispered the words that would show him Rori's actions that led to her blood being spilled here.

Instantly, a vision played out of Rori tucked beneath Aimon's great legs, hidden from view from anyone who might enter the rooftop. He flicked a glance at the only door that he assumed led to the cathedral below. Hunter might use that as a doorway, but had he come here searching for Rori? Therron returned to the vision, watching in horror as Rori used a dagger to remove the tracking device embedded in her abdomen. Tears silently rolled over his cheeks to drip onto her dried blood.

Next, she struggled with something in her neck, and he felt her anguish and fear as she withdrew a tiny piece of metal. This, she encased in amethyst and hung the pendant around her neck. Hunter's mind control device.

Therron leaned back and breathed a sigh of relief that she'd rid herself of Hunter's control. At least he could release that stress from his mind. Hunter wouldn't be able to destroy her as easily as Maxx had the scyvers.

The vision shifted to Aimon cleansing Rori with his tears and ended with Rori slumping against him, exhausted from her ordeal. Of where she went afterward, there was nothing.

Therron swished his hand and a small glass vial appeared between his fingertips. He carefully collected the glittery dust until the vial was full, then he secured a silver stopper and wrapped a powerful spell around it to prevent anyone but him to touch the vial.

"Neat trick. Any chance you might show me how to do that?"

Therron spun around, nearly losing his balance with his swift movement. Kaen strolled toward him, his hands outstretched to show he was weaponless. "I was hoping you'd return. I owe you an apology."

Stunned by the sincerity in his tone, Therron only stared at him as he rose. He placed the vial in his pocket with the dragon scale and ring.

Finding his words, Therron said, "You do, but what made you come to this realization?"

Kaen shrugged. "I'm a fairly new Dragon Lord, and quite young, to hear Lucien tell it. I sometimes act before I think. I'd heard the Darathi Vorsi Prince was in London, and I was jealous of Lucien getting the glory. Turns out, it was all for naught."

"A true lord does not attack an unarmed man, no matter what the circumstances. You should remember that, at least."

Kaen placed his hand over his heart and bowed his head. "I will, thank you." His gaze swept the rooftop. "Where is everyone?"

"I was hoping you could tell me."

"I don't know, but to make up for my earlier indiscretion, I will ask around. Will you be at the SIRE building in London?"

Therron shook his head. "I am returning to Elvenwood." He scanned the rooftop again, his mind and heart divided on his next steps. "Any information you find, can you give to Cian and Nikala? Also, can you pass along a message for Nikala from me? Tell her Hunter might've implanted one of those devices so that she and the other soldiers can hear each other. She'll understand what it means. It's important she know."

"Got it. Anything else?"

Yes, so much. Tell Rori he loved her, that he would move worlds for her, that he missed her. But Therron didn't tell Kaen any of this.

"Just that. I'm sure I'll see you once I return." Therron strode past him and used the door leading to the cathedral as a doorway to Elvenwood. He'd prefer the immature dragon lord didn't see him create a portal from nothing.

The void vibrated with his entry, and he felt a shift in the in-between. He hastened his steps, hurrying when he knew he should relax, but he was eager to get the business in Elvenwood concluded.

The in-between stretched into a doorway, and Therron stepped into his rooms at the palace. It took him a moment to adjust to the dimmed lights. He would never get used to the time difference between the human realm and Cilachaem. What was mid-morning in the human realm was the middle of the night in Elvenwood. Which gave him time to investigate without interference.

He changed into his elven robes and placed the ring, dragon scale, and vial of Rori's blood in a secure casket the size of his palm. He opened a drawer in his bureau and heard the tinkling of glass. Intrigued, he pulled the drawer fully open and stared at a pair of small bottles. They were familiar, but his thoughts spun in circles trying to place them, and why they'd be hidden in his drawer.

He placed the casket to the back of the drawer and withdrew the two bottles. Small sigils were inscribed in the lids, and immediately he recalled the impromptu search he and Cian had made for Thad. A search of Elvenwood City that had brought them to Gentle Galo's lounge. With all the events taking place since that day, he'd forgotten all about the potions he now held. He returned the bottles to the drawer, setting them on a piece of cloth to keep them from rolling around. In the morning, he'd pay Galo a visit and get answers about the contents of the bottles.

He locked the drawer and put an especially nasty spell on the bureau to keep out anyone snooping in his belongings. Privacy was a luxury he never took for granted, and in short supply at the palace. Once certain his treasures wouldn't be disturbed, he left his rooms and headed for the library. A chill rattled his bones at the memory of Hensen turning into a puddle of black goo. Now Therron knew the source of the dark magic that sought Rori, but he was no closer to stopping Hunter for good.

It rankled that the man kept two steps ahead of them. He strode through the silent library without glancing at the spot where Hensen had died. His target was the forbidden section. Once he passed through the alcove's entrance, he stood with hands on hips, lips pressed thin. All the books

Hunter had stolen from the library seemed to be returned. That, at least, was a relief. He'd worried that when he and Cian destroyed the manor home in Scotland, they'd also destroyed a part of Elvenwood's history.

"Can't sleep?"

Therron peered over the back of an overstuffed chair to find Rainne reclining with a stack of books on her belly.

"That can't be comfortable." He stepped around the chair to sit opposite her. Pora, her strange cat, wound his way around Therron's legs, his tail flicking.

"Books make a wonderful pillow if you know which ones to choose." She sat up with an elegance that he admired. Not a single book fell to the floor. "Does your father know you've returned?"

"No, but I'm sure I'll have to see him at some point. Has his mood changed?"

Rainne shook her head, her eyes softened. "A lot has happened since you were here." She held up her hand with one finger extended. "First, Taryn and Rhoane healed the elvenwood tree. There was a disc hidden inside that was causing its illness. Second, they created quite a scandal by turning into dragons and flying off. Of course, this was after your mother ordered them put into the dungeons." Two fingers were raised. At the third, Therron stopped her.

"My mother did what?"

Rainne settled in and told him an astonishing tale about how after Taryn and Rhoane healed the elvenwood tree, it made blooms that had curative properties. At first, it seemed to help his father, but after a few days, he backslid and his madness was worse than before. Of course, now his mother blamed Taryn and Rhoane, but with them gone, she raged at anyone within a few paces. Theo and Rainne were keeping well away from not only her, but his father, too.

Therron kept his focus on his father and mother, ignoring the part about Taryn and Rhoane becoming dragons. After the past few days, he was no longer shocked by such admissions. Although, the words had caused his breathing to deepen. If only Taryn and Rhoane were still there so that he could ask the dozens of questions that demanded answers.

"Theo and I became betrothed." Rainne whispered this, her eyes downcast. "It's something we desire, but your mother practically forced it upon us."

"But surely, this is wonderful news." He reached forward and clasped her hands. "I am happy for you, truly."

She didn't meet his eyes. "Therron, before Taryn left, she told us—Theo and me—that he would rule Elvenwood." And now she did look up. "But Rori is your curse breaker. You'll reign after your father passes."

Therron grimaced to hear the softly spoken words. "I don't believe I'm meant to rule." He held her gaze with an intensity he hoped she understood. "It's imperative we tell no one about this. Does Mother know what Taryn told you?"

"No, and Theo doesn't wish to speak of it. I can't blame him, with Thaddeus still missing and all."

"Good. This is our secret for now. But I feel it's your destiny—yours and Theo's—to rule Elvenwood." He placed his hand over his heart. "Just as I know it's my destiny to not claim the Forest Throne."

Rainne's eyes grew large and filled with tears. "Have you seen your death foretold?"

At this, Therron grinned. "I have seen many remarkable things, but not my death. May that be many years from now." He rose and kissed her on the forehead. "Welcome to the family, sister."

She chuckled and picked up a book. "I've been an only child my whole life. This will take some getting used to."

"You've survived the elven court for a fortnight at least. You will survive having siblings. And just to be safe, it would be wise for you and Theo to prepare to rule."

Therron left her in the library and made his way to the great elvenwood tree. It was dark with only a few candles lit near the revered tree, and he approached with caution. Huge white blooms dangled from leaves and he reached to touch one. Immediately, he smelled Rori's floral scent and felt her presence. He turned in all directions, expecting to see her, but he was alone.

She is with you, young prince. As she ever more will be.

Again, Therron spun to see who was speaking, and again, he was alone.

"Show yourself." His fingers fluttered above his waist, but he wasn't wearing a sword.

Open your eyes. See me. Really see me, and then you will see yourself.

Open his eyes? They were open; that's how he knew he was alone.

You are never alone. Nor will you ever be again.

Therron's gaze settled on the elvenwood tree, and he stepped closer. "Are you…speaking to me?"

I have been your entire life, but you never chose to listen. Lady Delarainne hears me, as does your curse breaker. They listen with their hearts, as well as their ears.

He stroked a finger along the smooth bark of the tree, stopping at a fresh scar in the wood. "You're injured."

I'm healing.

"Is this from when Taryn and Rhoane removed the disc?"

It is. They gave me a great gift. A small branch swooped down and handed Therron one of the huge flowers. *They allowed me to be what I was all along, but didn't recognize in myself.*

Therron held the bloom in his hand as if it were made of fine glass. Listen with his heart. All he heard was the heavy thumping of the organ. Then, ever so slowly, his heart rate calmed and he heard the unfurling of leathery wings. Hundreds, if not thousands of them.

Prince Rhoane of the Eleri wears the Crown of Awakening for now. But he will soon know his destiny, just as you'll know yours. A slim green tendril caressed his cheek where the scar marked him as the cursed prince. Instead of irritating his skin, the tendril soothed it.

Footsteps echoed down the hallway, and Therron pressed a hand upon the tree's trunk before hurrying to the shadows. He tucked the bloom into an inner pocket as best he could without damaging the thing, and waited.

The king approached, with several of his privy council keeping step. "Make sure the soldiers are ready by the next full moon. We'll meet the traitors at the Vale of Dorn. They won't survive this time."

The councilors nodded and agreed with the king, but Therron saw the looks of dismay flicker across their features. Whatever his father was planning, at least the privy council did not agree with him. But they were too weak to tell the king as much.

Therron didn't have to guess too hard who the traitors were—the queens of Faerie. Once he was done with his investigations in the palace, he'd go to Midna and warn her of his father's plans. The next full moon was a fortnight away. He inhaled the bloom that rested in his pocket and savored the scent of Rori. His curse gave him three moonturns—his father's madness just two weeks.

❧ 25 ❧

The two men hovered over Rori like anxious coworkers checking her work on what should've been a group project. She snarled up at them, giving her best assassin glare. They knew her history. Hells, they knew more about her than she did. That, more than anything, annoyed her. It also intrigued the futnucker out of her. When she had a minute, and didn't have two dragons breathing down her neck—literally—she'd research what the hell a Stone Guardian was, and then she'd learn everything she could about dragon lords and shifter princes from other worlds.

"Do you mind?" She cocked her chin toward the other side of the desk. "I'll let you know what I find."

She'd been searching Hunter's laptop for the better part of two days. Most of his notes were written in some archaic code only he understood, but every so often, she found a gem. Like she had that morning when she stumbled upon a file simply titled, Phase One.

It laid out Hunter's scheme for causing chaos and world

destruction on Earth. For such a brilliant man, he'd chosen the most basic form of annihilation: turn the people against each other. Start with exploiting humanity's weaknesses through fear, greed, and division. Then he planned to attack infrastructure, world economies, and supply chains.

Rori stared at the screen, mortified at what she read. Hunter hated the humans so much he wished to destroy an entire world. Same with Cilachaem. Although, she'd not found plans for her homeworld yet. She assumed it would be similar to what he'd planned for Earth, but with that madman, it was hard to tell and assumptions could get lots of people killed.

Sweat broke out along her back, and she twitched against the prickliness. "I need to tell my queens about all of this." She looked over the laptop to the men, who were now seated across from her. "Can you get this laptop to Cian in London? They can continue searching for answers while I'm in Faerie." Her gaze went to the line of vials at the edge of the desk. "It's time I returned these poor souls home. With any luck, I'll be able to free the ones already in Eirlys's care."

Neither she, nor Lucien or Aimon could sense life in the vials she'd stolen from Hunter, but that wouldn't stop her from trying to revive whatever was inside.

Aimon stood, his hand over his heart. "You're still weak, Aurora."

"Rori. Call me Rori."

"Yes, Rori. You're still recovering from your ordeal. I would be honored if you'd allow me to escort you home."

Rori glanced at Lucien, who nodded. "We've discussed this, and I understand your concern, but we believe Aimon will be safer in your kingdom. He is an elf, after all."

"An elf who can become a dragon. I'm still not sure how I feel about that."

The two men exchanged a glance that was full of meaning Rori wasn't privy to.

"I feel it's important you reconcile yourself to the fact that some elves, not all, can become dragons. Just as you have a unicorn soul, so do some elves have a dragon soul. It is possible even faeries do as well." Lucien's eyes clouded as if he were looking into the distance—or the future…she could never tell with the enigmatic lord. "Your own brother has something within him we cannot see, but we sense it."

"Cian?" Rori's brow scrunched. "Hunter said he was a failure. That he didn't have anything special about him." A smile broke out on her face. "Won't he be surprised when he discovers how wrong he was. Hunter is such a dick."

"I won't argue that. But Rori, no one must know about Cian. At least, not yet. When he reveals his true soul, it will be when he is ready."

Rori nodded her agreement and gathered her belongings. "Where's Uthran? I'd like to say goodbye. And to thank him for the cheeseburgers. They were delicious."

The little furry blue oewling waddled into the room, his eyes downcast. "Will you return?"

She went to him and enfolded him in her arms. "I hope so. But first, I have to save a few worlds. No big thing."

He gripped her tighter, surprising her with his strength. "I will learn to cook all your favorite meals so you will grow thick and strong. You're too skinny."

"I look forward to it." She rose and looked from Uthran to Aimon. Two creatures from other worlds. Both somehow found their way to Earth. Her life on Cilachaem and Earth seemed small in comparison to what lay beyond their galaxy. "Do you need to pack, Aimon?"

The dragon shifter shook his head. "I am sure my human clothing will not be appropriate for your queens. I will acquire clothing once there."

"Oh, the queens are going to love you." An idea pinged in her mind, but she shuttled it aside for the moment. Midna especially would like this polite, yet intriguing man.

She wrote two notes, one for Cian and the other for Therron, sealing them both with a drop of her blood and a spell that would allow only them to open the letter. These she gave to Lucien, along with the laptop, microchips, and trackers she'd taken from Hunter's lab.

Once that was done, she stood in the middle of the gorgeous room, slightly bereft. It had been her refuge the past few days while she rested and grew stronger. Whatever Hunter had given her had at last left her system, leaving her feeling clearer-minded and fully in control of her thoughts and actions.

Lucien led her to a small cupboard, where a secret doorway would allow them to travel to Faerie. She was no longer shocked to learn of how many illegal doorways existed in the human realm. There were probably just as many in Faerie and Elvenwood. She wondered whether the queens knew about them and chuckled to herself. Most likely, they did. Very little escaped their notice.

After a brief hug for Lucien, she said the words that would take her to the one place she knew she had to return, yet dreaded all the same.

"Are we going to the Seelie or Unseelie Court first?" Aimon asked, his eyes alight with excitement.

"Neither." She gripped Aimon's hand in her own to be certain she didn't lose him in the in-between.

The void swirled in front of them, and Rori took a shaky step into the darkness. Her heart trembled with what she knew had to be done. What needed to be said. The truths that would be faced.

The void shifted, and she drew in a deep breath to calm her nerves. It wouldn't do to have the snake-dragon-demon feel her anxiety and attack them. Even the thought of the creature made her healed wound throb, and she rolled her shoulders to release the tension that coiled in her body like a rattler ready to strike.

As serenity came haltingly to her, she realized the in-between was different. She didn't sense the snake-dragon-demon's presence, and a rainbow-hued glittery sort of light sped in all directions above their heads.

She looked at Aimon, his face illuminated by the shimmering glow.

"Does this feel different to you?"

"It's been over two centuries since I last traveled the portals, but yes. This is lighter, calmer. I almost feel giddy traveling through the void." He looked up at the soft rays. "Something has changed." He tapped his chest. "I feel it here."

"Yeah, I do too." A vision of Taryn and her great beast came to her. Rhoane was there, too, and they all fought the creature that had attacked Rori. It felt real, too real, as if it had just happened that morning. "I hope they're safe," she mumbled, forgetting that Aimon couldn't see the vision in her mind.

"They are," he answered, and she knew he knew who she meant.

"Have you met them?"

His eyes closed, and he lifted his face. She heard the murmuring of thousands of voices. "Not yet, but I will." A smile quirked his lips. "My people will soon, too."

"A premonition? Or do you know for a fact it will happen?"

"Both."

She chuckled and shrugged against all the things she didn't yet know. The world was an interesting place lately. She was learning to stay curious, but to also accept that there were things she might never understand.

She redoubled her focus on her destination. Then, so softly she almost missed it, she heard Therron's voice as if he spoke only to her in the great vastness of nothingness. She not only heard him, but felt his embrace. If she wasn't certain he wasn't there with her, she would've looked to see him holding her protectively in his arms. His words wound through her, bringing a sense of peace she'd longed for ever since Hunter first took her.

Therron. She saw him seated on the great Forest Throne, a golden crown held above his head. Dark wings spread behind him, but they didn't terrify her as she thought they might. They were fitting. A part of him. A part of her. Then the vision blipped out, and she was left with silence and a lingering warmth where his phantom hug had once been. Two visions in such a short span of time. It had to mean something, but right then, she wasn't afforded the luxury of exploring what, exactly, it meant. For her, for

Therron, for their futures. For now, she would trust it was something good.

The in-between grew lighter, and the calm of a minute earlier vanished. No more running. No more hiding.

"We're here." Rori released Aimon's hand as she stepped from the doorway into a small shed built for the exclusive use of Queen Eirlys's favorite personal guard.

"Where are we?" Aimon looked at the confined space, frowning.

"You'll see in about a min—"

The door burst open and a sword pointed at their faces. Holding the sword was the one person Rori feared and loved most in all the worlds.

"Hi, Mum." Rori took a step toward the sharp blade and pushed it aside before crumbling into her mother's arms.

26

The lounge was dark at this time of day, which was precisely why Therron chose to interrogate Galo now rather than when the club was full. He strolled through the main room as if he owned the place, surveying the seating arrangements and private booths as if he might redecorate. It was all a ruse. He knew Gentle Galo was watching him from his hidden room above the lounge, and Therron wanted to give the impression he was there for a business proposition.

The bottles sat heavy in his pocket, wrapped in silk cloth to keep them from making noise or breaking unexpectedly. He'd spent a short time in the library looking at Eleri runes, but they weren't *exactly* the same. Small changes, ones that could easily be mistaken, frustrated Therron. The runes on the vials Acelyne had used to kidnap Hunter's victims were precise, but these…it was as if they were made by an amateur.

Or someone not from Cilachaem.

The thought wormed its way through Therron's skull. It

was a possibility he hadn't considered until just then. His hand brushed the pocket of his trousers where the bottles were hidden. Their importance ratcheted up.

Finished with his perusal of the lounge, Therron strode to the door that led to the workrooms in the back where Galo's factory made the cider his patrons adored. The hairs on Therron's neck rose as he reached for the handle, but he didn't pause in his step or react to the unseen threat. Someone was using magic on him. Not on the door, on him.

They were clumsy in their attempt to dissuade him from entering the back rooms. He pushed open the door and the prickling snapped as if the magic had been broken off. An angry itch remained, but he ignored it. His focus was on the dozen or so crates stacked against the far wall. The rest of the warehouse was empty.

When he'd been there with Cian, stacks and stacks of wooden crates had filled the space. Therron's eyes narrowed in thought. Something changed.

"Your Highness!" Galo's effusive voice boomed from the other end of the warehouse as he bounded toward Therron.

"Galo, please. We've been friends too long for you to start with protocol now." He clasped the man's hand in his own and half-embraced him. "Where's your inventory? You were doing a booming trade last time I was here."

Galo's soft-brown eyes darkened and his plump lips quivered. "I was hoping you'd know something about that." His gaze went to Therron's trouser pocket.

"Why would I have information about your business dealings?"

"I assumed you'd spoken to Dithers."

The palace seneschal. Therron recalled that Galo had said something about him being difficult lately.

Galo shifted from foot to foot, making his clothing vibrate. Today he wore a kaftan in a shade brighter than a spring leaf, with bright pink fronds splayed at every angle. It reminded Therron of a woman he'd seen in Rome from the bus window. She wore a cloth wrapped around her head and walked with the elegance of a royal. Suddenly Galo's attire no longer seemed quaint.

"I've been busy lately. So, no, I haven't spoken with Dithers." He reached out to smooth Galo's sleeve. "But I think there is a lot you haven't told Dithers. I would be honored if you shared this information with me." He withdrew the two bottles and dangled them in front of Galo's doughy face.

Galo swallowed hard and glanced around the warehouse. "Did you find your brother?"

"What's in these, Galo? Where did they come from?"

"Not here." He led Therron to his office and locked the door behind him.

Therron felt the man's magic envelop the room before he sat in his expansive chair and beckoned Therron take a seat opposite his desk.

Once seated, Galo steepled his fingers and sighed, his face turned toward the ceiling.

"You're stalling. Why?"

When he looked at Therron, there were tears in his eyes. "My business is failing. My clientele, they no longer want only cider." He pointed to the bottles Therron still held. "Acelyne procured those potions. She called them amrita. I don't know what's in them, she never told me, or where they're manufactured. But I do know my patrons loved them. Said they made them feel invincible. Calmed their inner demons, they said."

Therron's nerves spiked, and he strove to stay calm while Galo spoke. "Who could make such a potion on Cilachaem? One of the troll tribes to the south? Sprites? Do you think they're fae made?"

Galo's shoulders slumped. "I don't know. I asked every time that witch brought a new shipment, but she never said." He leaned forward as if to share a secret. "One drop per glass of cider is all it took. One. Drop. Whatever that stuff is, it's potent." He leaned back with a sniff. "If you're thinking of partaking of any, that is."

"I have no desire to imbibe a potion I don't know the provenance of."

"If you're not going to use them, then I will." He held out his beefy hand. "You did steal them from me, after all. They're technically mine."

Therron wrapped the bottles in the silk and tucked them into his pocket. "Not anymore. Was Acelyne the only one to deliver the potions?"

"Another lad would on occasion. Disagreeable chap. I think he worked for the Seelie queen or something. Always bragging about how important he was, that one. Bit of a prick, if you ask me."

Therron's brain whirled with possibilities, landing on one name that chilled his blood. "Was he called Dorchmeir by any chance?"

"Yeah, that's the one. Got special clearance from Dithers on accounta he was fae'n all."

Damn. That complicated matters. If Dorchmeir had

been involved, then it stood to reason the potions were fae made. He could ask Meg whether she knew anything about them, or whether she was involved. It would break Rori's heart if she was. He knew they were close. But there wasn't anyone on Cilachaem more skilled with potions than Meg.

"Do you have any of the crates they were delivered in?" He had to find proof it wasn't Meg.

"There might be a few left in the back." Galo waved him toward the door. "Look wherever you like. Unless something changes soon, I won't be in business long enough for Dithers to extort money from me anymore."

Therron leaned back, arms crossed. "If you're a legitimate business, there's nothing to gain by extortion. What exactly were you doing here?" And how much of Dithers's activity did the king and queen know about? He didn't want to believe his parents were privy to Dithers's dealings, but they had to have been.

"I ran a good business for half a century until your brother showed up. It was hims who brought in the seedier clientele. It was hims who insisted I listen to Acelyne about her mystical potions." Galo pointed a thumb at Therron. "If'n you ever see him, you tell him he's not welcome here no more."

Thaddeus had known about the potions.

"Did Thad imbibe these potions regularly?"

Galo's laughter shook his kaftan so that the colors blended into a lime-pink blur. "Gods, no. He never touched the stuff. Said he wasn't that stupid." His laugher quieted and he rubbed his face with both hands. "I was a fool and now I'm about to lose everything. I never shoulda listened to them. Acelyne said I was special, that she would only sell the potions to me. I believed her. Or wanted to believe her. Said I was her beta test. I didn't know what that meant, but it sounded nice."

A beta test. Something about that phrase pinged in Therron's mind. Beta wasn't an elven word, nor had he ever heard it in Faerie. But he knew it from somewhere.

"Thank you, Galo. I'll have a talk with Dithers and see what we can do to keep you from losing your club." He rose, his mind still stuck on the word beta.

"I appreciate that. I never believed the rumors about you. You've always been more than fair in our dealings."

Therron chuckled. He'd heard the rumors about him, too. Most were spread by his own brother Thad. "I'll see myself out. I want to take a look at those crates first."

"Therron." Galo's voice was suddenly soft. "I'm not sure if Thaddeus knew it, but that last night? Acelyne put a few drops of potion in his drink. As a lark, she'd said. I didn't stop her. I'm sorry." Fresh tears sparkled in his eyes. He genuinely cared for Thad.

That alone broke Therron's heart a tiny bit.

"It's not your fault, Galo. Acelyne wasn't a nice person. Count yourself lucky you're still alive after knowing her. She didn't often leave witnesses."

Galo gulped and nodded, his eyes huge with worry. "You said she's dead, right?"

"Yes. Very much so. You can begin anew. No more deals with Dithers. No more potions, yeah?"

"Of course, Your Highness."

Therron left the office and searched the warehouse, but the only crates he found were those marked for Galo's cider. It was as if any evidence of the potions had been wiped from the place. With both Acelyne and Dorchmeir dead, that left only one other person who might know about the potions. Dithers.

Therron hurried back to the palace, dodging courtiers as he rushed to the seneschal's offices. Elves bustled about their day, but there was no sign of Dithers. After a brief enquiry where he might be, which produced blank stares and no answers, Therron went to find Theo. His baby brother needed to be brought up to speed on everything that had happened since Therron had left the palace.

"Therron, darling." His mother called from the other side of the hallway, and Therron turned to face her. He gave the requisite bow and endured her frosty hug and kiss. "I'm so pleased to see you've returned. Were you coming to alert me to your presence?"

By her tone, she knew he'd been there for quite a few hours. "Yes, Mother, as a matter of fact, I was. I arrived in the middle of the night and wanted to wait until you'd had a chance to greet the day before I interrupted your peace."

"And why would you do such a thing? You know I love your visits." She peered past him. "Where is your whore? Have you come to your senses and left the fae assassin?"

Therron sighed and shoved his fists into his pockets. "She is well, thank you for asking. We'll return together in due time, but I'm afraid my visit will be short. There are intrigues afoot that I must sort out first." He brushed her cheek with his lips and started down the hallway before turning and asking, as innocently as possible, "Have you seen Dithers this morning?"

Queen Helena's brows furrowed. "I haven't. He should be in his offices by now, though."

"I was just there. He's not in yet."

"Strange." His mother pushed past him and strode down the hall.

Therron followed her up a flight of stairs, down a plain corridor, and then down a flight of stairs before she finally stopped at a marginally decorated door.

"Open it."

Therron did as told and opened the door, allowing his mother to pass through before him. The stench hit him immediately, and he instinctively reached to shield his mother from what she would find. He was too late. She stared at the bloated body of Dithers with a horrified look on her pretty face.

"Who would want to kill Dithers? He was a sweet old man who never left the palace." She looked at Therron with wide, innocent eyes.

Whether she knew it or not, she'd just admitted to knowing that Dithers was not at all what he appeared. Therron's first clue was that from where he stood, it wasn't obvious that Dithers had been murdered. Yet for some reason, his mother instantly made that conclusion.

Her eyes narrowed and she glared at him. "Did you do this, Therronysus?"

He should've expected the accusation, yet he was surprised by it. "No, Mother, I didn't."

But someone had. Therron didn't suspect his mother, but he felt certain in his gut that she knew who had killed Dithers. Which meant there was someone else who knew about the potions.

27

Their tea had long since gone cold, their breakfast scones barely touched. Rori sat across from her mother and watched the emotions play across her beautiful face. She'd never truly seen her mother before, but now, sitting at her table in the house she lived in alone, far away from court, Rori saw Labhruinn MacNair for what she really was. A woman. One who had known love and heartbreak, who was feared and revered, who could wield a sword better than anyone Rori could recall. A woman who now knew the truth and extent of the betrayal her husband had committed in the last two decades. Possibly even longer.

She'd told her mum almost everything. Leaving out Acelyne and Meg's relationship to Hunter, and also omitting Nikala's name when talking about Hunter's victims. Her mum had enough to process without the added responsibility of knowing Acelyne and Meg were related to her children. As for Nikala, Rori didn't want her name sullied before Labhruinn MacNair had a chance to meet Cian's love interest. Once their mum met Nikala and saw her not as Hunter's weapon, then she and Cian could decide when best to tell their mum the truth. If ever. It was for the best. She hoped.

Her mum sighed and ran a hand through her still glorious auburn hair. "Well. You've given me quite a lot to think about." She reached over and clasped Rori's hands. "It wasn't your fault, my love. None of this. Don't you ever think for even a second you are at fault."

Rori nodded, but the words bounced through her skull, never landing quite right. Hunter had said it was all her fault, but he was a liar. Hunter needed her blood, but he was a manipulator. She repeated the statements and returned to what her mother had said.

"I know. Deep down, I know, but I spent fifteen years thinking I'd caused something. That doesn't go away overnight."

Her mum stared her down, and Rori kept her gaze. "You. Are. Fucking. Amazing. Say it with me."

"I am fucking amazing," Rori repeated, stifling a giggle. "You're pretty amazing, too."

Labhruinn leaned back, grinning. "I know." She lifted her chin in the direction of the lounge. "Now, tell me about this hot dragon you brought home."

Rori sighed and rolled her eyes, something she hadn't done since she lived at home. Old habits were hard to break. "He's from another world, got stuck in the human realm, and I'm taking him to Midna's court." Rori leaned in close and whispered conspiratorially, "I think she'll fancy him, don't you?"

Her mum gave a slow shake of her head and smiled.

"You are such a troublemaker. Now you're playing match-maker, too?"

"Couldn't hurt. Want to come with us? First, I'm going to Eirlys's court to see if we can free the imprisoned fae."

"Sure. Let me grab my coat." She rose from the table and stopped midway. "I still can't believe your great-great-great-infinity-grandmother gave you a unicorn soul. That's pretty sweet. I do wonder what Cian's hiding. He was always such a precocious child. Even more so than you."

Rori busied herself clearing the table and washing up while her mum got ready. It involved much more than just grabbing her coat, but Rori knew it would and didn't mind. Sitting and talking with her mum had been cathartic, and possibly even healing. She missed their talks, and the comfortable silences they once shared. Whatever reasons she'd had for staying away seemed dumb now.

Her mum popped her head out of her bedroom door. "Is Meg involved? I'd hate to think I was duped by two of my best mates."

"Meg knows nothing. As for Maxx, she's trying to do the right thing. Hunter was blackmailing her and threatening her child."

Labhruinn stepped into the small hallway. "Now that, I can understand. Hagan—erm—Hunter knew I would kill him if I found out what he was doing. It's just..." She closed her eyes and exhaled sharply. "You were my children. My babies. I should've known."

Rori went to her mum and hugged her hard. "He is a master manipulator. He hid his actions too well. Why would you suspect the man who swore he loved you? It's not your fault. None of this is your fault." She repeated her mother's words from earlier.

Labhruinn chuckled and kissed Rori on the cheek. "Wise words, my daughter. Come on, let's go see the queen."

Rori and Aimon followed Labhruinn to the shed in silence. Once at the palace, Rori would need to figure out how her blood played into freeing the kidnapped fae. She knew the words to speak, the cadence and timbre, but the blood…that was the kicker. Aimon had cried directly onto her wounds; surely, she wasn't expected to bleed on all the amulets. Then again, maybe that was exactly how it worked. She flexed her fingers as if preparing them for the pricking that was soon to come.

The trip to the palace took only seconds, but again, Rori felt lighter in the in-between. Something monumental had happened; she just didn't know what. The unknowing made her anxious.

"Calm down, Rori. You'll do fine." Her mum smoothed her hair as they stepped into Eirlys's Room of Mirrors. "The trapped fae are lucky to have you."

"They're not just faeries." Rori recalled Rhoane's face as he recognized the rune for dragon. "We don't know what to expect when those amulets are opened."

Labhruinn shared a look with Aimon, her eyes unreadable. "Then we'll be prepared, won't we?"

The door opened and a guard of four waited for them outside. When they saw their former commander, a few inclined their head, and all four thumped their fist to their chest. Without a word, Labhruinn led the small group to the throne room. Esme rushed to join Rori, but for once didn't babble. In fact, she kept her head lowered and only raised it to sneak a peek at Labhruinn. Rori slipped her hand into Esme's and gave a soft squeeze. She always forgot how much her mum was respected and feared at court. To her, Labhruinn MacNair was just Mum.

As a group, they entered the throne room and found Eirlys in deep conversation with an elegantly dressed woman. When she saw Rori and her mum, the queen waved the woman off and stepped down from the dais.

"I was not expecting you this morning, Labhruinn. Nor you, Rori." Her gaze went to Aimon. "And who is this delightful gentleman?"

"I am Aimon, Your Majesty." Aimon bowed low with his left hand and leg stretched outward.

Rori had seen a few elves bow in the same manner, but only to other elves. He was a mystery, that was certain.

"And you may call me Queen Eirlys. For now." Her cheeky grin suggested the possibility of a more intimate address if the occasion arose.

Rori took in the courtiers lingering in the room, catching Tug's worried glance. He motioned her over, and she cocked her head toward Eirlys. Once she was done with the queen, she'd see what her best friend needed. He didn't usually hang out at the palace, but it wasn't just that or his deep frown that made her concerned. She didn't see Meg with him.

"Rori," Eirlys said sharply, and she pulled her attention to the queen.

"We need to speak privately." Rori didn't have time for Eirlys's flirting or queenly attitude. If Aimon wished to bed her, he could do it after she completed her task.

Eirlys studied Rori a moment before leading them to the small room behind the throne room.

Once there, Eirlys crossed her arms, her gaze wandering to Aimon. "What is so alarming you interrupt my afternoon with a stranger and your mother in tow?"

"I have news from the human realm, but first—I know how to free the poor souls in the amulets. Do you have a room prepared?" Rori answered plainly.

Eirlys's expression changed from stern queen to alarmed mother, and she moved swiftly to a locked safe hidden behind a portrait. The door to the safe swung open and the queen retrieved the caskets, handing them to Aimon. He didn't ask what he carried, but obediently followed the queen through the palace to a wing Rori had not been to in several years. Not only had the queen made arrangements in advance of Rori's arrival, she also had several of her guard stationed outside the healing ward to keep out courtiers with nothing better to do than gossip.

Her mum slipped an arm around her shoulders and leaned in to whisper, "I believe in you, Rori. Trust your instincts."

"Thanks, Mum." Rori gave her mother a grateful smile. Knowing that she was there, and that she had faith in her, meant the world to her. More than she'd ever realized.

This was it. The moment of truth. Either she released all the trapped victims, or she failed. Failure meant death. Quite possibly hers or theirs or both. She couldn't fail.

28

The clear blue waters of the lake lapped over her bare feet, and Nikala raised her head to the sunshine that beat down on them with soothing warmth. It was still early summer, not yet too hot, just enough heat to take the chill off her confession. She'd only told Cian about the oath Therron accidentally bound them to, and that she couldn't lie to Therron, nor he to her. She knew she had to tell Cian everything, but fear choked the words in her throat. She would, she promised herself, and soon. Because if she didn't, she would lose the one good thing in her life. Forever.

Cian sat beside her, his face showing all his emotions as he processed her words. After they left the lab in Rome, she had asked him if they could go somewhere private to talk and he'd brought her through a doorway to a villa in Lake Como, as if that were a normal thing.

The villa belonged to a Hollywood star who Cian had helped with something Nikala didn't really wish to know the particulars of. The friend kept the villa as a vacation home, and allowed Cian to use it whenever he wished. He swore to her he never had. When he admitted that this was his first visit and she was the only woman he'd ever consider bringing to the gorgeous home, it made her feel even worse.

He'd brought her somewhere private, where they wouldn't be found. Somewhere safe. And she'd repaid his kindness with only telling half the truth. She was a terrible person.

He hadn't pressed her last night, but there was a tension to him that she had felt when she curled up to his body in bed. Breakfast was small grunts and not meeting her worried gaze.

She was being stupid, she knew, and yet it had been difficult to even admit as much as she had. Cian didn't understand that trust had been tortured out of her. It wasn't something that came back as easy as you please. She was trying; she truly was. And bless him for having the patience he did because fuck, this sucked.

Guilt slid over her as she sat on the bank, her toes playing in the cool water. She had to tell him everything. Her mouth went dry and lips felt like sandpaper scratching against itself each time she spoke.

"There's more." She rested her head on her bent knees and looked at him sideways. "After Therron accidentally bound us to the oath, we were whisked away to Faerie."

His jaw tightened, but he said nothing.

"Midna's palace, specifically." Why was it so hard to say simple words? Because they weren't so simple. "That's where we met Ishnara. She's a fae queen, long dead. But her ghost is stuck in your world because she cursed Therron's family. It got a little convoluted, and I'm not entirely sure why she placed the curse, but she can't leave until it's broken."

Cian ran a finger over his upper lip, his eyes dark in thought. "Let me get this straight. Ishnara isn't a ghost here on Earth? She's in Faerie, and you somehow went to Midna's palace? Did you see Midna?"

Nikala raised her head with a soft shake. "We saw her, but she couldn't see us. Like I said, it was confusing." She took a long breath. This was the part she dreaded confessing. But, she'd promised herself no more lies. Their relationship deserved the truth. "Her sister Mairead is my mother."

She let her confession sink in, all the while watching his face. Emotions played across his features, from confusion, to realization, to...she wasn't sure what, exactly. A broad smile showed his teeth.

"See? You are a princess."

His chuckle went straight to her belly, and then lower, tickling her with desire.

"Does Hunter know?"

"I don't think so. Malcolm never told anyone I was his daughter, and I highly doubt he would've given that information to Hunter. Before his death, he gave me this." She pulled a tightly folded piece of paper from her jeans pocket. "His last confession. He acknowledged me as his daughter, but said nothing about my mother."

"That guy, back in Rome, he called you the prodigal daughter. Sounds like he knows."

Nikala gave a swift shake of her head. "Everyone believes I'm Hunter's daughter. I never corrected them.

Neither did Malcolm or Hunter. It suited everyone's needs to avoid the truth, I guess."

She handed the note to Cian, and he gently undid the folds until the paper was fully open. His eyes tracked the words, his brow furrowed. When he finished, he refolded the note and handed it back to her without saying a word.

"Remember that amulet I wore when we first met?" At his nod, she continued, "My mother was trapped inside. After I read the note from Malcolm, she showed me a vision and spoke in my mind. Almost as if they had a pact that I was to be kept secret."

"For your protection." Cian gazed across the lake, his eyes shifting left and right. "I can see why you'd keep it from me." He turned back toward her, his expression soft. "Thank you for trusting me with this. I'll say nothing until you feel it's time. At some point, you'll have to tell Midna, though."

She shivered at the thought and adjusted herself on the sand. "That's what Therron said, but what if she rejects me?"

"She might. But her sister is the one great love of her life. She'll eventually do what's right."

Nikala chewed a nail, wincing when she tore it from the skin. "Were you…did you and Midna ever…?" She couldn't say the words. Didn't want to know.

"Were we lovers? No. Not for lack of her trying." He grinned, but it didn't warm Nikala's insides—did the opposite, in fact. "Sorry. Being a self-absorbed twat doesn't always land the way you'd like. No. I never slept with her or participated in any of her álainn obedience sex parties."

"Sorry, her what?" Sex parties! Therron never mentioned those.

"Midna has what she calls her álainn obedience, her beautiful obedients. They are faeries—and the odd elf sometimes—who come to her court to learn to control their emotions, or to be better rulers, or for whatever personal reason they might have. But they submit willingly to being essentially sex slaves. It's been the Unseelie tradition for millennia. No one knows exactly when it started, but some say with the fae queen who cursed Therron's family."

"Ishnara."

Cian's brows twitched. "The ghost queen. It's an interesting time we're living in, isn't it?"

The question was rhetorical, but he wasn't wrong. They sat next to each other, looking out over the lake, each lost in their own thoughts. Cian stood and held his hand out for her to take. She rose, and he gathered her into his arms to carry her as if she were a baby. Neither of them spoke as they went inside and he laid her down on the massive bed that could easily sleep eight.

Even though a wall of windows faced the lake, the villa had complete privacy. Even the little beach was private property for the sole use of the villa's occupants. She relaxed into the soft mattress and watched Cian's face as he undressed her. Once she was naked, he slowly disrobed, taking far too long on each button, and knowing it was driving her wild having to wait.

His cock sprang loose from his trousers, and she lost interest in anything else he might be doing. Her pussy clenched with anticipation, and she squirmed atop the soft duvet. Cian grinned as he made slow, sensual progress to the bed. He crawled on all fours toward her, his eyes glinting from an internal light.

His hands ran up her calves to her thighs, where he pressed them open to give him better access to her aching channel. She resisted the urge to buck her hips in an attempt to force him closer, and instead clenched a handful of bed linens to keep from screaming out to hurry the damn hell up.

The bastard knew she was impatient for his touch, and took his sweet time inching up the bed until his lips were a breath away from her vagina. One more second, and she would shriek.

The first flick of his tongue made her jump. The second made her wriggle. The third made her tighten in all the best ways. She gave in to the torment, oohing at the heat of his mouth, sighing at the feel of his fingers sliding into her. He sucked and flicked, tickled her insides with his talented fingers, and hummed against her clit until she came in a rush, pulsing around his fingers, filling his mouth with her juices.

Her heart jackhammered in her chest, and her mind spiraled with emotions and thoughts she'd kept tightly sealed. It was the release she needed. She lay on the bed gasping, her hand over her chest. Telling him her truth about her mother had released something in her, making her feel hella vulnerable, but she wasn't afraid.

Cian pulled himself up her body, his cock resting at the apex of her legs. His slick lips bent toward her, and she greedily sucked her own juices from him. She'd never liked that before, but with him, it tasted different. Everything was different with him. He made her feel safe in a world that she'd only ever viewed as kill or be killed. He made her dream of a life beyond what she'd been twisted to become.

"I love you." She stroked his face, watching his eyes. They didn't flinch or narrow, but darkened with desire.

"That's damn good. Because I love you, Nikala St. James." A wicked smile quirked his lips. "Or should I say, Your Highness?"

"Stop. Seriously. Forget I even told you." But it felt nice. Natural.

He slid his cock inside her, and she gasped at the sudden entry. Immediately, her body responded, and she clenched his cock with her inner muscles. Veins protruded on his neck and his face reddened.

"Fuck, Nikala. You drive me wild." His pumps were hard and fast, with a desperation she knew all too well. She thrust her hips to match his pace, and he groaned into her shoulder. "Can't hold it."

"Let go, Cian." It was more than a plea...it was a declaration.

They both had a past they'd have to live with, but for them to truly have a future, they had to release the hold the past had on them.

Cian cried out as he filled her womb with his seed. A momentary blip of sadness flicked across her thoughts, and she blotted it out before it could ruin the mood.

"What is it?"

Damn the man, he'd seen the blip.

"Nothing."

"It's something. Tell me." He held her face, his body hovering above hers, his half-flaccid cock still inside her.

"Kids." She gave a brief shake of the head. "I don't want them. Don't even know if I'm capable of having them. But if you want them…?" She left the question hanging between them.

"Children?" He stared at the ceiling a moment before returning his gaze to her. "I never thought about it, to be honest." Then his face softened, and he looked at her anew, this time with compassion. "You are everything I've ever wanted. You're all I will ever need. If somewhere down the road we feel differently, that's a conversation we'll have then. It's you I love, Nikala. Not some dream of a future with a dozen kids, two dogs, one cat, and a goat."

"A goat?" Her laughter bubbled up from her belly, causing his cock to slip from her pussy.

"We are anything but conventional, my darling." He kissed her nose and flopped to lay on his back at her side. He held her hand in his, his thumb rubbing over her knuckles. "We have the rest of our lives to decide who and what we want to be." With his free hand, he pointed to the room. "Hell, we could buy a place like this and live out our life in quiet solitude."

"We'd die of boredom." But it wasn't such a terrible idea. She turned to face him. "I was serious that I don't know if I'm capable of having children. I've never seen a doctor, gynecologist or otherwise. I don't even know if I have a uterus. Probably not since I can't ever remember having a period." She watched him closely, but he showed no emotions that would suggest horror or sadness, just curiosity.

"I'm not a healer, but we can find one in Faerie and have you checked over if you'd like. Meg is excellent. She's set far too many of my bones and stitched me up more times than I care to remember."

"That would be nice. Thank you." She pressed a hand to her forehead. "Think she could see if I have any trackers implanted inside me?" She said it half-jokingly, but seeing the trackers at Hunter's place in Venice made her wonder what he'd implanted—trackers or otherwise—into her body. A swirl of panic went through her, and she stiffened.

"What's wrong?" Cian kissed her forehead.

"You said in Faerie. It's a shock to realize I'll need to go there at some point. How do you tell a queen that you're her niece? Especially if Mairead is still trapped in the amulet?"

"Rori will figure out how to free them. And when she does, everything will be explained to Midna. Fear not, my love."

He pulled her atop him, and she straddled his hardening cock. Enough talking for now.

His phone pinged, and she glanced at the screen before catching herself. It was a message from Dony.

Nikala lifted herself and slid her pussy over his glorious cock. A moan escaped her lips, and she arched to take him deeper. A groan came from Cian, and she grinned. She sat upright in time to see him set the phone down.

"Checking messages mid coitus?" She kept her tone light, but it annoyed her that his attention could be so easily pulled from their lovemaking.

"Considering the events of the past few days, yes. I thought it prudent to keep abreast of any events that might need our attention." His hands slid up her thighs to her waist and gripped her hard; she clenched against his cock. "Vixen. You make it difficult to forget there's a world we need to protect."

"Two worlds. What did the message say?"

He thrust his hips up, taking her by surprise. She grunted and ground against him, her clit hitting just the right spot to make her crazy with need.

"Dony said there's a mysterious man waiting for us at the pub. Been there an hour and won't leave until we return. Has something for us." His words were stilted and kept cadence with his pumping up and down.

"He'll just have to wait. I have something for us, too." She leaned forward and took his bottom lip between her teeth.

"I'll let her know it might be some time before we return to London."

"How long do you think we can delay?"

A low growl rumbled up Cian's chest, and he grinned. "At least the day. I'll tell her we'll be back by noon tomorrow."

"What if it's important?" She arched and moaned, her need building despite the topic of conversation.

"It can wait. I just found out my girlfriend is a fae princess. I think that warrants us a few hours to celebrate, don't you?"

She gave him a devilish grin, her eyes narrowed. "Does being a princess mean I get to boss you around?"

He thrust his cock deeper. "Oh, yes, Your Highness."

"I'm going to like this. Fuck me, Cian."

"As you command."

Her breasts pressed between them, and she swished her pelvis in a circular motion. His hands kneaded her skin, his groans coming faster and louder with each press of her clit against his pubis. She panted against his mouth, her tongue searching for his as they kissed.

Harder, faster…a wild need overcame her, and she forgot about the world for one glorious, climax-filled moment. All thoughts centered on Cian. He was her everything.

❧ 29 ❧

Rori steadied her nerves and reminded herself she one hundred percent believed she could release those trapped in the glass vials. It didn't matter that her confidence was shaky when it came to waking them. That was a future problem. First, free the victims. Don't kill them. Free them. She repeated the belief she would succeed. She had to. Nothing else mattered.

Her gaze went to four faerie healers who stood to the side, and she inclined her head to let them know she was about to begin.

Eirlys beckoned the healers to her. "Your care will begin once Rori has released the fae. We don't know what condition they will be in, so clear your minds of any preconceived idea of what healing they may need."

The healers nodded and glanced at Rori, expectant.

At Eirlys's instruction, Aimon laid out the vials, one to a bed. Rori knew some of them contained more than one victim, but there was no way to tell. The three Rori had brought to Eirlys from the human realm were put at the far end of the ward nearest the windows. Finally, Eirlys reached into a hidden pocket close to her heart and withdrew the sleeping princess.

"We will start with Arianna first," Eirlys declared.

Rori's heart sank. She was afraid the queen would suggest her daughter be revived before the others. She would've rather had a chance to warm up with someone other than the crown princess, heir to the throne.

"Of course." She went to an empty bed, and Eirlys gently lay her daughter on the pillow. Rori withdrew the dagger at her hip and pricked her forefinger. A drop of blood formed and she prayed to the First Goddess to please, please, please don't let her kill Arianna. "The words I'm about to say are dark magic. I understand they are forbidden, but they are what's needed to break Acelyne's spell."

Her mum, Aimon, and Eirlys all nodded. The queen watched her with keen interest, and Rori knew she'd try to memorize the counterspell. It would do no good, as Eirlys should well know. Rori had already said the words once, but that time she didn't know she needed her unicorn blood to complete the spell.

Out of caution, she kept her voice low, hoping Eirlys couldn't hear what she said. As she spoke, she touched her forefinger to Arianna's forehead. She was so tiny, the blot covered nearly her entire head and part of her face. Sweat pricked across Rori's shoulders and ran down her temples as she concentrated on the healing or awakening, or whatever it was she was trying to do. People seemed to forget she was trained to kill, not heal.

Yet it came to her naturally. The words, the cadence, the emotion behind the spell: she felt the magic and what it could do—it was an extension of her…not just an intangible bit of enchantment, but a physicality she'd never experienced before. Colorful threads stretched from her to Arianna, embracing her, swirling in a gentle storm of healing that Rori created.

It was intoxicating, this sense of power she had from her own magic. Magic that, until only a few weeks ago, she'd feared as something illicit, illegal, deadly. Now, what came from her protected life. She breathed deep and wiped perspiration from her forehead.

"Awaken, Arianna. Return to the world of the living." Rori whispered the last of the counterspell and sat back, waiting.

Her colorful streaks of magic increased in speed and then settled, cradling the sleeping princess. Ever so slowly, the streaks elongated and as they did, Arianna's body grew until she was the size she'd been when Acelyne kidnapped her.

"My darling." Eirlys reached for her daughter and held her close in a loving embrace. After a moment, Arianna's wings fluttered, and everyone gathered near exclaimed with relief. Eirlys lay her daughter down and stared at her for one agonizing moment before turning to Rori. "Why doesn't she wake?"

Rori stroked Arianna's cheek, feeling the warmth beneath her fingertips. "I don't know. She's been asleep for so long, it might take a day or so for her to fully regain consciousness."

Hells, she hadn't even been sure the counterspell would work. She was elated with the results, but she couldn't tell

Eirlys that, especially not with the queen so eager to have her daughter fully recovered.

"Perhaps I can help." Aimon kneeled next to the bed and wiped a tear from his eye. He placed the tear upon Arianna's forehead and sat back. When nothing happened, he rose, his eyes downcast. "I'm sorry, Your Majesty. I had hoped it would work."

"Why would your tears revive my daughter?" Eirlys regarded him with renewed interest. "Where did you say you were from?"

"I came with Rori from the human realm." He stepped back until he was level with Rori's mum.

She didn't call him out for telling Eirlys part of his truth, but she sure as cockles would ask him why later.

"Perhaps Rori should see to the others. The healers will watch over Arianna in the meantime," Labhruinn suggested, and Rori cast her mother a grateful look.

She shook off her sense of failure and went to the three beds nearest the windows. She picked up the amulet with the symbol for dragon and set it back on the pillow. She'd return to that one later just in case she released a full-grown dragon in the ward; she'd rather not have two epic missteps back-to-back. Although, she didn't believe she'd failed. It had felt right, and she was certain she'd performed the counterspell correctly. Those in the amulets had been drugged by Acelyne. It was entirely possible they would need an antidote.

"Is Meg available? Acelyne drugged her victims before kidnapping them. We need Meg to whip up a potion to cleanse them of any residual aftereffects."

Eirlys rubbed her fingers along her chin. "I haven't seen Meg lately, but I'll send a message to her cottage."

"Meg's missing," Tug's quiet voice said from where he hovered behind those gathered at Arianna's bedside. "I been lookin' for her, but she's nae anywhere."

Rori rose and went to her friend. "How long has she been gone?"

Tug's shoulders rose and lowered. "A few days. We was ta meet at her cottage, but when I gets there, she's nae around. Left me cookies in ta oven all burnt n'such."

Rori shared a look with her mother. "As soon as I'm done here, I'll help you find Meg. She probably got called to help someone and forgot to leave you a note." Even though Meg had never done such a thing before, Rori desperately hoped she had now.

"Will ye be long? It's just…Ima worried som'tin fierce for her."

Rori took his big hand and smoothed it between hers. "I know you are, my friend. We'll find her."

He nodded and sniffled, but he didn't argue. Rori stroked his chin, wiping a tear from his soft-brown eye. Her first priority was to Eirlys, but right then, her heart desperately wanted to go with Tug to find their friend. Her mum moved beside Tug and wrapped an arm around his middle in as much of a hug as she could.

Eirlys motioned to the healers. "Get started on something that could gently cleanse their systems. We don't know what Acelyne used, keep that in mind."

Two of the healers left the room.

With two gone, and the other pair watching over Arianna, Rori alone was left to care for the rest of the victims. Her gaze went to Aimon, and she straightened her shoulders. She wasn't totally alone, but she wished she had Therron there to help.

She went to another bed and held the amulet with the vines. Elven. Another prick of her finger which she then pressed atop the stopper, and she spoke the counterspell. This time, instead of feeling peaceful, she encountered resistance from whatever was inside. Her confidence faltered, and the colorful swirling turned ashen. A deep breath helped clear her doubt, and she refocused on the spell. This time, the vial dissolved and a fully grown elf lay upon the bed. His shining gold hair reminded her of Therron.

He was bigger than Therron in size, but not height. He wore well-made clothing in the colors of the royal household, and Rori's heart went cold. "I think this is Therron's brother Thaddeus. He's been missing for a while."

Eirlys leaned over her shoulder and harrumphed. "He better not be dead, or King Thane will have my head. Literally."

Rori felt for a pulse and put a hand near his nose. His breathing was ragged, and he had a weak heartbeat. "He's alive." The shade of his skin was the color of paste, though. Elves were often pale, but not deathly so. "But he's sick." She looked up at her queen. "If I had to guess, he wasn't well before he was kidnapped."

Eirlys swore loudly, shocking the two healers. "One of you, work on this one. He cannot die, do you understand? Can. Not. Die."

The healer rushed to Thaddeus's side. Rori felt the healer's magic and backed away so that her own power didn't interfere. She sat on the next bed, her confidence restored.

This was the faerie. She closed her eyes and cleared her mind of Thaddeus. Before she even finished the counter-spell, a fae woman with strawberry-blonde hair lay on the bed, her face the picture of serenity.

Eirlys inhaled sharply and rushed to the other side of the bed. "First Goddess protect me. What is going on here?"

Labhruinn covered a gasp and gripped Rori's shoulder. "That's Midna's sister, Mairead."

"Have all the high-ranking royals been kidnapped by that madwoman?" Eirlys smoothed Mairead's hair from her face. "We'll take care of you, darling. This I promise." She looked up at one of her guard. "Send word to Midna that Mairead has been found. No details, only that she is here."

"Wait." Labhruinn held out her hand. "Is that wise, Eirlys? Midna will come at once. Do you want her to see her beloved sister in this condition?"

"If it were my loved one, I would be even more angry if I wasn't told."

Rori stood to face her mother. "I agree with Eirlys that Midna deserves to know. Even in this state, at least Midna's heart will be settled knowing her sister is no longer missing —or dead. However, right now, she knows nothing of my being here, or what I'm doing. Let me finish releasing the others and I'll go personally to tell Midna. A few hours won't change anything."

Her mum's eyes narrowed, and she scrunched her lips. "She won't be pleased. Be prepared for her anger." This was said to Rori, and she shuddered.

"I can handle her." She knew releasing the trapped beings would come with hidden risks. She never expected it might be the Unseelie queen. "I think news like this is better received in person by someone other than a guard." Rori gave Eirlys a meaningful raise of her eyebrow and the queen waved the guard away. Rori watched as he retreated to his position with the other soldiers.

"Take Aimon with you," Labhruinn suggested with a sly smile.

"He can stay here," Eirlys insisted.

"But you have Arianna to look after."

Whatever mischief her mother was up to, Rori stayed out of the crosshairs. "I need to keep going."

Rori let the women continue their verbal chess and moved from bed to bed, releasing those trapped inside. The victims ranged from fae to elves to dwarves and brownies, and everything in between. Rori released an ogre, three orcs, five giants, and several sprites. There was also a creature no one could name, and at least a dozen human-looking people who Rori couldn't be certain came from Earth. Even with Aimon's tears, they'd not been able to wake a single victim.

Four hours later, her body shaking from exhaustion, Rori returned to the bed with the vial marked with the dragon rune.

"Last one, and then we can search for Meg." She looked up at Tug, who had stayed in the healing ward the entire time, his body slumping with each passing hour.

"You're in no condition to travel, let alone search for anyone. I'll go with Tug." Her mum looked at Tug with a hopeful expression. "That is, if you don't mind an old lady helping out."

Tug's entire demeanor changed, and he stood tall. "I'd be honored, Lady MacNair." He very nearly saluted, and Rori felt a swell of love for her friend.

"I'm not a lady, darling. I've told you this. Just Labhruinn is fine."

"But ye are. I was there when ta queen tapped yer shoulders with her sword."

Rori slid a glance to her mum, questions dancing on her lips. Labhruinn MacNair, a lady! "When did this happen? And why wasn't I invited?"

Eirlys cleared her throat. "That might have something to do with me, I'm afraid. I gave your mother the honor five days past. She earned it through her service to me, and I thought it would be a nice way to commend her for excellence."

"It was a blatant bribe to get me to return to service. Of which I am grateful, but the answer is still no."

Eirlys huffed and pouted like a spoiled princess.

"If you've no objection, there is still one vial we need to open." Rori would get to the bottom of the ladyship title later. Her heartbeat ramped up, and she took her mum's hand. She sat with a weariness that was more than just physical. "Stay with me. Be wary."

Her mum nodded and asked one of the guard for a sword.

Rori held the vial for Aimon to see, and he sucked in a breath. "You recognize this, don't you?"

"A darathi."

"Just in case it's not sleeping, don't let it kill anyone."

He gave a reassuring nod and stood on the other side of the bed. Rori repeated the words she'd said dozens of times already and let her magic flow to the amulet. She pressed a drop of blood on the stopper, silently praying to the First Goddess to protect those in the palace. The inky blackness inside the glass began to swirl, and she held her breath.

Agonizingly slowly, the amulet began to crumble before turning to mist like all the others had done. Rori waited to see a talon or a snout, but neither presented itself. Instead, laying on the pillow, was an egg about the size of her head. Its shell wasn't like an ostrich or goose, but was black as pitch and etched with what looked like scales.

"Blessed be." Aimon knelt and reached toward the thing, but stopped short from touching it. "It's still warm. Thank the gods, there is still time. It must be kept in a fireplace. Hurry." He turned to Rori. "You alone can touch it. No one else. This is most important."

"Me? Why?" Rori looked from him to the egg and back, her stomach twisting with anxious excitement she didn't understand.

"Trust me, please. Only you or Therron may touch the egg." Then Aimon looked directly at the queen. "I need your word the egg will not be disturbed."

"Yes, yes, of course." Eirlys stared at the thing as if it were a diamond and she were appraising its value. Her fingers stretched as if to stroke it, but Aimon held out his hand to prevent the queen from touching the egg.

"Only Rori or Therron, Your Majesty."

Eirlys pouted, but nodded her understanding. She withdrew her hands and clasped them in front of her.

Rori gently lifted the egg and glanced around the room, looking for the nearest fireplace. One of the healers pointed to the other end of the room, and she raced toward a huge fireplace with a roaring fire already lit. Her exhaustion slipped away with each step.

A dragon egg. Snickertits and futnuckers. A real live dragon egg.

Aimon tsked at the size of the fireplace and insisted they move the egg to a smaller room that could withstand the heat day and night. And would be easier to guard. Eirlys directed them to a room a few doors down from the healing ward. It held two slim beds and a small table with a wash-basin sitting atop. A small window allowed some light, and in the fireplace, there was already a robust fire glowing brightly. Rori guessed it was where the healers would catch a few hours' sleep between shifts.

Aimon instructed Rori to put the egg into the fire without any care that she might be burned. "Trust me, Rori. You will not be harmed."

She didn't have his confidence, but after all the hours she spent releasing Acelyne's victims from the vials, she didn't have the energy to argue. Plus, it seemed right. Her instinct told her to trust him, and she did. Cautiously, she knelt in front of the flames and reached forward, hesitating at the first flick of heat.

"Continue…that's it. See? You're unharmed." Aimon's voice guided her as she placed the egg directly on the grate inside the fireplace.

It was warm, a little too much so for her liking, but as he said, her arms were unmarked when she withdrew them from the flames. She stared at him, and then at the egg, and back to him.

"Keep a fire going at all times. This is imperative," Aimon instructed the guards standing nearby.

"Is that truly what I think it is?" Eirlys stood in front of the fire, her eyes wide with awe.

"It is, Your Majesty. And more precious than all the gold in your treasury."

"Where did it come from?" Rori stared at the flames, her heart beating in time to their dancing. "Cilachaem doesn't have dragons."

Aimon put a hand on her forearm and waited until she looked at him. "At the moment, no, but there were once thousands of darathi on this world, and will be once more in time."

She nodded, knowing he spoke the truth. A vision of the sky filled with flying beasts came to her, with a magnificent midnight-blue dragon leading the horde.

"This is your egg, Aurora. Yours and Therron's."

"What?"

She'd heard wrong. Her mind was fuzzy from the healing. She thought she'd heard him say this was hers and Therron's egg, as if that made perfect sense.

❧ 30 ❧

The fire licked up the egg's sides, turning the onyx shell deep amber. Rori stared at the egg as if it could give her answers. Aimon had tried to explain what he'd meant, but she shut him down. She was too tired, her mind too scrambled with the spells and healing to understand what he was saying. A hearty meal, perhaps a good night's rest, she'd told him, and she'd be ready for whatever nonsense he spouted.

Her sleep had been fitful at best, and her stomach too sour for food. And so here she stood, confused, hungry, and tired.

Therron. She sent the thought out to the ether. *I need you.* But she didn't send that last part.

Rori, where are you? Therron's voice whispered in her mind, and she nearly cried with happiness to hear him.

The Seelie Palace. I've released all of Acelyne's victims. She didn't tell him of the ones she'd taken from Hunter's labs. Of those, there were no survivors, only tiny corpses if anything at all. They'd had a midnight ceremony where

Eirlys blessed the beings and used her power to turn them into sparkling lights that rose to the heavens. *They have yet to wake.*

I'll be there as soon as I can. Wait for me.

I'm leaving for Midna's soon.

Silence answered.

Therron?

More silence. A wild idea formed that she should go to Elvenwood. Therron might be there, and if not, then she could ask Eiodian to return with her to the Seelie Palace. He was the best healer she'd ever met. If he couldn't wake the sleeping victims, she didn't know who could. Besides Meg. Together, they would be unstoppable.

"We're ready, Rori," Aimon said from the doorway, and she jumped at the intrusion. "I didn't mean to startle you."

"I was just thinking about how best to tell Midna."

"I don't envy you that conversation. Some of the courtiers told me she is quite formidable." He held out his arms. "What do you think?"

He wore a collarless tunic in varying shades of green, a color she didn't think suited him well at all. Nor did the cut of the tunic do anything for his fit body. The loose trousers were even worse.

"Did Eirlys have this commissioned?"

He nodded and Rori snort-laughed.

"It looks great. Come on, let's get this over with."

If Aimon didn't realize Eirlys was setting him up, she wasn't about to tell him. Midna could make up her own mind if she found the dragon shifter attractive. They walked through the silent palace, and Rori instinctively scanned the rooms. Tug and her mum left earlier that morning, and Rori felt the sting of guilt. She should be the one searching for Meg. He was her best friend and Meg was like family. But he'd been happy to have her mum join him, a little too happy, if she were honest. And, she reminded herself, Meg was one of Labhruinn's best friends.

The guilt worsened—Meg wasn't like family; she was family. She'd have to divulge the truth of that sooner rather than later. It wasn't a conversation she was looking forward to. Almost less than the one she'd have with Midna in a short while.

They used Eirlys's Room of Mirrors and arrived at Midna's palace within minutes. Aimon chortled at their use of doorways.

"It is so much easier to fly. I wish you had wings, Rori."

"Same, my friend." She clapped him on the back. Then, in a more serious tone, she said, "Midna can be a bit much. She's a highly sexualized creature, but I think that's just a front. What I'm trying to say is, don't be offended if she insists you sleep with her."

"Why would I be offended?"

"You'll see." She grinned enigmatically and led him out of the room.

A squad of Midna's guards waited for them and escorted the pair to Midna's private rooms. Rori suppressed a gasp when they walked into the sitting room. In the previous times Rori had been privileged enough to be in the queen's personal space, the rooms were tidy—immaculate, even— now, it was chaos. Clothes were strewn across couches and chairs, servants hustled here and there in a tizzy. Rori stared at the mayhem, searching for but not finding Midna in the madness.

"Rori, I'm so happy you're here. Help me with this, won't you?" Midna appeared as if from thin air and scared the crap out of Rori. It was due to her training that she didn't yelp, although she did almost pull a dagger on the unsuspecting queen.

"What's going on?" Rori pointed to the room. "Are you moving palaces for the summer?"

"Of course not. Tonight is the new moon. I must refresh my energy and repay my álainn obedience for their good service." Midna cocked her head and scrutinized Aimon's clothing. "Who is this?"

"Your Majesty," Rori began with a flourish, "may I present to you my friend Aimon."

Midna's eyes narrowed and a small smile played at her lips. "Did you come from the Seelie Court?" At Rori's nod, Midna continued. "I see. Most unfortunate." She clapped her hands and a maid appeared instantly. "Get some garments for this gentleman. Nobility, I should think." She gazed at Aimon, and he smirked. "No, not nobility. Royal. Elven."

The servant bowed and scampered away without a word.

Rori gaped at her queen. "Damn. You're good." Rori had guessed he was a prince, but because he'd never told her personally, she kept her opinion to herself. It was nice to know she wasn't wrong.

"I am honored to make your acquaintance." He waved a hand at the room. "Is there anything I can do to help?"

Midna's grin would've put the Cheshire Cat out of business. "If you wouldn't mind?" She turned her back to him and presented her gown with about a thousand tiny buttons.

Rori hid her relief that she wouldn't have to fight with the blasted things. Aimon, however, had the deft fingers of a dactlys and managed the buttons within a minute.

Midna flicked a glance to Aimon. "You may stay with me, if you wish. I would be honored if you shared my bed tonight. After the celebrations, I will be ravenous."

"It's a sex party, Aimon," Rori stated bluntly. Better he know what he was getting into and not be surprised. "Multiple partners, choose your own adventure kind of thing."

Midna sniffed. "I wouldn't put it so obscenely. It is a necessary part of being the Unseelie queen."

"It exhausts you, Midna. You give too much of yourself. Even though you think it refills your well, it depletes you." Rori put her hand on Midna's arm to soothe her harsh words. "You deserve love, too."

"I love my subjects, Rori. You wouldn't understand. If I'm not mistaken, you refused me, as did your brother, and that wicked thief Therron." Midna turned to Aimon. "Since you're an elven prince, you must know that rascal Therron Mistwalker, cursed prince of Elvenwood."

"Therron and I have met, yes. Though under unconventional circumstances." Aimon glanced at Rori with a curious expression. "He and I share a common interest."

"Ah, I see. You are in love with Rori. Fair enough." Midna held up her hands. "I won't be heartbroken again. Therefore, I will not pursue you."

Aimon chuckled, low and deep and sexy as hell. "I am fond of Rori, yes, but her heart is woven with only one other, and I would never try to sever that bond. I'm honored you asked me to join in your festivities tonight, but I'm afraid I am not looking for that kind of relationship. If it is as Rori says, perhaps you need only one person to fulfill you, not many."

"I think you both have forgotten I am queen here. I do not have to listen to some mysterious and quite handsome elven prince tell me what I need. Stay or go, it matters not to me."

Midna was a master planner, manipulator—whatever word she spun, it was the same result: Midna always got her way. And now she was playing her usual game of pretending to not care.

"Your Majesty," Rori said with emphasis on those two words. "I can't stay because I must go to Elvenwood. If Aimon wishes to stay with you, that is his choice." She looked at the elven prince. "Or you could come to Elvenwood with me."

He looked from her to Midna, his face softening. There was a connection between them, that much was obvious. Rori nodded her acceptance of the mission and turned to leave. Halfway to the door, she remembered why they'd come to Midna's and stopped dead in her steps. Her gut twisted and for two full breaths, she debated not telling the queen that her sister was lying comatose at Eirlys's palace.

"Your Majesty," Rori returned to Midna's side and took her hand in her own, "I came here to tell you that Mairead has been found."

Midna's eyes grew wide with anxiety and dread. "Where is she?"

"She's at Eirlys's palace. She was one of the kidnapped fae."

Midna started to pull her hands from Rori's grip, and she held fast.

"She's free from the amulet, but not yet awakened." Rori searched Midna's eyes, her heart pinching at the pain she saw. "I was able to release them, but they remain in a deep sleep. She is being looked after and well cared for. There is nothing you can do right now for your sister." She kept her gaze level with Midna's.

Tears flowed elegantly over Midna's cheeks. "But she is alive?"

"Yes."

"I need to see her."

"Of course. Aimon can go with you to Eirlys's court."

Midna looked around her room as if lost. "My subjects are expecting a celebration tonight. I hate to disappoint them."

"Your Majesty, there is no harm in putting your subjects' needs first. Nor is there shame in canceling the festivities for your sister. Only you can decide which you choose." Aimon's eyes darkened as he looked intensely at the queen. "There is nothing you can do for your sister right now. We have used the most powerful healing at our disposal. The patients will waken when it is their time. Eirlys has talented healers looking after your sister."

The queen looked small and frightened and innocent as she stood between Rori and Aimon. She'd never noticed before that they were of the same height. She'd always thought of Midna as larger than life. Midna's wings vibrated and her hair turned a silvery shade of white.

Aimon placed his arm around Midna and pulled her into a close embrace. The queen was so distraught, she allowed him to escort her to a sofa, where servants cleared a space for the pair and he sat with Midna cuddled into him.

The servants barely paid the couple any heed, but Rori watched them with a mixture of awe and hope. Off to the side, standing close enough he could attend Midna if she desired, Rori saw the fae who had always been part of Midna's orgies, the gorgeous creature she'd once worried was her own brother servicing the queen, and her heart broke at the expression on his face. Despair burrowed into the lines on his forehead, but she also saw resignation in his eyes. He loved his queen enough to know when to step aside for her happiness.

His gaze landed on Rori, and she inclined her head in silent acknowledgment that she understood his sorrow. To lose someone you loved was never easy. It didn't matter how they were taken, through death or by a stranger who gave care and comfort…it hurt. Rori had always wondered why Midna didn't love the fae in return, and now she saw clearly that even though the queen loved all her subjects, and especially her álainn obedience, the love she gave and received wasn't the deep, forever type of emotional bond Rori knew Midna craved. Most people craved, she would imagine.

She had it with Therron, but not because of a curse—although even if it was the damned curse, she didn't care anymore. She loved him, truly, madly, deeply.

Cian and Nikala had the same bond. She thought of her mother and father, and wondered whether they'd had that bond at one time. Somehow she doubted Hunter ever had, but her mum most certainly did. In a way, her mum was the handsome fae who stood looking forlorn and a little lost.

She snickered as she imagined introducing the two in the hopes they might find a spark together in their desolation.

At some point, she'd become a hopeful romantic. Possibly at the same point she'd admitted to herself that having someone in her life to care for her, and look after her, wasn't such a terrible thing. She'd spent so long convincing herself she needed no one, that she was a lone wolf, that she'd almost believed it. Almost, but never entirely. Damn that thief Therron. He'd waltzed right into her life and stolen her heart.

31

The city of Elvenwood was just waking across the wide canyon that separated the palace from the city proper. Therron dragged a hand through his short hair and let out a long breath. He'd spent the previous day doing damage control. His mother relented in her blaming him for Dithers's death, but kept a frosty distance from him. He'd had a meeting with his father that led to nothing of importance considering the king could barely string two sentences together.

Whatever reprieve he'd been given from the bloom Taryn had created with the elvenwood tree, that was long past. More than ever, King Thane was mad.

It divided Therron's loyalties. He should stay and watch over the king, but without Rori publicly declaring her love for him and breaking the curse, he had no true power at the palace. Now, with his mother acting strangely and knowing there was someone at the palace who knew about Acelyne's potions, quite possibly his mother, he felt the need to follow that line of investigation.

And then there was Rori. He'd heard her in his mind, but then she went silent. He'd told her to wait for him. He scrubbed a hand over his face. Too many threads pulling him in opposite directions. At least he'd been able to meet with Theo and Rainne and tell them everything he'd learned at Galo's, and what was happening in the human realm. They were caught up on all the events in case Therron couldn't return for some reason.

With the way events were playing out, he worried for both realms. All the realms, actually. Known and unknown.

Theo had repeated to Therron the remarkable story Rainne shared of how Taryn and Rhoane turned into dragons and flew off for Faerie. Adding that, upon their return, his mother ordered the guard to shoot them from the sky. Therron's back twitched and he adjusted his shoulders to relieve the incessant itch. He cycled his thoughts back to Rhoane, and his insistence Therron was Eleri. Once he returned from Faerie, he would research whether being Eleri had anything to do with having a dragon soul.

"Your bath is ready, sir." A servant bowed to him and left his rooms.

Therron stripped off the clothes he used to love, but now felt like a prison. The long robe used to represent freedom to him, but with each passing moment at the palace, he saw all the ways elves held themselves above others, including in their garments. There was no personalization, no individuality, only a uniformness that marked them as elven.

He stepped into the steaming water and allowed his body to adjust to the temperature before sliding all the way into the tub. His muscles relaxed, but his mind continued to spin.

Gentle Galo didn't care about dress codes or uniformity—something Therron had once abhorred but now saw as wonderfully quirky. He and Theo had discussed the elven elitism, and his baby brother agreed that the elven culture needed to change. They clung to the old ways so hard it was stifling them as a race.

He washed his hair and rinsed with fresh water the servant had left on a table beside the tub. His mother would be livid if she knew he was bathing himself, but that was her problem. Therron had tasted freedom from such things on his travels outside the elven kingdom. He was more than capable of washing his own body. And dressing himself. And about a million other things his mother was either incapable of, or refused doing on her own. Neither of which Therron saw as a positive trait.

It hurt his heart to contemplate that his mother might be involved with the troubles that were plaguing Cilachaem. His father had mentioned briefly the need to invade the faerie lands, but Therron had told him there was no need. The king had looked at him as if he saw—truly saw—his son and nodded sagely, but then his eyes clouded again and the moment was lost. His mutterings of war began anew.

"Care for some company?"

Therron jerked his attention to the doorway where Rori leaned against the frame, a wicked smile on her lips.

"Absolutely." Therron scooched back to allow her room and watched with keen interest as she shed her clothing piece by piece. She still wore human clothes, but not the same ones he last saw her in. His heart pinched at the memory of what Hunter had done to her. "I thought you were at Midna's."

She pulled her glorious cobalt hair into a high bun and gingerly entered the tub. "So you did hear me. I wasn't sure since you went silent."

"I didn't go silent." They shared a look, and Therron's nerves snapped. "You're here now. We can talk all we'd like."

It felt so good to see her and hear her voice. He reached for her and pulled her near.

"I've missed you." She stretched her legs to either side of him and wrapped her arms around his shoulders. "You have no idea how much."

"I'm pretty sure I know exactly how much." His lips closed on hers, and she moaned against him.

His cock twitched, and she smiled. A moment later, she adjusted herself and slid over his erection. Therron's groan rumbled between their mouths. Rori's tongue swirled along his, teasing, tasting, turning him on until he was mad with desire.

"I'd say you missed me a whole lot." She arched away from him while simultaneously grinding her pelvis against his body, taking him deeper.

His breath came in short gasps as his need grew. Water sloshed over the sides of the tub, soaking her clothes, but she didn't seem to notice or care. Therron thrust up as much as he could. She had him pinned to the porcelain basin, but he didn't mind one little bit. Her pussy clenched around his cock, and she gasped.

Her nails dug into his shoulders and she leaned forward, her mouth searching for his. Their lips crushed together in a fevered need to close any gaps between them. Rori ground against him in a rhythmic motion that kept him firmly inside her and drove him wild. His fingers scraped down her back, and she whimpered. A moment later, he gripped her hips and she broke contact with his mouth to cry out.

"Bloody hell, Therron. You feel so good. We're so good. I need this."

"We need this." Therron pushed upward, and she bit her lip.

His need spiraled out of control. The heat of the bath, the nearness of his love…it all combined to make him light-headed. She arched again, and he grasped her nipple with his mouth, lashing his tongue against the sweet bud.

"Oh fudgesticks, yessssss." Rori's entire body went rigid for a heartbeat before vibrating with her release. Her cries and whimpers were music to his ears.

His grip on her waist increased, and he withheld his own release to enjoy the sensations of her pussy clenching against his aching cock. When he couldn't hold it a moment longer, he let go with a low groan that shook them both.

She rested her head against his shoulder, her breaths coming hard and fast. His heartbeat matched hers in its rampant pace. When she looked at him, her face was soft and dewy, her brilliant blue eyes full of emotion. She stroked a hand over his cheek, and he felt her magic healing the scratches the scyver had left. Then she smoothed his scar and he saw something new in her eyes, something he didn't recognize. It wasn't fear or anxiety. More like awe.

"What is it?" The tremor in his voice gave away the insecurity he fought to hide. Just like she hid her unicorn soul, he also hid something within himself that he feared if she found it, she might find reason not to love him.

"You are the most remarkable man I've ever met. Just when I think I couldn't love you more, you prove I can." Her lips brushed his, and he sucked them into his mouth. She giggled but didn't fight him.

Lucien's admonition to accept his true self floated through his mind, and with Rori's declaration, he believed it possible she would never leave him. Still, the fear rested just inside his every thought. A unicorn was one thing, but what he feared was inside himself…that was something else entirely. A beast. A monster. A myth.

When she withdrew from the kiss, he helped her out of the tub and dried her off with a soft towel. He held her close, never wanting to let go. His eyes searched hers, the questions he longed to ask resting on his tongue. They could wait another few minutes until she was ready. He didn't want to barrage her with an interrogation so soon after their reunion.

"I released all the trapped beings in the vials."

She said it so plainly that he thought he misheard. Then the words sunk in and he pulled back to study her features.

"Did they all survive?"

"The ones we brought to Eirlys, yes. But the ones I took from Hunter's lab in Venice." She shook her head sadly. "There was no help for them. But," she held up a hand to prevent his next question, "I wasn't able to wake them. That's not all." She picked up her soggy shirt and tossed it into the air before using her magic to dry it. She did the same to the rest of her clothes before finishing what she was saying. "Your brother Thaddeus is one of Acelyne's victims."

Even though he knew it was true, and had expected to

hear the words, they still hit him in the solar plexus like a brutal punch.

"Is he well?"

"No." She took his hand and kissed his knuckles. "I'm sorry, Therron. I think he was sick before Acelyne kidnapped him."

Therron walked naked to his room and opened the bureau drawer. He withdrew the two bottles he'd stolen from Gentle Galo's lounge. "Acelyne poisoned him with something. I found these at Galo's, but he doesn't know where they came from. Acelyne would bring him crates full of the stuff. He called it amrita. I couldn't find any information on it."

Rori took one of the bottles to inspect. "I came here to ask Eiodian if he could help Eirlys's healers revive the victims. Do you think he could do tests or something on what's in these bottles to find an antidote or cure? If she gave some to Thaddeus, she probably gave the same stuff to all of us."

He reached for his trousers and a tunic. "Possibly. But I doubt Eiodian would go to Faerie. He's needed here to deal with my father's madness." Therron held the second bottle. "This changes things, and yet, it changes nothing. We need to let Theo and Rainne know these new developments." He took the bottle from her and returned them both to the drawer. "Anything else happen at the Seelie Palace I should know about?"

He turned toward her and froze at the terrified look on her face. An instant later, it melted into a cheeky smile. "So much." She took his clothing and lay it over a chair before striding to his bed and climbing atop the linens. "Why don't you call for some food and then join me? We can have breakfast, make a little love, and tell each other everything that's happened since we last saw each other."

Therron's blood warmed and he felt the stirrings of an erection. Before either of them could change their minds, he dashed to his bed and joined Rori. He'd call for food later, but right then, there was something even more delicious he needed to taste.

He lay her back on a pile of pillows, noting the sweet smile that danced on her lips. Slowly, he left a trail of kisses down her chest to her abdomen and then lower. Her scent drove him wild, but he kept a steady pace, knowing full well he was teasing her mercilessly. By the way she gripped the duvet cover, he didn't think she minded.

Rori splayed her legs open, and he nestled between them. There was nowhere else he'd rather be than right there, with her. The rest of the world could wait for an afternoon. He lowered his head and breathed in her essence, his cock painfully hard against the soft mattress. The first flick of his tongue to her outer lips sent desire spinning through him.

His back itched as if something wished to rip through his flesh, and he shifted as if to scratch an itch that couldn't be satiated. Though he tried his best to ignore the sensation, the more he sucked and licked, the more he felt as if he were floating, his mind dizzy, his body weightless. Rori's whimpers and cries filled him in unexpected ways—as if her pleasure were his own. Her release vibrated throughout his body; her desire compounded his own.

With her juices still wet on his lips, she pulled him even with her and sucked his mouth as if milking the sweetness of their lovemaking. Then she wrapped her legs around him, and he slid into her waiting pussy. He felt her ache, her need, and returned it.

She watched him with those incredible eyes that seemed to see everything, visible or not. His back twitched, and she grinned as if she knew what lurked in the depths of his soul. He thrust into her, his release building, and she matched his tempo with each press of her hips upward. It was too much. His breathing quickened, his blood warming until it felt like fire beneath his skin.

Rori never looked away. The serene smile on her lips never faltered. Sweat ran in rivulets down his back, and she traced her hands through the slickness.

"Let go, Therron."

The words were whispered for only him to hear.

He wanted to. The gods knew, he did. But if he truly let go, he feared the beast would rip through his skin and leave him nothing more than a lifeless carcass.

❦ 32 ❦

The sun was hours from setting and Rori was restless. They'd spent most of the day in Therron's bed, nourishing their bodies with more than just food. He told her about the lab and Maxx; she told him about Hunter's torture. She was surprised to learn he already knew some of the story—some sort of elven magic that allowed him to project past events from a connection to the person. In this case, her blood.

They'd made love several times, each amazing, but she kept circling back to the moment when she'd told him to let go and she saw terror in his eyes. She'd meant to orgasm, but now, after half a day of pondering his reaction, she knew she'd meant it for something far more important. Every time she tried to bring it up, the words sat heavy on her lips.

She told him nearly everything that had happened at the Seelie Palace, but how the futnucker did she tell him that she found a dragon's egg—their egg, allegedly—in one of the vials without sounding like a complete loon? Her heart beat in her throat and she choked, trying to swallow. She wanted him to know. He needed to know. But her gut told her it would be best if he found out in person where he could see and touch the blasted thing. Then maybe she would understand what frightened him so much.

"Meg is missing." She traced his bicep with her forefinger. "Mum and Tug went to look for her. Midna is having one of her sex parties tonight. I think Aimon's still there, but he might've gone back to Eirlys's since he wasn't interested in participating in the festivities."

"Aimon? You took a dragon to Faerie?" Therron scraped his hands through his short hair. "Rori, there are no dragons in Cilachaem. What were you thinking?"

Rori blinked at him several times before dawning crossed her features. "Ooohh, you don't know. I didn't realize you only saw Aimon in his dragon form. He's an elven prince from another world."

Therron sputtered, but no tangible words came out. Finally, he managed, "This is insane. My father's looking for a reason for war, and you might've just brought it to his doorstep."

"Aimon is harmless. He healed me, and tried to help with the victims, but in the end it didn't work." She didn't understand his irrational behavior. Cilachaem had trolls and orcs and all kinds of creatures. Why his father would cause a war over a single dragon shifter made no sense.

"Fine. There's an elven dragon at Midna's court. Any other surprises?"

"Hmmm, I think that's it. Oh, Mairead was one of the

victims." How she'd forgotten about that detail, she wasn't sure. That's right. Therron's wicked tongue and that delightful cock of his. She was lucky she could form two sentences after their day of debauchery. "Mairead is Midna's sister."

"I know who Mairead is." His look softened, and he looked away. "Midna must be inconsolable."

"She is, but she said she needs to be there for her subjects tonight. Something about the new moon and repaying them for being amazing sex slaves."

Therron nodded, but she wasn't sure he was even listening. A buzz of jealousy went through her, but she shut it down. Therron had never participated in Midna's midnight orgies and it would do no good to start imagining him at one now.

"Something wrong?" She smoothed a hand over his arm, and he jerked his attention to her.

"Nothing. I was just thinking…two high-ranking royals. Why did Hunter need them?"

"For the same demented reason he needed any one of the others. He's cruel."

Therron leaned forward and brushed her lips with his. Her body immediately warmed and she felt the familiar tingle between her legs. He was turning her into his own kind of sex slave, and she didn't mind at all.

"More?"

He shook his head, his brows furrowed, but a chuckle came from his chest. "Not that I wouldn't love to, but we really should see to saving our world and the human realm." He nipped her nose with his teeth and she play-yelped.

"If you insist. I mean, if we don't, who will?" She rolled

off the bed and strolled to where she'd left her clothes that morning. "Should I dress in elven garb?"

"Absolutely not."

"Wow. Sassy Therron. I like it. Is there a reason you're trying to piss off your mother?"

"I'm hoping we won't see her. After that business with Dithers, I'm still quite vexed with her."

Rori nodded, but said nothing. Strange potions, a dead seneschal, the king mad…it was a bit much, even for the elven court. If he didn't want to see the queen, that was fine by her. Their last meeting hadn't gone so well. She'd prefer to avoid any more altercations with both the king and queen.

Therron pulled on his trousers and tunic before he reached into the depths of the drawer where he kept the bottles and pulled out a wooden box about the size of her hand.

She cocked her head. "More treasures of ill repute?"

"Something like that." He grinned and opened the box. The grin slipped, and he stared at the contents. "What the hell?"

Rori peered into the box and shuddered. "Isn't that the ring Rowan wore?"

"The ring he stole from my brother Theo." Therron held the other two items in the box in place with his fingers, and tipped the ring along with bits of broken obsidian and black dust into the palm of his hand. "What could cause this?"

Rori pressed a fingertip into the glittery substance. Immediately, the vision she'd seen when she traveled through the in-between to Faerie returned with a vengeance. This time, she clearly saw Taryn and Rhoane defeating the snake-dragon-demon, but then she saw them remove the disc they'd been searching for and the horrid monster dissolved, turning into the rainbow-hued lights that now illuminated the in-between. The next vision was of the ring in Therron's box cracking and turning to dust.

"Remarkable." Therron watched her as if he saw the vision, too. "The ring controlled the demon from the void. Once Taryn and Rhoane—"

"And Kaida."

"And Kaida destroyed it, the ring no longer held power." He returned the bits of obsidian and black dust to the box with the now impotent silver ring.

"You saw the vision, too?"

"I did."

"Huh. Weird, right?"

"That I saw the vision or the ring breaking?"

"Both. What are those?" Rori pointed to a brown disc that made her heart stutter. Next to it was a tiny vial, no bigger than her thumbnail. She wrapped her fingers around the amethyst she'd created in Paris.

Therron cleared his throat and held out the two items. "I found some of your dried blood atop the cathedral in Paris and put it in here. It's silly, I know, but it made me feel closer to you." He glanced at her with apprehension, and she felt her heart pinch.

"You must've been mad with worry. I wanted to reach out, I truly did, but feared Hunter would find you."

"I know. Lucien told me you were safe, but still…I couldn't be sure until I saw you this morning." He stroked her cheek, and she leaned into his touch. The bed was so close… "This is a dragon scale." He held up the brown disc.

"You're shitting me." But she knew it was true. And she knew whose scale it was.

"I would never lie to you. Lucien sent me a message embedded in the scale." He swiped a hand across his unmarked cheek. "Then a scyver attacked me. Thank you for healing me."

The ease with which he held the dragon scale made her believe he wouldn't think she was insane for telling him there was a dragon egg waiting for them at the Seelie Court. Although they told each other of their time apart, she suspected there was still so much she didn't know about his time in London, and that he didn't know about her time first with Hunter, and then in Faerie. Things forgotten in the moment that they'd remember later. Trivial things. Perhaps even some important things. Memory was funny that way. It didn't bother her, just made her curious to know more.

She glanced around his room, her gaze lingering on his bed. Her body warmed and a smile flitted across her lips.

"I know what you're thinking and there will be time for that later. Right now, we need to talk to Theo and Rainne." He pocketed the scale and vial. "I'll give him the ring for safekeeping. We don't know its power or if it can be restored."

Rori suppressed a shudder. She liked knowing the snake-dragon-demon thing was dead. Her shoulder throbbed as if in agreement.

They took the servants' corridors to avoid seeing the queen and found Theo in his tower, studying the stars. Rainne sat in a chair nearby, with her cat Pora curled in her lap. Therron gave Theo the ring and explained what had happened to it. Neither Theo nor Rainne seemed surprised by anything they told them, and Rori wondered what, exactly, they'd witnessed at the elven court to be so calm about it all. Even learning his brother was lying comatose in Faerie didn't alarm Theo. He took in the information like a true king—without drama, but to be assessed and acted upon in due course.

Rori realized with a start that if she broke Therron's curse, he would become heir to the elven throne, and yet, watching Theo and Rainne, she couldn't help sensing it was their destiny to rule the elven kingdom. She reached a hand to Therron and gripped it harder than she should. Events were moving too fast to contemplate and yet at a snail's pace.

They left Theo and Rainne in the tower and made their way to the healing wards. As they passed the great elven-wood tree, Rori's steps slowed.

"Is something the matter?" Therron scanned the halls for potential threats.

"He's healed." Rori looked up to the ceiling, where branches stretched far and wide. Huge white blossoms dotted the green canopy. "Taryn and Rhoane healed him." She didn't know how she knew, but she just knew. She went to the tree and put her arms around the trunk. "I'm happy you're feeling better." She kissed the bark and placed her cheek against the tree.

Therron joined her and held her hand in his, with his other circling around the massive trunk. "He says he's happy you're feeling better, too."

Rori heard the tree in her mind saying as much. "I know."

You and young Therron have much more to do, and time is not on your side.

What are we supposed to do now?

Stop the madman. Prevent a war.

Oh, that's all? She snickered but found nothing funny about his warning. *We're working on it. Be well, friend.* She squeezed the tree once more before disengaging and taking Therron's hand in her own. Stop the madman—that was Hunter. Prevent a war—that was King Thane.

"Our dads are kinda dicks."

Therron led her up the stairs and kissed her hand. "Not kinda. They are total dicks."

Snickertits, but she loved him. They would win. They had to.

Unlike the circuitous route it took to find Theo and Rainne, their search for Eiodian was much simpler. He was in the healing wards, studying the fang that had once been impaled in Rori's shoulder. Again, it throbbed as if in memory and she wondered whether there was something lasting from the wound. But sentient injuries weren't something she'd ever heard of. Didn't mean it couldn't happen; she just hoped it never did.

As Therron had warned, Eiodian refused to leave Elvenwood.

"My duty is first to your father, the king." The healer held up the bottle Therron had given him. "But I will do what I can to learn what this is and find an antidote or cure." He glanced over their shoulders and smiled. "Ah, here's the patient."

Therron and Rori turned in unison to see an attractive young man walking toward them. Messy black hair flopped across his forehead, and deep-brown eyes watched them with apprehension. Rori glanced at Therron, who shook his head, and then back to Eiodian.

"I don't know this man."

"Oh, but you do." He indicated the man join them. "Rajesh, this is Prince Therron and his beloved Aurora MacNair. Her brother Cian is the man who brought you here."

Rori's mouth dropped open. "You're the lycan? But how?"

"I'm fully restored." Rajesh placed his hand over his heart and inclined his head to her and Therron. "I am so grateful for everything you did for me." He tapped his chest. "I can feel you both in here. Without your healing, I wouldn't have made it."

"Taryn and Rhoane had a lot to do with your recovery." Therron gripped the man's hand. "We're grateful to have helped."

"Your magic? Did it come back?" Rori remembered all too well the stump she'd envisioned when the group was healing him. Charred and blistered, it looked beyond repair.

"For the most part, but I'll tell you honestly, if it hadn't, I would be just as happy. It was my magic that got me into trouble in the first place."

Rori felt a pinch of guilt. "I'm sorry Hunter did that to you."

Rajesh looked at her as if she said frogs could fly. "But you have nothing to apologize for. It was that horrid man who stole my magic, not you. Please don't feel guilty on my behalf. I have nothing but love for the pair of you." He looked over their shoulders. "And for Rhoane, Taryn, and their wild beast Kaida. She kept me company when I felt most assured I would die. I'd like to thank them in person."

Eiodian cleared his throat. "I'm afraid they're gone. I didn't tell you for fear you might backslide. You were making such good progress. I apologize for the deception."

Rajesh took this in with a look of sorrow crossing his features. "I understand. Probably would've done the same thing in your position." He patted his waist, his hands running down the tunic he wore. His gaze lingered on Rori's jeans. "You're from Earth. Er, the human realm."

"I'm from Faerie, but I spend time in the human realm." It was too long a tale to explain, so she kept her explanation short. "Cian said he found you in London."

"I would like to return." His gaze flicked to Eiodian. "If you feel I'm ready?"

Eiodian sighed and scrubbed a hand over his face. "There's nothing more I can do for you here, but I worry about you doing too much once you're home."

"Home." The word sounded like a whispered wish on Rajesh's lips. "My poor wife and children are probably worried sick about me."

"We'll take you home," Rori blurted. "I'm sure you'll heal even quicker once you're with your loved ones." She implored Eiodian and Therron to agree. She might've even batted an eyelash or two.

"Fine. Take him, but I would like progress updates."

Rori clapped her hands and nearly hugged the stoic elf. "Thank you, Eiodian. You're a fantastic healer. He's going to be fine. Aren't you?" She gave Rajesh an encouraging smile.

"Absolutely."

She pretended to ignore the lack of certainty in his

voice. If only for Eiodian's sake, she'd make sure to check in on Rajesh as often as she could. Her enthusiasm for returning him to London wasn't purely altruistic. She was looking forward to seeing Cian and Nikala even though there was still much to do in Faerie. Like stop a madman. Prevent a war.

33

The doorway lengthened, and Therron stepped from the darkness into the musty cellar. Rajesh stumbled into the cellar, coughing and sputtering. He'd been a lycan the first time Cian had taken him through, but as a man, he didn't understand or enjoy the trip. As he'd said many times in the minutes it took to go from Elvenwood to London.

"If I never do that again, it will be too soon. Bloody hell, that is—why is that a thing? Who invented it?"

Rori patted him on the shoulder and gave a sympathetic chortle. "You get used to it. My first use of the doorways, I didn't breathe the entire time. But now, I prefer it."

"You're insane, Aurora MacNair. Certifiable."

"I know." She grinned. "I'll be checking in on you. No tricks, okay? Stay away from scyvers and magic. I mean it."

Rajesh grimaced. "I'll do what I can. But when the full moon comes, I'm not sure I can ignore the call."

It was something they'd spoken about at length, with no real solution. He was a lycan. Therron just hoped he had enough time before the next full moon to recover completely. He would need the strength to fight his impulses.

At the top of the stairs, Donyatella gave Rajesh a quick once-over before turning her attention to Therron. She directed him to a booth, where two gentlemen sat talking. Rori bid Rajesh farewell and strolled to the table. Therron followed, unease gripping his guts like an ogre a turkey leg at the Beltane feasts.

"Who's this?" Rori indicated Kaen.

Lucien gave Therron a questioning glance. "You didn't tell her?"

"Tell me what?"

His gut twisted. "Not yet. I was distracted."

"Well, since His Highness seems to have forgotten his manners, let me introduce you to Kaen Dalwood, one of the Dragon Lords of London."

"So, he's like you, but from here." Rori held out her hand. "Nice to meet you."

"Please. Join us." Kaen slid over to leave enough room for only Rori. She ignored him, and Therron curled his fists to keep from punching the man.

"I don't suppose these are needed now, but I have the letters you gave me to deliver to Therron and Cian." Lucien withdrew two sealed parchments from his pocket and handed them to Rori.

Her eyes narrowed, and she glanced up at Therron. "You never got this? But, in the in-between, I felt you."

"I sent that message before returning to Elvenwood. I didn't know where you were, but hoped it would reach you safely. I'm assuming it did?"

Her cheeks turned a sweet shade of pink. "This is for you." She handed him one of the notes and tucked the other into her trouser pocket. "Do you still have the other thing I left with you?" This was directed to Lucien.

He handed her a leather satchel, and she slipped the strap over her shoulder.

Therron felt Rori's magic in the parchment he held. His name was written on one side, and on the other, Rori had sealed the letter with her own blood. Her magic was soothing, but with a warning for anyone who was not him to leave well enough alone. Therron put the note in a hidden pocket of his tunic for later reading. He assumed whatever she had to say, he already knew. In case he was wrong, he didn't feel like sharing the contents with the two dragon lords.

"Where is Aimon?" Kaen asked.

"I left him at Midna's palace. I hope he's okay."

"I still can't believe you let her take a dragon to Faerie." Therron still believed Aimon's presence could cause trouble in Elvenwood. Though, he couldn't say for certain why. It probably had something to do with his mother ordering the palace guards to shoot Taryn and Rhoane from the sky when they flew off in their dragon forms. If only he'd had more time to grill Theo about what, exactly, had happened with the pair.

"If you think a woman like Rori allows anyone to let her do anything, then you really don't know her." Lucien crossed his arms with a silent challenge to Therron.

"Boys. Please. No fighting at the table. Lucien and Kaen, scoot over so that Therron and I can sit together." Rori scowled at both him and Lucien.

"Aimon is one of us," Lucien began. "Although he is an elf who can shift into a dragon. He went with Rori in his elven form."

"Let's hope he has the sense to remain in that form."

Lucien shook his head and explained Aimon's history to Therron. He listened with equal growing concern and fascination. A lone darathi from another world trapped in the human realm. It was almost too remarkable to be believed. Yet, had he not just met Taryn and Rhoane, he wouldn't have believed other worlds existed. Theo had always tried to tell him, but he'd not listened to his baby brother.

Donyatella brought them food, some kind of steaming meat dish with a flaky crust and smashed potatoes, and a thick, foamy drink. He thanked her, grateful for the refreshments. While he ate, he listened to Rori banter with the two dragon lords, his gut tightening with each minute that passed.

He knew his jealousy was misplaced, but it was easier than admitting the truth to himself. Lucien was a dragon lord, capable of becoming a dragon at his will. How could Rori not be impressed by that? The words of his mother echoed through his skull that he was a placeholder. Merely the heir until such a time as he would pass and then his brother would take the throne.

His whole life he'd been told he would never be more than a cursed prince. It was hard to shake off the past when the woman he loved—his curse breaker—was loathed by the two people who should've shown him unconditional love and acceptance. A momentary flutter in his skull pulled up the memory of his father demanding that he'd been promised Thad would sit on the Forest Throne. The king hadn't answered Therron when he asked who had promised him such a thing, but it didn't take a genius to figure it out. Why Hunter would give such assurances, that was the true riddle.

He winced at Kaen's boisterous laughter. The fool man was trying too hard to impress Rori, and he felt a twinge of embarrassment for the lad. Therron got up to use the facilities, and Lucien followed.

"She loves you, Therron," Lucien said once they were clear of the table. "But her love is new. She's been a spy for much longer than she's been in love, and that independence doesn't go away. Perhaps not ever. If you're honest with yourself, it's one of the reasons you love her, too."

Blood and ashes. The man was right, and that irritated Therron even more.

"If you're implying you know her better than I, then please, elucidate me on all her wonderful qualities, because I'm certain I could school you on certain aspects of Rori you'll never comprehend. I know she loves me." He just worried she wouldn't love all of him once the beast was revealed.

"What about the other part of my message?" Lucien watched him like a hawk choosing which hare to capture first.

"I know my true fate. Once Rori declares her love publicly, then I'll be the proper heir of Elvenwood."

Lucien sighed and shook his head. He opened his mouth to speak, but whatever he was about to say went unspoken. The dragon lord stared behind him, and Therron looked to see what had caused his abrupt silence.

Cian and Nikala approached, both looking relaxed,

and…strange for the pair…happy. Therron noticed the change in their gaits, the way they held hands, the softness of their bodies. Two highly skilled assassins, who he had the unfortunate pleasure of seeing in action, looked like a moonstruck couple courting each other. He abandoned his plan of escaping the dragon lords and returned to the table with Lucien right behind him.

"Dony says you need to see us?" Cian gave Therron a questioning glance. "And you aren't supposed to be here." Cian's gaze then went to his sister. "Nor you. What the hell, Rori?"

"Last I checked, you're not the boss of me. I'm fine, by the way. Thanks for asking."

"Fine is debatable."

Rori scooted from the booth and gave her brother a fierce hug. "I missed you, too." She peeked over his shoulder. "And you, Nikala."

A look passed between the women, and Therron's heart ached at what they both had suffered at the hands of Hunter Pearson. The man would pay dearly for his cruelty.

Outside, a horrendous sound roared, unlike anything Therron had heard in nature. In this city? It was an everyday occurrence, but this was close. Far too close.

Nikala swore beneath her breath and pointed to Therron. "I'm happy you're alive, Rori, but you both need to go back to Elvenwood and stay there. I mean it."

Without waiting for their reply, she darted from the pub, with Cian following. A second later, Lucien ran from the booth and out the door. Therron ignored Nikala's command and sprinted to catch up with the others. He heard Rori give the satchel to the man behind the bar and threaten him with death if it was harmed. A moment later, she was at his side, her daggers drawn.

Nikala stared up the street that led to SIRE, her face a mixture of rage and disappointment. When she saw him, she stepped forward and thumped him on the chest. "Are you daft? I said leave." To Rori, she pleaded, "It's not safe for you here."

"It's not safe for us anywhere at the moment," Therron said. "And last I looked, you are not my queen. I refuse to run away when I can help."

"Gah! Hunter's men are here and it's you two they want. Hell, Hunter probably wants you to use as bait or leverage while he tortures Rori. You don't want to see that. Trust me."

"Then let's not give them what they want." He stood tall and faced her, his resolve set.

Nikala swore a stream of words that would make Therron's mother cower. When finished, she looked at Lucien. "Who are you?"

A roar sounded and drew Nikala's attention. "Dammit." She glanced at Cian. "I'm out of ammo. How about you?"

"A few shots left, maybe."

She cricked her neck and glared at Therron. "Guess you get to help."

Therron turned to Rori. "She's not wrong. I only went back to Elvenwood because Hunter's men were looking for me in Rome. With you here, they'll do whatever it takes to snatch you for Hunter. Stay close."

Her eyes grew cold, and she glared up the road. "I will never let them take me. Or you." She grinned at him. "He got the jump on both of us once already. It's time we turn the tables on that asshole."

"Agreed."

The roar came closer, a cacophony of sound similar to a thunderstorm across the tops of the mountains. Therron relaxed his shoulders and swung his arms in preparation for whatever was to come. It could've been a stampede of wild beasts, or those wretched two-wheeled vehicles that nearly ran him over every time he crossed one of London's streets. Horrible things.

Three motorbikes swarmed down the cobbled lane, their riders all clad in black with close-cropped hair like the man he fought in Geneva. Three more rode toward them from the other direction, effectively boxing them in.

The fact that enhanced soldiers were in London didn't surprise him. They were like lice, irritating as hell and diffi-cult to get rid of. The leader pointed to Therron, his muscled arm bulging from his rolled-up shirt.

As one, the others turned toward him, and he felt their rage like a blow to his sternum. Whatever Cian and Nikala had done in Rome, they blamed him for it.

"Get him!" the leader called out.

The motorbikes revved and raced toward Therron's group. He withdrew his sword and waited. Rori took up her stance at his side while Nikala, Cian, and Lucien were near one another, yet apart. The feel of someone's magic swirled close, surprising him. He'd been told over and over again not to use magic in the human realm.

The riders raced toward them, their bikes louder now that they were mere strides from his group. Cian crouched and sprang up to tackle one man, sending his bike sliding across the pavement. Another came near Therron, and he waited until he was nearly on him to swing his sword, slicing the man's arm clean off. He lost control of the motorbike and slammed onto the pavement, his head busting open like a melon. Therron spun around for the next attacker, his coat flaring out behind him.

An image came to him of midnight-blue wings spread wide from his back, and he caught Lucien's stunned expression. Therron's scar burned against his cheek, and he glanced over his shoulder to see whether the vision was real. Rori stood still in the middle of the mayhem, her expression one of wonder.

Behind her, another man on a motorbike raced straight at her.

"Rori, look out!"

She turned and threw a dagger, impaling the man in the throat.

Without missing a beat, she ran forward and leapt up to kick the man in the chest. He flew backward off the motorbike and tumbled ass over head until he lay on his back. Rori somersaulted toward him and withdrew her dagger before making a clean slice across his neck, killing him.

Seeing her brutal efficiency sent conflicting emotions through him that he didn't have time to sort through. Pride at her prowess, and cautious worry that she could kill someone without remorse. He reminded himself that she was a spy and assassin. It was literally her job to be this good.

He pulled his attention from the woman he loved and back to the battle. One of Hunter's band of merry soldiers gunned his motorbike straight toward Therron. For one mad moment, he considered letting the soldier capture him so that he could confront Hunter, but this wasn't the time. He steadied himself and held his sword in front of him with both hands. An internal light lit the blade, sending rays as bright as the sun outward. The man screamed and covered his eyes, losing control of the motorbike. The sound of metal crunching could be heard over the man's wails. Therron swooped low and stabbed the fallen man in his chest.

Rori stepped to his side, and he was aware of the similarities between him and her. She'd been trained in espionage; he'd been trained in warfare. Two sides of the same coin for different reasons. Both fatal.

Therron cast a glance to Nikala and Cian. They were embroiled in fistfights, which left only the leader.

He approached with a sinuous walk like a snake. If it was meant to be threatening, it only made him look ridiculous, and Therron chuckled.

"You won't be laughing when we take you to Hunter, pretty boy." His gaze flicked to Rori. "You and the girl."

Rori spun a dagger in the air, catching it with her forefinger and thumb. "You calling me a girl? I guess a dumbass like you wouldn't know a woman if she bit you in the scrotum."

"Now, now, little lady. Step aside and let the men handle this."

Rori scoffed and flipped her dagger again. "Whatever. You'll be dead in a minute." She moved several steps back, but close enough to intervene if necessary.

Therron kept quiet as he stalked the man, circling him with his sword held at his side. A firearm sat in a holster across the man's chest, and another gripped to his thigh, but the soldier didn't reach for them.

The scuffling behind him ended, and he heard heavy breathing coming from the victors. He flicked his gaze in that direction, and spied Cian wipe blood from Nikala's chin. Lucien and Kaen stood in the shadows of the pub, and Therron saw two of Dony's boys just inside the doorway. Useless twats. He wasn't a fan of their policy to not get involved. What Hunter did in the human realm affected everyone.

The soldier lunged and grabbed Therron's blade between the flats of his palms. The move was meant to surprise Therron, but his swordmaster had taught him well. Instead of faltering as was expected, Therron spun, ripping the sword from the man's grip, slicing his skin.

The soldier swore and shook his hands, blood dripping from the wounds. He reached for the gun at his thigh, but Therron was too quick. He plunged the blade into the man's chest and gave it a vicious twist. The sound of bones crunching echoed in the small courtyard, and the man dropped to his knees. His gaze locked to Therron's, his lips parted as if to speak.

Therron kicked the man and withdrew his sword, wiping it on the soldier's trousers before sheathing it at his waist.

"Damn, Therron." Cian clapped him on the back. "Honestly, I didn't know you had it in you. That was pretty slick for a thief."

Therron ignored Cian's pseudo-compliment. He sought Rori and felt a rush of relief that she was unharmed.

"I knew you had it in you." She slipped her hand into his.

Therron's gaze locked to Lucien's, who stared at him, an inner light shining from the shadows of his eyes.

At first, he thought the vision of the midnight-blue dragon was Lucien, but he knew deep down, it was his dragon he saw. And Lucien knew it. The dragon lord inclined his head and disappeared into the pub. Damn the man. There was no way Therron could deny his destiny now.

$\maltese$ 34 $\maltese$

Stone Guardians, and now this. There wasn't enough coffee in the world to prepare Nikala for this morning's surprise visitor. A dragon lord. Bloody hell, what next? Nikala looked to the ceiling and begged the gods not to answer. She could only imagine what would walk through the door, and it wouldn't be as attractive or polite as Lucien de Montague, she was certain of that. The other lord wasn't half bad looking, either. Unfortunately, he left for some unfinished business that didn't involve them.

Rori handed a laptop to her, and she nearly giggled at the sight of the familiar machine.

"This is Hunter's. Where did it come from?"

"I took it from Hunter's lab when I escaped." Rori shrugged as if it were no big deal.

"Well done." Nikala stroked the thing as if it were a favorite pet. "Do we know the password?"

"I changed it before leaving the lab." Rori pointed to the desk, and Nikala set the laptop next to hers.

Rori leaned over and opened the lid, and then typed in

a mix of symbols and letters. Cool relief spread through Nikala when the window opened.

"We're in. Ohmyfuckinggod, we're in." Nikala nearly fist pumped the air. "This is huge. Finally, we can get a jump on that motherfucker."

Cian grinned at her, and she shared a moment of jubilant excitement. This was the break they needed.

"Does it say where Hunter might be hiding?" Therron asked, and Cian frowned at the elf.

"If it did, do you expect us to tell you? For all we know, you'd race after him half-cocked and put everyone in danger. Again." Cian crossed his arms.

"I know you're vexed with me, fine. I understand your ire, but Rori and I returned for very good reasons. We brought the lycan you rescued back home. Surely you can understand why that was more important than staying on Cilachaem."

She knew Cian could, but he wouldn't tell Therron as much. Stupid pride or something equally as macho. She rolled her eyes at the man she loved.

"You knew Hunter's thugs were looking for you. You could have at least stayed more than an hour in Faerie."

In truth, Therron had been gone for as long as they'd been at Lake Como, but Cian wouldn't let his anger go. As for her, she was glad Hunter's men had attacked them. That was six fewer she and Cian would have to hunt down.

"If I am guilty of anything, I shouldn't have killed the leader until he confessed where we can find Hunter." Therron looked contrite, and she felt a pang of sympathy for him. He didn't need Cian's attitude.

Nikala checked her phone and sighed. "Still no sign of

Hunter, and the laptop doesn't help. I know all his hidey-holes, but if he were there, they would show on my app." She tapped the screen on her phone. "Unless something's wrong with the app, or Hunter somehow managed to remove my tracker."

"Rori removed both a tracker and microchip all on her own. It's possible," Lucien said.

Cian stared at the dragon lord before turning his attention to his sister. "You removed them? Where were they?"

"A glass tube was in my belly, and what I assume was a mind fuck microchip was embedded in the base of my skull." Rori tapped the back of her neck to illustrate where she'd removed the microchip. "Aimon helped heal me with his tears."

"His tears?" Nikala snorted. Now she'd heard everything.

"Dragon tears are potent. Nearly as strong as unicorn blood," Lucien said without emotion.

Nikala flicked a glance to Rori, but she didn't react. Her poker face game was strong.

Cian cocked his head. "Aimon's also a dragon lord?"

"He is a prince of his kingdom, but not a dragon lord," Lucien corrected.

"This is tedious. Lord, prince, blah, blah, blah," Nikala mocked as she scanned the laptop. "Aren't there any dragon ladies or princesses in your kingdoms?" She'd meant it as a joke, but her gaze swept past Therron, and a chill slithered down her back. She hadn't told him she confessed everything to Cian, but she saw in his expression he was eager to know that she had.

Cian paced the office, making a lap around the sofas

and stopping at the credenza that held drinks. He poured himself a soda and asked whether anyone else wanted a refreshment. She asked for a soda, watching him the whole while. She knew he was processing something and would share it when it made sense in his mind. It was hell to wait, but usually worth it.

"Hunter might be in Faerie." Cian set her glass on the huge desk and faced the others. "It's been several days and we can't find him. The only logical explanation is he returned to Cilachaem and is either hiding out somewhere in Faerie, or the elven kingdom."

Therron's jaw tightened, and he crossed his arms as if to fight off the very idea of Hunter being in his homeland. But, according to him, he saw a shadowy vision of Hunter standing behind the king in the throne room. Either Hunter was very good at projecting himself, or he was in Elvenwood at some point.

"I told Mum almost everything. If Hunter is in Faerie, she'll find him. She's none too pleased he resurrected from the dead." Rori took a sip of her soda and covered a burp. "Though, I'm sure that was the least surprising thing she learned from me." Her gaze softened, and Nikala wondered what Rori hadn't told her mum.

"Fuck, that must've been difficult. I'm sorry you had to go alone, Rori." Cian ruffled his baby sister's hair. "But I'm glad you finally went to see her."

"It was a good talk." Rori flicked a glance to Nikala. "I didn't tell her that you were Hunter's pet project. I didn't want her to have any preconceived ideas of who or what you are before she meets you."

Nikala felt a ball of tension release, and she breathed out

slowly. She hadn't realized she was worried about Labhruinn knowing who she was. "Thank you, Rori. That means the world."

Rori grinned. "I got your back."

Nikala looked at those in the room. They all had her back, and she had theirs. It was the first time in her life she had others who cared about her and it felt refreshingly good. Scary as fuck, but nice.

She checked her app again, as if Hunter might suddenly ping a location. Nothing.

Therron approached, holding a small bottle in his hand. He'd changed into human clothing and adjusted his coat as if it sat uncomfortably on his shoulders. "Can you check your magic box for any mention of amrita? I confiscated this potion from a lounge in Elvenwood City and think perhaps it might have originated from here. He called it a beta test, but I don't know what that is."

Cian jerked his attention to Therron. "Beta is like a practice run. They were trying it out on elves to see how it affected them."

"Galo said Acelyne gave some of this to Thad before she kidnapped him. He didn't know who the manufacturer was, but Acelyne or another courier would deliver it to him on a regular basis. He hasn't received a shipment since Acelyne's death."

Nikala listened with keen interest. There was more Therron wasn't telling, she was sure of it. She typed the word amrita into the search function. "Hmm, amrita means elixir of life in Sanskrit. But there's nothing in Hunter's files that mention it." Just to be safe, she pulled Malcolm's laptop to her and repeated her search. This time, dozens of hits pinged. "Got something." She looked at the others, hopeful. "Malcolm was involved somehow. There's a warehouse in Amsterdam. I have the address."

"Amsterdam?" Cian frowned. "A human contact of mine told me about a potion she was given once in Amsterdam. Made her feel out of it, like a bad acid trip."

"That doesn't sound like something an elixir of life would do. Malcolm, what the hell were you up to?"

"What are we waiting for? Let's go find out." Rori strode to the door.

Lucien placed his hand over his heart and lowered his head. "I cannot join you in Amsterdam as that is not my territory." He looked at Therron. "I will be in London for a short while longer. When you return, there are things I would like to discuss with you."

Therron seemed irritated but gave a quick nod. "Will you be at the pub?"

"If that suits you." Lucien bowed to the group and left without any explanation.

Nikala wasn't the only one giving Therron a curious glance. Cian and Rori both stared at him, but he declined to elaborate. Sensing this was a topic he didn't want to share, she reached to turn off Hunter's laptop and froze.

"Guys. You might want to see this." She pointed at a message that popped up on the screen. "I didn't do anything, it just appeared."

Cian, Rori, and Therron shuffled behind her and peered over her shoulder at the screen.

"What the futnucker does that mean?"

"Shit."

"Blood and ashes."

"Exactly." Nikala shut both computers and locked them in the safe before turning to the others. "Wherever Hunter is, I think this proves he's still very much in control."

She ushered them out of the office and locked the door behind her. In her mind, flashing like a neon sign on the Vegas Strip, was the pop-up countdown from Hunter's laptop. Twenty-three hours, and twenty-three minutes. That was it. Just a countdown for less than one day. Fuck.

Malcolm's—now Nikala's—receptionist Darla sat behind the enormous desk and smiled at the group. Nikala felt the familiar pang of guilt that she had no idea what Darla did, nor did she know what jobs to give her. Maybe have her search Hunter's laptop for a clue what the countdown meant? But then she'd be giving the young woman access to a lot of information she wasn't ready for. Hell, Nikala wasn't prepared for half of what she saw in his files. She needed time to process, but as ever, time was a luxury she couldn't afford.

"Molly called for you, ma'am." Darla handed her a slip of paper. "Said it wasn't urgent."

Nikala scanned the paper, reading exactly what Darla had just said, and pocketed it. "Thanks. We should be back in a few hours."

Molly could help. She knew what was happening, and what was at stake. When they returned, she'd call her and ask for her advice. Where the hell was Maxx? They needed her. She knew more about Hunter than any of them. Nikala stepped from the lift and scanned the lobby out of habit. Maxx had said she needed a few days with family. Nikala would be a right twat if she demanded she leave her husband and son. But if they didn't decipher the countdown, there might not be a future for any of them. She dug her nails into her palms and swallowed a stream of swear words.

Damn Hunter for still being one step ahead of them.

They were quiet as they made their way to the pub. That morning's fight with Hunter's thugs had rattled them all, not because of the very public brawl, but that they would feel brazen enough to attack in broad daylight. Hunter was getting desperate. And a desperate madman was a dangerous man. Then the mysterious countdown on his computer had upset them all over again. She felt it in their stiff gaits and the way each one of them scrutinized every shadow they passed.

The crossing through from London to Amsterdam took only minutes, but it felt like days in the black hole of nothingness. Rori swore there were rainbow lights flickering overhead, but Nikala saw nothing, heard nothing, smelled nothing in the void. It was a silent hell she would gladly avoid for the rest of her life if she could, but these lunatics seemed to enjoy popping from one place to another.

"There might be scyvers nearby," Cian warned as they made their way out of the pub that was the portal location in Amsterdam.

"I thought Maxx killed all of them." Therron said it with a bitterness that was palpable.

"She killed Hunter's creations, but those they infected are still alive," Nikala explained.

"Maxx killed the scyvers? Why?" Rori scanned the street as they hurried along a canal toward the eastern side of the city.

"Mercy, she said." Therron practically spat the words.

"That seems harsh. Surely, they could've been rehabilitated."

"Thank you." Therron glared at Nikala as if she'd personally flipped the switch to kill the scyvers.

"Children. What's done is done. Let's focus on our objective here." Cian turned them down a side street that was less populated than the major walkway they were traveling.

A few steps in, four men ambled out of a doorway, their gait unsteady. Nikala's skin prickled with apprehension. She recognized the dazed look in their eyes, the rictus grins on their scabby faces. Scyvers.

One of the men lunged at Cian, and he neatly avoided colliding with him. Without mussing his hair, he shifted, grabbing the scyver by the head and giving a savage twist. A sharp snap echoed down the quiet street, and Nikala's gut churned. No one had used magic, and yet she felt the familiar stirrings to kill the magic users. She stared in horror as Cian brought down another scyver, and Rori dispatched a third with her daggers. Therron reached for his hidden sword, but before he had it unsheathed, Cian slashed the last scyver's throat with a butterfly knife she'd never seen before.

He's keeping secrets from you. Kill him. Hunter's voice taunted her. She knew it wasn't real, yet her body reacted as if he stood before her in his torture dungeon. She was alone, cold, abused. Afraid.

You're wrong. We promised no secrets.

Kill him. He doesn't love you. He lies.

"No." Nikala put her hands over her ears, but the voice didn't stop. It egged her on, mocking her love, telling her she was worthless and unlovable. "NO!"

As if in a dream where someone else controlled her actions, she snatched Cian's blade from his grip and pushed him against the side of the building, the sharp edge at his throat.

His eyes grew large, but he didn't panic or fight back. "Nikala?"

"I don't want to. But he insists."

Understanding dawned on Cian's features. "I see. Then do it. Kill me, Nikala."

"No, don't kill him. Nikala, what the fuck are you doing?" Rori grabbed her arm, and Nikala shook her off.

"Rori, stay out of this," Cian warned, his eyes never leaving Nikala's. "I can handle it."

"You can't. I can't. I'm sorry, Cian." Nikala's hand trembled as she held the blade, nicking his skin. At the sight of his blood, her need to kill heightened. Tears flowed over her cheeks, and she angrily wiped them with her sleeve. "He's in my head."

"But you're stronger than him. He knows it, and so do you."

Cian was wrong. She couldn't fight Hunter. No matter how many times she'd tried in the past, she always failed. He was too powerful, his hold over her absolute. This was her final test. Kill Cian and subject herself to Hunter's control forever.

You've always been mine, Nikala. Now, prove it.

Therron stepped into view. "Nikala, look at me."

She glanced his way, the blade digging into Cian's throat.

"Do you want to kill Cian?"

Such a simple question. He knew she couldn't lie to him. Part of her wanted desperately to tell him yes, but the oath that bonded them prevented her from saying the words Hunter was trying to manipulate her to say. The battle between Hunter and her was shredding her mind. Inside her skull felt like a volcano about to erupt. She fought through Hunter's mind fuckery, scarring herself in the process. Each step toward the truth was a million tiny cuts against her psyche.

She bit her lip and shook her head.

Bitch! Hunter shrieked at her. *Traitorous cunt. How dare you disobey me? You belong to me.*

"Cian's right. You're stronger than Hunter. I can't lie to you, Nikala, but you have to believe it." Therron kept his gaze on her, steady and intense.

She swallowed a sob that threatened to break her.

Therron couldn't lie to her. She had to stop lying to herself.

Kill him. He's nothing. You're nothing.

"Nikala." Cian's sweet voice pulled her attention to his calm face. "I love you. You love me. Forever. We promised, remember? Now, fight him."

He's lying. You're unlovable. You're pathetic. A monster.

Cian's focus never left her as he reached for her hand and gripped her wrist. She fought against him as he slowly moved the knife from his throat down his stupid white shirt and beneath his suit jacket. The blade stopped above his heart.

"Take it," Cian said. "It belongs to you anyway, princess."

From her periphery, she saw someone step into the street and immediately back away. It wouldn't be long before the local police showed up. She gripped Cian's suit jacket with her left hand as if that were the only thing keeping her grounded. Through the soft skin of his throat, his heartbeat fluttered. He was scared yet remained calm for her sake. He loved her. Hunter was the liar.

Hunter was nothing.

No!

Yes!

She backed away and threw the knife to the ground, her heart pumping hard, her breathing ragged. Cian enveloped her in a fierce hug that took her breath away. He held her face and searched her eyes, his own full of emotion.

She'd done it. She'd defeated Hunter. And yet…it felt like a hollow victory. The next time, they might not get so lucky.

❧ 36 ☙

Cian wiped blood from his neck and watched passively as Rori and Therron rolled the dead scyvers into the canal. They'd be dissolved in a matter of minutes—he hoped. Their attack was startling in its brevity. They must've been young scyvers, not yet used to their enhanced strength. It was all too eerily reminiscent of the night he fought the scyvers in Brugge. That was the night he learned about Malcolm Dagniss's involvement with the kidnapped fae. That night had led him to Nikala.

He tightened his grip around her shoulder and assured her for the hundredth time that he didn't blame her. He knew she wouldn't kill him. For a moment, he'd thought she might, but she fought Hunter's control. This time.

"Therron, take Nikala back to London and stay with her. She's rattled and needs a soothing presence." He would rather he went with Nikala, but in her current state, he didn't fully trust that she wouldn't try to kill him again. They both needed a little distance to come down from their respective adrenaline rushes.

"I can go with her," Rori offered.

"No, it should be Therron. I need you with me here." He felt the elf would be safest with Nikala, all things considered. "When we return, why don't we see about removing any trackers or mind fucks Hunter implanted into you." He held Nikala's chin and rubbed his nose against hers. "We'll heal whatever that asshole did."

Nikala nodded but said nothing. She followed Therron like a lost puppy, and Cian's heart broke for her.

"Do you really think that's safe? What if she tries to kill Therron?"

"She won't. Come on, the warehouse is just up here." Cian strode away, and Rori followed.

"You will tell me what's going on at some point, right?"

"To be honest, I don't fully understand it, nor do I think does Nikala or Therron. He was going to force a truth oath on us, and it backfired. So now, he and Nikala are bound to tell each other the truth—on pain of death, it would seem. Since he bound them, she's been acting strangely when he's around. Softer." He looked at his baby sister. "It's nothing to be jealous of, so don't worry your pretty little head about that."

"Oh, I'm not jealous. I'm fascinated. What on earth made Therron invoke a truth oath?"

"You, actually." He told her how Therron was going to reveal her secret, but didn't trust Maxx, and so he invoked the truth oath. He left out Nikala and Therron's impromptu trip to Faerie where Nikala learned about her mother. That was Therron and Nikala's story to share.

Cian stopped at the address of the warehouse and looked at the unremarkable door. On either side were red brick buildings with large windows on the first floor, and a hook hanging from a thick pole at the roofline. This area of Amsterdam was once full of warehouses and used the canal as easy access to the docks. He wondered how many of the buildings were now converted to housing. Or if those neighbors knew what was being manufactured inside the building.

Instead of knocking, Cian used a thread of magic to unlock the door, and they entered unobstructed. He carefully locked the door behind them before directing Rori to search the rooms to their right while he searched to the left. In the first room, couches and chairs were strewn about haphazardly. Empty condom wrappers and beer bottles mixed with fast-food bags on every surface. The floor was littered with more detritus Cian was careful to avoid. He spied a single needle, but even one was more than he liked.

As his contact had said, it looked like a place where druggies might hang out. Not a crack house, but close.

"All clear." Rori popped her head in the doorway farthest from the entry. "This room's disgusting. All mine were clean and tidy." She kicked at a fast-food bag. "What kinds of drugs are they making here?"

"Dunno. Let's look upstairs." He heard floorboards creak above him and put a finger to his lips. The downstairs might be empty, but the floors above were definitely not.

They made their way up the stairs without a sound. At the landing, Cian stopped to listen. The layout was similar to the floor below, with rooms on either side. Rori crept to the open door at the front of the building and peeked inside. She held up three fingers. Cian checked the opposite side of the landing and shook his head. They searched this area first, finding crates filled with bottles similar to the one Therron took from Gentle Galo.

At least they knew where the potions were coming from. But what they had yet to discover was how involved Malcolm was, what the potions were, and why they were being smuggled into Elvenwood. And why were elves the test subjects?

Next, they went to the room with the three workers. Cian stood tall and adjusted his suit jacket. He strutted into the room as if he owned the whole damn block. One of the workers looked up in alarm and warned the other two. All three wore white coveralls and orange hats.

"Malcolm sent me," Cian said in Dutch, hoping that would defuse the situation.

"Where is Mr. Dagniss?" An older gentleman stepped away from a large silver vat. "We have sent messages, but he does not answer."

From the corner of his eye, he saw Rori slip behind the vat closest to the door and scale a ladder barely visible to him where he stood. She was silent as a cat as she made her way across a slim metal walkway that connected the six vats from one end of the room to the other. The machines blipped and blooped, their contents bubbling behind a small window that allowed Cian to see inside.

"He is not well—hence why I am here."

"And you are?" The man's eyes narrowed, and suspicion rolled off him like an odor.

"Victor Stanstead." Cian walked to the vat closest to him and poked the window. "You're behind on your shipments. This is unacceptable."

The man lifted his hands, shrugging. "We do not have

permission to ship, we have no way of contacting Mr. Dagniss, what are we to do?"

Rori dropped down from the farthest vat and snuck into the office at the back of the room. A large window showed her clearly snooping around the desk, and Cian drew the three men's attention to himself.

"What to do?" he practically shouted. "Don't have parties every night. The downstairs is disgusting. Mr. Dagniss would be quite disappointed to see how you've disrespected his warehouse." Cian searched the contents on a nearby desk and flipped over papers. "Filth! Nothing but disorganization and chaos. I should fire the lot of you this moment."

One of the men looked alarmed and turned on the youngest. "I told you he would find out." Then to Cian, he said in English, "It weren't me, sir. Was him that thought it would be a laugh to have some friends over. I told him it were a bad idea."

Cian glared at the younger man. "Entertaining friends here as if this is your home? You know what's in this vat, right? You are aware what it can do to your so-called friends, right?"

The man stared him down and shook his head. "I actually don't, innit? Don't know nuttin' but to put this in this and that in that, but don't think too hard 'bout what's what."

"He tried it," the panicked man said. "Didn't you? Tell him. Tell him what it did to you."

"Made me see unicorns." The younger man grinned as if he were still tripping. "It were grand."

The elder man in charge shook his head with disgust.

"Randall, if I've told you once, I've told you a thousand times. This isn't for you or your friends." But his scolding lacked conviction.

"Has everyone here been sampling the goods?"

The three looked properly chastised, but not sorry.

"Victor," Rori said from behind the men. They turned in unison to stare at her. "It's a potion to help ease the scyvers' pain." She pointed to the open laptop she held. "Malcom created it as a way to help, not hurt."

"That's private property." The elder reached for the laptop, but Rori stepped out of his grasp.

"Don't worry, Gramps. I'm not interested in your porn." She flashed him a charming smile. "But you definitely have a type." At this, she winked at the two younger men.

Rori handed the laptop to Cian, and he skimmed through the pages detailing what ingredients were used, for what purpose, and where the potion was distributed. Rori was right—Malcolm had made the amrita for scyvers. Humans consuming it was an unintended consequence, and one that Malcolm regretted. Nowhere did he see anything about it being tested on elves or fae.

Cian pinned the older man with a stern glare. "When was Hunter Pearson last here?"

By the way the man's face lost all color, Cian assumed a short while ago.

"I don't know who that is. We only deal with Malcolm Dagniss."

"And I'm Tinkerbell," Rori drawled. "Did the magical potion tell you to say that?"

"We know Hunter is involved, so you might as well be upfront with us. What's your name?"

The man shifted and glanced at the doorway as if he might make a run for it. Rori stepped into his path, arms crossed.

"He's called Elmond, sir." The chatty lad piped up. "I'm Dermott, and that's Randall. We don't mean no trouble, sir. Please tell Mr. Pearson we're working on his special batches."

"Shut your filthy whore mouth," Elmond commanded in English, and Dermott snapped his mouth closed. "Look, we know we're not supposed to be taking orders from Mr. Pearson, but he pays a helluva lot more than Mr. Dagniss. It's the same elixir, so what's the harm to make a little extra, right?"

"It's the same? All of it, no matter where it goes?" Rori strolled around the men, her eyes narrowed.

Cian knew that look. She was plotting something he hoped wouldn't get them killed.

"Yes. All the same." Elmond glanced to the floor, and Cian sighed loudly.

"Tell us the truth."

"Sometimes, Mr. Pearson will arrive unannounced, just as you have done, and add an ingredient to one of the vats. We never know when he'll show up, or what he adds." Elmond put his hand to his heart. "This is the truth. I swear it."

"And these special vats, those go where?" Cian searched the computer for specific keywords about Faerie, Elvenwood, etc., but nothing popped up. Hunter must use code words. He typed in Eris, and again, nothing.

"We don't know. A courier collects the crates, puts them on a barge, and that's the last we see of it."

Rori flicked her wrist and a thread of magic circled the men, paralyzing them where they stood. Her next flick made a bubble around the three, effectively cutting them off from hearing what happened outside of her magic.

"What's all this? I thought you were afraid of your wild magic?" Cian turned his back on the men in the off chance they could read lips.

"Turns out, it's not wild." She leaned in close and whispered, "I'm a freaking unicorn. But don't tell anyone."

Cian chuckled and put his arm around her. "I already knew. Therron told us. That's what he was swearing Maxx and Molly to secrecy about."

"Oh. Well, since you already knew, then you should also know that unicorn blood is very potent." She pointed to the vats. "What if—and hear me out about this—what if I put my blood in those vats? The healing properties of my unicorn blood will mix with the amrita. Anyone who drinks it should be healed from whatever affliction scyvers suffer from."

"Or you might kill them." Cian didn't like the idea of using Rori's blood for anything until they knew for certain what it would do. "You might make their suffering worse."

"Either way, we have to try. Malcolm was close but never got the formula just right. What if all he needed was one teeny tiny drop of pure unicorn blood?" She nudged him in the belly. "I know this will work. What's the point of being a unicorn if you can't spread glittery healing rainbows? That's pretty cool, right?"

"All right, all right, settle down, Prancer." He rubbed his chin and gave her idea some thought. It was mad, but not barking. And it just might work. Both on Earth, and in

Elvenwood. "What if it does something bad instead of good? This could backfire on us."

"How do you think I was able to free the kidnapped beings? It wasn't just the dark counterspell, it was my blood."

"Dark magic?"

She gazed at him, her eyes softening. "Oh. I forgot you don't know. Actually, there's a lot I need to tell you. We'll catch up later, but trust me, it won't backfire. And hey, if it does, you have your flippy floppy stabby stabby."

"You are such a child. It's called a butterfly knife."

"I know." She grinned at him like she used to when they were kids and he was trying to teach her something important that she'd already figured out on her own.

"Fine. We'll give it a try. What should we do with them? We don't want them knowing you've altered their mixture."

"Once I'm done, erase any memory they have of us being here." She patted him on the back. "You remember how, don't you?"

"Shut up."

She snorted a laugh and raced to the farthest vat. He returned the laptop to the office and typed in several commands that would allow Nikala to access the laptop from her own. As long as the men didn't suspect anything, they had no reason to search for his back door access.

He waited until Rori was finished and had left the room before he touched each man's forehead with his fingertip. He not only erased all memory of him and Rori being there but implanted the suggestion that they should distribute the amrita as soon as possible. Next, he told each man that Nikala was to be trusted and was handling the amrita production from now on. Lastly, he put into their minds that should Hunter arrive unannounced, they were to call Nikala's mobile number immediately to let her know.

When he and Rori returned to London, he'd have Nikala send an email from Malcolm's account with instructions and payment details. Then, once this batch of amrita was finished, they would end production. He only hoped that Rori's plan worked. As he left the warehouse, he made a mental note to have Nikala search Hunter's laptop for Eris. The number twenty-three wasn't a coincidence.

"Back to London?" Rori asked.

"Yeah." He put his arm across his sister's shoulders. She'd lost weight while in Hunter's lab. One more reason to kill the sonofabitch. "This magical unicorn blood you have, do you think it could rid Nikala of Hunter's control?"

Rori's lips quirked in a half smile. "I was thinking the exact same thing. Wouldn't hurt to try. We could use Lucien's help, if you don't mind."

"As long as you don't kill her, I don't care who helps."

He felt the tension in Rori's shoulders and regretted his words. He kissed the top of her head and whispered, "I love you. Never forget it."

She squeezed his middle. "Love you too. Are you ready to hear about my time with Hunter?"

He wasn't. Would never be ready for what he knew was coming. After seeing the cellar in Hunter's mansion in Scotland, he knew what to expect and shuddered. Rori and Nikala had survived Hunter's torture, but at too high a cost. He had to be stopped. No matter what.

❧ 37 ❧

Four pairs of eyes looked at her as if she were a bug pinned to a board. Nikala trembled with the prospect that she would have to allow them free rein over her body and her mind. Cian and Rori, she didn't mind, but Therron and Lucien? They were strangers. What if they found something horrific that she didn't even know she was hiding? What if she tried to kill them? All of them, including Cian. Again.

Overriding her concerns was one word: Freedom. Freedom from Hunter's control. Freedom to live her life however the hell she wanted. Freedom to love unconditionally. Right now, she was still tethered to a man who wished only manipulation and subservience on her.

"Let's get it over with." She directed them to the conference room. "Would it be best if I lie on the table, or a bed?"

Lucien looked to Cian for the answer. He cleared his throat and cricked his neck.

"The bed. Nikala should be as comfortable as possible."

Interesting. She'd thought for sure he'd suggest the table.

He'd returned from Amsterdam determined to heal her of Hunter's mind fuckery, with some wild idea that Rori could cleanse her blood, body, and soul. Nikala didn't argue because, honestly, she was willing to try anything at this point.

She lay with her head at the foot of the bed, fully clothed, and closed her eyes. Lucien placed his hands on her skull and gave a gentle massage. A moan escaped her lips; she sucked it back in, but it was too late. Cian's hands stiffened on her abdomen, and she made a conscious effort not to enjoy their touch too much. But it was a really nice massage. Cian could learn from the dragon lord.

"Cian, if it will upset you, perhaps you should wait in the other room," Therron's quiet voice said from her right.

"Not a chance." Cian's hands softened, and she rubbed her fingertips along his thigh to let him know she appreciated him being there.

A flicker of panic made her go cold, and she sat up, disrupting the men. "What if I try to kill you again?"

"We'll deal with that if it happens. You overcame the urge in Amsterdam, you can do it again here. Besides, I've used magic on you many times in the past and nothing was triggered." Cian smirked.

"That's different. It was in a safe environment." She gave him a knowing look. It was always when they made love.

"Then tell yourself we are safe. We are helping you. We do not wish you harm. The mind is a powerful tool, Nikala." Lucien directed her to lay down again.

Once settled, she repeated the mantra Lucien had said and relaxed into the mattress. Rori sat on the bed near her side and took Nikala's hand in her own. Therron began to sing, low and in a language she didn't understand, but seemed familiar. Lucien massaged her scalp while Therron and Cian pressed lightly against her abdomen, thighs, and torso, each being careful to avoid her breasts.

Her breathing evened with her repeated mantra. A prick in her brain brought her out of her relaxed state, but Lucien told her it was all part of the process. His soothing voice swept away her worry, and she sunk deeper into the duvet.

Someone's magic swept across her skin, and she felt the stirrings of her mania to kill. She took a long drag of air and said her mantra, but this time, she reached for their magic as if to pull it on like a jumper. A sense of nurturing and profound love wrapped around her, and she guessed it was Rori's magic she held close.

"Let us heal you. Let us in," Rori whispered.

Therron's song swam through her mind, making everything distorted. Another prick against her skull, this time more insistent, angry even. A vision came to her of when she was still a child, but on the cusp of becoming a teenager. Hunter held a long syringe, the thick needle pointed at her skull. He warned it might pinch and stuck the thing several inches into her head. She held the scream that begged to be loosed, knowing she would be punished if she cried out.

The pain hit Nikala again, harder this time, and she bit her lips to keep quiet.

"Don't hold it in, darling," Cian cooed. "You're safe here."

Tears tracked down the side of her face to puddle in her hair. The memories cascaded across her mind—some too fast to capture, others lingering longer than she'd like. She saw the torture, the tests, the violent things Hunter did to her in the name of science, and she cried for the innocent young girl who only wanted to please her abuser. She cried for the lost years filled with loneliness and pain. So much pain. She felt it all again as if it were happening to her now. But it wasn't real, not this time. Now it was only her memories tormenting her. She'd survived. If their healing succeeded, she might even thrive.

Rori's grip tightened on her hand, and she heard her crying quietly. Even if she knew how, she couldn't stop the images from being shared with Rori. She, more than anyone there, understood Nikala's torment.

Another vision, this time of Hunter strapping her to a chair, her eyes held open with a metal contraption that reminded her of an inside-out spider. He played a video on loop, forcing her to watch it over and over until she could no longer keep awake. Cold water splashed her face, stinging her open eyes, and she was made to keep watching the recording.

Words came to her, Hunter's kill code.

She memorized them, her heart thumping with anticipation of hearing Hunter in her mind telling her to forget the words, kill those helping her, anything. But her mind was strangely silent.

As if he couldn't reach her here in this safe space.

The realization was jarring. It wasn't someone's magic that prevented him from trying to control her; it was her own belief that she was with people who wanted only the best for her and who loved her.

Fresh tears tracked down her face. If only she'd realized it sooner. But then, maybe she needed to almost kill Cian to finally break through her fear of Hunter.

"I know the words," she whispered, too afraid to speak aloud lest her tormentor heard. "I can undo them."

And she could. Somehow, she knew she could undo the programming he'd set in her brain. While the others worked to heal what Hunter had broken, she worked to reverse his cruelty.

"I don't see a microchip, but there is a dark blot in her brain guarded by powerful magic. I worry if I try to remove the spell, it could harm her," Lucien said. It sounded like he was far away.

"Do it," Nikala stuttered.

"I'll help." Cian moved to the end of the bed.

A moment later, Therron moved to the end of the bed with the men. Three pairs of hands held Nikala's head as if she were a precious vase that could shatter at any moment.

"I'm here, Nikala. I won't let you go." Rori smoothed her hand, and she felt the love she infused into her words.

A sharp pain ricocheted in her skull, and she swallowed a gasp. They were close; she could sense it.

"Harder." Nikala gritted through the pain.

"Nay, lass." Cian bent and kissed her cheek. "This is not the time for heroics. We don't know what kind of dark magic Hunter used, and I will not lose you to him."

She nodded and silently repeated the words she could use to reverse Hunter's mind control. They became her new mantra, and she whispered them while envisioning the words written in golden light across her closed lids.

Therron's song rose in tempo, and she changed her cadence to match his song. The bond he'd accidentally forced upon her sparked to life, and she was momentarily in Therron's mind. She saw his childhood, his father's madness, his love for his brothers, and his deep affection for Rori. A heartbeat later, she was back in her own mind, but now she wasn't alone. Therron stood with her, incorporating her words into his song. Then he was gone, and she faced Hunter alone on a dark lake as clear as glass.

He laughed at her attempt to push him from her mind. His *he-he-he* echoed across the strange lake. She refused to reply. Instead, she searched deeper into the programming, knowing there was a flaw somewhere she could exploit.

"Almost there," Lucien whispered.

"I see it. Here, let me." Cian's magic coated her skull, but it wasn't the gentle touch she recognized from their lovemaking. It was darker, sinister even. It burned brightly in the darkness.

Kill him.

No.

She trusted him.

She loved him.

He was her forever.

Cold spread over her brain, and she shivered against it. Pain, deep and abiding, dug into her skull, and then through her body, damaging everything in its path.

Softer magic flowed through her, luminescent in its innocence. Dark and light twined and twisted, erasing her pain, cleansing her blood, body, and soul. Just as Rori had promised.

"It's gone." Cian's magic retreated haltingly. "You should be healed now."

She was, yet she wasn't. There was more. Nikala delved deeper, into the void they'd created by removing Hunter's dark magic. He shrieked at her to stop, even telling her she would die if she kept going. That only served to spur her efforts faster, farther, into the deepest, darkest part of herself where she'd never allowed herself to tread before.

Hunter stood on the lake, shaking his fist at her.

She pointed to him and shouted, "You have no control over me! Not now. Not ever again."

"You are mine. Mine!"

"I belong to no one. I am whole. I am flawed. I am perfect exactly as I am."

"You are worthless."

"And you're a scared old man who knows he's lost."

Light shone where he'd been standing, and Nikala ran full-out toward it. The warmth of the light's rays curled around her skin, and she felt pricks all across her body, especially in her skull.

"What the hell?" From far away, Cian spoke, but she was too far in the void to answer.

He touched her shoulder and pulled back, swearing beneath his breath.

"Leave her. She's found the key," Therron said.

"How do you know?" Cian's voice sounded concerned, and she fought against breaking the contact she had in her mind to tell him she would be okay.

"Look."

Rori now. Whatever she saw, Nikala couldn't see, but a rising heat emanated from her skull.

Where Hunter had stood, she now saw her mother, Mairead.

"Well done, dearest. You've found your magic at last."

Nikala paused in her steps, confused. "What do you mean?"

Streaks of color—golds, silvers, emeralds, rubies, and sapphires—whipped around them in a torrent of motion that made Nikala dizzy.

"Hunter blocked your magic from you in a most grievous way. It was only through your own cleverness that you were able to undo that block." Mairead reached for her, and she lunged toward her mother, eager to hold her in her arms.

When she reached the woman, she vanished, leaving Nikala all alone on the strange, pitch-hued lake.

Hunter's laugh echoed, making ripples across the glassy surface.

Nikala held herself taller and pulled the colors into herself. She envisioned Hunter's damaged face, the sneer he certainly wore, and threw her hands wide, sending her magic outward in a rainbow of cleansing healing. The image of Hunter splintered and shattered into thousands of minia-ture shards before lighting like sparks from an open flame and disintegrating to nothingness.

"Is this you, Rori?" Therron asked.

"Not my magic." A gentle chuckle. "But I forgot, Nikala shares my blood. She was Hunter's first test subject after me. My blood was the first he gave her."

"It's probably how she survived all those tests," Therron said, sadness in his tone.

"And how she'll survive this. She's so much stronger than she ever allowed herself to believe." Cian. Her love. Her life.

Nikala stood alone on the dark lake, unafraid. Her magic pulled back into herself, and she methodically went from the tip of her toes to the top of her scalp, burning away the scars Hunter left, figuratively and literally. Every wound he'd ever inflicted, she healed. Each mark on her skin he left, she smoothed. When she got to the dark stain in her brain, she filled it with color so bright it hurt her eyes.

Her body shook violently against the bed. Cian called out, but she couldn't answer. He tried to wrap her in his magic, but she rebuffed it. This was something she needed to do alone. Only once she was rid of every speck of Hunter's disease would she allow him in. Tendrils of dark magic slithered from the void and burned like paper caught in a flame. The ashes blew away with a single puff of air.

She heard Cian begging for access, and she willed him to understand this was what needed to be done.

"Cian, all is well." Therron consoled Nikala's greatest love. "She is healing herself."

"Impossible." Lucien gasped, and Nikala never felt so proud of herself.

Anything is possible with love. She sent the thought to the others, knowing it was the one truth she'd always denied.

Find me, Mairead whispered in her mind. *I'm waiting for you in Faerie.*

Another truth she could no longer deny. She would have to travel to Faerie sooner rather than later.

I'll find you. Then she would be fully whole.

38

Rori twisted a lock of cobalt hair around her finger, her mind churning like cogs in an expensive watch. Cian and Nikala sat at her huge desk, each searching a computer for Hunter or any mention of Eris. Rori still didn't quite understand the connection, but the number twenty-three and chaos…now, those she was familiar with. She worked the puzzle again, still coming up short of a full picture.

Therron paced the room, his impatience palpable. She watched him walk from one end of the large window to the other, his gaze set on something she couldn't see. A shudder ran the length of her at the memory of seeing midnight-blue wings spread from behind him during their fight with Hunter's soldiers. Lucien knew, somehow, but he'd left too quickly after healing Nikala for Rori to ask him what it meant. As for Therron, she hadn't found the courage yet to ask, nor to tell him about the egg.

Her heart knew the truth—Therron was the same as Aimon. An elf with a dragon soul. Like her being fae with a unicorn soul. She didn't know yet what it meant, but she was determined to find out.

"Want some company?" Molly nudged in beside her on the sofa, and Rori spread the blanket covering her to encompass her friend. "You look pretty serious. Care to share?"

"I'm putting all the pieces together, trying to sort out our next move."

"Ah. Maybe I can help. What have you got?"

Rori gave her a grateful smile. Sometimes, it only took saying things out loud to fully hear and understand them. At this point, she'd take all the help she could get. "Hunter is missing. Has been since I escaped his lab in Venice. There's some sort of countdown happening in…" She called out to Nikala, "How much longer until the countdown ends?"

Nikala peered at Hunter's screen. "Nine hours, forty-two minutes, forty-seven seconds."

"What's going to happen?" Molly asked.

"No idea. A countdown just popped up on the screen." Rori snuggled deeper into the blanket. "What else? Rowan is dead. Meg is missing. I freed the trapped fae and others, but can't wake them."

"Say that again." Therron turned from the window. "Rori, you're brilliant."

"I mean, yes, but also, why?"

"If you were a maniacal despot who needed somewhere safe to heal after being injured by a fatal fae, where would you hide?" Therron looked at them all in turn. "A dead man's cottage."

"Holy cats, Therron, you're right!" Rori smacked her head. "Why didn't I think of that sooner?"

"Probably because, like the rest of us, we're dealing with a lot right now." Cian rose from behind the desk and stretched his arms wide. "I guess it's time to go to Faerie." He looked at Nikala. "Are you ready for this?"

Her face paled, and she shook her head. "Will we see the queens?"

"Not unless you want to. Their palaces are equidistant from Rowan's cottage. He lived in a charming vale far from everyone. Liked it that way, he said. Which, now that I say that out loud, sounds exactly like where Hunter would go to heal." Cian took Nikala's hand in his, and she visibly relaxed.

Rori caught Therron's concerned expression and studied the three of them. There was something going on with Nikala that she wasn't a part of, and that didn't sit well with her. She tossed the blanket onto Molly and stood.

"What are we waiting for? Let's go." Irritation laced her words. She was being kept in the dark; whether intentionally or not, it sucked. She'd rather confront her despot father than sit around and watch Cian and Therron fuss over Nikala. Oof. That was some serious jealousy. Rori checked herself and mentally reminded herself she had nothing to worry about. Therron loved her. Cian loved Nikala. And Nikala loved Cian. But damn, still didn't feel nice.

"You can stay here." Cian stroked Nikala's hand as if soothing a child. "We can handle this on our own."

Nikala stared at the laptop before answering. "No, I

need to go. If Hunter is there, I have to show him I'm not afraid—that he no longer controls me."

Rori swallowed a lump of something nasty. Guilt, irritation, jealousy…she wasn't sure what exactly, but it didn't taste good. This wasn't like her. She wasn't the type to worry over other women getting more attention than her. Even if she'd spent a vast amount of her energy helping to heal said woman. Wasn't it her unicorn blood that had given Nikala the strength to confront Hunter? Yes. But did Rori get any kudos for that? No. Not even a pat on the back. Everyone had been too busy fussing over Nikala to care about Rori.

And now she feared she was losing Therron.

All true, but she'd never loved someone like she loved Therron. Just the thought of that love being taken away made her tremble with anxiety. Love made her weak. Exposed. Vulnerable.

Fuck this. She checked she had her daggers and went to the door. "I'm leaving. If you're coming, then get a move on. Meg is in danger."

Cian glared at her, and she returned the look.

"She's right. We're wasting time." Nikala took a deep breath and settled her shoulders. "Just to Rowan's?"

"Just to Rowan's." Cian kissed Nikala and led her to the door where Rori stood, seething. "You might want to stay here if you can't control your temper." His look was challenging.

"You're hiding something from me." She flicked a look at Nikala. "You all are. What happened while I was being tortured at Hunter's?"

Cian's face immediately softened. "Geez, Rori. Don't get it twisted. We're not hiding anything, but there are some things that need to be told organically—not forced. You seem to forget it's literally our jobs to deceive. Yes, we love you, but that instinct doesn't magically go away." He motioned to the office. "And we've been a bit distracted with other things."

"Whatever." She was being ridiculous, but her feelings were hurt and she didn't understand why. Instead of waiting for any more of Cian's pathetic excuses, she strode to the lift and jammed her thumb against the button.

"How are we going to get to Rowan's?" Nikala asked.

"Therron knows the way," Rori said over her shoulder. He'd been distant to her since they healed Nikala and even now, he stood behind the couple, not with Rori.

"You do as well, Rori." Therron finally stepped to her side and took her hand. "What is vexing you?"

She glared at him as if the answer should've been obvious. "Nothing."

By the time they reached the pub, her emotions had reached a boiling point. She was tetchy and irritable and nothing felt right.

"I'm serious, Rori. If you can't control your emotions, you need to stay here. We have to be focused when we confront Hunter." Cian placed his hands on her shoulders and looked her dead in the eye. "Can you do that? Can you set aside whatever's bothering you and do what needs to be done?"

This close, with his intense gaze holding her captive, she felt his apprehension as if it were her own. He was scared. For her. For Nikala. For Therron. But not for himself.

A vision seared her mind of Cian struck by a blinding

light. She shielded herself against it by folding into Cian's arms, but the light only got brighter.

"Rori, what's wrong?"

The vision faded, but the message remained burned in her brain. "Don't go to Rowan's." She pulled back and stared at her brother. "Stay here."

"I was literally just telling you to stay here."

"I know. I'm jumpy for some reason. Maybe it's seeing Hunter again after what he did in Venice, I'm not sure. But…" She blinked several times, trying to find the words. "If you go, you'll die."

Cian's gaze didn't falter. A second later, he laughed loud enough it made her jump.

"Is that all? Well, let's be getting on, then. If I have a date with destiny, I don't want to be late."

"Cian, I'm serious. I saw a vision. You die."

He held her face between his hands. "I decide when I die. Not that piece of trash who calls himself Hunter Pearson. Me. And I don't wish to die today."

Therron slipped her hand into his and gave a slight squeeze. "None of us will die. When we confront Hunter, it will be together, as one."

She turned to give him a grateful smile, but she knew in her heart what she saw in the vision was true. Cian would die.

39

The in-between stretched with silence, and an uncomfortable itch scratched up Nikala's spine. Her mother had told her to meet her in Faerie, but she wasn't ready yet to face the queens. Not until she knew Hunter was dead. She cricked her neck and told herself Rori was wrong—whatever vision she thought she saw, it was Hunter who would die this day, not Cian.

He'd almost died once when they fought Yash and Jude in the London warehouse, and that nearly broke her. And then there was whatever the fuck her little stunt was in Amsterdam. She touched her temple as if to make certain Hunter was gone from her mind for good. There was no way to tell without confronting the bastard.

A light elongated in front of them, and Therron stepped through first, followed by Rori, then her, and Cian last. She took in the room, noting the overflowing bookshelves, thick rugs, dark wood, and assorted random objects that made her nerves squirm. Yup, they were in Rowan's space. His creepy presence was everywhere. She twitched her back to alleviate the itch, but it stubbornly remained.

"We'll look upstairs; you check this floor," Cian said, but Therron stopped him.

"We stay together. It will take longer, but if we encounter Hunter, we can't be separated. He's counting on that."

"Fine. Lead the way, Your Highness." Bitterness edged Cian's words.

Therron was right. They were stronger together. She, for one, was grateful to have the other three with her. Her healing was too fresh, too untested.

Rori slid her hand in Nikala's and looked up at her. "Sorry I'm being a twat. I don't know what's gotten into me."

"You're allowed to be angry, Rori. We all are. Just don't let him get the best of you. He doesn't deserve a second of your precious attention."

Rori scrunched her lips, her eyes soft. "Thank you."

They walked behind the men, checking all the rooms and finding no one. Once they cleared the ground floor, they made their way upstairs. Again, all the rooms were empty.

"I was so certain he was here," Therron said with no small amount of anger.

"There's a cellar." Rori led them to a door hidden behind a tapestry, and Nikala's nerves snapped.

"Hunter loves a cellar." It was meant as a joke but landed flat.

They crept down the rickety stairs, pausing each time one of them creaked. It took far too long, but finally the four of them stepped into what could only be described as a cavern. This space looked as though it ran beneath the entire planet. It would take years to search.

Cian swirled his hand, and a thread of golden magic floated through the air. A moment later, he snapped his fingers and the cellar collapsed to just three rooms.

She held in her gasp, but was secretly impressed with his ease of magic use. One day, she'd be just as comfortable with her own magic. That day was not today.

They found Meg in the second room, bound, gagged, and unconscious. From the bruises on her arms and face, she'd been beaten.

"I will kill him with my bare hands." Rori swore as she gently untied the ropes around Meg's wrists. "How dare he. How very dare he do this to his own flesh and blood."

Cian's head snapped up from where he was working on the ropes binding Meg's ankles. "What?"

Rori made the scrunchy face again. "I kinda left that part out. Acelyne and Meg are Hunter's half-sisters. Our aunts."

Cian sat back and stared at his sister as if she'd lost her mind. "How long have you known?"

"He admitted it between beatings. Meg never knew. Still doesn't, as far as I'm aware. And I didn't tell Mum yet. It's complicated, but Grandpa MacNair and their mum hooked up without their dad knowing anything about it. He raised Acelyne and Meg as his own. Meg never betrayed us. I can see that's what you're thinking, but she's innocent." Rori brushed a lock of autumn hair from the woman's face. "That's probably why he did this to her. She refused to heal him."

Hunter was truly depraved. She'd always wondered how he slept at night, knowing what he'd done to her, but she wasn't his flesh and blood. But what he'd done to Rori and now Meg confirmed that he had no conscience. He loved no one but himself. Cared for no one but himself. He was a malignant narcissist of the worst sort. If only she'd been able to kill him, then none of this would be happening. They had to stop him before any more lives were ruined or lost.

Therron carried Meg upstairs, and they headed for the room with Rowan's secret doorway.

"Wait." Rori held up her hand.

Nikala looked at Cian, but he shrugged. "What is it, Rori?"

"I don't know. I feel it," she thumped her chest, "in here." She pointed to a sofa. "Put Meg there, and cover her with a thick blanket."

"Rori, you're not thinking of running off to the forest again, are you? That didn't end so well last time." Cian's tone was tight, as if he meant it as a joke, but also was dead serious.

"He's here." Rori turned to look at them, her face ashen. "He's in the forest where I killed Acelyne. He's…mourning her."

"Are you sure?" There was no joking in Cian's voice now.

Therron covered Meg with several blankets and tucked them around her before he stood, his face as equally as ashen as Rori's. Nikala's nerves tightened and she felt the familiar obedience that had been drilled into her since childhood rear its ugly head. Only this time, she was in control and beat the impulse down. Her hands shook as she walked with the others out a side door to a beautiful land-scape that could only be described as enchanted.

It was her first true glimpse of Faerie, and she saw immediately why the others loved this land so much. Lush greens buttressed up against meadows of wildflowers, much like the one where she'd first seen the image of her mother. To their left, a forest of trees in every shade from rust to evergreen stretched as far as the eye could see. It was just coming on twilight and a cloudless blue sky was turning a delicate shade of rose. But beyond the beauty, there was a stillness. A calm that immediately soothed her aching soul.

She was home.

Cian watched her, a small smile on his lips.

She nodded and held in an urge to run off through the meadows.

The beauty was marred by a sight that didn't seem real, but was not only real, but horrifying. A fiery arrow shot from the forest, heading directly for her love. Her scream sounded hollow, as if it came from someone else. Cian turned to see what drew her attention, and she reached out to pull him back, but it was too late. The arrow hit Cian directly in the heart, making an odd thud as it penetrated his body. The awful thud would echo in her mind for all time. Cian's eyes opened wide in surprise, and Nikala screamed a second time. Time slowed, and she saw what happened next in a capsule of a moment.

"Rori, no!" Therron grabbed Rori to keep her from running off.

She turned on him as if to argue, but when her gaze landed on Cian, she crumpled to the ground. Therron spun his hands, making a magic ball between them and then flung it outward, sending shards of flames to the forest. A cry came from the forest, followed by a dark flash.

"He's gone." Rori sobbed and hunched over her stricken brother. "That coward fled. Couldn't even face us. Had to attack from behind the trees." Her words came between hiccups and sobs.

Cian lay on the soft grass and gasped for air. His hands curled around the hilt of the arrow; his face paled and mouth frothed with bloodied foam.

Nikala knelt opposite to Rori. "Save him, Rori. Use your magic or your healing or whatever the fuck you call it and save him!" Tears shimmered in her eyes, and she blinked rapidly. "I can't lose you, Cian. You're my forever plan. You're my forever love. Please, don't die."

"Your forever love?" Cian choked out. "Forever and ever? Like in the fairytales?" A gurgled chuckle sounded from his chest, and he wheezed. His face turned a sickly blue, and red filled his eyes.

"Yes, Cian. Forever and ever. You can call me princess and tease me. Just please, don't leave me. You're my family."

He gripped her hand, squeezing so hard it hurt, but she said nothing. His head rolled to the side to face his sister.

"Love you, Rori," Cian forced out. "So much." Then he turned to Nikala. "Tell her. Tell them all."

"Yes, I will. Just please don't die." She knew what he meant and trembled inside.

"I love you, Nikala St. James. Forever and ever." Cian held her hand for one achingly short moment, and then his body went slack.

"No!" Nikala screamed to the skies. "Fuck you, Hunter! Fuck you to the seventh level of hell, you fucking asshole!"

She didn't care if he'd left Faerie; she knew he could hear her. Somehow, she knew.

Rori reached across her brother and clasped Nikala's hand in hers. Therron knelt beside Rori, and she felt his magic alongside Rori's.

"He'll pay, Nikala. With his life." Rori's hold increased and her hand trembled. "I warned him. I told Cian not to come."

"We can heal him, right? There are healers in—what was that place you released the fae? There. Let's go there."

Nikala gazed at her love, at the torment etched into his features from his last moments. She stroked a hand over his hair, wishing for one more minute, just one more day. Tears welled in her eyes, making her vision wobbly; for once, she didn't care who saw her cry, didn't care if they thought her weak.

Rori pressed a hand upon Cian's chest above his heart and spoke low. "May the First Goddess embrace you upon your journey into the mist. May the First God light the fire that keeps you warm. May your heart be free of ache, your soul cleansed of burden. Fly with the fae folk in the realm beyond the veils and may you never again suffer any ails." She kissed her thumb and placed it first to her forehead, then to her lips, and finally to her heart.

Nikala heard the words for the first time but knew them. They were part of her, embedded in her soul, but she couldn't say from where.

Rori's tears fell upon Cian's face as she bent low to kiss his forehead. Nikala looked up to see Therron leaning over Cian, his arms spread to encompass Rori as well as Nikala.

"We're your family, Nikala. Forever." Rori placed her hand over Cian's heart. "Forever and ever."

Nikala smiled and wiped her nose on her shoulder. Tears streamed over her cheeks to fall upon Cian's blue tunic. Smoke rose from where her tears landed, and Rori pulled back with a gasp. Therron made a weird sound and pointed to where smoke rose from Cian's face. A heartbeat later, his entire body was consumed with rising smoke.

"Stop this!" Rori roared at whatever might be the cause of her brother combusting.

"Step away, Rori. Nikala, you too." Therron gently lifted them.

Reluctantly, Nikala stood and moved back several paces. Cian's body fell in on itself and flames burst forth. She screamed—or it was Rori; she couldn't tell—but the heartbreak was shared by them both.

It was devastating to watch. Yet Nikala couldn't look away.

Cian's fiery corpse rose from the ground, where ashes made a grotesque outline where his body had been. Higher and higher it went.

"What's happening?" Nikala stared at the sky, more confused and frightened than she'd ever been in her life.

"I don't know," Rori said, and Therron agreed.

"How can you not know? This is your stupid world." Nikala glared at the couple. She needed someone to blame, but there was no one.

Her gaze returned to Cian, who now floated at least fifty feet in the air. The sparks around his body intensified until he was a glowing ball of fire as bright as the sun. Nikala shielded her eyes, but didn't look away.

Rays of light streaked outward and then, the ball of light collapsed into a sphere of darkness.

The black ball dissipated as if it were blown away by the breeze, and a fiery bird rose high into the air until it was out of sight. No one moved. Nikala barely breathed.

"A phoenix," Therron mused. "That's what Ishnara couldn't see in him. Blood and ashes, what a sight."

The next minute, the bird swooped low, its red and gold feathers touching the tops of the flowers in the meadow. Then it landed in front of Nikala with a low, sweeping movement as if it bowed.

Another bright light, this one singeing Nikala's heart with its intensity, and there stood her beloved. Unmarked. Unharmed. Alive.

❦ 40 ❦

Cian gripped the back of the chair as if his life depended on it. In a very real way, it did. He kept his face placid, his tone neutral in an effort to hide how difficult it was to stay upright. Who knew dying was so taxing?

What a freak show experience that had been. One minute, dead. The next, he was exploding into a bird with swooping feathers and fire for lungs. A phoenix. Him. No one saw that coming. And, fortunately for him, only the four of them knew. They decided as a group that for now, they'd keep it to themselves. Hunter had already left Faerie, which meant Cian was safe from that threat for the minute.

His gaze went to the inert form on the sofa. Poor Meg. His aunt. Another shocker. It explained why he and Rori had always felt a connection to the witch. And why Rori was such a gifted healer. He didn't think his mum would be too upset to learn that her best friend was his and Rori's aunt. His heart twisted, and he gripped the chair hard enough his knuckles turned white.

His mum was strong, but he could only imagine what she was going through after learning what her husband had become. Once they found Hunter, he'd return to Faerie and give her whatever support she needed. As much as it pained him, their first priority was finding Hunter and ending his spree of malevolent chaos.

They had a ticking clock—literally—to beat.

"Therron, you and Rori take Meg to the Seelie Palace. She's known there and will be more comfortable with Eirlys than Midna. Plus, Tug is there and he's got to be worried out of his mind by now. Nikala and I will return to London and continue our search for Hunter."

"Are you sure?" Rori pierced him with a knowing look. "You were dead five minutes ago. Are you fit for travel?"

"Does it matter? Hunter is out there. Something is going to happen in the next few hours, and Meg doesn't look so great."

"You don't look so great."

"Stop being stubborn, Rori, and please, for once, do what I'm asking you to do. Not as your older brother, or hell, even as your superior, but as someone who desperately needs to figure this shit out and we're wasting time."

Therron scooped Meg into his arms. "We'll see you in London as soon as we get Meg settled."

Rori glared at him, but relented and followed Therron to Rowan's study.

"Are you sure about this? Rori's right. You look terrible, and if you grip that chair any harder, you're going to break it." Nikala rubbed his arm, and he leaned into her touch.

"You're going to heal me once we're back in London."

"I can't. Cian, please, don't ask me to. I'm not a healer."

"You're fae, Nikala. All fae have inherent healing abilities. Plus, you're royalty, so you're probably stronger in healing than most folks." He didn't mention that her aunt healed her subjects every few weeks through sex parties, but it did give him an idea. "They're gone. Let's go."

"Seriously, why didn't you want to go to the Seelie Palace with Rori and Therron? There are healers there who are way more experienced than me."

"Are you ready for that? Eirlys would take one look at you and know you're fae. Not only that, but I'd be willing to guess that she'd figure out real quick you're related to Midna. Never underestimate the fae queens."

Nikala visibly shivered, and he placed his arm around her. For comfort, and also support for himself. Walking was damn hard.

"I'm not ready for whatever that will entail. But I would endure it for you."

"I know that, and I love you for it. But you're going to have to trust me when I say you can heal me. Remember, you have Rori's unicorn blood in your veins."

Nikala snorted. "Yeah, like a drop. How potent can that be?"

"We'll find out." He smiled mysteriously and opened a doorway to the pub in London.

By the time they reached the office at SIRE, he had expended the last of his energy reserves. What good was being a phoenix if it took ages to recover from dying? They passed Darla at the reception desk, and he told her they weren't to be disturbed.

Nikala led him to the sofa, but he shook his head and directed her to the room where they'd healed her the day before. If Malcolm saw fit to put a bedroom in the office suite, they might as well use it.

"Get naked." Cian unbuttoned his suit jacket and tossed it on a chair. His white shirt followed. His shoes and trousers caused him some consternation, but he managed them eventually.

"Sex?" Nikala glared at him. "You died, Cian. Dead. Done for." She ran a finger along her neck and cricked her head to the side, her tongue sticking out. "D.E.A.D. Dead. Then, miraculously, you turned into some mythological creature that, I don't know, combusts into flames whenever you die? And all you can think about is sex?"

He took her hands in his own. "It isn't about sex, it's about connection. Sex has potent healing power. Use this emotion to heal me. Channel it for good, yeah?"

He pulled her T-shirt over her head and helped her unfasten her bra before sliding her jeans over her hips. Despite her lecture, he smelled her scent and knew she wanted this, too.

He stood in front of her, skimming his fingertips over her smooth skin. Every mark Hunter had given her, the visible scars, and he hoped invisible ones, she'd healed on her own. She was a marvel.

"What if I hurt you?"

"You won't."

She chewed a nail, indecision clear in her features.

"What's the worst that could happen? If you kill me, I'll simply turn into a fiery chicken and combust, then boom! I'm me again. Problem solved."

"Not funny."

"It's a little funny."

"No, it's not."

"Yes." He pulled her close, his mouth seeking hers. "It is."

Her hands tangled in his hair, and she pressed her body against his. "How does this work?"

"Just love me."

"Now that, I can do." Her hand slid down his chest. "Your heartbeat is weak. Like, scary slow."

He kept hold of her and walked backward to the bed and lay them on their sides on the soft mattress. Her mouth was warm and inviting, her hands careful as they stroked his nakedness. Their arms and legs entwined as they kissed, the pace slow, unrushed. Her magic cloaked them like a comfortable blanket, and he knew she was ready.

He shifted and lifted her leg over his hip. She moaned and inched closer, making it easier for him to slide his cock into her wet pussy. He'd die a thousand deaths just to feel the soft warmth of her healing.

They rocked together, their tongues dancing, heat building. Cian's magic flowed into Nikala's until it became one indistinguishable thread. He pulled it inside himself, slowly so as not to cause more harm. Turning into a phoenix had its advantages, he was sure, but it came with some drawbacks as well. When he had more than a minute to spare, he'd research what having a phoenix soul entailed. Molly could help. Hell, MI6 probably had an entire department devoted to mythical beasts.

Nikala moaned, and he focused on their lovemaking. Education would come later. Right then, it was about him and Nikala.

Her magic spiked and she gave a small cry.

"What's wrong?"

"I don't know." She twitched her shoulders and rolled them over to straddle him. "Ahh, better."

He studied her face as she ground against him. It was a mix of pleasure and pain, but he sensed nothing in their magic that should be causing her distress. Her features relaxed as she ran her hand over her breasts and down, lower, to find her clit. A sly smile danced on her lips, and Cian let his apprehension go.

Watching her pleasure herself while his cock was deep inside her was the sexiest thing he'd ever witnessed. Their magic continued to work through his body, healing what Hunter's fiery arrow had broken, strengthening him for what was to come.

Nikala's movements became more frantic, her moans more insistent. Cian stroked her thighs, his gaze never leaving her face. It was a sight he would never tire of.

Her pussy clenched against him, and he knew she was getting close. Their magic intensified with her coming orgasm, whirling through his blood like a tempest, and he gasped at the sheer force of their combined power. *Invincible* whipped through his mind, and it felt right.

Together, they were unstoppable.

Nikala thrust her pelvis hard into him, her fingers working a frenzy against her clit. She groaned and whimpered, her face creased with that indescribable pleasure/pain that came with mind-blowing orgasms. Silently, he willed her to come, to release whatever was causing her discomfort.

She came hard, not with a cry or shouts, but with a series of relieved shallow breaths and a slow smile. Her face crumbled and fear filled her eyes. Cian tensed, wary of what might happen next.

Nikala arched and cried out, but didn't lose contact with him. Behind her, silken wings unfolded and glistened in the dim lights.

"The fuck?" Nikala twisted to see her wings, the movement erotic against his cock.

"Your wings. All fae have them, but only royalty show them." Cian stared at her in awe. "You never cease to amaze me."

She flexed and shrugged her shoulders, delighting in the tiny flutters it made.

"You have wings, too?"

"Sure do. But they're safely tucked away."

Her face softened, and she looked at him with an apology dancing in her eyes. "You didn't finish." Her gaze flicked to where their bodies were connected, his cock to her pussy.

"I told you, it wasn't about sex. It was about connection." He placed her hand over his heart.

"It's strong and a steady beat. Did we do that?"

"We did." He reached up and traced his thumb over her cheek. "I love you."

"Marry me." She grinned, and he blinked in surprise. "Don't pretend you didn't ask me just a few days ago when you were banging me in the conference room. You thought I didn't hear, but I have excellent hearing." She winked. "Don't tell Therron."

A chuckle rumbled from his chest, and he shook his head. "Your secret is safe with me. All your secrets are."

"I'm serious. Marry me. You can wear a tux and I'll wear

a poufy dress. Then you'll be mine forever. I'll be your faerie princess and we'll live happily ever after." She fluttered her wings and grinned deviously. "We'll get married in Faerie with my mother and the queens, and all your family and friends there. A meadow at sunset."

"You've thought about this a lot."

"Actually, it all just came to me right now." She cocked her head. "Well? Will you?"

He pulled her down until their lips met and she sucked him into her hot mouth. His cock stirred and she wriggled her ass. Tease.

"I would love nothing more than to stay in this bed all day ravishing you, but we've two worlds to save, and there's that countdown we still don't know what it means." He kissed her nose. "As for your proposal, yes, of course. I will marry you here, there, anywhere."

Her face brightened, and a wide smile lit up her entire being. "What do I do with these? They're fun and all, but highly impractical." She cocked her head toward her wings.

"I'll show you how to conceal them. I need a shower, how about you?"

They left their clothing on the floor and walked through the office to the shower with Cian moaning the entire time about the ridiculous layout of the office. Bed on one side, shower on the other. It didn't make sense.

"Change it. Get a contractor in here and move stuff around. Or we find a different building." Nikala turned on the shower and pointed to her wings. "There isn't room in the shower for you, me, and these."

He instructed her how to fold her wings so they appeared to be beneath her skin, but could be unfurled at a moment's notice. It took her three tries before she had it just right. In the shower, Nikala made certain he finished, delighting him with her talented mouth and hands before pulling him close to pin her against the slick wall.

Her legs wrapped around his hips, and he breathed heavily as he thrust into her. It reminded him of their first time in his flat when she'd refused to take off her shirt for fear he'd see her scars. How far she'd come, they both had, in so short a time.

He came with a loud grunt and kissed her softly as the water ran in rivulets down their faces. Her fingers traced along his back, where his wings lay dormant. He knew what she was doing and allowed it.

"When you marry me, you'll be a prince, right?" She blinked at him.

"I suppose so."

"Then you'll show your wings, too."

It seemed important to her, yet he didn't understand why. He released her from the wall and she untangled her legs from around his body to stand. She seemed delicate… fragile almost. When she looked up at him, he saw the same fierceness in her eyes that he'd fallen in love with. This was a new Nikala, and he was excited to know more about her.

41

What the fuck had gotten into her? Nikala pulled on a black T-shirt and shook out her wet hair. Mooning over wings like a love-struck schoolgirl. Something had happened in their healing lovemaking, something even more profound than when she'd confronted Hunter on the strange lake. Whatever it was, she didn't hate it. As long as it didn't change her too much.

She didn't mind the softened edges, to be honest. She'd even told Cian she would wear a poufy skirt! A snort-giggle escaped her lips, and she rolled her eyes at how ridiculous she was being. Love made her stupid.

And she really didn't mind.

Cian dressed in a pair of casual trousers and a black T-shirt similar to hers. Instead of the brogues he always wore, suede loafers covered his feet. She eyed him critically, wondering whether something had shifted in him, too.

"Nice outfit. No suit today?"

"I thought I might try something different." He smoothed the shirt over his abdomen. "I feel exposed."

"You look hot."

He cocked his head and grinned. "Thank you."

"If you two are finished?" Maxx said from the doorway, and they turned in unison to see the spy scowling. "While you've been playing dress-up, there's been an event."

"An event?" Cian looked at Nikala, and her heart thumped to her belly. "The countdown."

"Fuck." She'd thought they had more time.

She raced from the dressing room to the safe and pressed a trembling fingertip to the pad. The door swung open and she grabbed both laptops. Maxx strolled to the television and clicked the remote. At the same time Nikala opened Hunter's laptop and typed in the password, images flashed across the television screen, showing a massive explosion.

"No." Cian stepped closer to the telly. "Where's Molly? Is she safe?"

"I am." Molly entered the office, with Darla at her side. "I wasn't at work when it happened."

"What happened?" Nikala's heart beat in her throat. She scanned the laptop for the countdown, but there was no longer a pop-up on the screen. "It's gone. The countdown, it's gone."

"Because the time passed." Cian pointed to the telly.

"You mean?" Nikala couldn't say the words.

"Hunter's first attack was MI6." Maxx turned to face them. "What better way to send a message than to destroy the one place that held scads of information about you?"

Tears streaked down Molly's face, and she crumbled

onto a sofa, with Darla sitting beside her. They held hands and cried together.

"Your friends. Fuck, Molly, I'm so sorry." Nikala glanced from them to the television, her stomach roiling with disgust. Fire and smoke rose from the building that was merely a mile from where they were. She went to the window and looked up the Thames to see the carnage for herself. Guilt sliced through her, and she rubbed her arms as if to wipe it away. "It's our fault. If we hadn't been…busy, we could've stopped it."

"No, Nikala. We couldn't have," Cian said. "We had no idea what he was planning. It didn't matter what we were doing, or where we were. This was still going to happen. You can't blame yourself. That helps no one."

He was right, but damn, it still felt like it was her fault.

The laptop pinged, and she dreaded looking to see why.

Cian strode to the desk and swore beneath his breath. "Maxx, there's a new countdown."

Maxx joined him, and Nikala forced herself to turn around.

"Twenty-three days, twenty-three hours, twenty-three minutes. Fucker. Why not add twenty-three seconds? What a complete—" Maxx shook her head. "At least this time we have a chance to prepare."

Nikala stared at the two laptops. "Even with all that knowledge inside these machines, how the hell are we supposed to predict what Hunter would do next?"

"We change the game," Maxx said simply. "We take control."

Cian slipped his hand into hers. "We become the hunters."

Nikala knew what they said was true—they had to beat Hunter at his own game. Cian was right: dead dads were dicks. Alive ones even worse. Tempered excitement spiraled through her. Malcolm. She'd only seen his ghost at SIRE's warehouse, but he could help. He knew Hunter better than anyone. He was their ace in the game.

Her gaze went to Molly and Darla. They were part of her family now, too. Family. What a wild fucking idea. She'd always had Malcolm, but he kept her at a distance to assuage his own guilt. No matter what happened in the past, he was still her father. And now, she had Maxx, Rori, Therron, Molly, Darla, and her beloved Cian. It was a rag tag family at best, but she'd die fighting for them. If they didn't end Hunter—utterly and completely—then everything she loved would be destroyed. Forever.

ABOUT THE AUTHOR

Tameri Etherton is a USA Today Bestselling and award-winning author of dangerous fantasy and paranormal romance with magical ever afters. She grew up inventing fictional worlds where the impossible was possible.
It's been said she leaves a trail of glitter in her wake as she creates new adventures for her kickass heroines, and the rogues who steal their hearts.
She lives an enchanted life traveling the world with her very own prince charming. When at home, she enjoys many cups of tea and cuddles from their two massive Maine Coons, Pora and Ember.
Read more from Tameri Etherton and explore the Aetherverse at
www.TameriEtherton.com
Join Tameri's newsletter to get exclusive content, enter giveaways, and receive free books and excerpts.

AUTHOR NOTES

This book! I've been dreaming of this book, and these characters for so long, I feared I'd never complete their story. But here it is in all it's messy glory!

Whatever possessed me to write four main characters was madness. Yet I loved every singly minute of it. Nikala's sass, Rori's sweetness that she tries (and fails) to hide, Cian's overt sexiness, and Therron's complicated past made this journey so much fun to travel along. There's still a bit more to say from each of them, and they'll all learn their fates in Fatal Destiny. I can't wait.

Thank you, my darling reader, for being so freaking patient! You've waited a long time for this book, and my sincerest hope is that it delivers everything you wanted and more. Without you, there's no Fatal Fae.

Thank you to my lovely editor Faith Williams at the Atwater Group who always works her magic. Any typos or errors are solely mine since I'm a revision gremlin and always need to add just one more thing.

The gorgeous cover was designed by Lori Grundy at Cover Reveal Designs.

I'd like to thank my Dazzling Dragons. Having such fabulous readers is an honor.

To my amazing husband David. Thank you for being

my sounding board, my therapist, my business partner, my very own Prince Charming, and my favorite human. I love you. Forever and ever.

Otherworldly portals. Mysterious powers. Evil hungrily awaits her return.

Taryn's simple life is all she's ever known. Living above a busy London pub with her grandfather, they're ripped from their reality and plunged into a strange world to jumpstart an ancient prophecy. And when he's killed defending her from a vicious intruder's magic, Taryn's left nearly alone… and forced to trust a rugged savior.

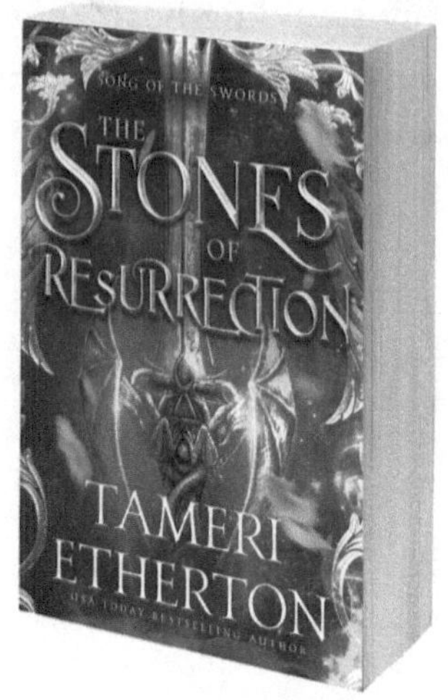

Rhoane has one job. Sworn to protect the young woman who has returned to fulfill her destiny, the assassin dare not let his feelings get in the way of her training. But he knows the time will come when she accepts her power and recognizes he's her fated mate.

As Taryn learns her life on Earth was a lie, she must unlock her hidden talents to save an entire world from destruction. And though Rhoane will show no mercy to anyone who stands in her way, he fears her biggest threat comes from the family she has never known.

Will the destined pair rise to stop the annihilation of a vast kingdom?

The Stones of Resurrection is the enthralling first book in the Song of the Swords fantasy series. If you like ensemble casts, intense action, and dark family sagas, then you'll love Tameri Etherton's epic tale.

She's in for the fight of her life...

Every sunset, Rainne is cursed to change from an elf maiden into a lust-fueled ogress. She keeps her ogre desires under control until an elf prince arrives and upsets her precariously balanced life.

The ogress in her desires Prince Theo and will break every rule, entertain every taboo, and defy death to have him.

Theo needs a reason to return to the luxurious palace of Elvenwood, and the lovely Lady Delarainne is the perfect excuse.

The only problem? There's a mysterious woman following them and he's determined to learn her secrets.

If Rainne doesn't break the curse, she'll lose more than just Theo--she'll lose her elven soul to the greedy ogress that wants to consume all that she holds dear.

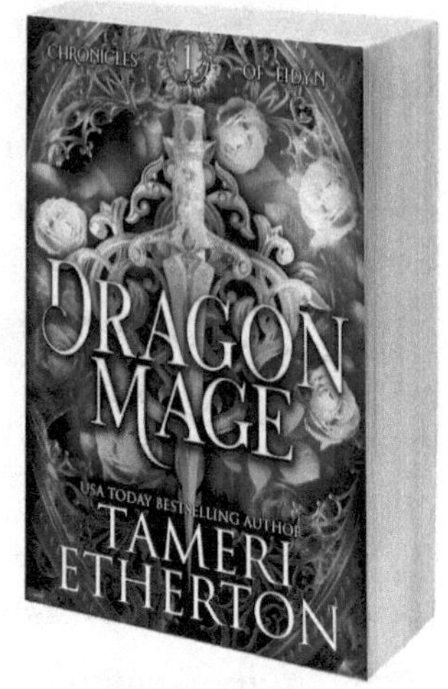

Her secret could destroy a kingdom. His trust could cost her everything.

Amaleigh never wanted to be a thief, but survival left her little choice. A single stolen dagger was supposed to buy her freedom. Instead, it exposed the truth hidden within her: the dragon she never knew existed. When her wings unfurl for the first time, she's faced with an impossible choice—kill her best friend, Prince Gwilym, or become a pawn in her ruthless boss's deadly schemes.

Forced to flee, she abandons everything—including the one man she ever loved, and the only man she ever betrayed, Gwilym.

Seven years later, Amaleigh is still running. World after world, she's chased by guilt, grief, and the fire locked inside her soul. All she wants is to stop running, to find a place to belong. But her heart won't let her forget the one man she left behind.

Gwilym's life is in danger, and the only person he trusts to save him had to flee for her life after refusing to assassinate him. But he can't forget the bond they shared or the way she's always made him feel whole. He knows Amaleigh is his only hope. To save his life and protect his kingdom, he must convince her to return to the place she's sworn to forget.

With time running out for Gwilym and his father,

Amaleigh faces a perilous choice. Can she confront the haunted city that stole her family before palace intrigues claim her as their next victim? If she fails, she risks losing the chance to heal her past and open her heart.

As danger closes in and their enemies grow bolder, Amaleigh and Gwilym are forced to confront the truth about their past and the undeniable connection that still burns between them. But love comes at a cost, and the secrets they keep could tear them apart—or heal the kingdom.

For fans of slow-burn romance, heart-pounding adventure, and forbidden love, this fantasy romance will sweep you away!

Indulge in a mesmerizing tale of passion and danger, where an enchanted apple holds the key to forbidden desires.

Lady Eira Cannaid, blessed with unparalleled beauty, conceals the scars of her abusive past. Longing for escape, she is enticed to the grand palace, where a glittering ball promises a respite from the uncertainty of her days. But beneath the dazzling facade lies a treacherous plot woven by her scheming stepmother, who seeks to elevate her own status by sacrificing Eira's innocence to the king.

Lurking in the shadows is the king's heir, a prince willing to court the ire of his father to claim what he believes is rightfully his—and he'll do anything to ruin Eira before his father has the chance.

To evade the prince's threats, the shackles of an unwanted marriage, and her stepmother's malicious machinations, Eira must place her trust in a mysterious stranger. A captivating huntsman, whose intentions remain as enigmatic as his alluring presence. He could be her savior, or the instrument of her downfall.

Eira's journey towards a blissful ending is fraught with treachery, deceit, and betrayal at every turn. She will risk everything to claim her freedom, embarking on a perilous path that starts with an enchanted apple destined to seal her fate.

Enchant plunges readers into a spellbinding series of courtly intrigue, concealed royalty, and an intoxicating enemies-to-lovers romance. Immerse yourself in this enchanting tale, perfect for fans of fairytale retellings, where passion and peril intertwine in an irresistible dance. But beware, within these pages, mature content awaits, exploring profound and sensual encounters that will leave you breathless.

www.ingramcontent.com/pod-product-compliance
Lightning Source LLC
Chambersburg PA
CBHW050615170726

48283CB00001B/251